D0442797

EVERYDAY MAGIC

He runs with A-list stars, but will he run her life?

EVERYDAY MAGIC

Emily Albright

MeritPress | fw

Published by
Merit Press
an imprint of F+W Media, Inc.
10151 Carver Road, Suite 200
Blue Ash, OH 45242. U.S.A.
www.meritpressbooks.com

ISBN 10: 1-4405-9873-8
ISBN 13: 978-1-4405-9873-9
eISBN 10: 1-4405-9874-6
eISBN 13: 978-1-4405-9874-6

Printed in the United States of America.

10 9 8 7 6 5 4 3 2 1

Cover design by Sylvia McArdle.

Dedication

For Gene and Sue, thank you for *everything*.
(And yes, I really mean it.)

Acknowledgments

I couldn't have done this without my amazing critique partners: Amy McKinley, Kristin Kisska, and Victoria Van Tiem. You ladies are the absolute best. I feel lucky to count such talented women amongst my friends. I thank you with all my heart.

A ginormous thank you to my agent, Jessica Watterson. You have the best ideas, come up with the perfect little ways to tweak, and are always full of encouragement. I'm so glad to have you on my team.

My Life Raft ladies: B, Amanda, Anise, Kimberly, Tara, Samantha, Colleen, Heather, and Kelly. You've kept me sane on this crazy journey. I don't even want to think where I'd be if it weren't for you ladies. You're all rock stars in my book.

To Jacquelyn Mitchard and her wonderful team at Merit Press and F+W Media, thank you for making Preston and Maggie shine.

For my parents, I'm so blessed to call you Mom and Dad. You both fostered a lifelong love of reading in me and always told me I could do anything I set my mind to. Now, because of your love, I'm living my dream. Thank you.

To my hubby and kidlet, thank you for understanding when the house gets a little trashed and we have to get takeout because I'm so deep in my writing cave that I didn't realize how late it was. I couldn't do this without either of you. I love you both beyond all reason.

And you, dear readers, you guys are the absolute best. So many of you have contacted me and I can't even begin to describe the warm fuzzies it makes me feel. Thank you for being your awesome selves—never change.

Chapter One

First Impressions

My life had never been my own. Not really. It'd been carefully plotted and planned for me from infancy. Even down to where I got my haircut. Only the best would do for members of the McKendrick family. We were Hollywood royalty. Well, Dad was.

All I wanted was to escape.

From my hilltop vantage, I pushed my bangs off my face and looked down at the sprawling estate, tucked below into the green valley just on the outskirts of Inverness. Our rented manor house neighbored the massive property. Curious what the owners were like, my mind imagined some rich couple with impeccable fashion taste and servants galore.

With a sigh, I turned and sat on the nearby boulder. I pulled out my sketchbook and flipped past the drawing of fabulous outfits I'd designed and scratched my pencil across the page in a rough line drawing of the beautiful house.

I glanced up at the white façade, then back at my drawing. Erasing a wayward line, the little bits of crumbled eraser scattered off the page with a puff of my breath. Closing my eyes, I lifted my face to the sun. There was something magic here that I'd never felt before. Like I could taste my freedom on the very air.

Here, in Scotland, no one knew who I was. The potential this offered was staggering. Back in L.A., everyone knew I was Scott McKendrick's daughter. Perhaps here, I'd finally be able to step out from his looming shadow and just be me . . . Maggie.

My phone chimed and I pulled it from my hoodie pocket. With a flick of my finger I lit the screen.

Dad: Don't forget, cast and crew dinner tonight. Be there.

I rolled my eyes. *Like I'd dare forget.* If I did, the ugly side of my father, the one I hated and avoided at all costs, would rear its nasty head.

Me: I'll be there.

I set my phone aside and grabbed my pencil, continuing the sketch, the house slowly taking shape. Nearly done, I checked the time on my phone and bit my lower lip. The minutes had vanished.

Packing up, my notebook slid into my bag and caught on a loose sheet of paper. I grabbed it, smoothed out the crumpled bumps, and smiled when I read the letterhead: *Thrippletons School of Fashion and Design*. Dad didn't know it yet, but my dreams were coming true.

He'd consider it a rebellion. But for the first time, I'd found something worth fighting for. This mattered. This was my dream. This was my chance to escape.

My eyes scanned the words, still not believing they were real. *Dear Ms. McKendrick, it's my great pleasure to offer you acceptance to Thrippletons.* The worn piece of paper was always with me, like a talisman.

Dad would be furious. I dreaded telling him.

A ladybug scuttled beside me on my gray stone seat. I set my letter down and picked him up, passing him from palm to palm, loving the tickle of his little feet. Looking into his little face, I said, "I should get a say in what's best for me and my future, right?"

This was ultimately my decision, not Dad's. Not even if he threatened or bullied me. The small red bug reached the tip of my finger and took flight. Smiling, I grabbed my letter and tucked it away in my gray messenger bag.

In a perfect world he'd be happy for me. But this wasn't a perfect world and my dad was way closer to an ogre than a perfect father.

I slid off the rock and into the tall grass, inhaling the sweet scent of flowers and countryside. This world seemed so much richer and more colorful than back home. The people here moved at a slower pace and were nicer. More real. With a sigh, I picked a red poppy and ran my finger over the wrinkled petals. Tucking it behind my ear, I lay back, not ready to leave my little haven. Possible scenarios of telling my dad ran through my head. Even Mom was nervous for him to find out.

When I was eleven Dad decided entertainment law was my calling. He'd been liberally greasing the wheels at UCLA as a generous donor since I'd started high school to ensure he'd get exactly what he wanted. But that was my father—he threw a wad of cash at things and made them happen. Or made them disappear.

The sun's warm rays touched my skin and I repressed a shiver. I knew, without a doubt, that if Dad didn't unleash his anger on me, he'd take it out on Mom or my brother, Marc. We often paid for each other's transgressions.

"Ugh, I should get moving." I still had to make the walk back, and tardiness was unacceptable to my father.

A muffled throat clearing told me I wasn't alone anymore.

Tilting my head back, I moved my eyes from a cat-shaped cloud, trying to catch Marc before he could sneak up on me. I knew he was there.

"Have you fallen and now you can't get up?"

Not my brother.

My intruder was tall and cute and apparently sassy.

I sat up like a shot and shook my head mutely, taking him in and wondering where he came from. His English accent told me he wasn't Scottish.

With a step toward me, he grinned and held out his hand. "Well, I'm relieved to see you aren't in any danger. I'm Preston Browne."

Cautiously, I took his hand, letting him pull me to a stand. "So what, you just randomly wander the countryside looking for damsels in distress?"

His face lit up as he laughed, and I froze, unexpectedly delighted by the rich sound.

"Ah, no, I'm staying at Chillingham Manor." He gestured to the grand estate I'd just been sketching. "And you are?"

"I'm Maggie." I purposefully didn't give him my last name. The fewer people who knew I was a McKendrick, the better.

"So, what brings you to Inverness?" He tucked a hand into the pocket of his khakis.

I dusted off my backside, then ran a hand through my hair, hoping I didn't have any stray bits of grass in my usually messy bob. "Um, summer vacation. You?"

This Preston fellow had disheveled blond hair with a slight wave to it and warm brown eyes. I had to admit, he was easy to look at.

"Same. I just arrived the other day. My aunt lives at Chillingham, we visit every summer."

"Lucky you. It looks amazing." I straightened the T-shirt I'd reimagined into a tunic top with extra pieces of sheer fabric gusseted at the seams. Finding treasures to turn into fun pieces was one of my favorite things to do.

Wrinkling his nose, he shook his head. "Well, not that lucky. My daft git of a cousin is here for the summer as well. We don't get on very well."

"Mags!" A voice called in the distance.

Preston turned in the direction of the summons.

"Oh, um, that'd be my brother. I should probably . . . go." I walked toward the edge of the slope and stopped, turning back. "It was nice meeting you, Preston."

"You too, see you 'round." One corner of his lips lifted.

I turned and ran down the hill, nearly rolling into Marc, who was getting ready to climb up and get me.

"What were you doing up there?"

I turned back, the hilltop now abandoned. The wind rustled the long grass and poppies where we'd stood. Grinning, I said, "Just admiring the view." Which was true, until Preston arrived; then my admiration may have slightly shifted focus.

"Dad sent me to find you. He says he expects you to mingle tonight. I know how you love to mingle." He nudged his shoulder against mine, teasing me.

I threw back my head as a tortured groan left my lips. Hobnobbing with the rich and famous was not my ideal way to spend an evening. Quite the opposite, actually. I mean really, they're just people. The way the media and fans fawned over them like they were gods never made sense to me. They were simply the popular kids in the big high school of life.

Why Dad even wanted the two of us there was beyond me. We didn't contribute anything. Well, Marc was an accomplished flirt, but I'd just sit there, painfully trying to make small talk.

Then again, Dad was grooming Marc to be quite the cinematographer. In fifth grade Marc expressed an infinitesimal interest in cameras and film. Dad took to calling him his "little director of photography."

Truthfully, Marc wanted to be like our mother, who was an award-winning director of photography, or DP, but Dad, as always, managed to take the credit.

"All right, come on." I looped my arm in his as we carefully picked our way through the bracken back to the house.

I glanced at the hill one last time and smiled. *Preston.* This summer might turn out better than I thought.

I clutched Marc's shirtsleeve as I nearly pitched forward over a hidden branch. "I'm surprised you didn't try to stay at Berkeley with your friends this summer."

"I did try, but Dad wouldn't let me. He says he wants to bond. Not that I like his way of bonding, but, it's Scotland, so at least that's cool. I figure if I can stay outta Dad's way, the summer could be pretty kickass. Just gotta find a way to avoid the set and find me a hot little redhead to fill my time."

"That's my plan, too. Well . . . minus the redhead. I just want to stay under his radar."

"Talking about radar, when are you planning to tell Dad about Thrippletons?"

I stopped walking, my mouth popping open. "What? How did you know?"

The corner of his lip twitched. "Mom. She thought you'd already told me and she just started brainstorming ways you could tell Dad." He leaned down and blew my long bangs, that I'd been growing out forever, off my face. "Were you at least going to tell me before Dad?"

"Of course! Are you kidding? I'm gonna need your help telling him."

"Yeah, you are." He threw an arm around me and squeezed me to his side in a hug.

Marc and I had always been close. Probably because there was only a couple years separating us. We were practically raised as twins. He was planned, I wasn't.

"Just make sure I'm there when you tell him." He ducked under a branch and reached back to hold it out of the way for me to step under. "It's gonna be ugly and I want to make sure you and Mom are okay."

"Thanks, Marc." I never doubted his loyalty.

"Come on, Magpie. We don't wanna be late." He yanked a strand of my hair and grinned.

The lengthy gravel drive to our rental manor was filling with long black town cars and SUVs. It was already starting. I didn't know if other directors liked to do a dinner before the shoot, but Dad sure did. He felt it got the cast and crew in the right frame of mind and all on the same page. Or, in my opinion, under his control on his "tight ship."

Marc and I snuck around to the back entrance as the guests stood around and chatted in the driveway before making their way to the large black double entry doors.

In the kitchen caterers careened about and waitstaff stood, getting their orders from our mom.

"Hurry, quick, maybe she won't see us." I eyed the stairs leading to our rooms, not wanting to hear the usual lecture on behavior. We were eighteen and twenty; we knew how to deal with Dad.

Marc nonchalantly plucked a coconut shrimp off a platter and headed to the staircase. He looked like he belonged here.

Me? Not so much. I looked like I shouldn't even work here, considering I slammed into a tall-hatted chef and slipped on a slick spot in my escape to the stairs. Glancing back, I caught Mom's eye and bit my lip. *Damn it.* Marc was already halfway to the second floor and shaking his head at me.

"Hold it right there you two." She held up a finger signaling us to stop. Once she'd finished giving her instructions she came to us and leaned on the railing, ready to give us ours. Her long brown hair covered her shoulders, but not the worry etched in her face. "Where do you think you're going?"

"Upstairs, to get dressed, of course," Marc said, his face the picture of innocence.

Mom's blue eyes glinted. They matched the loose sapphire maxi dress she'd changed into, the one I'd created for her. Dad would probably make her change before dinner into some designer label.

For as long as I could remember my nickname from Grandma had been Diana's mini-me. Aside from having the same hair and eye color as Mom, I didn't really see it. She was elegant and serene. I was, well . . . not.

"I don't need to remind you to be on your best behavior, do I?"

"Mom, we know better than to piss Dad off." I leaned back as she reached to tuck a wavy strand of hair behind my ear.

She turned her nervous gaze on Marc. "Whatever you do, no cussing. Just don't upset him. You know how he gets."

Marc nodded and put a hand on her shoulder. "It's gonna be okay. Breathe, Mom."

"I know. I just hate these things. Someone's bound to say something that'll set him off." Mom put her hand over Marc's and smiled. "Off you go, get dressed."

We both shared Mom's fear. One minute Dad would be fine, the next he'd be all red-faced and angry, yelling and verbally abusing anyone in the vicinity. Even his cast and crew weren't immune. But Hollywood revered him as a genius, despite knowing he had a temper like a firecracker. He never failed to bring in serious box-office results, so they ignored it.

Just like we tried to.

I slipped into my room, opened the large wooden wardrobe, and noticed my reflection in the mounted mirror. The red poppy from earlier pulled my attention. I'd forgotten it was there. Reaching up, I untangled it from my hair and held it between my fingers. It made me think of Preston. My lips quirked up at the memory of him.

If I was very lucky, and had a little magic on my side, he might help me steer clear of Dad for the summer. I knew I couldn't avoid the truth forever; my Thrippletons plans would come out eventually. But in the meantime, I had three months to play until the inevitable fallout. And I intended to live for the moment and soak up every tiny hint of fun I could.

Because my world was about to change.

Chapter Two

Falling

The walk from the outskirts of Inverness into the city proper was a short one. My feet crunched along the gravelly shoulder of the road and I raised a hand to cover my mouth as I yawned. After spending last night with Dad's guests, I craved alone time. My batteries were severely depleted and I needed a recharge.

Dad had been in his element, socializing, laughing, having fun. He could turn on the charm when it suited him. Only those of us who knew him didn't buy it. The full production team hadn't arrived yet, but it'd still been a large number of bodies settled at the long wooden trestle table.

I kicked at a large rock as a car passed me, whipping my hair into my face, where it stuck in my lip gloss. Around me the world was a misty, fog-covered green. Everything here was much quieter and somehow seemed softer than California. I liked it.

Last night, Marc had spent the evening flirting and chatting up some girl from the crew. Just the way she'd looked at him, I knew she'd have spent the night with him if he'd asked. I wouldn't be surprised if he had.

That was my brother in a nutshell: he liked the ladies and boy, did they like him. Probably didn't hurt that he was dark haired, blue eyed, and spent most of his free time back home at the beach on a surfboard, flaunting his perfect abs.

My evening had been spent as the invisible woman. Wedged between a sound guy and one of the producers, they'd leaned around me to talk to each other. Awkward.

Metal bracelets slid up my arm with a tinkling sound as I ran a hand through my hair. I'd much prefer an evening in my room refashioning something from my thrift store hauls or drawing in my sketchbook. Which reminded me, I need to grab a new one while I was out.

The edge of town was steps away. I shook my head and tried to enjoy the present. I could smell coffee on the air. Lifting my chin toward the sky, I smiled, feeling more myself than I had in a long time.

It's perfection here.

A man in a deerstalker hat smiled as he walked a small white dog. "Morning, miss."

"Morning." Just being here I could feel my creative juices flowing, surging inside of me like a supernatural power. I needed to create. *And that dude could seriously use a new hat.*

As a little girl I'd been convinced that if I wished hard enough, fairies would give me magical powers to turn my father into a kind man. Didn't work.

Further down the path, I stepped into a secondhand store packed with treasures. After an hour of wandering, my fingers brushing the well-worn fabrics, I made my purchases. A long gold chain necklace and a bunch of really cool dresses and shirts that I intended to tear apart and make into my own creations.

I adjusted my purse on my shoulder and stepped onto the sidewalk; a short distance up the path I saw a sign: The Paper Bookworm. That sounded promising. Through the front windows the store appeared to be packed with various stationery bits and bobs. In the back, hundreds of books lined tall shelves. I stepped inside, a delicate chime announcing my arrival.

A woman, roughly the age of my grandmother, called from behind the counter. "Morning, lass. Holler if ya need anythin', ya ken?" I hadn't been in Scotland that long, but the accent was getting easier to decipher. It must be a sign.

I nodded. "Thanks." I tested the smooth samples of paper with my fingertips. All the blank sheets held so much potential. Give me some colored pencils and I'd happily start sketching all the designs dancing about my brain.

Loosening my lightweight scarf, I grabbed a wire-bound sketchbook and held it under my arm. It was just like my nearly full one at home. Pleased, I wandered into the book section. Gently, I tipped a novel from the shelf so I could see its cover.

"Check out the used bookstore a few blocks over, they have everything." The words were whispered near my ear.

I whirled to find a grinning Preston. Biting my lip to suppress a laugh, I said, "Hey."

Hair rumpled, he leaned in and softly said, "Seriously, Draxton's is the place to go."

"What are you doing in here then?" My eyes darted away, then back to him. *He's a lot taller than I remember.*

"I saw you through the window as I was walking by. Thought I'd pop in and say hello." He smirked, his eyes glinting.

In his accent, it sounded like "ello." Which was insanely cute, especially when added to the dimple that appeared in his cheek.

With a breath, he continued, "Wanted to offer my assistance in case you were in danger of falling down again."

"Doing good, still standing. It was Preston, right?" As if I could actually forget.

He nodded. "Why don't you check out and I'll take you over to Draxton's. My best mate is a complete bookworm and loves it in there. Come on."

I chewed at the inside of my cheek. Could I trust him? He seemed like a nice guy. I may not be looking for a book necessarily, but I did want to spend more time with him.

"Okay, why not." Shooting him a pretend warning look, I added, "Just don't go all psycho killer on me, okay?"

He shrugged his shoulders. "You're in luck, I'm more of a sunshine and kittens kind of guy than serial killer."

"Sunshine and kittens, eh? That sends a whole different set of concerns running through my mind." Laughing, I shook my head and went to pay for my sketchbook, grabbing a pack of watercolor pencils on the way.

Outside I followed Preston and asked, "So, what's your story? Are you a student? Do you work?"

He nodded. "I'm in my last year at Oxford."

Oxford, wow, impressive. "What's your major?"

He tucked closer to me as a large moving truck lumbered past on the skinny road. His arm pressed into mine, sending an unexpected jolt through me.

"I'm studying engineering, mostly structural engineering. What about you? Are you a student?"

I met his brown eyes. "I start college in the fall."

"Oh? Where?"

I pursed my lips, not sure if I should admit to Thrippletons with Dad still in the dark. If I started telling people, it upped the risk that he'd find out before I was ready for him to know. "Well, if my dad gets his way, I'll be going to UCLA."

He scrunched his brows together. "So, that'd be . . . California?" His face told me he was nowhere near certain on his guess.

I nodded.

"When it comes to the geography of the States I'm absolute rubbish. But, I do know where California is." He looked pleased with himself as he made sure it was safe to cross the street. "One of my mates is in Seattle with his girlfriend right now. That's pretty close to California, right?"

"Well, it's on the same coast. They're a state apart, though."

"So, what are you going to be studying at UCLA?"

"Um, the plan is entertainment law."

He looked me up and down, his eyes narrowing. "No offense, but you don't seem uptight enough to be a lawyer."

I sniffed a laugh and said, "That's what I keep trying to tell my dad, but he thinks I'd be perfect. He's not exactly the best listener."

He tilted his head. "What about your mum?"

I shrugged. "My mom knows it's not my first choice, but my dad is very . . . persuasive. He's always so certain he knows best." Telling him the truth, that my dad would use *any* means necessary to get me to do what he wanted, wasn't going to happen.

Holding open the door to the used bookstore, he asked, "If you could choose, what would you do?"

"Something where I can be creative." I slid past, brushing against him with a shy smile.

"Ah, now *that* I can see. You look more the imaginative and whimsical type." He reached up and gave a gentle tug on my hedgehog-patterned yellow scarf.

I couldn't explain it, but this Preston, a perfect stranger, made me feel . . . safe. Something my dad had never managed to do. I found myself wanting to tell Preston things. It was disarming. Especially since past experiences had me distrusting men in general.

Dad would certainly never approve of him.

Just inside the door of Draxton's I stopped, my mouth popping open as I looked around. A massive number of books lined the shelves and every available surface in neat piles. "Holy crow, you weren't kidding when you said they had everything."

Preston followed my glance and gave a wave to the man behind the counter. "If you like books, this is the place to come."

I looked up at him. "Are you a big reader?"

He shrugged and took a couple steps in. "I used to read more than I do now. Seems like the only books I pick up these days are textbooks."

On the stand beside me was a coffee-table book with what looked like an x-rayed dress on the front. I flipped the cover open and checked out a couple pages before following Preston up a flight of stairs.

"Do you read much?" He turned to smile at me.

"Probably not as much as I should. I spend more time with my sketchbook." I lifted my hand not laden with bags and ran it through my hair, tucking the shoulder-length strands behind my ears.

"I keep telling myself when I graduate I'll make time for books. That's the plan anyway." He leaned against the railing. "Anything in particular you were looking for?"

"Not really. Earlier I was just browsing. I saw the sketchbooks and paper through the window and went in." I lifted my paper sack, my cheeks flushing at his attention.

Reaching a hand up, he rubbed the back of his neck. The growing smile on his face had warm fuzzies coursing through me.

I didn't want to even start liking Preston. Not like *that*. I couldn't.

The last time I dated a guy it turned ugly. Thompson made me think he was really into me, but ultimately he used me as a stepping stone to get close to my father. He wanted Dad to kick-start his career. When I refused to introduce them, Thompson dumped me . . . while on a group date. I'd ended up walking home in the dark, alone. I was never part of the popular group, but his actions made it infinitely worse.

The next morning I'd walked into school a social pariah. Kids snickered behind their hands and pointed. I prayed for the ground to swallow me up whole. Unfortunately, it hadn't.

From then on it became routine; if someone was nice to me, for any reason, nine times out of ten, they wanted something from my father. I was just the quickest, easiest path. Trusting people was not something I did easily anymore.

This was one of the many reasons why I needed to separate myself from my father's world. Getting out of L.A. was my first step. I wanted to live someplace where people had aspirations beyond acting and getting rich and famous.

"So, what do you say?" Preston's words shot me back to the present like a bullet.

"Sure." I had no idea what I was agreeing to, but I didn't want him to think I'd zoned out on him like he was boring me.

"I have no idea what to get her. She likes anything that's spooky and creepy. She's really into the paranormal."

Helping him pick out a present, gotcha. For a girl. I should've known he had a girlfriend.

My long bangs slid, covering my eyes and I sighed, grabbing a clip from my pocket, to secure them. "Well, since we're in a bookstore, how about a book."

"She has nearly everything, so a book might be a good gift. I could stick a few gift vouchers to some of her favorite restaurants in it too. Come on." He turned down an aisle and glanced back to make sure I was following.

He pointed to the sign labeling the section as horror. Mouth twitching, he met my gaze. "My sister used to do everything she could to scare me when I was little. She once read me a bedtime story from a Stephen King book. Scarred me for life. My mum was livid."

His sister. A shot of relief hit me, but I quickly tamped it down. *Not what I'm here for.* "Well, that wasn't very nice." I chuckled. "Bet you slept like a baby after that."

"My parents made her crash on my floor in her sleeping bag, since I didn't want to be alone and was begging to sleep with them." Brown eyes glinted at me and crinkled around the edges. "She was so pissed."

"How old were you?"

He pursed his lips in thought. "Um, I think I was about seven; she was twelve. She never did it again, though."

"Sounds a little like Marc and me. I have a . . . somewhat irrational fear of bugs. Thanks to him, no doubt. I'm not an outdoorsy girl, at all." I laughed. "Anytime he found a bug he knew I'd freak out over he'd leave it in my room. Usually in my bed."

Preston's mouth popped open. "That's cruel."

"Right? To this day, I still have to pull all my blankets back and check everything. You think your sister scarred you?" I chuckled, enjoying the moment.

He laughed and reached over, nonchalantly tucking a strand of hair behind my ear. "I'd slay any bug you needed."

I held my breath, unable to breathe at the sudden and unexpected close contact. As he pulled his arm back, I could see the realization of what he'd just done flash through his eyes.

Clearing his throat, he looked at his feet and shook his head before glancing at me again. "I'm really sorry about that. It's crazy, I didn't mean . . ." He studied my face before softly adding, "It's absolutely barmy, but I feel like I've known you a long time."

My face flushed and I averted my eyes, unsure what to say.

I wasn't seeking anything romantic, but admittedly, Preston was the kind of guy I usually went for, cute, kind, and clever, a deadly combination. Especially when intelligence was my weakness.

"Um, we should probably pick out a book." He ran a hand through his blond waves as I nodded.

"Hmm, well, you can't go wrong with Poe. Oh, no, I know, I had to read *The Turn of the Screw* by Henry James for school, that was super creepy. About a governess at a haunted house where the evil that's inside it wants to possess her two mute charges. At the end you're not sure if it really happened or if the governess went insane."

"I've heard of it, but I never read it. Sounds right up Hal's alley though; she does a bit of ghost hunting when she has free time.

Let's go see if we can find it. James, James, James . . ." He scanned the rows of alphabetized books, holding a finger out as he checked the author names on the spines.

"Wait, your sister is a ghost hunter, that's so cool."

"Yeah, I've actually gone with her several times, it's fun."

I watched him as he continued to scan the shelf, torn between wanting to know him better and knowing it couldn't go anywhere. Dad wouldn't let it. And chances were, Preston was like all the other people I'd known, and he'd change once he found out my dad was a big-time director.

"Aha! Henry James, here it is." He held up the black paperback with a triumphant smile.

We finished up in no time and were back outside, bags in hand. "Thanks for all your help." He glanced across the street and smiled. "What do you say, I buy you a coffee to pay you back for your time?"

My eyes darted to the Starbucks sign and I nodded, catching my bottom lip between my teeth. "Okay."

Once inside, I ordered my summer favorite, a venti vanilla macchiato with whip, iced.

I should probably skip the whip cream . . . nah. I wasn't one of those super skinny mini girls, and my curves did tend to make me a little self-conscious. My horrid ex Thompson informed me my weight was another reason he'd broken up with me. Mom had been furious when she'd finally heard the full story.

I wouldn't call myself fat though; models and actors probably would. I was definitely . . . *feminine.* That was Mom's coded way of saying I had boobs and a butt.

"So, did you drive into town?" Preston asked between sips of his drink.

"I walked. Too beautiful of a morning not to."

"Why don't I give you a lift back?"

Smiling, I nodded. "That'd be great."

I knew it'd probably come back to bite me on the butt, but I wasn't quite ready to say goodbye. His offer of a ride was the perfect excuse to find out more about him.

Chapter Three

Chance Encounters

I sat atop the poppy-covered hillside, the large gray stone once again my seat. Refining my sketch of Chillingham manor, I took in the scenery. Totally hoping to catch a glimpse of Preston. Despite my going on daily walks nearby, he hadn't popped up in my sights in nearly a week. He'd been on my mind practically the whole time, though.

"Did you hear Ben Chambers was here?"

I jumped at the intrusion.

Marc reached my side and plopped down beside me.

Ben Chambers was the male lead for Dad's movie. I don't know what the dude version of "It Girl" is, but that's essentially what he was. Wrapping up a press tour for a different project had delayed his arrival on Dad's set.

"No, I hadn't heard." I popped open the metal buttons on my army jacket. "Is that what you hiked up here to tell me?"

"No. I got bored and wanted to get out. I decided to come bug you."

"Well, mission accomplished." I glanced up, then turned back to my sketch to fix the tall chimney. "So, did you meet him?"

"Ben? No. Dad just texted me wanting me to come welcome him. I've heard he's a lot shorter than he looks on TV." Marc's brows lowered. "You know he'll want you to meet him too."

"Guess we should head back then." I sighed, irritation flooding my system.

"Finish what you're doing, then we'll go."

Nodding, I took a pull from my water bottle. "How's lighting girl?"

"Who?"

I chuckled and continued working. "Seriously? Jeez, the girl you were flirting with at the cast and crew dinner."

"Oh, her." Marc waved it off. "Nothing happened. Turns out she has a boyfriend."

"Really? She sure was flirting and giving you the eye for someone who's not single. I guess the search for your redhead continues."

"Damn straight." He gave a playful shove to my shoulder, nearly knocking me off my perch and sending my pencil skidding off the page.

Grumbling, I erased the dark line and scowled at Marc. He wasn't helping my creative flow. He pulled an apple from my bag and bit into it, making a juicy suck before he pulled it away. The sound of people eating repulsed me. Putting my pencil and sketch away, I vowed to come back without a sidekick.

"Let's go meet Dad's Mr. Chambers. Want to grab some lunch after?" I asked, my rumbly stomach feeling like it was trying to ingest my spine.

Shrugging, he nodded.

The breeze lifted my hair as I stood and tied my jacket around my waist. I looked to Chillingham, wondering if Preston was inside.

"Race you down!" Marc grinned.

With my sandals there was no way I was running anywhere. Instead I clambered along behind him, secretly hoping he'd trip and take a little tumble.

At the bottom Marc waited, hands on his knees, slightly breathless. "Come on, poky."

"Oh, bite me." I stuck my tongue out at him as I reached his side.

We neared the house, the long grass swishing as we walked. Marc smacked my arm. "There he is."

Grateful he didn't point, I looked in the direction my obnoxious brother was staring. Sure enough, standing near his shiny sports car was Ben Chambers, teen heartthrob extraordinaire. *Huh, he is kinda short. Cute, but short.*

"Let's go meet him." Marc, though trying to play it off, was clearly excited.

"You go. I'm gonna go grab the keys for the car, then I'll swing 'round the front." I didn't care if I met Ben Chambers or not. Chances were it'd happen eventually during the shoot. Guys like him were a dime a dozen at my high school. I knew exactly what he'd be like. In my experience they were all vain peacocks only concerned with preening themselves and doing whatever it took to get ahead.

Technically, Dad only told Marc to come meet him. *Like that'll fly.*

Mom stood in the kitchen, fridge open, pulling out sandwich makings and setting them on the granite counter.

"Hey Mom." I grabbed the keys to one of our rental cars off the hook by the door. "S'okay if Marc and I run into town for lunch?"

"You're not staying here? I've got turkey and ham."

Wrinkling my nose, I shook my head. "Nope. We'll catch you a little later."

"Drive carefully," she called as I spun out the door, keys jingling.

The BMW purred to life and I smiled. This car was a sweet ride; even though it still felt so weird to drive from what I considered the passenger side. I pulled to the front of the house, where Dad, Marc, and Ben stood laughing and chatting. I sat, waiting for Marc to finish up, knowing I was probably stepping over Dad's tolerance line by not getting out and going over.

I grabbed my phone and pulled up Facebook. Scrolling through posts of people from my high school only proved to be more of their typical drivel, bragging about auditions they'd nailed and photos of the exclusive parties they'd attended. I sighed and put it away in time to see my dad coming my way.

His stride was purposeful and once he left Ben's side, his smile vanished. Control freak was too tame a word for Dad. He wanted his say in everything I did. That's how my future got decided *for* me, not *with* me. He knew I liked to sketch and design, but still never asked what I wanted to do with my life. My art was a hobby, nothing more to him.

With the press of a button, the window rolled down. I couldn't meet his gaze. "Hey, Dad."

Reaching in he grabbed my chin and made me look at him. "Get out of the car and come meet Ben."

"Okay." I tightly smiled, wanting to smack his hand away but not daring to, not with the chilling edge that tinged his words.

Telling him no wasn't an option. Well, at least it wasn't an option if I wanted any freedom this summer. I may have been legally an adult, but my father didn't care. If he wanted to, he could make my summer one long confinement to the house.

Dad waited for me to kill the engine and climb out. As we walked toward Ben and Marc, he slung his arm over my shoulder, to give the impression of tenderness. "Ben, this is my daughter, Margaret."

"Maggie." I quickly corrected, then bit my lower lip and shot a nervous glance in Dad's direction. I may get in trouble, but Margaret made me feel like I should be wearing a shawl and knitting in a rocker.

Ben offered a hand to me, his green eyes twinkling. "Hey there."

"Hi." I tucked my keys in the pocket of my magenta shorts before shaking his hand. The warmth from his palm spread into mine, making me shiver. Okay, so he's *really* cute. He stared me in the eye as he held on to me longer than was necessary.

He cleared his throat and released my hand.

"You liking Scotland?" I asked, trying to make conversation.

Ben nodded. "It's a beautiful country. I was up here a couple years ago filming a miniseries, and I fell in love with it."

"Mags, Marc says you're heading out for lunch, why don't you take Ben with you?" Dad gave me a grin that could only be described as cheesy. And yet, I couldn't mistake the threat buried deep behind it.

"Yeah, that's a great idea." Marc smiled.

If I didn't know better I'd think Marc had a little man-crush on Ben. *He's probably just picturing all the girls Ben could score him.* Like he needed any help in that department. "We're just heading into town, nothing fancy, but you're more than welcome to join us."

Ben glanced at his watch. "I'd really love to, but I've got a conference call in just a bit." His gaze lingered on mine. "Maybe next time, though."

I nodded as Marc said, "Anytime."

Once Ben drove off, Marc and I set out for town.

"Okay, what's the deal?" I glanced over from the driver's seat. "Why were you salivating over him like that?"

"What? Who?" Marc continued when he caught the expression on my face, sighing. "He's a cool guy and he's always got some hot chick on his arm. He could totally hook me up. I mean, I've got game, but he's at a whole 'nother level."

I so called it. Snorting a little as I laughed, I said, "I love it when you show your deep side."

• • •

The restaurant Marc chose reminded me of a Panera. We walked in and the smell of fresh-baked bread nearly knocked me over. Warm colors covered the walls and a mishmash of tables and booths filled the eating area.

With our order in, we turned to find a place to sit and—my eyes darted to the blond guy in the corner.

Preston.

He was thumbing through his phone, a smile on his face. Telling myself not to stare, I tore my eyes away and focused on where Marc was wandering.

As he picked a table and sat down I stopped him. "Can I sit on that side?"

His brows drew together. "I guess so, why?"

"I just . . . want to be able to see out the windows." Or a view of Preston, but he totally didn't need to know that. Besides, I shouldn't care if I could see Preston or not.

Seconds later, a waitress in a black ball cap came out with a tray laden with plates, definitely more than we ordered. She placed ours on the table, told us to enjoy our meal, then turned and headed over to Preston.

He looked up and thanked her with a smile. He really did have a nice smile. It was probably his lips—*Oh. Crap.* I gave a little wave and mouthed "hi." What else could I do now that he'd caught me staring?

His eyebrows rose as he motioned, silently asking if he could come join us. I nodded, smiling far too big, but I couldn't stop myself.

"Well, hello there. I was wondering when I'd see you again." He approached, plate and drink in hand.

Marc eyed him up, clearly wondering who the hell he was and glancing at me with a question in his eye. With zero time to prep him, I prayed he'd keep his mouth shut about Dad.

I scooted over so our guest could slide in beside me. "Marc, this is Preston, he's our neighbor for the summer. And this is Marc, my obnoxious, bug-loving, older brother." I grinned.

Marc's brow furrowed, unsure, but he still reached his hand over the table for a shake. I could only imagine how tightly he must be grasping Preston's hand.

My brother didn't know I'd been keeping our father's identity a secret. Inside, my stomach clenched with nerves, anxious at the possibility of Marc spilling the beans and Preston suddenly looking at me differently. Like an opportunity.

"Nice to meet you," Preston said with a smile, then shifted his gaze to me. "How've you been?"

I nodded. "Good, just hanging out and keeping out of trouble. You?"

"Forced family time. My sister just got engaged, so we've been away celebrating with her."

As we caught up I could feel Marc's eyes watching me. I knew exactly what he'd say when we were alone again. At least I hoped he'd wait until we were alone.

"So, Marc, are you liking Inverness?"

Marc shrugged and took a bite of his BLT. "It's okay."

Chuckling, I amended his answer. "Marc's disappointed that he hasn't found a cute little redhead yet."

"Ah." Preston's eyes lit up. "Do you fancy redheads?"

"Thanks a lot, Mags." He turned to me, eyes slivered.

I full-out laughed. "Oh, what? Since when have you been shy?"

A smile cracked Marc's lips and he nodded, relaxing into our conversation. "Okay, I'll admit it, I've always had a thing for redheads. I figured Scotland would be the perfect place to find one."

Preston chuckled. It was an inviting warm sound that made me feel like I'd just finished a perfect mug of cocoa, complete with marshmallows. "I have a good friend back at school you'd probably take a liking to. She's got a boyfriend though."

Once Marc chilled out and dropped the overprotective big brother routine, they actually got along quite well and no mention of Dad was made. *Thank God.*

Before we left, Preston stopped me at the door. "What would you think about meeting up on purpose next time?"

I tucked my hands into my shallow pockets. *Seriously, what's the point of these?* "What did you have in mind?"

"Coffee, tomorrow? Right here?"

"Ten?" I offered, feeling myself get sucked into his warm caramel-flecked eyes.

A smile spread over his lips. "Sounds great."

"Here, um, let me give you my number just in case." This was more forward than I ever was, but I didn't care. I liked him.

He handed his phone to me with a fresh contact page up, ready for my info. I punched it all in and handed it back to him with a smile. "There you go."

Preston's fingers grazed mine as he took his mobile back. A zing of energy radiated up my arm and spread through my body straight down to my toes.

"I'll see you tomorrow then." Preston grinned, the dimple appearing in his cheek.

"Tomorrow," I said with a nod, completely unable to wipe the grin off my face. I watched as he left, turning back once to wave at us.

I sighed. Grateful Dad hadn't come up in conversation and that my secret was still safe.

"You *like* him, don't deny it." Marc crossed his arms over his chest and snickered at my side.

I'd forgotten Marc was standing there, watching my descent into a ball of giddy, girly emotions. I shrugged. "He's a very nice guy."

Marc scoffed. "Right, nice guy, that's all it is."

"Shut up." I smacked his arm. "Maybe you don't know me as well as you think you do."

"Hmm, let's see." He tapped his lips with a pointer finger and squinted like he was thinking hard. "Cute, friendly, has some semblance of a fashion sense, and clearly he's smarter than Thompson, so already he's screaming your type. What did you tell me you were the other day, a sadiesexual?"

I rolled my eyes. "Sapiosexual. I can't help it, intelligence is sexy."

"Yeah, so I still don't need to know what you find sexy," he said, tucking the front of his shirt in his waistband. A group of teen girls were eyeing him and giggling. When he winked at them I grabbed his arm.

"Oh please, you should know better than that. They're like sixteen."

Glancing back, he shook his head. "Really? I was thinking at the youngest maybe eighteen."

Outside the restaurant I pulled my hair into a messy pony, my long bangs instantly slipping free and falling into my face. "When in doubt, don't even encourage."

"True. Come on, I need to run to the grocery store, I'm running out of deodorant."

I followed along behind him, pondering my date with Preston tomorrow. *Is it a date?* Did I want it to be a date? *No, not a date.* Better not to complicate things.

At the very least Preston would keep my mind off Dad and the inevitability of him discovering I'd stuffed his UCLA plans in the trash.

My stomach fluttered and I smiled, mentally planning my outfit. How many more hours until it was time for coffee?

Chapter Four

Opening Up

The car idled in the parking spot as I checked my hair in the vanity mirror. I'd parked a good distance away from the restaurant, not wanting Preston to catch me here this early. Mostly I'd wanted to avoid Dad. I'd been invited to the set and when I told Dad I'd already made plans he was less than thrilled. I figured it'd be better to be out of sight before he could find me.

I smoothed the front of the heart-print dress I'd created, straightened my long necklaces, and checked my makeup. It'd only taken fourteen outfit changes to settle on my look. *Why am I stressing over this?*

Just the thought of Dad finding out about Preston or Preston discovering who my father really was made me shudder. Eyes closed, I took a deep breath. This guy had me seriously frazzled. I didn't even want a boyfriend.

A knock on my window and my eyes shot open. Preston was looking at me, grinning. He looked even cuter than he did yesterday. I gave a weak wave and unlocked the car.

"You beat me," he said as he opened my door with a grin.

"Just barely." I offered a shy smile, vowing next time to park *much* further away.

He gestured toward the sidewalk. "Shall we?"

I nodded, hit with a nervous energy. We walked side-by-side toward the restaurant. I passed my small pocketbook from hand to hand, trying to figure out what to say. My brain glommed on to our conversation about college the other day.

"So, why structural engineering?"

"Oh, um, I guess I've always had a mind for math and science, but really it's the challenge of helping design buildings that are safe during natural disasters, yet still beautiful in a minimalistic sort of way. It allows for creativity, which I like."

"That makes sense." I totally understood his need to create beautiful things.

"As a child, I remember seeing photos of buildings that'd gone through earthquakes, I think it was California." He glanced at me with his brows raised. "I became fascinated by the idea of making them withstand that kind of force while protecting the people inside."

"I can see how that'd be interesting. My parents still talk about the one in '92." I passed through the door he held open. The warmth was a nice change from the cool, misty morning. "I'm just grateful we haven't had any big ones since."

The smell of baked goods enveloped us as we ordered our coffee. After doctoring it up, we sat at a booth across from each other, just a couple seats away from where we'd sat yesterday.

"So what about you? You mentioned your father wanting you to go to law school but you clearly aren't into that."

My nerves frayed like a piece of yarn. I didn't want to talk about Dad. I could feel myself clam up at the possibility.

Much to my relief, he continued, "I know you like the creative stuff, but what excites you?"

You. I had to look away.

Studying the black lid of my cup, I ran my finger over the hole in the spout, hoping he didn't notice my instant blush. "I love art, drawing, designing, making beautiful things. In a perfect world, I'd go into fashion design."

He smiled and took a sip, the soft crinkles reappearing at the corners of his eyes. The lines told me he smiled a lot, which I loved. "I can see how you'd have a flair for that. You always look so put together."

The smile was instant on my lips. "Thanks."

"Okay, big question, if this is what you really want, why are you letting your father send you to a school you don't want to go to?"

I shrugged. "It's been his plan since I was young, but really, that's not me. I may be independent and strong willed at times, but I don't want to argue my whole life." I softly laughed. "I just can't figure out how to tell him I'm not going to UCLA."

His brow scrunched and he looked pretty adorable. "If you're not going through with your dad's idea, what are you doing in the fall?"

Shaking my head, I decided I wanted to share a tiny bit of my plans. I couldn't explain it; he had a calm comforting affect on me. So I went with it. "Um, well I've been accepted to a design school. I used the check my dad intended for UCLA to secure my spot." I'd been vague enough on the details, and thank God, Dad had been super busy and handed over a signed blank check and told me to figure out the rest. Mom had covertly helped me with the paperwork.

When he finds out . . . icy tendrils of dread coursed through me at the mere thought. I prayed Marc and Mom could talk him down fast or Dad would make sure I'd suffer for my disobedience.

It wasn't that long ago that Marc had drawn Dad's ire and we'd all paid the price. With Marc it was different. Dad could no longer physically take his anger out on him. Instead he'd get to Marc by hurting Mom and me.

Just before I'd graduated Marc had gone out partying with Santos Turgen, a down-on-his-luck actor who'd gotten on Dad's shit-list, hence the down on his luck. When photos of them came out, Dad lost it. In his eyes Marc was associating with an enemy. No matter that they were friends before any of the drama went down.

Dad had found me, thrust the magazine in my face and questioned me about it. I still remember the pinch of his fingers on my skin as he shook me when I told him I didn't know anything. Mom had rushed in and pulled him off me, which had earned her a slug in the shoulder. Before he'd left my room he'd punched a hole in my wall.

When Marc had returned home that night Dad confronted him, shouting and yelling. When Marc saw the bruises on Mom, as well as my arms and wrists, he stormed up to Dad, furious. I thought he was going to punch him. Instead he ended up getting kicked out, Dad telling him to go play with Santos.

"But he knows . . . nothing of your plans?" Preston's voice pulled me from my memory. Concern flashed through his eyes.

I shook my head and swallowed. "Nothing."

"When are you going to tell him?"

A nervous chuckle escaped me. "I should probably do it sooner rather than later, right?"

"One might argue that." The way his brown eyes sparkled sucked me right in. "But I suppose you could always wait until the last minute and make a well-timed exit, too."

I paused, wondering if he'd put the pieces together. No, we'd barely talked, he couldn't. Shaking my head, I tried to shrug it off. "And *that* seems to be the way I'm leaning. Maybe I should just send a postcard after I get there." I puffed my long bangs off my face.

"Now there's a solid plan." The corner of his lips quirked up, revealing that dang dimple. If I'd been standing I'm sure my knees would've wobbled. I liked me some adorable dimples.

His lips pulled my gaze. They looked soft and I found myself curious how they'd feel against mine. My teeth captured my bottom lip and it slowly slid free. At the clearing of his throat, I startled, feeling caught. I took a drink of my coffee while searching for words. "So, you said you had a sister. What does she do besides the ghost hunting?"

"Well, during the day she works for a bank, but at night she goes off on cases with her paranormal group."

I smiled. "That's still so cool."

"Haley and her group go out on investigations, then return to reveal their findings. It's actually how she met her fiancé. He owns a giant estate in Derbyshire and asked her group to come check out some weird things they'd had happening."

This was something I could seriously get into. "Have they ever found anything?"

"They've gotten a few super creepy things. Disembodied voices, shadow figures, that sort of thing. One time when she took me out with her, I was about thirteen, I swear to you, something yanked the back of my shirt. Just reached out and grabbed me. You can even see my shirt being pulled back on the video."

"That's awesome!" I grinned. "I've always wanted to go on one of those investigations."

His smile lit up his face. "It doesn't freak you out?"

"Not at all. My grandfather lived in this eerie old house near the beach in California. When we'd stay there as kids, I'd hear voices at night, talking in the attic and I always saw this woman in a long silky nightgown slowly walking the halls. They chalked it up to an over-active imagination, but I'm still not convinced."

"Well, if Haley has any investigations this summer I'll let you know and maybe we can tag along. They always like having extra hands."

A pulse of excitement coursed through me. "That'd be amazing."

"What are you doing tomorrow?"

"Um, I don't think I have plans. Why?" I smiled, inhaling deeply.

I totally like him.

There was no point denying it.

I had three months to enjoy as much time with Preston as I could before we'd both go off to school. And in that time I also had to sort out how to tell my dad I wouldn't be going home with them in the fall, and pray I survived his backlash.

"Come to Chillingham around noon? I'll have a surprise for you."

Chapter Five

A Fresh Chance

The dark wooden doors loomed before me as I crunched my way across Chillingham's pebbled drive. Preston was in there somewhere, expecting me. *Why am I so nervous?* My heart accelerated as I stepped onto the porch and wiped my clammy palms against my skinny jeans. *Do I just . . . knock?*

Blowing out a deep breath, I wrapped my fingers around the metal lion knocker and announced my arrival.

Through the doors a muffled voice said, "I've got it, Curtis."

I smiled. *Preston's waiting for me?* Warmth spread from my fingers down to my toes. The door opened to reveal a skinny guy with short dark hair and bad skin.

So not Preston.

"Well, hello there, love." He leered, licking his lips. "And who might you be?"

I took an involuntary step back. "Hi, I'm Maggie. Um . . . is Preston here?"

"Preston? No, I don't think I've seen him, must've run into town. I'm Tanner. Tanner Bunbury. Is there anything *I* can do for you?" He took a step out the door, closing the distance I'd put between us.

Crossing my arms over my chest, I looked into the house, hoping Preston might come running. Something in this guy's eyes gave me the heebie-jeebies. "Well, Preston's expecting me. Would you mind double-checking?"

Tanner turned slightly and spoke over his shoulder. "Curtis?"

"Yes, sir?" A tall, Italian-looking man snapped his heels together beside Tanner.

"Would you please track down Preston and let my cousin know he has a lovely guest waiting for him?" He threw a wink in my direction.

"Of course, sir." The stiff-suited gentleman nodded and turned from the door.

"Oh and, Curtis, there's no need to rush. *Maggie* and I can get to know each other." He averted his attentions back to me and straightened his white button-down. "Why don't you step inside? I'll have tea brought to the parlor. We can wait for him there."

The way my name spread across his lips felt oily and dirty. How could Preston and this guy be related? I sighed and looked behind me, tempted to just come back another day. Trouble was, I really wanted to see Preston.

Biting my bottom lip, my desire won out. I nodded, but kept my arms crossed, not wanting to touch him.

Tanner smiled, lips tight, and dropped his arm, instead gesturing me to go in.

Just over the threshold I jumped as he called to a passing maid. "Celia, please have a tea tray brought to the east parlor."

The maid nodded and scurried off.

"So, what brings you to Scotland?" Tanner asked as we walked down a long hallway.

Where's Preston? He knew I was coming. I pulled my phone from my pocket, unsure what I intended to do with it. My number was in his phone, his was not in mine.

Tanner stopped and turned to eye me, clearly wondering why I'd gone mute.

"Oh, um, summer vacation."

The door behind Tanner opened and Preston's face popped out. "Found you."

"Hey." Beyond happy to see him, I couldn't suppress my giant grin.

Tanner scowled up at Preston, his upper lip curling back. "Cousin, there was no need to rush. I could've kept her perfectly entertained. Did you run? You look out of breath." Clearly the thought of exertion was distasteful to him.

"Why wouldn't I rush?" Wrinkling his brow, Preston turned his face to Tanner. "Admit it, if she was here to see you, you'd be just as eager as I am." Preston smiled my way. "And I didn't just run, I rode like a bat out of hell as well."

Gone was the uneasy dread filling the pit of my stomach. Fluttery wings of excitement took its place. He really did want to see me.

Meeting my eyes, Preston continued with a smile. "Sorry I'm late. I had to finish setting things up."

"I guess that's my cue to leave." Tanner turned from Preston, not smiling, and tucked his hands in the pockets of his khakis. "Maggie, it was a pleasure. One I hope to have repeated very often."

I nodded and watched as he stiffly walked down the hallway away from us. The more distance spread between us, the lighter I felt.

"Sorry about that. I told you he was a total git." Preston held out his hand to me. I took it and he threaded his fingers through mine, tangling us together. "You ready?"

"For what?" My heart jumped at his touch.

His eyes widened and with a mischievous smile he whispered, "It's a surprise."

Laughter escaped my lips as he pulled me through room after ornate room at a breakneck pace. Slightly winded, we stopped in front of a tall portrait of a man on a horse. With a cocked eyebrow, Preston dropped my hand and reached behind the gilt frame and popped a lever, allowing the painting to swing forward into the room.

I gasped, not expecting that. A smile curled my lips as I looked up at him. "Okay, that's pretty cool."

"Just wait." Reaching for me again, he pulled me into a tunnel built between the walls.

"Let me grab a torch."

Seriously? They still use torches? He grabbed a flashlight off a small alcove just inside the door and I grinned. *That's right, flashlights are torches here.*

The painting closed on its own behind us, plunging the small passage in darkness. I wondered if it was supposed to do that or if it had some invisible help. My grip tightened on Preston as a slightly musty smell hit me. With a soft click, light illuminated his face. He had a slight scruff to his chin that I hadn't noticed until the beam caught it.

We stood watching each other, letting our eyes adjust. Taking a step toward me, he reached up to tuck a strand of hair that'd escaped my ponytail behind my ear. His fingertips grazed my neck and I sucked in a breath, startled by his nearness. The scent of him filled my head and holy hell did he smell good, citrus and woodsy, like he'd been outside all morning. It made me want to get closer. *Much* closer.

Softly, he asked, "Shall we?"

I nodded, not trusting my voice.

Preston turned and led the way down a set of steps. He kept my hand in his, which I was grateful for. I ran my free hand along a rough stone wall, my fingertips feeling tingly, just like my stomach. We made a couple turns, passing a couple other corridors, making me wonder where they led to.

A sliver of light lit the horizon. It looked like the outline of a door.

"We're almost there," Preston whispered. Why he was whispering was beyond me; we seemed to be alone down here. Maybe the mysterious atmosphere just necessitated it.

As we approached the exit, Preston pulled me in front of him, making me lead the way but still holding my hand.

"Go ahead and open it," he said, with a smile in his voice.

Palms flat on the door, I pushed. The wood groaned as it dragged along the cement floor. The sunlight momentarily blinded me as a rush of breath hit my face before I could focus. *Did we just go to the stables?* It only took me a moment to realize a large horse was pushing his muzzle into the opening.

"Whoa, horse." I stepped back, bumping into Preston's chest.

"Here you go, Ajax." Preston stretched around me and ran his hand down the velvety nose, then reached back inside the door and into a burlap sack. He pulled out a couple apples. "Good boy."

The horse nickered happily as another came over to loudly protest the unfairness.

"I didn't forget you, Collette." The cream-colored horse plucked the last shiny red apple from Preston's palm and contentedly munched away. Preston turned to me. "Do you ride?"

I watched him stroke Ajax, the sun making the horse's russet coat shimmer. Reaching to Collette, I ran my hand over her nose. "I took riding lessons for years. I loved it."

A bully from school had led to my quitting. She hated me because of who my father was and had threatened to have her dad and older brother beat up my brother. I was terrified for Marc. At the time I was eight and didn't realize she was completely full of crap. I'd begged Mom to let me quit. She'd finally relented after I came home sobbing after every class, refusing to tell her why.

I missed riding.

"Brilliant. Here, let me help you on." At Collette's side he did a quick check of the stirrups and then reached down, making a step with his hands. Looking at him uncertainly, I placed my foot in his care. With ease he lifted me into the saddle, surprising me. As did the muscles peeking out from under the sleeves of his thin green T-shirt.

"How far are we riding?" I asked, needing to stop myself from wondering how muscled the rest of his body was.

"It's not far, but it'd take too long to walk there."

Both now mounted and ready to go, I smiled. He looked *really* good on a horse. He clicked his tongue and Ajax trotted forward. Colette needed no prodding; she seemed to want to follow wherever Ajax led. The parallel wasn't lost on me.

I gently guided Colette to pull alongside Preston so we could talk. "Has your sister ever brought her paranormal group here to investigate?"

"Chillingham?" Preston's lips curled as he huffed a laugh. "My aunt would never allow that. Far too stuffy. If there were anything here she'd find a way to get rid of it. I'd be more afraid of her than any spirit."

"Really? If she's so scary, why do you come?"

"Mostly 'cause it's tradition. We've come up here every summer since we were kids. Nowadays it's really the only time I see my family. And my mum, despite their arguing, likes spending time with her sister. Same certainly can't be said for her son."

"What do your parents do?" As soon as I asked, I regretted it. Now he'd undoubtedly ask about mine.

"My dad's a researcher with the National Health Department. Mum does a lot of volunteer work and takes care of my dad and our estate. How about your parents?"

"They both work in the entertainment industry," I evaded.

"That's cool. What areas?"

Dangit.

"Um, Mom's a director of photography. Dad's . . . well, he kinda gets his hands into a little bit of everything." *Please don't want to know more.*

He nodded. "So being a California girl with parents working in show business, do you get to meet a lot of celebrities?"

I shrugged. "A few, but not really." Okay, that was a teensy bit of a fib. But I didn't want him to look at me any differently. 'Cause I *really* liked the way he was looking at me now. Seriously, the way his brown eyes caught and held mine, and the smile on his lips, I'd do anything to make that never go away.

If he knew, everything would change. He'd change.

It always did. I stopped being a friend, and became someone who had the right connections. And I was sick of it. I didn't want to lose what I might have found with Preston. He had to get to know me without the influence of my father's celebrity.

We rode on across heather-dotted landscapes and through treed glens, talking about movies we liked and musicians.

"Just up here." He beckoned toward a line of softly waving willow trees. Preston guided Ajax toward the tallest tree. The tendrils of leaves made an arch in the front, inviting you inside the green copse. I squinted my eyes. There was something red laid out underneath the tree.

Closer, I could see it was a blanket. A wicker basket sat on a corner. "Are we having a picnic?" I asked, turning in the saddle, wanting to see his face and feeling a little silly for stating the obvious.

"Yeah, I hope you don't mind." A look of insecurity flashed through his eyes before he shifted his gaze. "I guess I just wanted to show this place to you. It's one of my secret spots. I come here when I have to get away. I thought you might like it."

I loved that he brought me here and that he prepared a picnic for us. His rambling was also pretty cute. "It's lovely."

It really was. The shaky leaves rustled with the breeze as the tree's long arms swayed, picked up in the soft airstream.

Preston jumped down from Ajax and came to my side. Reaching up, he clasped my waist. I shivered at the warmth of his hands seeping through my thin tank top. I braced myself on his shoulders as he guided me down with a smile. We stood momentarily frozen until he cleared his throat and released me, making me drop my arms.

For a second I thought he might try to kiss me. I couldn't deny I was disappointed he didn't.

I shook my head at myself. It wasn't that long ago I'd sworn off men completely. A large part of me was still wary. Romance had never worked for me. And yet, a tiny part of me hoped that just this once, with Preston, it would.

Chapter Six

Preferences

Preston secured the horses, then came back and grabbed my hand, guiding me to the plaid blanket. A slow stream meandered past us on the other side of the trees. Some of the long, slender boughs dipped into the water and were pulled along in the flow. I knew how they felt. Our whole family got pulled along in the undercurrent that was Dad's life and work. Hell, even just his personality. It was too exhausting to fight, and far too dangerous.

"I wasn't sure what you liked, so it's a bit of a mishmash." Kneeling down, he opened the picnic basket and started pulling out glass containers.

Stirred from my thoughts, I sat and popped the lids open, laying them out. With a chuckle, I said, "When it comes to food, I'm fairly easy to please. Just no onions."

"Onions?" He looked to me, his lips twitching. "How can you not like onions?"

I shrugged. "Really, I think it's mostly the smell. It feels like it coats my nostrils and I can never get it out." *Yeah, now that's a sexy thing to talk about, nostrils.* I rolled my eyes at myself.

"Well, we're in luck, there's no onions. But, I've got grapes, cheese and gherkins, apples, sliced turkey, pasta salad, cucumber sandwiches, biscuits, homemade lemon squash, water, strawberries . . ."

Leaning over, I looked into the basket. "Goodness, is that thing bottomless? How many people are you expecting?"

His cheeks pinked. "So, I may have overpacked. I just wanted to make sure I had at least something you liked."

I leaned back, secretly thrilled. "This is all very sweet. You did a terrific job."

With a huge grin, he handed me a plate and we started to dish up. Above us a little bird hopped from branch to branch. I smiled as it perched next to a friend. "It's so peaceful here. I can see why you like it so much. But I'm curious, what do you come here to escape?"

He paused, a square of cheese ready to pop in his mouth. "My family, mostly. That sounds beastly of me. It's just, there's so many of us, and when we holiday, they're always around. It's nice to get away and have some quiet. This house, despite being large, is so loud. My aunt and Mum bicker all the time. Tanner and I . . . well, we hate each other and spend the summer seeing who can make whose life the most miserable. And Haley brought her fiancé this year so . . ." His lips quirked and he looked away, clearing his throat. "Never mind, I won't elaborate on that. It just gets overwhelming."

"Sounds like it. You must be anxious to get back to school and your regular life."

"Normally I am, but this year it's a little . . . different."

"How so?" I grabbed a strawberry and bit off the juicy bottom.

He looked at me like it should be obvious. "Well, you're here."

Heat crawled into my cheeks, making me look away. We'd known each other such a short time, but his face and voice seemed to consume my thoughts. I could almost forget about telling Dad my plans for Thrippletons and what his reaction would be.

Preston cleared his throat. "Where is this fashion school you're wanting to go to?"

I shook my head, debating with myself. "Um, it's in the UK, but I'm not telling which one. If I tell, two things would inevitably happen: One, something would make my plans fall apart. And two, my dad would find out and all hell would break loose."

"Did you ever think that your dad just might be cool about this?"

"Um, no. He's not the warm, fuzzy, happy-if-you're-happy kind of guy."

He shook his head. "Hmm, I guess I just don't understand it." Pausing, he looked away. "I get the impression that there's more to the story but you don't want to tell me." His gold-flecked eyes flicked up to mine. "You *can* tell me, you know. I'm a very good secret keeper."

"Thanks." I nodded and looked down, picking at a frayed fingernail. He was definitely trying to sort me out.

"So, are you at least excited to start school?"

My shoulders lifted. "I am. I'm looking forward to a fresh start and living my own life, not one that's been planned out by someone else or that I've been dragged to because . . ." I stopped myself from mentioning Dad. "Because it's a good idea. This is just mine."

Preston leaned closer and softly said, "I hope you'll be happy wherever you end up."

I forgot to breathe until he moved away. "Thanks." My voice sounded off. Clearing my throat, I said, "Tell me about your friends. You said one was in Seattle." I nipped off the end of a pickle, enjoying the tangy crunch.

"That'd be Edmund. His girlfriend's from there and she went home after classes ended. I guess she wasn't sure if she was coming back in the fall and Edmund chased after her to change her mind. That and he was unable to be apart from her for . . . well, possibly forever, I suppose."

I smiled, wishing I had a guy like that. "That's awfully romantic."

He rubbed his hand on the back of his head, ruffling his short waves. "It is. They're really great together. He's lucky, she definitely brings out the best in him."

"That's wonderful." I reached out and plucked a blade of grass and ran my fingernail along the seam in the middle, splitting it apart. *My parents certainly don't have that.* It's nice to know it actually exists. "I think that's one of the best things. The idea that just being with someone makes you a better person. I hope one day someone feels that way about me."

"I don't think you'll have to worry about that."

• • •

Still floating from my date with Preston, I sighed and looked up at the sky, pinked from the setting sun, feeling content. I bounded in the front door of my family's rental manor and—"Oh my gosh! I'm so sorry." My hand flew to my mouth in shock, as I'd just slammed into someone. The person turned around and, crap . . . it was Ben Chambers. "Um, hi." My voice came out stiff and awkward.

Ben stood about three inches taller than me. Which was nothing when compared to Preston; now that boy was tall. All my life I'd hated being so short, but next to a towering hot Brit dude I discovered I actually kind of liked it.

Ben smiled. "I was hoping to run into you again."

"Yeah, sorry, for *actually* running into you, I wasn't expecting anyone to be there." I gave a small laugh and looked up the stairs. "Um, can I get you something?"

He shook his head. "We had a long day on set and your dad's just grabbing something to help me better grasp my character."

"Ah." I leaned back on my booted heels and tucked my hands in my back pockets. "Well, I guess I'll see you around then." I took a step away when his hand shot out and stopped me. His skin was hot on my cool forearm.

"Would you be interested in grabbing dinner? I'm starving and I hate eating alone." The way he wrinkled his nose was cute.

After our picnic Preston had taken me for a long horseback ride around the estate, and I was getting kind of hungry. "Um." I looked behind myself, wondering when and where my dad would pop up. Did I really want to get dinner with Ben? He was a massive celebrity and that status meant dealing with the press, which I hated. "What did you have in mind?"

His shoulders lifted in a shrug. "Are you in the mood for anything?"

"Maybe something quick and easy? Wherever your usual posse of paparazzi won't be."

Chuckling, he tucked his hands in his pockets and flashed a crooked grin my way. "Ah, well, they haven't quite found us yet. It won't be long before they do, but I plan to enjoy it while it lasts. What do you say we track down a pizza joint?"

The look on his face was hopeful. I'd just end up scrounging in the kitchen and making a sandwich. *Pizza sounds way better.* "Okay, let me go grab a jacket and clean up, I'll be right back."

When I reached the top of the stairs Marc was leaning against the wall, his dark hair in a perfect state of messiness. He nudged my shoulder and whispered, "I thought you said you'd never date a celebrity."

I shot a glare at him. "It's not a date."

"You're getting dinner together. Alone. It's a date." He smirked and followed me into my room.

Stopping at my armoire, I smoothed my hair in the mirror fastened to the inside of the door.

"See, you're even primping."

I spun from my reflection to face him. "Marc, shut it. I'm just getting pizza with him." I grabbed the gray hoodie off the hook and shut the door harder than I intended. "You're just jealous I'm going with your man crush."

Marc scowled and shook his head. "Whatever."

"Why don't you come with us?" I grinned.

"And intrude on your hot date? Never." He smirked at me, pushing my buttons, which was something he excelled at.

"Go pick on someone else. I'm not in the mood and I'm not going to give you the reaction you want." I stuck my tongue out at him as I headed back to the entryway. My arms slid into my well-worn jacket and I zipped it halfway up. Reaching into my pocket, I pulled out the lightweight circle scarf I'd stuffed in there and looped it around my neck twice. I loved the funky vintage octopus printed on the thin cream fabric.

Marc didn't follow me to the stairs; instead he stopped at the door to his room. "Have fun, but some advice, you probably shouldn't kiss him on a first date. You don't want him to get the wrong idea." He ducked out of sight before I could even think of flipping him the bird. *Jerk face.*

At the bottom of the stairs Ben and Dad were chatting. Ben held on to what looked like a packet of printed pages. They were doing some sci-fi action-y flick . . . *The Moons of* . . . something.

Dad glanced up to me and grinned, the edges of his eyes crinkling. He looked on the verge of actual giddiness. "There you are."

"Here I am." I held my arms out in a gesture of "ta-da" as I reached the bottom of the stairs. "You ready?"

Ben nodded. "Let's go."

"Don't keep her out too late," Dad cautioned, still struggling to suppress his smile.

My gaze darted to his. What was with the doting daddy act?

"I won't, sir." Ben's hand slid onto the small of my back, guiding me to the front door. I was struck by how odd his touch felt. I barely knew him and this felt way too intimate for having just met.

When we got into his convertible I buckled in, grateful to have a little space. As we drove away I looked back. My father waved on the porch, illuminated by the lights flanking the doors. *Okay, that's weird.*

Ben reached and cranked up the heater. Thank goodness; it was chilly and my California body still hadn't adjusted to the highland climate.

"Thanks for coming with me." He smiled.

"Sure." My brows scrunched together. "So, do you have some sort of issue with eating alone or what?"

Both hands on the leather-bound steering wheel, he kept his gaze on the road. "Um, kind of. Being alone is . . . difficult for me. I'm not really sure why."

"That's pretty much the opposite of me. I hate crowds and . . . well people, sometimes." A nervous laugh escaped my lips. "I'd much rather be alone with my sketchbook and pencils."

"You're an artist?" He turned with a grin, looking relieved at the topic shift.

"I suppose you could say that." When I was growing up all my art teachers raved about my drawings and paintings. I'd actually won a few contests. Even back then, my favorite part was drawing people and dressing them up in fun clothes. I put much more detail into the attire than any other aspect of my pieces.

"I'd love to see some of your work."

"Oh." I wasn't expecting him to show an interest. "These days most of my drawings are designs for clothes." We hit the edge of town just as the sun was in its final descent.

"Then you want to be a designer?"

I sat mute, knowing I had to be super careful with what I said next. He had a direct line to my father and I didn't want anything to accidentally slip out. My teeth nibbled my lip, trying to sort an answer. "Um, I haven't decided yet."

We fell silent. I found myself wishing Preston were here. True, he didn't have the full story either, but at least I didn't have to censor myself as much, which was such an amazing feeling. Add in my attraction to him and it was quite the powerful combo.

I cleared my throat, trying to focus my thoughts back to the present company. "So, what made you want to do Dad's movie?"

"Honestly? I've always wanted to work with your mom, she's an amazing director of photography and she only works with your father. When this came along, I liked the script and it fit into my schedule." He flashed a smile, his teeth perfectly straight and gleaming white.

We parked in front of a row of buildings all squished together. In the fading sunlight I couldn't tell if they were connected or not. The glowing windows of an Italian restaurant lit up the sidewalk and the smell of basil and tomatoes wafted on the cool breeze.

"Oh my gosh, that smells delicious." I tucked my hair behind my ears, inhaling the lovely aroma as I stepped up onto the pathway.

Ben matched my smile and sniffed the air. "Mm, let's go."

I pulled the restaurant door open and he grabbed on to it, holding it for me to enter. Feeling awkward to be here with him, I shyly met his eyes. "Thanks." Despite my connection to fame, I still didn't hang out with celebrities.

My plan was to survive dinner and not talk about anything that could get back to my dad's ears and kill my plans for my future.

These lies and omissions were getting awfully heavy. And I was sick of having to drag them along everywhere I went.

Chapter Seven

Family Business

Little Sicily, the pizza place, was deserted. It was also very red. Red tablecloths, red chairs, red candles, red carpets, pretty much everything. But the food was delicious.

Ben and I shared a large vegetarian pizza and talked about California and the things we loved and hated about home.

"I don't miss L.A. I never really do when I leave," Ben admitted after wiping his lips with his red cloth napkin.

"I don't either. Not even a little." I looked at the candle on the table. With one puff of air I could easily snuff it out. I fought back the urge.

"Things move slower here, and it's a really nice change. The people seem more . . . real." His eyes took on a faraway look.

His admission surprised me and piqued my curiosity. I'd have thought with his mega success he'd love California. I wanted to get to know him better, which I hadn't expected.

"If you could go anywhere, be anything you wanted, what would you choose?" I propped my head in my hand and took a sip from my straw.

His brow scrunched in thought. When his green eyes met mine his lips curled into a half-smile. "You have to promise not to laugh."

"Okay." I tilted my head, confused. "Why would I laugh?"

Sighing, he looked away. "Because, growing up I wanted to be a makeup artist."

"Really? A makeup artist instead of a glamour boy actor?" I grinned. "I'm guessing there's a story there?"

His gaze dropped to the tabletop as he idly straightened scattered crumbs into a pile with the tip of his finger. "Yeah, my mom. I'd sit with her when I was little and we'd talk about our day while she got ready to go to work at night. She was a bartender and worked late hours. The old lady across the hallway used to come and stay with me while she was gone. And I loved those moments, watching my mom and just catching up." Glancing at me, he shrugged. "Now, if I could, I'd love to work on a special effects team. What they do is nothing short of amazing."

I could see he was passionate about this, yet he was trying to play it off. "Why don't you do it then?"

He shook his head. "Acting pays more and it *is* fun, don't get me wrong. Sometimes I just wish my life was a little more behind the camera. Plus, with the money I make from acting my mom doesn't have to bartend anymore. I can easily take care of her."

"I think she's lucky to have you." My heart melted at his words. A soft smile crossed my lips that I couldn't have stopped even if I wanted to.

"Nah, I'm the lucky one."

"What about your dad?"

"Not in the picture." He took a sip of his drink. "He left when I was a baby."

"That's definitely his loss."

Ben glanced down his straight nose at me and sat back in his seat. "You're not what I was expecting."

"Oh? What were you expecting?"

"Some rich girl who wanted to be seen with me or who was more interested in watching her carbs than carrying on a conversation. How did you turn out so normal with Scott McKendrick for your father?"

Because my father is a giant bully and I've kept my distance from anything to do with him or his career. Shaking my head free of those thoughts, I said, "Well, to be fair, you aren't the typical celebrity I'm used to either."

The green of his eyes gleamed. "Normal, that's all I want to be. Just a normal guy."

"Well, you're definitely in the wrong line of work for that." I chuckled.

Laughing, he threw some cash on the table. "Touché. Come on, I should get you back. I don't want to get on your dad's bad side, it's not pretty."

Hmm, so he'd actually seen it. Under my breath, I muttered, "Tell me about it."

Ben stood and stared a moment, assessing me. Just how much of Dad's bad side had he seen? As a family we all tried to not provoke him. We tiptoed around, never really sure what might set him off. Did his actors and crew do the same?

This evening had completely taken me by surprise. I'd expected a career-obsessed narcissist, but instead I got . . . Ben. Who was actually pretty cool.

I wonder if Dad will be waiting up for us? He certainly seemed interested in my going out with him tonight. My red flags had shot up at his overeager attentiveness. Something was up, I just wasn't sure what.

• • •

My slippers scuffed against the kitchen's hardwood floor as I made my way in for coffee. I wrapped my blue robe tighter to ward off the morning chill. The damn rooster from the barn started cock-a-doodle-dooing as soon as the sun poked its head over the horizon. Actually, I think he might have let a few screeches loose while it was still dark out. The sleep deprivation may be clouding my brain, but I'm fairly certain that blasted bird had it in for me.

"Good morning, star shine." Mom's tired eyes met mine over her mug of coffee. "Sleep well?"

I grunted.

Dad lowered his paper with a sly grin. "How was your date with Ben?"

Opening my mouth to correct him, I stopped myself. Instead I got some coffee, lips zipped.

From a young age I'd discovered the consequences of trying to set Dad straight. It usually involved a lengthy passive-aggressive lecture on why I'm wrong and always ended with him informing me I'm too stupid to keep up with his intellectual prowess.

"You went on a date with Ben Chambers?" Mom set her mug down, a little sloshing over the side. Her eyes darted to Dad before she quickly set to cleaning up the spill. "He doesn't seem quite your type."

Dad opened his paper and cleared his throat. "Always in the dark aren't you, Diana?" He smirked and shook the newsprint to straighten out the crinkles. "Just keep your mouth shut when you have no clue what's going on."

Mom's eyes dropped to her lap and she looked like she wanted to leave, but Dad wouldn't let that happen. He'd call her back and belittle her even more until she did exactly what he wanted, sat there and looked pretty.

"Sorry, mom. I should've told you before I left last night." The words spilled out with the need to diffuse the situation.

My grandmother had once told me that before Mom married Dad she'd been a force to be reckoned with in Hollywood. You couldn't tell that by the woman sitting before me now. She'd gone from being a successful, sought-after director of photography to only working on Dad's projects.

She still got lots of offers. Dad just *encouraged* her to turn them down.

I hated him for what he'd done to her. I couldn't understand why she'd married him in the first place.

Marc chose that moment to come sauntering in the room and pluck an orange from the fruit bowl. "Good morning." He took in Mom's and my faces and looked to Dad, jaw clenched. "What'd I miss?"

"Mags was just about to tell us about her date." Dad slid his juice glass to my mother, indicating he wanted a refill. I struggled to keep the anger out of my expression. To him she primarily filled three roles: his personal maid whenever necessary, an accessory while entertaining, and a doormat for all the times in between.

Mom said the man she fell in love with was kind and funny, easygoing even. After I'd been born, when his career really began to rocket off, that's when he changed. But part of me worried. I knew I'd been a surprise pregnancy.

Did he consider me a mistake?

Secretly, I hoped it meant she'd had a steamy affair that I was the result of. Anything so I wasn't his daughter. But I knew my mother would never do that.

Grabbing his glass, Mom rushed to do his bidding.

Marc slid his chair out and sat. He popped the orange peel off, the citrusy smell wafting around him. Mom sat back down and handed Dad his refreshed juice, not meeting his eyes.

Dad cleared his throat, still waiting for me to speak.

"It wasn't anything special, really. He just didn't want to eat alone, so we grabbed a pizza. It was perfectly innocent and very non-datelike."

Mom's eyes darted to Dad, gauging his reaction. Clearly he was in a surly mood this morning. I hoped my answer didn't upset him.

Dad's eyes stayed on me as he placed his hand on Mom's. She recoiled ever so slightly at his touch. "If Ben Chambers wants to date you I'd think you'd be thrilled. It's not like the boys are lined up to take you out." He chuckled and stood, dumping his untouched juice in the sink.

My shoulders rolled forward and I looked to my lap, not meeting his eyes. I couldn't. I knew I didn't need a string of guys vying for my attention, nor did I want that, but Dad's words still stung. All I wanted was someone kind and caring. Preston's face appeared in my mind. *Maybe he'd be the one to prove him wrong.*

Under the table Marc grabbed my hand and gave it a squeeze. When I looked up at him I saw his jaw tense and twitch.

"I'm off to the set. You two should stop by." He used two fingers on one hand forming a V to point to Marc and me before coming to my side. Tightly pinching my chin in his fingers, he tilted my head back. "I don't know what Ben sees in you, but you're gonna do whatever it takes to get into a serious relationship with him. You got me?"

His grip tightened painfully and I nodded ever so slightly just to make him stop. When he let go he patted my cheek and headed out the door. I opened and closed my jaw, wondering if his fingers left any bruises I'd need to hide later.

Mom turned to me, eyes soft and concerned. "Are you okay?"

I nodded and glanced to Marc, his face red and his eyes angry. The front door shut and Marc slammed a fist on the tabletop, rattling the glasses. "He's such an ass."

"Why do you stay? I don't get it." I rubbed my chin trying to ease the pain.

Mom sighed and reached across the table to grab my free hand. "It's not easy to explain."

"Try," Marc demanded.

Her eyes darted to his face. "He used to be so different. When we first met we'd go for long walks and just talk. He was always smiling and kind. He could be assertive, but he was never cruel."

"How could he have changed this much?" I asked, unable to picture my father like that.

"Everything changed when we had a two-year-old and a newborn. After the first Dragon Guardian film, it happened overnight. He was suddenly this hot, up-and-coming director. He was constantly working and overwhelmed."

"So that made him mean?" I asked, confused how that could cause such a drastic change.

"I chalked it up to the stress and how our life had so rapidly turned unrecognizable." She shrugged. "But I could see him slipping away from us with every accolade and award he'd get. I hoped he'd see what he was doing to us. I loved him so much." She cleared her throat and took a shaky breath.

Marc grabbed her hand and held it, as if offering her some of his strength.

"Plus, I'd left my career to stay home and raise the two of you. I had nothing to support us. I only went back once you guys were much older."

"We could've figured something out." I pulled my hand from hers to scratch my nose and watched as she shook her head.

"I was young, stupid, and believed that marriage was forever. I was taught it was something you worked at and you didn't quit just because it got hard. Just considering divorce made me feel like a failure. I thought maybe if I tried harder things would get better."

Marc sighed. "Why didn't you go to Grandma and Grandpa?"

Mom blew out a heavy breath, her eyes watery. "I was embarrassed. I didn't want them to know. And I definitely didn't want the two of you coming from a broken home. I thought you'd be better off with two parents and I just . . ." She looked down and sniffled. "He threatened to fight me for sole custody and said he'd win because of who he was and the size of his bank account."

"You could've won," I countered. "He's abusive, to all of us."

"It wasn't a risk I was willing to take." She looked me in the eyes and offered a gentle smile. "I couldn't lose you guys."

"We're not little kids anymore and you don't have to put up with him." I put my hand over their clasped ones.

"You're right." Mom put her free hand on my cheek. Voice soft, she said, "That's why I've decided to file for divorce when we get home."

"What?" Both Marc and I asked.

"I'm tired and I'm done."

My mouth popped open, then I smiled. "For real?"

"For real." Her blue eyes shimmered with unshed tears. "You guys are grown and making your own way. I'm steadily getting offers for really great projects. There's just no reason for me to stay and put up with his crap anymore. He'll never change."

Standing, I leaned over and hugged her sitting form. Marc did the same, enveloping us both. We looked like a mountain of happiness.

"I'm proud of you, Mom." Marc's face lit up.

"Me too."

A tear slid down Mom's cheek and she wiped it away. "Just promise you'll stay far away from him once I file. I'm not sure what he's capable of."

Her words sent a shiver up my spine. Less than three months until the shit would hit the fan. Lucky me, I'd be far away from the splash zone. My mind tumbled around mental images of my father angry. *What would he do to Mom?*

• • •

Bright stars twinkled on the other side of the wavy glass next to me. I sat in the window seat sketching, my phone at my side. Preston's face slowly appeared from the tip of my pencil onto my sketchpad. Just the sight of him made me happy. I wondered why he hadn't kissed me at our picnic. I'd certainly wanted him to. A loud chirp made my heart jump in my chest and alerted me to a new text.

Setting my pencil and pad aside, I glanced at the illuminated screen. The text was from a number not in my contacts.

Mystery Texter: What are you doing Saturday night?

I knew who I *hoped* was texting me.

Me: And you are?
Mystery Texter: Sorry, it's Preston. ;)

Warmth spiraled inside me, filling every inch of my skin. I held in an excited squeal as I added his name to the number. Before replying I took a steadying deep breath.

Me: Oh, hey! I don't think I have plans Saturday, why?
Preston: I was hoping you'd want to get together.
Me: Hmm, I might be able to make something work.
Preston: Can I pick you up at 8:00?
Me: See you then.

Rolling onto my back, I kicked my feet in the air and let out my pent-up squeal. Dad may have wanted guys lining up for me, but just perhaps, Preston was the only one I'd need.

Marc appeared in my doorway and cleared his throat. "You got a minute?" He smiled, amused by my spontaneous aerobics show. "Once you're done with your Jazzercise?"

My hand smoothed my hair as I sat up and made a face at him. Deep breath in and out, I composed myself.

I nodded and scooted over, playing it cool. "What's up?"

"We need to make a plan."

My brows scrunched together. "What kind of plan?"

"How we're gonna keep Mom safe."

I scrubbed my palms against my jeans, happiness pushed aside and worry now eating my insides. "I'll do anything, of course, but being over here I'm not sure how I'd be much help."

Closing the door, he crossed the room and sat beside me. "I'm going to ask Mom to move in with me and I might need your help convincing her."

"Really? What about Jack? Do you guys have enough room for all three of you?" Jack was Marc's best friend and they roomed together at Berkeley last year. This year they were renting an apartment.

He shook his head. "Jack will have to find a new place. He'll understand. He's been around our family long enough to know what Dad's like. I just . . . I want her where I can make sure she's safe."

Jack, despite teasing me growing up, had always been a good friend to both Marc and me. My junior year of high school he'd taken me to the prom. As friends only, but it'd definitely made a little soft spot in my heart for him.

"You're the best brother ever." I laid my head on his shoulder and huffed out a breath. "I wish we didn't have to deal with this at all. This may sound terrible, but it'd be so much easier if Dad would just disappear."

"If only. I'm just worried 'cause my place won't be as posh as Mom's used to."

"I don't think she'll be picky. She's scared, Marc, I could see it in her eyes."

Rubbing his forehead, he nodded. "I know. I saw it too. We also need to figure out when you're going to tell him about Thrippletons."

I leaned my head back and groaned. "I know I've got to do it, but I'm terrified."

"I think you should tell him soon. Give him time to cool down from it before Mom serves him with divorce papers. 'Cause if it's piled back to back . . . he might snap."

"That thought crossed my mind too. I'll do it soon. I promise."

He nodded. "And don't worry, I've got your back and so does Mom. You should get to follow your dreams."

Tears welled in my eyes. "Thanks."

"No worries, Mags. We'll get through this."

Marc watched out for me and was always there for me. No matter what. Even once when Jack's teasing had gone too far, Marc had gotten into a huge fight with him and didn't speak to him for a week.

"So, have you found your redhead yet?"

A sly grin lifted the corner of his mouth. "Maybe."

"Come on, spill it. I could use some good news."

"I sorta met someone." He shrugged. "But she seems to have zero interest in me."

I stuck out my bottom lip. "That sucks. Let me know if I can be of any help to the cause." I leaned into him, giving him a nudge.

"Any more news from Thrippletons?"

"Yeah, I got an email, I'm rooming with a girl, Daisy Michaels. Well, if I'm still alive after telling Dad." I tried to laugh it off, but it came out choked and shaky.

"Mags, it'll be fine. Even if it's not and he's pissed, I won't let him hurt you. Not again."

Chapter Eight

Impetus

Lying in bed, I stretched my arms out and touched a band of streaming sunlight. The days had moved at a glacial pace, but it was now Friday. Tomorrow was my date with Preston. I still hadn't told Dad about Thrippletons; he hadn't been around for me to tell. He'd either left early for the set or been busy with night shoots.

Truthfully, I hadn't minded the delay. Reaching up, I pressed my palms on the solid wood headboard and braced myself so I could stretch. *I can do this.* With closed eyes, I sucked in a breath, trying to instill courage I didn't feel.

I dragged my body from my warm cocoon, wrapped my robe around me, and went across the hall to knock on Marc's door.

"Yeah?" His voice sounded groggy.

Slipping inside, I sat on the side of his bed. "Marc, get up. I'm telling Dad."

He lifted his head, his dark hair sticking up at odd angles. On his cheek was the imprint of his hand. "Now? Why now? I'm sleeping."

"'Cause it's the only time I can catch Dad."

"Is he even still here?"

"I'm not sure, but if he is, I really want you there." My brows drew together in worry.

He rubbed the back of his hand across his nose. "M'kay. Gimme a minute . . . or five."

"Thanks." I whispered before hopping up to head downstairs. A part of me wanted Dad to be there, but a much bigger part hoped he'd already left. My stomach churned and my heartbeat flitted around like a drunk hummingbird.

Crap, should I have warned Mom first?

I sucked in a shaky breath, cautiously stepping on the creaky stairs. The paintings on the walls stared down at me. Their male inhabitants glared, as if judging my decision. Mom hummed a soft tune from the kitchen, unaware of the impending drama just around the corner.

I took a deep breath and reached up to straighten my hair, wondering if I should dart back upstairs and brush it.

My foot hit the bottom step and I paused, looking back for Marc, wanting strength in numbers, but Rip Van Winkle was still in bed.

"Morning, sweet pea." Mom smiled at me and scraped the scrambled eggs from her pan into a lidded dish.

I glanced at the table and saw Dad. Fear made my palms sweat and itch.

Now, actually faced with it, I wished he hadn't been here.

"Hey." I grabbed a clean plate from the stack on the counter and filled it with eggs, toast, and some fresh fruit, bypassing the sausage.

Dad looked up from his reading as I sat down. "Morning."

"How's the shoot going?" I nibbled on the toast, hoping to settle my tummy.

"It's good. We're a little behind schedule, but we'll catch up. That Ben of yours is quite the hard worker."

He's not mine. "That's great." The knots in my stomach pulled tighter.

Folding his paper he set it aside. "I've invited Ben for a family dinner tonight. I expect you to make an effort to actually look nice." He waved me off, then added, "Wear a *real* designer. Not one of your little . . . homemade things."

My forkful of eggs stopped at my lips. His dismissal made my eyes burn, but I let it go. I had bigger issues right now. "Of course."

"Marvelous." He glanced at his watch and started to stand. "I should get going."

"Dad, wait. I've been meaning to talk to you, it's important."

He settled back into his chair. Glancing at Mom, he gestured with his head and she came and sat beside him. "What is it?"

My eyes darted to the door, wishing Marc would get his ass down here. "Um, I . . . I have something I need to tell you." I popped my knuckles under the table, stalling.

Mom's eyebrows lowered and the look she gave me said she knew what was coming.

"Sorry, morning, everyone." Marc hurried into the room, still in his pajamas, hair a rumpled dark mess. He sat beside me with a supportive grin.

"Get on with it." Dad glanced at his watch again, then at me with an impatient look on his stubbled face. "I don't have time for this."

I took a deep breath, mentally bracing myself. Maybe if I put a super-positive spin on it, he'd react better.

In a rush, I said, "I have some completely amazing and life-changing news . . . I've been accepted to Thrippletons School of Fashion and Design. So, I won't be going back to California when the summer's over."

Dad leaned forward and threaded his fingers together. "I'm not sure I follow. Where is this completely amazing and life-changing school?" His tone was sarcastic, like he was just playing along with a charade.

"In England, Bampton to be precise."

"Mmhm, I see." He steepled his two pointer fingers together, then pressed them against his lips like he was deep in thought.

"Let me make sure I understand this. Your plan then, is not to attend UCLA and basically shit on all the work I've done."

My mouth stayed shut. I knew the last thing he wanted was for me to actually answer him.

"On all the connections I used to get you accepted there." He was smiling, but it wasn't a good smile. It was a threat of the storm he was about to unleash.

I looked down at my hands, wishing I was anywhere but here.

Dad stood, the chair scraping on the wood flooring. In a menacing whisper he said, "What happened to the money I gave you to reserve your place at UCLA?"

My stomach clenched and I glanced between Mom and Marc. Wincing, I said in a small voice, "I sent it to Thrippletons instead."

His fist came down on the table, rattling the dishes. "That was not your money. You had no right to send it to this *fashion* school." The words spat from his lips.

"You're right. I know you are, and I'm sorry, it's just . . . this is something I've wanted for so long. It's my dream." My voice quavered.

Mom tugged on Dad's arm, trying to get him to sit. His breathing turned shallow and fast.

Beside me Marc squeezed my hand, giving me a boost of courage to continue. "I never wanted to be a lawyer. That's not me."

Inhaling sharply, Dad lowered himself to his seat and rubbed a hand down his whiskery face. "This is a ridiculous idea, Margaret. You'll never make anything of yourself in fashion."

Marc sat up straighter. "You're wrong. She'll be amazing no matter what she does. She's always known what she wanted to do, you just never took the time to notice. Or maybe you just never cared."

Our father's face turned scarlet. His voice was soft, a clear indicator of his rising anger. The quieter he got, the scarier he got.

"You think you're so smart. You know everything, do you? Let me remind you who pays your tuition."

"Dad, please." I could feel tears threatening. My teeth sank into my bottom lip, fighting to hold them back.

"I won't pay for this." Dad stood again and walked away from the table. "This is a stupid idea from a foolish girl."

My eyes watered. "No, it's not."

"Fine, do what you want, I don't care. But if you don't go to UCLA you're on your own."

"Scott." Mom's voice pleaded with him.

"What?" Dad growled. "Do you think we should be supporting her forever? Diana, she has to learn to make it on her own."

Mom's face looked serene and calm. "But that's not really the issue here, is it? You and I have made more than enough money to support both our children for as long as they need it."

"She needs to learn—"

"This has nothing to do with her learning anything." She threw her arms up in frustration. "Your logic doesn't work, can't you see that? If you were so willing to pay for law school she still would've missed that *learning* opportunity. Plus, I helped her. She had my permission to send the check to Thrippletons."

Dad scoffed. "I always knew you were stupid, but this . . . this tops everything." His lip curled in distaste as he stared her down.

For the first time in a long time I saw my mother get angry. Her blue eyes sparked and she ran a hand through her hair, messing the long curls. She sat straighter, as if pulling on some well of strength deep within her.

"At least be honest, Scott. You just don't like it when someone doesn't follow your almighty decree. Cutting her off is your way of hurting her because you aren't getting *your* way."

Smack. It was a swift backhand to her face, knocking her head to the side. Slowly, she turned to face him, a glare in her eyes, but no fear.

In a quiet voice Dad said, "You always make me do this. When will you learn your opinion isn't necessary?"

Marc and I both shot out of our chairs. I went to Mom's side and Marc stood next to Dad, poised to take him on, fists clenched.

"Oh, what are you gonna do?" He sneered at Marc's angry face.

My normally quiet and meek mother flexed her jaw and stood, squaring off with my father. "Maggie is going to do amazing things, whether you believe in her or not."

"Whatever, I'm not paying for that bullshit."

Mom shrugged. "I want to make one thing very clear, Scott. That was the last time you'll ever lay a hand on me or my children. I'm done."

"I'll believe it when I see it. Just remember, darling, you're nothing without me." Dad jammed his keys into his pocket and left.

Once he was gone, Mom's hand reached up to cover the sting on her cheek. "Go pack your bags."

As much as I wished it would, this wouldn't go away easily. No, this was just the beginning and we were embarking on a long trip into hell.

• • •

The view from the hotel window was lovely. The sun was just setting and the River Ness lazily flowed just a few steps away. I sighed, spun around, and leaned on the glass-paneled door. Mom and I were sharing a suite and Marc took the adjoining room. We made it. We got out.

Mom approached me and brushed my bangs from my eyes before crossing her arms. "I should've done this a long time ago."

"Better late than never." I wrapped my arms around her and gave her a hug. "I'm proud of you."

She patted my arm. "Likewise, and don't you worry, we'll find a way to pay for Thrippletons. My money may get tied up for a little while with the divorce proceedings, but we'll sort something out."

This new school of mine wasn't cheap. Quite the opposite.

"It's okay. I'm sure I'll figure it out. It's what I want, so I'll make it happen." At least that's what I was telling myself.

Inside my mind raced. Where would I get the money? Loans? Maybe. With my parents' incomes I wouldn't qualify for any type of aid. I'd have to get a job, plain and simple. It'd be my first, but at eighteen, it was high time. No, it wouldn't be easy, but tons of people work and go to school. *I can do this.*

Across the room Mom's phone jingled a happy little chime. Letting go of me, she went over, looked at the screen, and sighed. She looked like she was debating whether to answer it.

"Who is it?" My guess was Dad.

"Who do you think?" She gave me a look and hit the Answer button.

Marc came to stand next to me and kicked off his flip-flops—can't take the California out of the boy. He crossed his arms over his chest and watched with a concerned look on his face. He mouthed, "Don't tell him where we're at."

"Scott." Mom's voice was hard.

We couldn't hear his reply, which was a good thing. It meant he hadn't started yelling.

"Well, I'm very sorry that we're not there to greet Ben, he's a very nice boy."

I'd forgotten Ben was coming to dinner. Ben was getting to see a very different side of my family.

"No, we won't be back tonight or any other night. You also need to find a new DP for your shoot, because I quit. I meant what I said, Scott. I'm done. We're done."

I didn't breathe. Marc didn't seem to be either. The silence as she listened went on too long. I jumped when she started speaking again.

"No, the reasons why I stayed and tolerated your bullying don't hold up anymore. I want a divorce."

Dad's voice was just barely audible, but it was a mumbled mess and I couldn't make anything out.

"No, stop right there. You don't get to talk to me like that anymore." And with a push of a button she disconnected the call. She let out a heavy breath and squeezed her eyes shut.

"Let's celebrate and get room service. I'm starved." Marc threw himself on the bed and reached for the phone.

For the past eighteen years a weight had been pushing us down, crushing us, but now there was a lightness to the air, to all of us. It was our first taste of freedom and it was definitely a magical moment.

I stretched out on the bed and listened as Marc ordered from the white-embossed navy menu.

Mom tapped the corner of her phone against her chin. "Your grandmother is going to be thrilled."

My phone chirped and I sat up so I could pull it from my back pocket. The past couple days my family had been in our own little bubble. I paused and took a deep breath, needing to prepare myself for the outside world again. Lighting up the screen, I saw a new text.

Ben: So, I'm following your Dad to a restaurant in town. Feeling kind of weird. Is everything okay with you guys?
Me: Yeah, we're good. Sorry we're not there.
Ben: Glad you're okay. Will you be back tonight? I'd love to see you.
Me: Um . . . I don't think so. We've checked into a hotel.
Ben: Oh . . .
Ben: Um, well, in that case, do you want to catch a movie this weekend? We could always get a DVD and hang at my place.
Me: I suppose so. Sunday work?
Ben: Perfect, see you then.

I didn't think much of Ben's invite. He was most likely just wanting the company, and he was definitely someone I could see myself being good friends with. I just hoped with him working so close to my Dad that it didn't get too complicated. Well, that or the more important thing: mess up things with Preston.

Preston . . . I smiled and shook my head. Boys should be the last thing on my mind right now.

Yes, I may have jumped one hurdle, but there were still several ahead of me. Like how to pay for Thrippletons and how to be a huge success and how to prove myself to Dad. No pressure there. Nope. None. Nada.

Chapter Nine

My Kind of Perfection

Preston and I traipsed across the south lawn at Chillingham Manor. The sky, dark and star spattered, added a bit of its own magic to the night. Thank God he'd told me to change my clothes. That sundress, although adorable, would've turned me into an icicle. Even in my warmer attire it was still a little chilly.

I grinned at Preston's back, loving how his hand felt in mine as he pulled me alongside him. Thankfully he'd picked me up at the hotel, no questions asked. Mom had been on the phone pretty much nonstop ever since we'd arrived, talking to lawyers and booking travel arrangements for her and Marc. Not that I minded, but it was kind of nice to get away from it for a few hours. I was counting on Preston's presence to chase away my worries about Dad's next move.

"What are we doing out here?"

"Just down these stairs and you'll see. We've got to hurry though, I don't want Tanner to know we're here." He looked fabulous in jeans and a charcoal, three-button hoodie. The maroon of his undershirt peeked from the open collar.

Just down the staircase sat a large illuminated fountain. As we approached, the top came into focus. It was a Pegasus posed in mid-flight. The water shot up around it on all sides, momentarily hiding its hooves.

"How beautiful." I looked up at him.

Stopping in front of the winged horse, he released my hand and looked up at the massive sculpture. "There's a legend attached to this fountain." He glanced at me before continuing. "It's said that if two soul mates come to this fountain on a full moon and kiss under the moonlit sky they'll be together forever."

I glanced up, looking at the full white orb glowing down on us. "Do you believe it?"

He sat on the large concrete bowl's edge and shrugged. "It's certainly a nice idea."

"What about soul mates?" I settled next to him. "Do you truly think there's only one person out there for everyone?"

"I don't know. It's a lovely thought, I suppose." He looked away, his voice slightly rough. "Maybe it's because I've never truly been in love, so I can't imagine connecting with someone on that level, but . . . I find it hard to believe I'd actually want to be with someone that long."

I scrunched up my face. "Ah, commitment issues, eh?"

"No." He was quick to jump in and correct me. "No, not at all. I've just never seen a couple who're still happy and in love after a long period of time. Take my parents; yes, they love each other, but it's more like the way you love a friend. They take care of each other, but there's no passion."

"But *you* only get to see the intimate side of the relationship *you're* in. You're not going to see that side of your parents," I countered. "I mean seriously, *really* think about it." I faked a shiver. "Kinda gross."

I wondered what he'd think if he knew anything about my parents' horrible relationship.

He rolled his shoulders and stretched his neck from side to side. "I want something different from what they have. When I fall in love . . ." He paused to look at me. "I believe true love is the closest to magic humans ever get. And I want that magic."

"That's a wonderful thought." I studied my fingernails, not sure I could meet his eyes. His fanciful idea was nice in theory, but seemed impractical. "I think love changes with time. That magic you talk about morphs into something else, a different kind of love, but it's *still* magic."

My grandparents had that. Up until the day my grandfather died, the look in his eyes whenever he saw her . . . *that's* the kind of love I wanted. It was their example that made me believe true love was possible. Lord knows my parents didn't show me that.

Preston studied me, taking every inch of me in like he didn't know what to make of me. We sat in silence, neither sure what to say when he stood and offered me his hand.

"All right, come on, up you go. This isn't our actual destination."

I looked around, only seeing darkness. "It's not? Where are we going?"

"Just over here, away from the lights a tick." He tucked one hand in his jeans pocket; the other held tight to mine as he guided me onto the grass.

A short distance off I saw a blanket. It looked almost like the one we'd picnicked on before, but in the dark it was impossible to tell. Set up just off to the side was a chubby little white and black telescope.

"I've got the scope lined up to show you Cassiopeia." He looked through the eyepiece before gesturing me over. "Here, take a look. It's the five brightest stars, they kind of make a really spread-out W."

It took me a moment to see it, but once I did, I leaned back and smiled. "That's cool." I peeked through the lens again, pleased with myself.

"Want to see another galaxy?"

I nodded, stood, and backed right into him, not realizing he was so close. Warm hands grasped my shoulders, steadying me. "Oh, I'm sorry."

"It's okay."

Stepping around me, he repositioned the telescope. I sidled a little closer. His arm brushed mine as he slightly shifted the angle.

"Okay, there it is." He leaned up and smiled. "It's the thing that looks like a bright star with a cloudy haze around it; that's the Andromeda Galaxy. It's basically our neighboring galaxy."

This time when I looked through he didn't take a step back; he stayed close, brushing up against me. I liked it. When I straightened up, he was right there. I wanted him to lean down and kiss me. "I-It's really beautiful."

"Did your brother ever find his redhead?" His face shifted slightly toward mine.

What? My brain couldn't follow where he was leading. Why was he talking about my brother when we were this close? My brow furrowed in confusion.

"Just curious." He shrugged and ran a knuckle down a tendril of hair that framed my face, then met my eyes. "I've always fancied brunettes myself."

He leaned closer, his breath on my lips and I could no longer fill my lungs.

Holy cannoli.

"Is that so?" My words came out on a breathy whisper.

The corner of his mouth turned up slightly. "Crazy about them. I fancy one in particular."

I leaned toward him and a massive explosion of butterflies swarmed my stomach. *Oh, God, this is it.*

It was a sudden movement that brought his lips to mine. I wasn't sure which one of us made the final lean, but I didn't care. His lips were on mine and they were just as soft and perfect as I'd imagined, better actually.

Strong arms wrapped around me just as my knees started to wobble, pulling me flush against his muscular body. A tingle shot straight through me, settling low in my stomach. I don't think I could've dreamed up something this perfect.

I parted my lips, wanting more, and he took full advantage of the opportunity. Deepening the kiss, his tongue danced with mine as his hand slid over my back, under my hair and came to cradle my head. I never wanted him to stop.

My arms wound around his neck and my fingers curled in the blond hair at his nape, gently scratching the tender skin there. A soft moan escaped his throat that did amazing things to my insides.

"Maggie." He pulled away just long enough to whisper my name, then crushed his lips to mine once again.

His fingertips pressed firmly into my side, grasping, searching for a way to get me closer. I'd kissed guys before, but never in my life had I been kissed like this. It was as if his soul was trying to reach mine.

Maybe there is such a thing as soul mates.

When he pulled away, I gasped at the loss of his mouth, wanting it back.

Eyes heavy-lidded and voice raspy, he asked, "Bloody hell, where did you learn to kiss like that?"

• • •

Preston drummed his fingers on the steering wheel to the song on the radio as he parked in front of the hotel. Being near him for the past few hours had considerably perked my spirits up. Of course our little impromptu make-out session hadn't hurt either. Reaching up, I briefly touched my lips, shocked that I could still feel the tingly sensation his kiss had left behind.

Looking at me, he smiled. "Okay, I'm curious. What's the deal with the hotel?" He pointed a finger to the tall building outside my window.

Crap. I hoped he wouldn't ask. Although, a tiny part of me was relieved he had.

Sighing, I shook my head and picked at my nail polish. "My parents are um . . . having some issues."

"I'm sorry. Is it bad?" He reached over the console of the Land Rover and momentarily placed a hand on my knee.

My eyes darted to his and I tried to shrug it off. "Well, it's not good. But . . ." I paused, not sure if I should continue. "Honestly, it's been brewing for a really long time. After I told my dad I wasn't going to UCLA everything just sort of . . . snowballed."

His brow furrowed. "He was that upset about your change of plans?"

I nodded. Normally I kept quiet. I didn't speak bad about my father unless it was to Marc. I knew what the repercussions were, but . . . this was Preston. Somehow I knew I could tell him anything and he'd be there, nonjudgmental.

In fact, a bigger part of me than I wanted to admit to, wanted him to know.

I toyed with the idea of telling him my dad was the great Scott McKendrick, but I wasn't ready yet. He'd stop looking at me in the wonderful way he did.

Words slipped from my lips before I could stop them. It showed just how much I desperately needed someone to talk to outside of my dysfunctional family. "My father isn't a nice man. He's a bully and . . ." I trailed off on a sigh and turned to look out the window, unable to continue.

I heard him shift in his seat before his hand came to rest on my shoulder. "Are you okay?"

With a glance at him I nodded and dropped my gaze to my lap. I couldn't make myself look him in the eye.

"Did he hurt you?" His voice had a hard edge as he asked.

The bruises Dad had left on my chin were nearly gone. A little concealer had easily covered the green remnants left behind. They hadn't been too bad to start with.

Shaking my head no, the threat of tears burned. I didn't want him to see me cry. I tried to pull myself together before I looked up. This whole situation made me feel weak and out of control. My voice sounded soft and a little shaky to my ears. "No, not really, he didn't hurt me, not this time. My mom wasn't quite as lucky."

Thanks to the shiner, courtesy of Dad, she hadn't left the hotel room since we'd checked in. The collection of sunglasses she'd amassed from just these incidences got left behind at the manor. In my bag my phone chimed, but I ignored it, not caring who it was from.

From the side of my vision I caught Preston running a hand through his hair, then over his face.

"Oh, God, Maggie, I'm so sorry. Is there anything I can do?"

I shook my head and pasted on a smile, determined to not let Dad ruin one more thing in my life. Turning to face him, I sniffled and said, "Yes. In the time we have left, let's just have fun. You make me smile and that's something I could use a lot more of."

He nodded, and grabbed my hand in his. Bringing it up to his lips, he kissed the back of it. His other hand cupped my cheek, his thumb gently rubbing against my skin. "Your wish is my command."

Leaning in, he pressed his lips to mine in a soft, sweet kiss.

I eagerly lost myself in him and his touch. My arms twined around his neck, pulling him closer as his fingers threaded through my hair, as if telling me he'd never let me go. Which was exactly what I wanted. Never to be let go. As long as he was kissing me like this I could easily imagine my crappy home life away.

Right now, it was just us in our own little world. And it was the only place I wanted to be.

Chapter Ten

A Fresh Perspective

I glanced to Ben, who sat beside me on the couch in his hotel suite. He tossed a handful of popcorn in his mouth, eyes fixed on the large flat screen. A DVD played, but I wasn't paying attention.

Last night had changed everything. It didn't help that my mind was everywhere but here. I kept thinking of Preston and how he'd kissed me. Of my mom and Marc and how soon they'd be leaving.

There was still the issue of my dad and how thrilled he'd been to see Ben and I together. I hated that I didn't know why. Was I somehow playing into his plan?

Yesterday with Preston had been so wonderful. *He* was wonderful. I liked him—really liked him. But now, being in a fancy hotel suite, hanging out with another guy, even just in a friends-only kind of way, made me feel a bit . . . guilty.

I wrapped my arms across my chest, as a weird, uneasy feeling coursed through me.

Ben was fun and seemed kind. I already thought of him as a friend. How he felt about me . . . well, I had no clue.

Three days had passed since we'd left the manor house. Dad hadn't bothered to contact us. Apparently he was as eager to be rid of us as we were him.

Inhaling deeply through my nose, I ran a hand through my hair and tried to focus on the movie, but my rebellious brain wouldn't slow down. If I wasn't thinking about our family, it got stuck on the fact there wasn't much summer left.

And that meant saying goodbye to Preston.

I worried I'd never see him again. But, we were both in England, we could work it out if we wanted to. *What if he doesn't want to?*

"Maggie?"

Startled, I whipped my head to face Ben. "Hmm?"

A slow smile cracked his lips. "You seem a million miles away right now. You okay?"

"I'm sorry." I pulled a throw pillow on my lap, needing the armor. "My thoughts are a little . . . jumbled."

"You want to talk about it? We could turn off the TV and you can tell me anything you want. I've been told I'm an excellent listener." He ran a hand through his dark hair, messing it up.

I smiled and shook my head. "Thanks, but I'm good."

"So, you're heading to school soon, right?" Ben asked, hitting the Mute button on the remote.

I didn't remember discussing my going off to school with him. "Yeah, how did you know?"

"Your dad said something about it yesterday. Said you weren't going to UCLA after all."

Ben never asked why we left the manor house. Thank God. Because as comfortable as I felt with Preston knowing, I didn't feel that way about Ben. He worked too closely with Dad and I didn't want to make things more awkward for him.

Wait, that meant Dad was talking about me? About my school?

"Um, what did he say?" The large screen cast a blue glow on Ben's face.

"Just that everything was in place for you to go to UCLA, and then you'd changed your mind."

I sighed. "Did he look mad?"

"I could tell he wasn't happy, but honestly, he's been in a serious mood the past few days."

What had Dad told him about our situation? And why on earth was he talking to Ben about me?

"So, if it's not UCLA, what's the deal with school?"

"Oh right . . . um, I'll be moving in about a month." I shoved a handful of popcorn in my mouth.

"That soon? Wow. I'm gonna miss you around here. Are you heading to a different school in California?"

I shook my head no, my mouth too full to speak.

"Really, where you going?"

I swallowed and took a drink to wash the salty taste away. "It's down south a ways. It's on the outskirts of a little town called Bampton. They actually filmed the outside scenes of *Downton Abbey* there." *Hmm, maybe I should've led in with that for Dad.* It would've been something he could easily understand and identify with.

A big grin filled his face. "That's great, I can come visit before we finish shooting. Well . . . that is if you want me to."

"When are you wrapping up?" I reached over and grabbed another handful. Neither of us was paying attention to the movie anymore.

"Only about a month and a half, maybe two, but I'll probably be back for reshoots. I'd love to come see you."

"Yeah, a friendly face would be nice." I smiled. "You know, I'm glad I got to know you. You're actually a very cool guy."

Ben's green eyes flicked to mine. "Thanks, I think."

"It's definitely a compliment." I turned back to the soundless movie and tossed a piece of popcorn into my mouth.

"Well then, I'm definitely coming to visit." He popped up and went to refill our water glasses from the small kitchen in his suite. "Why haven't you come to the set at all?"

I sighed and tucked my feet up so he could walk around me without tripping. "Truth?"

He nodded and sat again.

"'Cause my dad and I aren't close."

"Ah, I was hoping you might've come visit *me*." He didn't meet my eyes when he spoke.

My mouth popped open, unsure how to reply. Was he thinking we're more than friends? "Oh, um, I didn't realize you wanted me to."

He bumped his shoulder into mine. "I like having you around."

Any other girl would've been thrilled to hear him say those words to her. Especially if they thought his attentions were more than just the friendly kind. I wasn't that girl. I couldn't shake the worry that under his boy-next-door demeanor was a guy working for my dad. Just how far would he go to please him?

• • •

Dad finally came around to the hotel one evening after a long day on set. Not that anything happened beyond more yelling. Marc stood sentry beside Mom while she stood her ground and refused to allow Dad back in our lives. I stood back in my pajama pants and tank, just wanting Dad to leave.

Mom ran a hand through her chestnut hair. "And no, for the last time, Scott. I'm not coming back to the set. I told you, I'm done."

Apparently Dad didn't like the guy he'd flown in to replace her. Serves the jerk right.

"This isn't over, Diana." Dad turned on his heel and stormed out.

Minutes later a knock sounded on the door. Thinking it was Dad, I went to answer it.

"Preston?" I smiled, thrilled to see him.

If he'd been a few minutes earlier he'd have run smack-dab into my Dad and there'd be no hiding who my father was after that. My cover would've been blown and Preston would no longer think I was just normal Maggie.

"Hey, Mags." He rolled his shoulders forward as he tucked his hands in his pockets. "May I come in for a moment?"

"Of course." I motioned for him to follow me. I knew I needed to tell him. And I really did have every intention to, but fear got in my way every time. I liked him too much. And to have him treat me like Scott McKendrick's princess daughter just might kill me.

I guided him toward the living room of our suite, stopping at Mom and a grinning Marc.

There was no escaping introducing them. I doubted Mom would willingly talk about Dad, but there was always a chance. I scanned her face, just to make sure the fading bruises were covered. They were.

"Mom, this is Preston. Preston, this is my mom, Diana."

She shot me a pleased look as they shook hands. "Nice to finally meet you."

"It's a pleasure to meet you." His eyes crinkled around the edges. "I can't tell you how much I've enjoyed getting to know Maggie this summer." He darted a glance my way. "Your daughter is a very special girl."

Mom looked at me, a soft smile settling on her lips. "She is, but then again, I've always known how amazing she is."

Marc leaned against the wall, arms crossed, just taking it all in.

"We're gonna be in here." I pointed to the living room.

Mom nodded and I led the way, Preston following me. What brought him here? Not that I minded in the least. Sitting on the couch, he took his place beside me.

"I can't stay long. I'm actually driving back to campus tonight." He rubbed his denim-clad thighs as his warm chocolaty eyes met mine.

My breath caught in my throat.

I wasn't ready for him to go. There were still three weeks of summer. He couldn't go now. Tearing my eyes from his, I bit my bottom lip and picked at a frayed thread on the hem of my tank. I didn't want him to see my disappointment. "So, this is goodbye, then?"

"Well, not quite." The smile in his voice was evident. "Normally, I can't wait to get out of here and wouldn't be returning until next summer, but . . . I'll be back next week."

"Really?" My eyes drank in his happy face.

"Really." Reaching up he cupped my cheek. "I'm not ready to leave. I'm dreading it actually."

I wanted to pull him to me and kiss him, but Mom was just around the corner. His eyes darted to the arched entrance and he smiled like he could read my thoughts and dropped his hand.

"Are things any better with your dad?" He leaned closer as he spoke.

I shook my head and blew out a heavy breath. "We haven't really talked. We've barely seen him at all. I'm still trying to formulate a plan." The other night I'd told him how Dad refused to financially support my decision and about my job hunt.

"You'll make it work, I know you will." He squeezed my hand. "You can do anything you set your mind to."

I looked up into his eyes, my throat tightening from his unwavering belief.

"What do you say we get dinner when I get back?" He grabbed my hand and gave it a squeeze.

I smiled, my gaze trailing down to his lips. The memory of our kiss flashed in my mind. I could almost feel his warm hand on my neck, his fingers tangling in my hair. Shaking my head, I cleared my throat. "That'd be great."

"I should probably get on the road."

Nodding, I stood and walked him to the door, wanting him to stay. Hand on the knob, I looked up at him. "Drive safe."

He cupped my cheek and smiled. "I will." His eyes darted back to where my family was still within earshot. "Can you step into the hall a moment?"

"Sure."

His fingers grazed mine as he opened the door and gestured me through. It closed with a soft snick and I turned to face him and found myself wrapped in his arms. His lips covered mine and I happily curled myself into him.

When he pulled back his eyes glinted. "I couldn't leave without a proper goodbye."

"Thank God." I giggled. With a swift peck on the lips, he backed his way to the elevators and waved before stepping on.

Sighing, I went back into our suite and leaned against the door, the sensation of floating overtaking me.

Mom came into the room, leaned against the archway, and crossed her arms, smiling. "So, how much does he know?"

"He knows that we left Dad and how he's not a nice guy." This conversation was seriously killing my afterglow. "I haven't told him that Dad's a famous director." I fessed up to my worries of him treating me differently and how I'd cease to be a normal girl.

Mom came closer and straightened my hair. "I don't want you to get mad at me, but . . . isn't that kind of silly?" She cringed and lifted a hand to stop my protest. "Have you even considered giving him the benefit of the doubt? He's not part of the L.A., fawning, movie-obsessed, wannabe-famous crowd, so chances are, he's probably going to have a very different reaction."

My teeth sank into my bottom lip as waves of doubt crashed over me. She was so right.

"If it were me, I'd tell him. You don't want him to treat *you* differently, but how's he going to feel when he finds out you've kept something so big from him? Whether we like it or not, your father is a huge part of what makes you, you."

"I'm screwing this up, aren't I?"

Reaching out, she tucked my long bangs behind my ears. "Probably not, but if you wait any longer you might."

Preston was someone I'd instantly connected to. I trusted him, but apparently not enough. Keeping this from him definitely wasn't my best move.

Cold fingers of worry slithered up my spine. "But what if he does change?"

Chapter Eleven

Inevitable Endings

Preston and I sat on a humongous suede sectional in the media room of Chillingham Manor. It looked like the only modernized area the house could boast. After he picked me up we'd gone to the very red pizza place, grabbed a pizza, and brought it back. Now two empty plates sat on the coffee table and I sat with my head on Preston's shoulder, his arm around me, watching a movie.

There was no disguising how thrilled I was to have him back. The week had dragged on without him.

Preston's hand found mine and he laced our fingers together. "I talked to my sister, Haley, the other day. She and her team have an investigation coming up soon. She said you were more than welcome to come with us if you'd like."

"I'd love to. You'll be there, right?" I'd gladly hunt ghosties to see him.

"If you're going, I'll definitely be there."

"Good."

He rested his chin atop my head and I smiled as we turned our attentions back to the television. I struggled to focus. Being this close to him made all my senses go into rapid-fire mode and my brain no longer functioned at full capacity. His warmth seeped through my thin tee as his delicious scent surrounded me. It was too much.

As he lifted his head, I turned and our gazes locked. His eyes darted to my mouth, then back to my eyes. Tingles zip zapped through my nervous system as his fingers ran over the bare skin of my upper arms.

Please kiss me. I leaned closer, hoping he'd meet me.

"God, I missed you." His words left his lips on a whisper. Mere inches apart, he leaned the final way and pressed his mouth to mine. I couldn't stop the sigh that escaped on contact.

Fingers tangled into my hair and rapidly morphed our kiss into something so much more. Not releasing the back of my neck, he positioned himself so he was directly in front of me, kneeling on the floor. His tongue touched my lips, as if asking them to open. They gladly did.

Tingles like shockwaves shot down to settle low in my belly. This is exactly what I'd been craving. *Lord, can he kiss.* With him, this felt perfect.

My arms wound around his neck, holding on like my life depended on it. I didn't want to stop kissing him. Ever.

I *needed* to stay like this. I needed *him*. I wanted him.

A low growl sent a shiver over my skin. My lips curled against his in a smile. He pulled away, eyes glinting, and grinned. Leaning in again, this time he pressed me back into the couch. His warm, solid, and sexy-as-hell body contoured against mine perfectly.

Soft lips grazed my jawline, then skimmed down my neck, sprinkling more kisses and nips onto my collarbones. Sucking in a deep breath, he leaned up and rested his forehead against mine, our ragged breaths intermingling.

Never had anything felt like this. He electrified me.

Heavy-lidded eyes flicked up, matching my gaze. The flecks of gold scattered through the brown irises caught the light and shimmered. I loved his eyes.

The way he looked at me suggested he wanted so much more from me. Reaching up, I pulled his mouth back to mine and took control of the kiss.

That control was short lived as his warm hand found its way under my T-shirt to flatten against my stomach. My gasp broke the kiss. Slipping a finger into the waistband of my jeans, he caressed my sensitive skin. I shut my eyes and a soft moan tore from my throat, surprising me. Preston's lips crashed down upon mine, cutting off any embarrassment I may have felt.

I held him tight, my fingers curling in the blond waves at his nape. *How far am I going to let this go?* This was entirely new territory and it shocked me to discover just how far I *wanted* to take it.

At the clearing of a throat, a panting Preston leaned up and looked to the doorway. I followed his gaze, pulling my shirt down to cover the bare skin of my tummy.

Tanner. Preston's creep of a cousin leaned in the doorway, a leer on his face, watching us. *How long has he been there?*

Preston positioned himself to block me from Tanner's view the best he could. "What are you doing here?"

Tanner snorted a laugh. "Ah, cousin, looks like you've certainly got your hands full."

My lip curled in distaste. I sat up as Preston stalked to the door. "What do you want?"

Beady little eyes settled on me. "I'd tell you, but I doubt you'd be willing share, so why bother?"

"Out. Now." Hand on Tanner's chest, Preston shoved him into the hallway and slammed the door behind him. Taking a deep breath, he ran a hand over his face. "I'm so sorry, Mags. Tanner's a complete minger."

"So I've discovered." I wasn't one hundred percent sure what a "minger" was, but by the look on Preston's face, it wasn't nice. I looked away from his disheveled appearance and attempted to straighten my hair with my fingers. "It's fine, really."

Preston returned and settled beside me on the couch. His hand found mine. "No, it's not fine." His free hand came up to cup my cheek, his thumb running against my skin. "If there's ever a next time I'll deck him."

With school rapidly approaching, would we even get a next time?

• • •

It was our last night together as Preston was heading back to Oxford tomorrow. And so far we'd managed to completely avoid the topic. I knew if I voiced my thoughts I'd fall apart in front of him. And that so wasn't the last memory I wanted to leave him with. We stood in an elevator at the hotel, his hand tightly clasped in mine. The doors slid open and our last moments together loomed. Stepping out, we made our way to my family's suite.

"Um . . ." He tucked a hand in his pocket and pulled out a folded piece of paper. "Here's all my contact information. Promise me you'll keep in touch."

I opened it, smiling at all the ways to reach him. When I looked up, his brow was furrowed. Reaching out, his fingertips grazed my neck as he ran his fingers through my hair before tucking it behind my ear. My heart stuttered at his touch.

I nodded. In a strained, tight whisper I said, "I promise."

"I suppose I'll see you whenever Haley's investigation is." His feet shuffled against the carpeted hallway and he softly chuckled. "She'll be happy to see me on a case. She's always after me to come with them. Says she never has enough bodies to help out." He chuckled. "Nagging is what it is, really."

God, he's cute when he rambles.

Smiling, I grabbed his arm and pulled him closer.

The corners of his lips lifted as his face drew closer to mine. "I suppose I should—"

I popped up on my toes and pressed my lips to his, effectively stopping his words. Eagerly he returned the kiss as he wrapped his arms around me and pulled me against his chest. My fingers wound through his hair, tangling in the loose curls. If I hadn't been wearing boots my toes would have definitely curled.

Every time we kissed, I wanted more. The taste, the smell, the feel of him, it was all overwhelmingly perfect.

Behind us the door opened a crack. We pulled apart and turned to see Marc.

"Not trying to interrupt, but Dad's coming over to talk to Mom. You should probably cool it."

"Thanks, Marc." The door shut with a soft snick and I turned to face Preston. "I should head inside."

"You don't want me to meet your father, do you?"

I shook my head. "Not with everything going on."

This so wasn't how I wanted to say goodbye.

"Okay." He cupped my face in his hands. "But, I'm not going to say goodbye. Instead, I'll say see you 'round." He kissed my nose and leaned back.

"Yeah, see you around." My vision blurred. "I don't want you to go." My words came out strangled.

Sucking in a sharp breath, he took a step back and looked down at his shoes. What I wouldn't give to know the thoughts running through his head.

"I'll see you soon." He took a step toward the elevators and lifted a hand in a weak wave. "I promise." With that, he pushed the button and in seconds the doors for the first elevator opened. Just as he stepped in, the second elevator opened and Dad stepped out.

Chapter Twelve

Power Plays

Dad came down the hall toward me, his polo shirt untucked from his jeans. Stopping in front of me, he looked tall and intimidating. His graying facial hair was verging on an all-out beard. He needed a trim, as did his disheveled jaw-length hair. Then again, whenever he was working he had zero time for anything else.

"What are you doing out here?" Dad's brow furrowed.

"Oh, um, just saying goodbye to a friend." Okay, that's a lie. *Preston's so much more.*

"Since when do you have friends in Scotland?"

Still in jerk mode, I see. Not that he ever seemed to turn it off. They say little girls want to grow up and marry a man like their daddies . . . so not the case here. I wanted the complete opposite. In every way.

I crossed my arms over my chest, angry with him for . . . well, everything. "I'll go get Mom."

He ran a hand through his dark hair and sighed. "Margaret, I actually came here to talk to you."

Shit. What now?

"Me? Why?"

I leaned against the doorframe, waiting for him to go on.

"I have a business proposition for you." He continued after I nodded. "I'm willing to pay you to date Ben."

"*What?* Why?" My eyes darted to his, hoping I hadn't just angered him.

He sized me up with his gaze. "Because I want you to."

I shook my head, confused. Despite being terrified, I was determined to stand my ground. Mom had, so could I. "I don't understand why. You *wanting* me to isn't enough of a reason."

"Oh, is that right?" His nostrils flared as he grabbed my chin and pinched it between his fingers. "How about I make it enough of a reason. If you don't agree, I'll make this divorce a living hell for your mother."

The threat in his voice raised the hair on the back on my neck.

"She wants the house that she so painstakingly found and remodeled? Never gonna happen. *Anything* she wants, cars, pets, kitchen appliances, I don't care what it is, I'll fight tooth and nail for it. I can make sure this drags out so her whole life becomes one giant nightmare of dealing with me. She'll never be free, I'll make sure of it. And I'm sure you don't want that."

He stared me in the eye before letting go of me. I had to stop myself from rubbing my tender skin. "Are you . . . blackmailing me?"

"If that's what it takes, yes." He crossed his arms over his chest. "I had hoped you'd do this because I asked, but clearly, like your mother, you only think of yourself."

Are you freaking kidding me? My whole body vibrated from the anger thrumming through me. He was delusional. There was no other explanation.

Taking a step closer and backing me into the door, he growled. "Do you seriously need time to think about this? And here I thought you loved your mother." His tone was mocking and cold.

"Ben won't agree to this." My voice shook and I hated myself for showing fear. "He doesn't need people to pay girls to date him." Ben was my only chance. Surely he wouldn't go along with this.

Dad's eyes slivered and a sly smile filled his face. "Ben's already agreed."

My mouth popped open. *No.*

Is that why he'd been calling? To please my dad? Maybe Ben wasn't my friend like I'd thought.

"The money I'm offering would be more than enough to cover your tuition at this . . . *school* of yours. It's more than fair."

I knew if I questioned him it'd only anger him more, but I wanted to know. "What happened? Why are you so desperate?"

He looked me over from head to toe, a sneer forming on his lips. He wasn't pleased with what he saw. "That's not your concern."

The hell it isn't.

Pulling out his cell, he dialed and put it to his ear. "Think about it, Mags. I'll talk to you soon. Don't tell anyone about our conversation." With a sharp turn he headed back to the elevators, sauntering as if confident my agreement was in the bag. "Yeah, I'm on my way now."

"Didn't you want to see Mom?" I hollered at him.

"Not particularly, no." He vanished into the elevator without a second glance.

I went into the suite and slammed the door behind me, which only took a tiny edge off my fury. Mom and Marc were watching a show in the small sitting area so I avoided them by crawling straight into bed, fully dressed. Covers thrown over my head, the tears threatening to spill over.

Did I have any options? A tear escaped and I squeezed my eyes shut. Dad had me trapped, and he knew it. If I told Marc he'd get all protective and probably confront Dad, which would only cause trouble for him. I couldn't do that.

Part of me wanted to run and tell Mom, but that didn't feel like a good idea. She was already dealing with the divorce, currently being unemployed, having to move out, travel plans . . . the list was too long to go through. By agreeing to Dad's demands it'd make things easier for her. He wouldn't fight her. That made it worth it.

Why did Dad have to be this way? *Asshole.* I'd spent most my life hoping he'd wake up and be different. That'd he'd finally be the loving, caring father we deserved. But it was time to accept facts.

He's not a Dad. He's a monster.

Thoughts buzzed around my head, looking for a loophole. There had to be some way I could get out of this. Why would Ben agree to this?

Is he being blackmailed?

I closed my eyes and shook my head. What could Dad have on him? I sucked in a shaky breath. Then again, what if Ben's in on the plan? The thought alone pissed me off.

Sighing, I rubbed my eyes, the emotional buildup overtaking me. My little plan was my life preserver. It was the only thing that made sense in my topsy-turvy world. Move out on my own, be a fashion school rock star, and become a massive success.

And show Dad I don't need him or his money.

Could I actually fake-date Ben? If it made Mom's life easier and shielded her from Dad, I'd do pretty much anything. As for the money, I didn't want it, but, I couldn't deny that I needed it. Maybe I'd just use it for tuition and nothing else. All other expenses could come from whatever job I got. The leftover father funds I'd send to Mom. Hopefully they'd help her start over.

The way I saw it, I didn't have a choice. No wonder Dad had walked away like such a smug baboon. I had to agree to his scheme. *I have to date Ben.*

How do I explain this to Preston?

• • •

The early morning mist swirled around us. Fall had descended on the highlands over the last week, making it damp and even chillier. I stood in front of the hotel, eyes watering, and hugged

Mom and Marc. My bags were packed and in the back of a black town car Dad had sent. Neither Mom nor Marc was thrilled I'd let Dad hire a car for me. In all actuality it was part of his bribe. I wanted to tell them, but I couldn't. When I'd called Dad to agree to his plan he'd basically put a gag order on me. Telling them, or anyone, voided our agreement.

I looked between the long black town car and my family. Heavy stones of guilt filled my stomach, weighing me down. *This is it.* The start of my new adventure. *What I've wanted for so long.*

Oh, God, did I make a huge mistake?

"I hate you going alone." Mom straightened the collar of my jacket before cupping my cheeks.

No, if this keeps Mom safe and happy, it's worth it. At least I'd come up with a new plan . . . well, a tweaked plan.

"I'm still willing to go with her," Marc offered. Berkeley's fall term started three weeks ago. He should've been there, but after our familial explosion he decided to take the term off to help Mom adjust and get settled back home. He'd stepped up in ways that I didn't realize he was capable of.

I probably should've told him everything and sworn him to secrecy, but this whole scenario made me feel dirty, embarrassed, and scared of what Dad would do to sabotage Marc if he knew. No, it was better to deal with this on my own.

Waving them off, I zipped my jacket, putting on a brave face. "It's fine. I'll be fine. I don't have much stuff and I'm sure I can manage. Plus, you guys have to get ready to fly out. I don't want you to miss your flight because of me."

Marc hugged me again and Mom dabbed the corners of her eyes with her sleeve. "I'm going to worry about you nonstop. You better keep in touch."

I nodded, a lump in my throat. She pulled me close again, motioning Marc to her too. The three of us stood wrapped around each other. The driver closed the trunk and leaned against the door, waiting for us to finish.

"I've got to go." It came out hoarse. "I'll talk to you guys soon. Call me when you land in L.A."

Mom kissed my cheek and Marc stuffed his hands in his pockets as he took a step back. "See ya, Magpie. Call if you need anything."

When I turned to the car, the driver immediately opened the door. With a wave and unsteady smile, I climbed inside. The door shut with a muffled clap and I hit the button to roll down the window. Craning myself out, I waved as the car drove away and shouted, "I love you, guys!"

The hotel was out of sight when I clambered back inside, frozen and damp. Settling in my seat, I cranked the heat up and stuck my earbuds in. I wanted to zone out. I needed to. I had too many things rattling around my mind and none of them I wanted to dwell on.

The overall plan may have changed a bit, but it was still time to put it into action: move out, rock fashion school, be a success, survive dating Ben, and make sure Dad comes out of this with the world knowing just a bit more about him—the truth.

Chapter Thirteen

First-Time Freedoms

A massive, sprawling castle housed Thrippletons. It had every stereotypical thing you could think of: turrets, arrow slits, and a huge set of stairs leading to large wooden double doors. Cinderella could totally fly out of here any second in a fabulous gown and lose her slipper with no trouble. I stepped from the car and tilted my head back, taking it all in with a grin. There were even gargoyles perched at the corners.

Inside were all our classes and dorms. I'd seen pictures and browsed the website, but it still rendered me speechless.

I can't imagine this being someone's house. Seriously, who needs this much space?

The school was just outside Bampton, nestled in a lush green valley. After checking in, I carried my bags up the marble staircase in search of my room. I was on the second floor with the rest of the first-years. Being a two-year program was probably how they were able to accommodate all the students.

I pinched my schedule between my fingers and glanced at it. Across the top my dorm number and roommate's name were printed. Down a long hallway of mahogany doors, I eyed the coppery plaques, looking for room 218. The padded runner of carpet deadened my steps, and a little ways down sunlight spilled through an open door. I stopped just outside the sun's rays. 218. My new home.

From the entrance I could see the scale of the room. Large. It was clean but not ornate, fairly simple really. Wood floors, large rug, plain white walls, the only color in the room was the curtains, pale yellow and shimmery white floral swirls. There were two of everything: queen beds, desks, and wardrobes. A couple of naked dress forms stood near the large windows.

Poking my head in further, I saw a girl kneeled into one of the wardrobes, lining up an assortment of colorful shoes. When she sat back, her hair took me by surprise. It was styled in an A-line bob, but that wasn't what caught my attention. The soft pastel pink dye job did. Traces of platinum blonde peeked through some of the colored strands. It was pretty fabulous.

She turned and spied me. With a huge smile, she stood and rushed over. Her arms hugged me as she let out a squeal near my ear. "Margaret! I've been waiting for you. I'm so glad you're here. I hope you don't mind, but I already picked a bed. I suppose if you really want to we can switch out, but I thought you might like the one by the window. Oh, I'm Daisy Michaels, by the way, your roommate."

My brows raised, not expecting her exuberance. She looked at me expectantly so I assumed it was my turn. "Hi."

"We are going to have so much fun this year! I can feel it. I can't wait for classes to start, can you?" She bounced on her heels, her fitted white T-shirt amplifying her assets. "Hmm, you don't say much, do you?"

I laughed. "Um . . ."

"Come on in, put your bags down." She pulled a suitcase from my grasp and ushered me to the free bed. Her perkiness was unlike anything I'd ever encountered.

I plunked the bag I carried on my bed alongside the case she'd just released. Doing a quick spin, I grinned. She'd already added lots of details, making the room cool and cozy. Strands of fairy lights encircled the perimeter, undoubtedly offering a soft magical glow at night. On the door hung a dry erase board with "Home of Daisy and Margaret" written in a feminine scrawl.

I pointed to my name on the sign. "You can call me Maggie. Everyone does."

"Oh, that's grand." Her thick sooty eyelashes rested against her cheeks momentarily, then she was off again, changing the sign. "Margaret sounds like a little old lady, sorry." She covered her mouth with her hand and let out a girly giggle.

"Tell me about it," I snickered. "My parents named me after my mom's aunt that I met like, once."

"Aw, that's lovely." The words rolled off her tongue in a bouncy cadence thanks to her Irish accent. "So, I sorta Googled you." She looked at me with a pretense of bashfulness and cringed.

My heart plummeted to my toes.

"I can't believe I'm living with a real-life celebrity! What's Hollywood like? Have you met many stars? Oh, you must have so many stories! What's it like being Scott McKendrick's daughter? Do you have a steady boyfriend? Why Thrippletons?"

Sitting on the corner of her bed, I took a deep breath, disappointed that she clearly only liked me for my famous father. "Well, I'm not a celebrity, just the daughter of one. Um, L.A. is . . . busy and fast-paced I guess. And pretty warm." I shrugged. "I've met some celebrities and they're mostly regular people, just like you and me. My dad is . . ." I sighed, not sure what to say. "Not someone I'm super close to. So, I have zero pull with him and can't connect anyone up." *Please let that be the end of it.* "And, um, I picked Thrippletons because . . . well, because it's a great school and it's nowhere near California. As for a boyfriend, I'm not exactly sure."

I had no intention of mentioning Ben. He may be my media boyfriend, but in my real life, he was . . . gosh, I couldn't even call him a friend anymore, could I? Not when I hadn't a clue if he was on my side or in cahoots with my dad.

One of her well manicured brows lifted. "Hmm, sounds like there's a story there. How can you not be sure?"

"I met someone over the summer. But now that we're both back at school I don't know what that makes us." I caught the inside of my lower lip in my teeth as I rubbed a hand over her bubblegum-pink blanket. "What about you?"

"Single gal here, but I'm in the market for love and I've decided this is definitely goin' to be my year. I can *feel it.*" Clapping her hands, she went to my suitcases. "Let's get you unpacked and go grab some dinner. I'm famished."

Deep breath in, I nodded. She seemed sweet. Perhaps while she sorted her love life out she could help me with mine.

Please just let her be a friend and not another person who wants to use me.

• • •

The next morning I woke, curled up under my duvet, and smiled. Daisy and I'd been up way too late chatting and getting to know each other. She was an only child from Dublin and had gone to a super-fancy-schmancy boarding school. In most areas we were polar opposites, but turns out we shared a love for treasure hunting at thrift stores and reimagining our finds.

"Mornin'." Daisy stretched from her bed and popped up, fully energized. "You ready for this? Goodness, I'm so excited."

First day of classes. A thrill of anticipation raced through me. *I wonder how Preston's classes are?* He'd be starting his second week back.

"I'm a little nervous." I sat and grabbed my phone from the windowsill. Fourteen new messages. My pulse spiked. *One might be from Preston.* I'd emailed him after he left, just wanting to make sure I had his address correct.

"Something tells me that smile on your face has nothing to do with school." Daisy stood and wrapped her robe around herself.

Shaking my head, and trying to shrug it off like I didn't know what she was talking about. I tapped my email icon, and sitting at the top of my inbox was an email from Preston Browne. Sent super-early this morning. My lips spread in a grin and I opened it.

"Mmm, that's what I thought. It has to do with your maybe-fella, doesn't it?" Shaking her head, she grabbed her bathroom caddy. "I'll be in the shower." With a wink, she turned and did a little skip into our adjoining bathroom.

I quickly pulled up Preston's email and smoothed out my hair, as if he could see me.

From: Preston Browne
Sent: October 12, 2015 at 5:14 AM
To: Maggie
Subject: Good Luck!

Hey Maggie,
I know it's super early, but I really wanted to wish you a great first day of classes. I'll be thinking about you.

Yours,
Preston

Yours. Such a small word, yet it had the power to send goosebumps dancing across my skin. It definitely put a sigh on my lips and a bounce in my step. *And* he'd be thinking about me. A girly giggle escaped me.

Setting my phone aside, I'd look at Marc's and Mom's messages later. I already knew they'd made it home okay, so it didn't feel urgent. I went to my wardrobe and picked out skinny jeans, tank, sweater, and infinity scarf. When Daisy exited the bathroom, towel twined atop her head, she stopped and tugged a strand of my hair as I passed, clothes in hand.

"You know what would look grand on you?" She narrowed her eyes and leaned back. When I shook my head, she continued. "A fuchsia streak, no purple. I think it'd look totally fabulous with your brunette coloring."

Laughter barked from my lips. "Okay, we'll see."

"It'll happen. I *feel* it."

• • •

Daisy and I carried our dinner trays to the end of a long wooden table. The dining hall practically vibrated with all the conversations going on. The first week of school was over and I was thoroughly exhausted. But I loved my classes and I still couldn't believe I was here. So far my Design Studio and Figure Drawing classes were my favorites, but History of Fashion was close behind.

"I don't know if you'd be up for it, but I was wantin' to get out of Bampton this weekend. Maybe run to Oxford. There's some shopping I need to do." Daisy met my eyes to see if I was up for it.

My spoonful of soup paused midway to my lips. "Oxford?" *Preston.* "Is it close?"

I remembered his phone call the night after my first day of classes and smiled. We'd talked for over an hour. Telling each other about our classes and just catching up on what happened since we last saw each other. I tried telling him about my father, but the timing didn't seem right, that and Daisy came in and started teasing me and making kissy faces. Once I hung up she said if he wasn't already, he definitely wanted to be my boyfriend.

"'Bout thirty minutes east."

"Girls, I'm done for. Please tell me you have something brilliant planned this weekend. I *need* to get out of this place." Andrew plunked his tray down next to mine and sat. The three of us had all the same classes and I had to admit, he was fun. He'd approached us the first day, having decided Daisy's hair had called to him. His own dark, teased-until-standing 'do reminded me of Adam Lambert.

"I do." Daisy sang out. "Shopping in Oxford."

"Yes!" He dragged the end of the word out and clapped his hands. "Fabulous idea."

"Count me in." My brain raced with thoughts of Preston. Should I tell him I'll be in town? Hope I'll miraculously run into him? Surprise him?

Daisy and Andrew were making shopping plans while I zoned out to figure my next move. I felt weird calling him. Maybe email? Would he even want to hang out? What would we do? He probably had plans already. I should just skip it this ti—

"Oi, Mags. Earth to Mags . . ."

I focused on Daisy's face, only then realizing the two of them were done eating and my bowl of soup sat untouched. "Hmm? What'd I miss?"

"Dinner." Andrew chuckled. "Where'd you disappear to?"

Daisy's pert lips curled into a grin. "Probably daydreaming about a certain fella."

"I'm just tired." I nibbled my lip, self-conscious. "It's been a long week, sorry."

"Then you need to get into bed and get some good rest, 'cause we're power shopping tomorrow." Andrew put an arm around my shoulders and pulled me into a side hug.

Nodding, I took a bite, but my soup was too cold. I settled for the bread, knowing come the morning I'd be starving. "You're right, let's head up."

Back in our room, Daisy and I took turns in the bathroom and climbed into bed. I waited until her breathing turned even and into soft snores. Sitting up, I grabbed my iPad and opened a blank email.

Hey Preston,
I know it's last minute, but I'll be in Oxford tomorrow. Wanna meet up?

I deleted everything but the Hey Preston.

Hey Preston,
I didn't realize, but I'm actually close to Oxford. How did I never tell you I was going to Thrippletons?

Nope, rambling. Plus, I knew how I never got around to telling him. After avoiding the topic the first time, it never got brought up again. Not even when we were parting and exchanging contact info. There was a moment when I thought he was going to ask, but he didn't. And I felt weird bringing it up after essentially telling him he didn't need to know.

I stared at the blinking cursor under the greeting. The brightness of the screen made seeing in the darkness behind the computer nearly impossible. Sighing, I drummed my fingers lightly on the keys, the faint tappity-tap soothing my nerves.

Why was I blanking on this? It's just an email. *I doubt he'll even see it.* He has his friends, he's probably already doing something with them. Maybe I shouldn't bother him. Next time I can email him earlier and give him warning. I slid the tablet onto my desktop.

Nestled under the covers, I closed my eyes, but sleep didn't find me, not for a long time. My brain chugged along, second-guessing everything.

"Wake up!" A bubbly voice warbled near my face.

I opened my eyes to a blurry Daisy lit up from the sun shining through the window. "Oh, God, tell me it's not morning yet. I barely slept."

"It's nearly nine thirty. Come on, sleepy head. Up, up! There's shopping to do!" She pulled my arm, making me groan.

"Nuh uh, not going, too tired."

Yanking the covers back, she giggled. "Get up, you know you don't want to miss this. Andrew and I will come back with fabulous stuff and all bonded. Don't miss the bonding, Mags. We need to bond."

I laughed when she lined our noses up and twisted her head, distorting her features. It didn't matter that I didn't have the money to buy anything. Well, technically I did, but I wasn't going to use Dad's dirty money for anything other than tuition. Thinking about the check Dad had made out to me dredged up images of Ben. I hadn't talked to him and I really didn't want to.

The money in my bank account was for Mom. Well, as soon as I got the courage to tell her what Dad was doing to me.

I have to find a job.

"Maggie, girl time, shoppin' . . . come on." Daisy rocked me back and forth with gentle shoves.

"Okay, okay, for the sake of bonding, I'll get up." I sat up and the room tilted. I laid back down. "On second thought, I don't think my body's ready to do the human thing right now."

"Up. Now." Yanking on my arm, Daisy got me upright and heading for the shower.

When the warm water hit my body and my brain perked up, it went to one place. I should have emailed Preston.

Chapter Fourteen

The Ugliness of the Unexpected

Old buildings lined the streets of Oxford. They were beautiful, but at the moment they were acting like a wind tunnel. My long heavy-knit sweater didn't block the biting chill. At least the sun was shining. I dragged behind Andrew and Daisy, clutching my Starbucks like it was my lifeline. Probably because it was; the caffeine was the only thing keeping me upright.

"Come on, poky." Andrew looped his arm with mine and looked over his black Ray-Bans at me. We caught up with Daisy as she peeked into the window of some ritzy shop.

In California I wouldn't hesitate to go in. But here, in my current financial shape, I really hoped Daisy wouldn't make us.

"One day I'm going to have a shop like this." Daisy turned and leaned against the window with a determined gleam in her eye. "I'm going to be big. I can feel it."

Linking my arm with hers, I was now sandwiched between the two of them and said, "We're *all* going to be huge."

"You bet we are." Andrew ran his free hand through his hair, which was dramatically draped to one side and looking slightly emo. "Being this fabulous, it's just the natural progression."

Laughing, we continued on, passing an iconic red phone booth and going into a secondhand store. Not that I was planning on buying anything, but at least here I *could* if I wanted to.

As soon as we stepped through the door we all noticed the guy in the tight T-shirt behind the counter.

Daisy leaned and whispered into my ear. "Maybe he could be my Mr. Right."

"Um, I don't think so. I saw him first." An infatuated chuckle escaped Andrew's lips as tight-tee guy waved hello.

Separating, we wandered the store. Daisy found loads of cute seventies-esque clothes she intended to rehab. Andrew found a camel-colored wool car jacket that he decided his wardrobe couldn't do without. And I offered my opinions and company.

I pulled a scarf off its hook and wrapped it around my neck, loving the softness, despite the tag scratching me. *I wonder how close Preston is?* "So, I'm just curious, where is the university? Is it nearby?"

"We're in the middle of it." Andrew straightened the sunglasses that hung from the V of his T-shirt. "Parts of it thread into the city. But the main campus is just down the road a bit."

My heart did a flippity-flop. We were close. I pulled my phone from my pocket and tapped on Preston's name from my contacts. My finger hovered over the Call button. What if he didn't have time to see me? What if he was with another girl? *Definitely don't want to know about that.*

"Hmm, who do you know here, missy?" Andrew's eyes flashed to the cute guy behind the counter, then back to me. The whole time we'd been in here he'd been checking Mr. Muscles out.

"Just someone I met over the summer." I slid my phone back in my pocket and unwrapped the scarf from my neck, returning it to its peg, frustrated with myself. I just couldn't bring myself to call him.

Andrew left me by the scarves and sauntered closer to the counter, shooting a cocky grin to the clerk all while casually browsing. I smiled and shook my head. Andrew definitely went after what he wanted.

After we dragged Andrew out of the thrift shop, tight-tee guy's number scrawled in Sharpie on his hand, we spent the rest of the morning popping in and out of storefronts. Both Andrew and Daisy had several bags each. I had my purse.

We stopped in a small restaurant for lunch and sat at a booth overlooking the front pathway. I looked out, noticing lots of people roughly our age walking by.

"I've got to get a job." I ran a hand through my hair. The pressure just kept building. What if I couldn't make this work? Using Dad's bribe money to live on wasn't a choice.

"You know, I work in the fabric shop in Bampton, The Bolt. I'm sure I could talk my boss into taking you on." Andrew smiled over a turkey sandwich, a dollop of mayonnaise clinging to the corner of his mouth. "She likes me, but then again why wouldn't she," he added with a cheeky wink.

"Andrew, that'd be perfect! Do you really think you could manage it?" If I got this job it would ensure the only money I took from Dad would be for tuition. And *that* I intended to pay back. I didn't want any of his dirty money, but I did want to show him I could be successful and that fashion school wasn't a waste of my time.

He nodded. "Millie's a sweetie, and she likes helping Thrippletons students. Plus, once she meets you I'm sure she'll think of you as one of her kids. She does all of us."

"I would love to meet her. When can we go in?"

He glanced at his watch. "Well, the shop closes at seven, and she's only there until two. If we take off after lunch we can stop by on the way back to campus."

"Perfect!"

Daisy pursed her lips. "There's a couple more places I want to get to."

"We'll come back." I promised. *We'd better.* "Maybe next time I'll actually have a little money."

I tipped my water glass to my lips and glanced out the window.

Preston.

I choked on my water as my heart thundered in my chest. He was here. Just across the street, exiting a curry restaurant. My eyes fixed on him as he slid a pair of aviators on. He looked fabulous.

Pushing my chair out, I needed to see him. It'd be a surprise.

He looked like he was waiting for someone. Turning, he looked back at the door. A short blonde woman moved down a couple steps to join him, smiling. My heart skidded to a screeching stop. He helped her slide into her jacket, tucked a long strand of hair behind her ear, and matched her glowing grin.

I gasped, needing to breathe, but the air had been sucked from my lungs. The short blonde looked up at him and threaded her arm with his. He threw his head back with laughter as they looked both ways to cross the street.

He has a girlfriend?

My eyes burned. *I should've known.* Had the terrible ex, Thompson, taught me nothing? Of course he'd have a girl back on campus. I'd been nothing more than a summer fling. He was expecting me to go away. He hadn't asked where I was going again because it didn't matter. He had no intention of keeping anything going with me.

Dad was right—guys weren't lined up for me and neither was Preston. Apparently he wasn't as different as I thought.

I slumped down in my chair, praying he wouldn't see me. I didn't want to hear his excuses. No, make that I didn't want to hear his voice. Just the way he looked at her, smiling and happy, killed me.

"Um, Mags, you okay?"

It was then that I realized Andrew and Daisy had stopped talking and were staring at me like I'd lost my mind.

"Oh, um . . ." I didn't sit up straight until I was certain Preston had passed. Inside my heart had shattered into a heaping pile of broken glass. *How could I have fallen for his nice-guy routine?*

Andrew leaned over and looked out the window. "What was that about?"

My eyes darted to Daisy. "Um . . . I just thought I saw someone I knew."

"But you were hiding," Daisy pressed, brow furrowed.

I nibbled a bite off my sandwich and shrugged, hoping she'd drop it. Outwardly, I tried to act like nothing was wrong. Inside, everything had twisted around and turned inside out. *How could I have gotten this attached?* It was just a summer, not a love story.

So foolish. I should've learned my lesson and stuck to my rule of no more guys. With Preston, this felt a million times worse. I'd way more than liked him; that should've been a red flag right there.

Andrew and Daisy shared a look. I couldn't answer them. If I talked about him, hell if I spoke his name out loud, I'd likely burst into tears.

Crap. The backs of my eyes burned. They were coming anyway.

Standing, I grabbed my purse. "I'll be back. I'm gonna run to the ladies."

Not waiting for an answer, I made a mad dash for the restroom. Inside, I barricaded myself behind the solid stall door. It actually wasn't a stall, more a separate little room. Leaning against it, I inhaled a shaky breath as a tear trickled down my cheek. Squeezing my eyes shut, I willed myself to stop. It didn't work.

A creaky hinge signaled I wasn't alone. I held my breath. But I knew exactly who it was.

"Maggie? You okay?"

"No." My voice shook.

Daisy knocked on my door. "Don't tell me nothing happened. What was that?"

Shoulders slumping forward, I unlocked the door and came out. "Remember the guy I told you about, from this summer?"

"Course, the fella you weren't sure if he was more than just a friend. What just happened?" Everything sounded better in her lilt, happier somehow.

"I just saw him outside. He was smiling and laughing with another girl."

"So." She shrugged. "Maybe they're friends."

I crossed my arms over my chest. "They walked away arm in arm, flirting."

She shook her head and proceeded to sit on the tile counter between the two sinks. "How on earth can you know they were flirting through a window pane?"

"The way he looked at her." I squeezed my eyes shut. "It was the way he looked at me all summer. Ugh! I know not to trust men. I broke my one rule; maybe I deserve this." I looked toward the ceiling and shook my head.

"What was your rule?"

"No guys."

A soft, sultry laugh left Daisy's throat. "Something tells me that wouldn't have worked for very long. Boys can be a lot of fun."

"Boys can be a lot of heartache."

"True, but some of them are so very worth it."

• • •

I sat at a sketching table in a vacant design lab. Rows of the same tables, baskets of magazines, and a wall full of colorful fabric swatches filled the room. It was one of my favorite places. My thoughts came more clearly here. The paneled windows overlooked the well-tended lawns. Although, right now I couldn't see much through the fog.

The swivel chair groaned as I leaned back too far. School had been in session for a little over a month and I'd avoided all of Preston's calls. Granted, between classes, homework, and working at The Bolt, I usually couldn't answer.

My email replies were short and sweet. I hadn't wanted to answer at all, but it just felt too rude not to.

Maybe once the hurt had subsided we could be friends. I pulled out a sketch of some chunky knitwear wraps I'd been working on.

A loud buzz from my phone made me jump. A text from Mom lit up the screen. I smiled at the photo I had set for her number. It was Halloween last year; she'd dressed up as a jellyfish. A large, round, illuminated hat with glowing tentacles draped around her slim face. It'd turned out so pretty.

Mom: How's it going?
Me: Good. Working hard at The Bolt and school. Not sleeping nearly enough. ;)
Mom: Do you need anything?
Me: So far I'm okay. How're you?
Mom: Good, mostly. Getting to work on some fun projects. Finally getting to do that Georgian era period piece I always wanted to do.

I knew how much Mom loved her job as a director of photography. So knowing she was getting back to projects she felt passionate about, and not under Dad's thumb, thrilled me to no end.

Me: Yay! That's great! How's living with Marc?

Mom: Not ideal, but it works. He starts back at school winter term. I'm looking at some condos. I want to get out of his hair.
Me: How's the divorce coming?
Mom: My lawyer has filed and gotten the ball rolling. Your father gets back next week, so we'll see. How's Preston?
Me: Don't know. I haven't talked to him in a while.
Mom: I'm sorry, sweetie.

A number I didn't recognize flashed on my screen as the phone buzzed out a Morse code on the tabletop. "Hello?"

"Hi, may I speak with Maggie?" The caller was female, but that was all I could figure out.

I set my colored pencil down. "This is she."

"This is Haley Browne, Preston's sister. He passed your number along to me so I could call and give you all the details on our paranormal investigation. You still interested?"

My head reared back, shocked she'd called. Preston must not have informed her he'd moved on. Was it bad I still really wanted to go? "Um, yeah."

"Great." Papers rustled in the background. "We're doing it this weekend. You free?"

I wasn't scheduled at the shop, so I could easily manage it. My only worry was Preston being there. He'd mentioned that he rarely went with them, but I couldn't bring myself to ask her if he'd be there. "Yeah, that should work just fine."

What will I do if he's there?

"Great. Okay, do you have a pen and note paper?"

Flipping my sketchbook to the back cover, I grabbed my purple pencil. "Yup."

"Okay, Saturday at five meet us here." She rattled off an address in Oxford. "Then you can drive to the investigation location with us."

I scribbled down the directions and smiled, a zing of excitement ripping through me. "Okay, I'll be there."

"Now remember, this can get dangerous, so you really have to listen, be careful, and do as you're told." I heard voices in the background on her end, but couldn't make out what they were saying.

"Of course. I'll see you Saturday."

Another student entered the lab and sat on the far end of the row of tables. I clicked off the phone and sat there, my mind tripping over Preston. He hadn't struck me as a player at all. And I think that's what hurt the most.

Chapter Fifteen

The Unseen

The black cab I'd hired from the Oxford bus station pulled to a stop on a quiet drive dotted with lit street lamps. My phone chimed, alerting me to a new text, and I yanked it from my jacket pocket. Handing a tenner to the driver, I hopped from the cab, hoping that the investigation hadn't been canceled at the last minute.

> Ben: I was thinking about making a trip down to Bampton tomorrow. We've got some stuff to discuss. Think you can squeeze me in for lunch or dinner?

This was the first communication I'd had with him since Dad dropped the bomb that Ben had agreed to his plan. I was relieved he'd initiated contact. When I thought of him now I got a squirmy, uneasy feeling. *Why would a hot guy like him agree to this farce?*

> Me: Sure. Can I get back to you on which one? I've got a late night ahead of me so . . .
> Ben: Sounds cool. Talk to you tomorrow.

From the sidewalk, I tucked my cell away and looked up at the tall white townhouse before me. Warm light beckoned from the windows. As I stepped forward my gaze traveled down the tree-lined street, realizing the poshness surrounding me. *Is this Haley's place?* Her bank job must pay really well.

I went up the steps and rang the doorbell, hearing the muffled chimes inside.

The door popped open and I sucked in a sharp breath. The cold air hit my lungs, making me cough. It wasn't Haley that greeted me.

It was Preston.

My knees turned to jelly and my stomach lurched at the sight of him. I so wasn't ready to see him.

"What are you doing here?" My voice sounded odd to my ears.

A slow smile curled across his face. I couldn't stop myself from staring at those blasted lips and remembering how incredibly right they felt pressed against mine. A fluttery sensation settled low in my stomach and I hated my traitorous body and the fact that he had such an easy effect on me.

"Um, I live here, this is my flat. Well, actually it's my best mate's flat, but . . . oh, come inside." He ran a hand through his mop of blond hair and his eyes darted away from mine.

"Oh, I didn't realize we were meeting at *your* flat." I stepped in and glanced around the entry, needing to look anywhere but his eyes. "It's nice."

"Yeah, well, we didn't have much choice. We had to meet certain security standards."

I was just about to ask what he meant when Haley hollered from the other room. "Pres, is that Maggie?"

"Yeah." His gaze settled on me and he seemed reluctant to look away. "We'll be right in."

The rubber toes of my Converse captured my attention and I spoke to them. "I didn't realize you were coming tonight."

"Well, I knew you'd be here, and I wouldn't miss a chance to see you for the world."

What is he playing at?

• • •

The hotel and pub we were investigating was on the eastern outskirts of Oxford. Inside the bar, a row of orange vinyl barstools sat tucked under the polished bar top. Not that I could see them any more, but I remembered from our initial walk-through. The only light illuminating the room came from outside the windows and our flashlights.

Preston and I were the second team to investigate the building. One team was supervising the command station and the other was across the street at the cemetery. The owners of the pub believed spirits buried in the graveyard were making their way into the bar, so we were checking it out.

The wooden floor creaked as we made our way over the threshold and into the room. The outline of Preston's broad shoulders lowered as he took a seat on one of the barstools and motioned for me to join him. He sat the slim voice recorder he held on the wooden surface. "Let's do an EVP session."

EVP, or electronic voice phenomena, was basically catching disembodied voices on a recording device. I got the basic rundown of the tools they used while we set up. Plus, my slight affinity for paranormal television shows didn't hurt.

I sat at Preston's side, our shoulders touching, feeling silly about talking to thin air. Especially in front of him. If I'd been with any of the other members of the team I would've been fine. Preston had me nervous and completely off kilter. He had since the moment he opened the door. Heck, since the first time he snuck up on me on the hilltop, really.

"Hello, I'm Preston and this is my friend, Maggie. We're here to talk to you."

"Hello," I said to the room and held an electromagnetic frequency meter—EMF—in my hand. It beeped, so I flashed my light on it to see the needle had jumped. Preston leaned closer to get a better view. His breath brushed my cheek and I had to lean back, his nearness too much.

"Why don't you do a quick walk around the room and get base readings."

I happily got up and put some distance between us as I did a quick sweep around. My gray chucks softly tapped against the wood slatted floor. The only area that fluctuated was near the bar, and we narrowed it down to a mini fridge tucked under the counter.

Sitting down beside him again, I set the EMF on the bar.

"So, I've got two options for you." His low voice startled me.

I looked straight ahead, not daring a glance at him. "Oh?"

"I know you took the bus here, and I really hate the thought of you riding it back so early in the morning. In fact, I don't even know if there's a bus running that early."

"There's one leaving at 4:30."

He sucked a breath in through his teeth. "Ouch. That sounds miserable."

I shrugged. "It is what it is."

"Well, I'm offering you a bed at my place."

This time I did look at him, my eyes narrowing. *Is he asking what I think he's asking?*

"Not mine." He quickly added and glanced away. "Sorry, we have a guest room you can use."

"Okay." I dragged out the word, relieved and a little bummed at the same time.

With a slight laugh, he added, "Although, the alternative would be fine with me too." He shined the light on his face and flashed me his adorable grin until his dimple indented his cheek. "Or maybe not. Anyway, I was thinking tomorrow I could drive you back to . . . wait, I still don't know where you're going to school. Think you can let me in on the secret now?" He bumped his shoulder against mine.

I smiled. "I'm at Thrippletons."

"Oh really? That's a fabulous school." The beam of his flashlight shot to the corner and he studied the area, searching for something. "Did you just see a shadow over there?"

"Uh, no." I was too busy watching him. Hmm, maybe I wasn't cut out for this ghost hunter thing . . . at least not when Preston was around.

"So, anyways," he continued, "I was thinking, if you wanted, we could spend tomorrow exploring Oxford, then I could drive you back to Thrippletons. Maybe even get some supper in Bampton if you like."

I reached up and scratched my head, feeling like a bug had landed on my hair. The idea of spending the day with him sounded pretty fantastic. I opened my mouth to speak, wanting to ask him about the cute little blonde, but changed my mind.

"If you're busy, no worries. We could always do it another time." He shrugged and in the dim glow of my flashlight I could make out an uncertain, almost nervous look on his features.

All the signals were the same I'd been receiving throughout summer, but I still couldn't shake the doubt. I unscrewed the top of my flashlight, needing something to do with my hands. "Um, sure that'd be great. Although, I've already made dinner plans tomorrow. So, is that still okay?"

Damn this whole Ben situation anyway.

His smile was instantaneous. "That's great. Perfect."

Why on earth is he asking me out if he's seeing someone? It didn't make sense.

"Um, we should probably get back to work."

"Probably." I couldn't stop the smile.

"I hear you like to play with hair," Preston spoke to the air in the room. "I know it's not much, but you can touch mine if you'd like." The EMF needle warbled before settling on the number two.

Something brushed against my hair again. I reached up and fluffed it, trying to knock out whatever fly or gnat may have tangled in it. I flashed the beam of my light to the ceiling, thinking it might've been a cobweb, but it was clean. Moments later it happened again. My eyes widened as goosebumps prickled across my skin, uneasiness curling around me like fog. The EMF needle still hadn't gone back down.

"Um, Preston." I kept my voice calm. "Is there, by chance, anything in my hair?"

He cocked his head to the side. In the dimness, his outline leaned toward me. With a click of a button, his flashlight lit up. "Come here, let me check."

I angled myself toward him and he shined the light on me and ran his fingers through my hair. A jolt of desire coursed through me as flashbacks to our movie night at Chillingham and the way his fingers had tangled in my hair as we'd made out on the couch now assailed me.

"I don't see anything." His breath rushed across my lips.

I cleared my throat. "Well, then I'm pretty sure something just touched me. Twice."

Leaning back, he illuminated the ceiling. "There's no air vents. Do you feel a draft?"

I held out my hand, feeling around me. Nothing. "Um, nope."

A soft chuckle left his lips. "Hmm, if that was you who touched Maggie, I'd like to thank you. I did invite you to touch me, not her, but she does have lovely hair, doesn't she? It's very soft."

The corners of my lips turned up. His easy playful demeanor helped me relax. Not that I was freaking out necessarily, but my creep-o-meter was definitely in the red.

"Thanks for letting us know you're here. Can you touch Preston too?"

A few minutes of silence passed and Preston patted my knee. "Should we go upstairs?"

Nodding, I stood. "Sure, let's go."

He led the way up a creaky flight of steep stairs to the second level. Midway up I paused and tugged the back of Preston's shirt. "I swear it just happened again. Something touched my hair, this time on the other side."

He turned and the beams from our flashlights collided.

The EMF meter buzzed and chirped. Preston flashed his light on the needle. We watched it jump back and forth, but still stay relatively elevated.

"Preston and Maggie in the stairwell at the Drunken Unicorn pub." He tagged the voice recorder so we'd know where we were when it came time to review evidence. "High EMF readings."

"Is there anyone here with us?"

Preston faced me on the stairs, towering over me even more. "Can you tell us your name?"

A heavy thump came from the second floor. I froze, eyes wide, and watched Preston, needing his cue to decide on my reaction. This being so new for me, I wasn't sure what was normal. My senses were heightened by the darkness, the adrenaline coursing throughout my body, and the fact that Preston was so damn close to me. Part of me was ready to bolt at the slightest noise; the other was determined to prove to Preston that I could do this. Just like I intended to prove to Dad that I'd be a success in the fashion world.

His eyes never left mine. "You heard that, right?"

"Yes." My voice came out softer than I'd intended.

Turning back around, Preston climbed the stairs the rest of the way. I followed close behind. Once we reached the hallway another loud thud sounded, this time farther away. I wanted to grab his hand or hide my face in his shoulder, but thankfully I held myself in check.

"I think it came from this way. Keep your torch on."

I almost laughed. There was no way in hell I'd turn it off right now. I stayed at Preston's side as we walked down the long hardwood hallway. When we reached the end, it was empty and all the doors around us were shut.

We stood there looking around, unmoving. Footsteps echoed down the hallway on the wooden stairs we'd just come up.

"Oh my God, Preston, please tell me you hear that." I flashed my light in the direction we'd just traveled, not seeing anything.

"It sounds like . . ."

"—Boots." We spoke at the same time. The sound continued and grew louder as they reached the top of the stairs. I had to wonder how close they'd come.

Preston reached for his radio. "Hey, Haley, is there anyone else in the building?"

"Nope, it's just the two of you."

Chapter Sixteen

Friendly Meetings

The chirping coming from my phone woke me. My bleary eyes opened and for a moment I forgot where I was. I glanced around the plain room and spotted an old concert poster on the wall and vaguely remembered Preston carrying me in here after I'd fallen asleep on the ride back from the hair-loving ghost investigation.

Here I was, nestled in Preston's guest room in Oxford. I glanced out the window at the sun high in the blue sky and stretched. *How late had I slept?*

I grabbed my cell from beside my pillow and checked the clock. It wasn't even noon yet. Ben's name scrolled across the top of my screen, followed by a short message: *I'm guessing you're wanting to do dinner?*

Crap. I'd forgotten to text him. Truthfully I didn't want to deal with him and this whole situation. I knew we needed to talk though. You can't pull off a fake relationship without a game plan. My main goal was to find out whose side he was on. I swiped my finger across the screen to reply.

Me: Sorry. Yes, dinner's better for me.
Ben: 7:00 okay?

I caught my lip between my teeth, thinking. We needed more time. I'd decided today was the day for me to come clean with Preston about who my dad was.

Me: Can we make it 8:00?
Ben: Sure, see you then.

Despite being cozy and comfortable, I flipped the covers back. Preston might be up already and I didn't want to waste a minute of our time together. I smoothed my rumpled clothes, then stood and opened the door. Across the hall I spied a bathroom. I darted in, quickly finger-combed my hair, washed my face, reapplied the face powder and mascara that I thankfully always carried in my purse, then headed downstairs.

In the entry I heard what sounded like someone unloading the dishwasher. I poked my head around the corner and spied a girl with a spiky pixie cut, several mugs dangling from her fingers. "Um, hello."

She jumped and looked my way. "Who are you?"

I walked closer. "I'm Maggie. I'm a friend of Preston's."

"Oh, yeah." She snapped her fingers. "You guys went hunting ghosties last night, right?"

Nodding, I sat on the barstool in front of her.

"I'm Marissa. Preston and Edmund's flatmate." She set down a mug and reached her hand across the counter, smiling at me. Cocking her head to the side, she asked. "Did you spend the night here?"

"More like the morning." I chuckled, thinking of the sun just rising on the ride back.

One eyebrow rose as she tucked the mugs into the cupboard. "So, you and Pres, huh?"

"Oh, no, not like that. I, uh, stayed in the guest room." My cheeks warmed and I looked down to the marble countertop. Last night I'd gotten a hug, but nothing more. I had no clue what this day meant. Were we going out as friends or was this more of a date? I really wanted it to be a date.

"Ah, I see. Bollocks." Marissa ran a hand through her swoopy brown bangs and winked at me.

I chuckled. She certainly was blunt. The front door opened and I turned toward the arched doorway, waiting to see who was joining us.

"Rissa?" A breathless voice hollered.

"In the kitchen, babe."

A figure flew into the room and threw herself into Marissa's arms, planting a kiss on her. "I have the best news."

"We have a guest." Marissa smiled and pointed to me.

Smiling, I waved. "Hello."

Marissa jumped to make introductions. "This is my girlfriend, Caroline."

"Hello." Caroline looked to Marissa as if searching for answers.

"This is Preston's friend, Maggie." My new pixie-haired friend answered the unasked question.

Caroline's brown eyes widened. "Ah, *Maggie.*"

The way my name came off her glossy lips made me think she'd heard it before. Which honestly sent a thrill from my head to my toes.

"You want some coffee?" Marissa offered.

I nodded. "That'd be great. I'm still a little groggy."

"You slept here!" Caroline's eyes widened, her black bob swishing as she spun to face me, a huge grin on her face.

"Guest room." Marissa corrected as she poured me a mug of steaming deliciousness.

"Thanks." I took the cup and doctored it up.

Caroline's smile fell. "Mm, drats."

Did all his friends think he needed to get laid? What about the pretty blonde girl?

Marissa laughed, no doubt because of their similar responses.

Preston popped around the corner, his hand smoothing the messy bed head he had going on. "Hey, glad you're up."

As he approached me, I sat a little straighter. He still had crinkles on his cheek from his pillow. The sleep not completely gone from his eyes, he looked like a little kid. I couldn't stop the corners of my lips from curling even if I tried.

"Hey, Rissa, do you mind pouring me a mug?" When she handed him one, he used the sugar and cream she'd set out for me. "Mm, that's good, thanks."

I took another sip, enjoying the warmth as it coursed down my throat. "So, man with the plan, what are we doing today?"

He swallowed his mouthful and turned to me. "It's up to you. I could show you some of the places they filmed Harry Potter, if you're into that. There's the Bodleian Library, or the Bridge of Sighs, or we could go punting." He looked out the window. "It's a beautiful fall day. You name it, we'll do it."

"I was with you on most of those ideas, but I'm guessing 'punting' has nothing to do with a football."

The three of them chuckled.

"No, it's going out on River Cherwell in a boat. Basically you push yourself around with a long stick. We could even grab lunch. They have fabulous food there."

"That sounds like fun." Caroline hopped up and sat on the counter across from us, her dark skin illuminated from the sunlight streaming in the window. "Maybe we should join you." The look she gave Preston made me think she was teasing him.

The front door shut with a bang. "Caroline!"

She spared a quick glance at Marissa and hopped off the counter, heading for the door. "Suzy? What's wrong?"

With Caroline's arm draped around her shoulders, this Suzy girl walked in. I nearly gasped when I saw her. It was the girl I'd seen Preston with. The one who'd made him laugh and who he'd looked at so adoringly.

"Leo and I broke up." She sobbed and covered her face in her hands.

Wait, so she's not with Preston?

I'd gotten it wrong. It may be terrible, and I felt completely guilty about it, but my heart still soared at my newfound knowledge. He wasn't dating her. I'd jumped to a stupid conclusion and Daisy had been right. I looked heavenward. *Okay, lesson learned, don't make snap judgements.*

Marissa joined them and flanked Suzy from the other side. Both girls held her and tried to soothe her.

"Where's Evie?" Caroline glanced to Preston.

He shrugged. "Not a clue. You want me to call her?" When Caroline nodded, he pulled out his phone and made a couple taps, then put it up to his ear. I heard him fill the other person in on the drama. When he hung up he said, "She'll be here in just a bit, she's just getting out of a study group."

I felt like an eavesdropper who shouldn't be here. Leaning in to Preston I whispered, "Why don't we hang out some other time. I'm gonna go catch the bus. You should be here for your friend."

"No." He shook his head, his eyes widening. "This is a girl thing; I would only be in the way. Trust me. I'll be back in just a second." He walked over to the huddle of girls and I assumed told them we'd be taking off.

"Wait, she's here?" The distraught girl poked her head around Preston and gazed at me. A smile streaked across her face and she made her way over. "Hello, you must be Maggie. I'm Suzy. I've heard so much about you." She sniffed.

I loved how my name sounded in their accents. Suzy was no different. It seemed like they pronounced both the g's, making something simple sound somehow exotic.

"Hi." I wanted to hug her for what she was going through and for the fact that she wasn't dating Preston. "I'm so sorry to intrude on all . . . this."

She waved it away. "It's okay. I should've known better than to date one of my . . . oh, never mind. Do you and Preston have plans today?"

With how upset she'd been, I felt weird talking about Preston and me. "Um, I think we're going to go punting."

"How fun, you'll love it. Leo and I did that over the summer." Her eyes welled up again. "I'm sorry."

I put my hand on her shoulder and rubbed. "No, don't be. Breakups are awful." From the corner of my eye I noticed Preston smiling at us.

Suzy grinned and wiped at her nose with a rumpled tissue she fished from her pocket. "You're sweet." She turned to Preston and motioned for him to come over to us. "I like her, Pres. You guys go. Have fun."

"Thanks, Suze." With a shoulder squeeze for his friend, he grabbed my hand and guided me to our escape, out the front door.

• • •

Preston's SUV rumbled to a stop in the parking lot of a quaint three-gabled brick building. His keys jangled as he removed them from the ignition. I opened the door and climbed out, taking in the small building with its colorful flower boxes. Lining the edge of the path were wooden boats, or punts, I guess is what they're called.

"Should we eat first or go punting?" Preston asked as I met him at the front of the car. The green grass and fall-dappled trees felt too perfect next to the steadily flowing water.

"Let's eat." I smiled, enjoying the unseasonably warm day. "I'm starving."

"This way." He grabbed my hand, thrilling me to no end. *He's single.* Thank goodness I'd been wrong.

Inside, we reserved a boat and then were seated at a table with a long white tablecloth. All around us were matching tables with shiny glass centerpieces and glowing candles. At night it would be extremely romantic. Maybe one day Preston and I could come back.

"What do you think looks good?"

"Everything." I looked at him over my menu and grinned. It looked like lunch was a two-course meal. Which I was glad for; my stomach was seriously growling. At the very top it read: Autumn Menu. How cool, they had a menu for the different seasons. "What do you recommend?"

"Hmm, to start I love the artichoke soup, it's fabulous. For the main meal I've had the gnocchi and the tortellini, can't go wrong with either of those."

When the waiter returned we gave him our orders, then he spun away with our menus tucked under his arm. I looked across the table and met Preston's brown eyes. We hadn't been alone in over a month and I'd missed this, just us, together. A warm fuzzy feeling of contentment and happiness settled over me.

"So, Thrippletons, huh? That's actually really close to Oxford."

"Yeah, I was surprised. I expected it to be farther away."

"Well, next time you need a ride into town, just give me a call, I'd be happy to pick you up."

The waiter brought our drinks and I took a sip of my water. "That's awfully sweet, but I certainly don't expect you to drive all the way in to Bampton just to give me a ride."

He added cream and sugar to his tea, then glanced up and smiled. "Are you kidding? A half hour alone with you in the car is worth it." His eyes stayed on mine as he took a sip.

I laughed. "How are you single?"

"That is a great mystery." His deep rumbly laugh filled me with tingles. "What about you?"

My eyes darted away. "Oh, um . . . I had a not-so-nice boyfriend and he kind of had me swearing off guys for a while."

He reached over and slid his hand over mine. "I'm glad you got rid of him."

I raised my gaze to his. "Me too."

"That means you're taking a chance on me then?" His brows rose as he studied me.

I'm breaking my rules for you.

"So it would seem."

He released my hand and leaned back as a bowl of soup was set in front of him. "Thank God for that."

I looked up to the waiter after he placed mine. "Thank you."

With a nod, the stoic gray-haired man turned and left.

Preston blew on a spoonful of steaming soup and between breaths asked, "How's your family doing?"

I crinkled my nose and shrugged. "Mom and Marc are back in California and she's filed for divorce. Dad gets back sometime soon and . . . well, the only time I talk to him is when he wants something from me."

Should I tell him right now? I wanted to come clean about Ben and about Dad blackmailing me with threats of dragging out the divorce and making Mom fight tooth and nail to get rid of him, but I didn't know how to begin. I didn't want to pop out with "Yeah, my dad's blackmailing me and I don't know why. Totally sucks."

"That's got to be hard. I'm sorry." His eyes softened at the corners and I could tell he meant it. "How are you holding up?"

I set my spoon in my bowl. "Okay. I'm worried about Mom once Dad gets back. It's hard not being there and unable to help or do . . . anything."

Preston nodded and didn't press for answers, which I was thankful for.

The waiter brought the rest of our meal and took away our finished soup bowls. Preston got the tortellini and it looked yummy. My basil and pine nut gnocchi made my mouth water. I took a bite and closed my eyes, savoring the flavor.

"Oh, this is fabulous." When my eyes opened Preston's were watching me, a slight curl to his lips.

The look on his face made up my mind for me. I'd dragged this out long enough and I just couldn't keep lying to him. I needed to tell him.

He cleared his throat and loaded up his fork. "I'm glad you like it."

"I need to tell you something." Wiping at the corners of my mouth, I set my napkin down and took a drink. *Please let him take this well.*

Chapter Seventeen

A Recipe for Disaster

Our white-swathed table in the boathouse suddenly felt too small. I looked around the room at the other couples, waiting for Preston to say something after the bomb I'd just dropped. It's not every day someone tells you their dad is a big-time Hollywood director.

"Wait, so you're telling me your dad is *the* Scott McKendrick. The guy who did all those Dragon Guardian movies, right?" His brow scrunched and he met my fidgety gaze.

This was the test. Would this change everything? Would he see me differently? Nerves tightened in my stomach and I nodded. He didn't smile.

"Why did it take you so long to tell me?"

"Because I was afraid." I explained how people changed once they found out. How he was the last person I wanted to look at me differently. Waiting for his reaction, my stomach knotted. He sat quietly, like he was figuring out what to say.

"I get it." His hand reached under the table and covered both of mine. "I'm glad you told me, but honestly, Mags, I couldn't care less who your father is."

"Really?" My eyes darted to his, feeling like a weight had shifted. I still had too many other secrets I was keeping from him for it to totally be lifted.

"To me, he's just Maggie McKendrick's father. You're the important one." He squeezed my hands. "And I already seriously dislike him for his treatment of you and your family. He sounds like a major tosser."

A smile filled my face and I sucked in a breath. Mom had called it. He didn't care and he still liked me for me. "You really don't care, do you?"

He shook his head and reached a hand up to cup my cheek. "No, I do care . . . about you. *My* Maggie."

I couldn't meet his intense gaze for fear that I might spontaneously combust from the heat coursing through me.

"Let's finish lunch and get out of here," he added in a soft undertone.

I peeked up at him and nodded. I so badly wanted to tell him about Ben and the blackmail, but Dad's gag order stopped me. I didn't want to give him a reason to make Mom miserable.

We finished lunch and as we headed outside Preston stopped and retrieved our punting supplies, then we went to find our boat.

Preston set everything down on the pathway and stood to the side of the floating wooden punt, offering his hand to help me board. I clasped on to him and shakily stepped in, holding tight to the cushions they'd given me. I went to the far end of the long boat and turned around. It'd been explained to me that Preston would stand in the back, using the long metal pole he'd carried over, to push us around.

I sat facing him, with my back to where we'd be traveling. It was beautiful scenery, but given the choice I'd much rather stare at Preston. Especially since he'd be using his muscular arms to keep us moving along. *Too bad he's wearing a peacoat.*

"You ready?" he asked after untying us. At my nod he dipped the pole into the water and pushed off the river bottom.

"Have you done this before?" I admired the way he easily maneuvered us into the current and how he used the pole like a rudder.

"A couple times. Once with the whole gang and another time with my parents."

My phone rang and I pulled it out. Daisy's perky face appeared on the screen. "Oh my gosh, I've got to take this. It's my roommate, I forgot to tell her I wouldn't be home last night." I hit the Accept button and assured her I was okay and no, I hadn't been eaten by ghosts.

"Jayzus, you scared me. Where are you?"

"Um . . ." I looked around me and grinned. "Punting."

Preston chuckled and kept pushing us along. A line of pristine white swans swam past us. Wordlessly, I pointed to the lovely animals and grinned up at Preston, who nodded and kept silent as Daisy chattered in my ear, still irritated that she was just now getting in touch with me.

"Wait, who are you with?"

"A friend."

"Okay, I can totally hear the sunshine in your voice. Would this happen to be the summer romance you're not sure where you stand with?"

My cheeks flushed and I dragged my fingers in the smooth, cold water, trying to appear unaffected. "Yeah, that'd be the one."

"I think we need to have a chat about signals, my friend. I'll let you go, but I want all the details later."

Once I got off the phone I tucked it back in my jacket pocket and looked up to Preston, insanely happy at the moment.

"What?" he asked when he caught me staring at him.

I shook my head. "I'm just really glad that I'm here. That I'm with you."

The smile that crossed his face made him practically glow. "I'm glad you're here too."

Adjusting my position, I sat up straighter. "So tell me about this gang of yours. Is it all girls?"

Laughing, he raised his brows. "Almost. Edmund and I are the only guys. There's Marissa, you met her this morning, she's our other flatmate. Then there's Suzy, Caroline, and Evie. But those three live on campus. What about you?"

"I'm still meeting people, but my roommate's pretty cool. She's got this really awesome pastel pink hair. She's been trying to get me to dye mine."

"Really? What color?"

"Purple."

He laughed and raised an eyebrow. "Purple. That would certainly be eye catching."

"Wouldn't it though." I pulled up a clump of the mousy strands. I never liked the brown. I always wished it was blonde. "Who knows, I may let her do a small section."

"That could be very interesting."

Just the smile on his face made me want to do it. To see what he'd really think. A swan floated past and let out a honk, startling me.

"She's trying to get our friend, Andrew, to do blue. If we go anywhere together we might get mistaken for a pack of My Little Ponies."

Preston's laugh sent things uncoiling and bubbling low in my stomach. If we weren't in a boat, or rather a punt, I so would have kissed him. My gaze focused on his lips. I loved the way they curled up at the corners and the scruff on his face, oh Lord, how I wanted to feel it pressed against my skin.

I shook my head and picked at a leftover knotted end of yarn on the knitted red cowl around my neck. It might be a good thing we were in the middle of a river.

A boat full of people came at us from the opposite direction. The man doing the punting lifted a hand to wave at us. "Oi, mate, careful down there, it's muddy and we almost lost the pole a couple times."

Would that be a bad thing? I didn't mind the idea of getting trapped in the middle of a river with a hot guy.

Preston waved. "Thanks. I'll take care."

"What happens if you lose the pole?" I asked.

"We'd use the paddle they gave us to try to fish it out. At least that's what I'd try before paddling our way back."

Too bad we had a paddle.

"This is actually probably the last weekend this'll be open. They close for the late fall and winter."

I looked around us at the bright fall colors in the trees and just felt happy. Although that was probably more to do with the fact that I was with Preston. "Well, I'm glad we got out here this weekend then."

"There's a small area up ahead, that most people bring picnics to and hop off at in the summer. Maybe next spring we should do that."

A big smile filled my face and my stomach turned all fluttery. He was planning on still seeing me next year. *Holy shit.* Being in a boat was the only thing preventing me from doing a little happy dance. Well, that and not wanting to look idiotic.

Preston stared at me and I realized I hadn't answered him. Grinning, I bobbed my head and said, "That'd be fun. You can count me in."

• • •

We pulled back into the dock and my shoulders slumped. Our time together was running out. Preston hopped onto the bank and tied the boat to the side, once again offering me his hand. It was warm and slightly rough and much bigger than mine, which I loved. There was no way I'd ever tire of it twined with mine.

"I'm going to return everything. I'll be right back."

I nodded. The smile was impossible to keep off my lips. Today couldn't have been more perfect. Well, if he'd kiss me, that'd make it better. I turned just in time to see him jogging back to me.

"So, what time do you have to be back for your dinner plans?"

That took the smile off my face. I didn't want to see Ben. I didn't want to pretend to date him. And I didn't want this charade to destroy things between Preston and me. "Um, we're getting together at eight."

How am I going to get out of this mess? I had to tell Preston the rest of my story. I knew if I didn't, I risked losing him. Well, either way I might lose him.

Sighing, Preston reached for my hand. "I guess that means we should head back."

My face scrunched. "Probably."

He didn't release my hand once the whole drive. When his thumb rubbed lazy circles against my palm I nearly purred. I wanted to be closer to him.

We pulled through the gates and I glanced at the dash clock. Forty-five minutes and Ben would show up. I should run and freshen up a little.

Preston let go of my hand as he parked a little ways away from the main door. He turned the engine off and angled himself to face me. The only light came from the tall lights of the gravelly parking area. His voice broke the silence, coming out low and soft. "I'm not ready for today to end."

I slid closer in my seat and gave his hand a squeeze. "Me neither."

His eyes flashed to mine and the corner of his lips quirked up as he took my hand and placed it on the back of his neck. My teeth tugged my lower lip and I pulled him toward me. His mouth met mine and on contact a soft moan worked its way from my throat. This is exactly what I'd wanted all day. Heck, last night too.

Warm hands grasped my back, clutching my coat and guiding me over the center console. A hand shifted and snaked its way into my hair, holding me tight. It felt like he couldn't get me close enough. I shared the frustration.

His lips parted and mine eagerly followed. When our tongues touched he growled and deepened the kiss. I knew I had to leave, but God, I didn't want to. If only I could stay here with him.

"Maggie." He pulled back slightly, his voice a hoarse whisper. "I've been wanting to kiss you since I opened the door last night."

"Preston . . ." My voice wasn't any louder, and his mouth silenced the rest of my words. I flattened my palms against his chest. Everything about him was lean and muscular and . . . perfect. Correction: everything about him was just plain sexy.

A knock on the window caught our attention. Breathing heavily, we turned to look out my side of the car. Daisy and Andrew's smiling faces stared back at us.

"Just once I'd like not to get interrupted." Preston sighed and reached up to straighten my hair.

I snickered and leaned back into my seat, unlocking the door, which Andrew rushed to open.

"So, who're you swapping spit with?" He leaned into the SUV and grinned, the dome light shedding light on his face. Daisy's head appeared through the windshield and she gave a cheeky wave.

"Andrew, this is Preston. Preston, this is Andrew the Annoying." I grinned as they shook hands.

"Nice to meet you." The dimple in Preston's cheek made an appearance, which made me giddy at the sight.

"What are you two doing out here?"

Andrew eyed Preston, then smiled appreciatively. "We're just getting back from dinner."

Daisy yanked Andrew by the arm. "Give us some space, let me in."

When she leaned over me, I did the introductions as she batted her lashes. Turning to me she stage-whispered, "You're right, he *is* really cute. *Nice.*"

Chuckling, I shook my head. "Yeah, thanks, Dais." I turned to Preston. "I should go. These two aren't going to leave us alone, are you?" I asked Daisy.

"Not likely." Her pert nose crinkled and she laughed.

I pushed against Daisy's shoulders, getting her out of the car. "Give me just a minute."

With a giggle, she and Andrew took a couple steps away, allowing us a smidgen of privacy.

Closing the door, I turned back to Preston. "I'm sorry about them."

"It's fine." He reached and took my hand. "I'm glad I got to meet them."

Sighing, I looked out the window. "Really? I think it could've waited."

He chuckled and his thumb ran over my knuckles in a soft caress. "Hey, before you leave, um, my flatmates are throwing a small party next week. I was hoping you might come."

"What's the party for?"

He focused on our hands. "It's my birthday."

"Really, well happy early birthday."

His lips twitched and he raised his gaze to mine. "It's Friday. I'd really love for you to be there."

"Hmm." I pretended to think about it, then cracked a smile. "I don't have any plans. So, if you want me there, I'll be there."

With no warning he kissed me again. It didn't last as long, nor was it as intense, but it still made my knees weak. Pulling back, I touched my fingers to my bottom lip. "I have to go. I'll see you Friday." I hopped out, but leaned back in. "Thanks for the ride back and the wonderful day."

"Anytime," his low voice answered.

Daisy and Andrew were both chattering at me, one at each side, as soon as I closed the door. But their voices were only a distant murmur; my focus was still solely on Preston. He waved at me with a grin just before I was yanked up the front steps.

"He's cute."

"Does he have a brother you can set me up with?" Andrew's eyes widened and his dark brows bounced up and down.

Daisy zipped up the front of her black fleece. "How can you seriously be unsure if he likes you?"

"What? She's not sure?" Andrew leaned around me to see Daisy. "Am I missing something?"

I sighed. "Guys, I've got to get ready for dinner."

Daisy's brow furrowed. "Who are you getting dinner with?"

Cringing, I said. "Another guy."

"You're two-timing him?" Andrew, eyes wide, gestured with his thumb to the SUV now driving through the tall metal gates. "That cute, adorable guy who looks like one hell of a kisser?" He snorted a light laugh. "Just so you know, I wouldn't mind keeping Preston busy while you're off with bachelor number two."

"No, it's not like that. This other guy, he's just kind of . . . well, a friend, I suppose." I was forbidden to tell anyone about Dad's scheme and how I had to play my part or Mom's life would be torn apart by a messy divorce and a vindictive estranged husband. Right now, Ben was the one person I wanted to talk to about it. Well, *had* to talk to about it might be a better way to say it.

Behind us a horn honked. We all turned to see a sleek, black sports car pull up. Ben and Preston had to have passed each other on the road, which made my two very different lives feel like they were on a collision course. *God, I hate lying.*

Hopefully he wouldn't get out of the car. I didn't need to run in and freshen up after all, I just needed to get Ben out of here.

I turned to Daisy and gave her a quick hug. "He's early. I'm just gonna run over, I'll see you guys later."

Before I could turn around, her mouth popped open. "Is that . . . Oh. My. God. It is, it's Ben Chambers."

Chapter Eighteen

Between a Rock and a Hard Place

On the steps of Thrippletons, I gazed at the moon high in the starred sky, my brain racing. Blowing out a deep breath that curled in misty clouds on the air, panic welled inside me as Daisy and Andrew stood transfixed by the sight of a bonafide celebrity strutting toward them. I'd just dropped the news that I was kinda sorta seeing two guys at once. *What are they going to think when they just saw Preston and me making out, and now Ben Chambers appears to sweep me away?* A slimy, uneasy chill slithered up my spine. This was so bad.

Ben jogged up the stairs to my side and did the French cheek air-kiss-y thing. "Hey there, beautiful."

"Hi." I quickly made introductions. Daisy looked shell-shocked, Andrew intrigued. Both managed to mutter hellos.

Ben took them both in, his eyes pausing on Andrew, and he smiled. "I like your coat, man. It's nice."

Andrew pulled the leather jacket down, straightening it, then matched Ben's gaze, the corner of his mouth lifting. "Thanks." He was totally flirting.

Clearing his throat, Ben said, "Sorry to rush, we've got to get going. It was nice meeting you guys. I hope to see you again."

I looked down at my skinny jeans, chucks, and long flowy T-shirt tucked under my black jacket. Pulling at the red knitted cowl that suddenly felt as if it were choking me, I asked, "It's not fancy, is it? Should I change?"

"You look great." He reached for my hand with a tight smile. The friendly ease we had when he'd arrived was already vanishing.

His hand was cool and smooth, nothing like Preston's. As much as Dad wanted this, I still wanted to know why. I glanced at Ben. There was just nothing there. I mean, yes, he's cute and nice, but there wasn't any spark. You can't fake chemistry if you just don't have it.

"I'll be back a little later." I waved to my friends as Ben guided me to his car and opened my door. The two of them would pounce on me the minute I got back and I knew I was going to have to let them in on *everything*. The sense of vulnerability that came with that thought, I didn't like one bit. What if they didn't keep my secret?

Ben sat beside me and the car started with a roar. I looked over at his smiling face; he looked uncomfortable.

"How's school been?"

Nervous laughter burst from my mouth. "Is that really where we're going to start?"

"Yes. Let's start with the easy stuff and work our way into . . . whatever we're gonna call this." A sincere grin settled over his lips.

"Okay, um, it's been good. Although, my Design Studio instructor refuses to use nicknames. So, I'm Margaret with him and I hate it." I chuckled.

"Well, if that's the worst, I think you must be pretty happy."

My head bobbed. "I am. How've you been?"

"Good, I'll be heading back to L.A. . . . soon. Although, your dad thinks I should stay a little longer. Get to know you better. He's willing to pay for me to stay somewhere nearby." He flashed me a crooked smile that probably should've sent shivers through me, but didn't. It would've worked on any normal girl.

"Oh . . . okay." Awkwardness seeped into every beat of our stalled conversation.

His eyes darted between the road and me. "Um, I've made arrangements for us to have dinner at one of the old estates out here."

"*You* arranged it? When did you find time for that?" I knew Dad's shooting schedule rarely left his principals with much down time.

He looked to me, his face slightly lit by the dash lights and grinned. "Okay, yes, guilty, it was my assistant. And I'm sure she did a lovely job. I figured we'd need some privacy to plan things out. Which we definitely won't get in a restaurant. Now if I can just find our way there we'll be good to go." He looked to the muted GPS screen and turned right, taking us outside the Bampton city limits.

We pulled off at a large gray stone house. The sign at the entrance told me this was the Watford House Bed and Breakfast, which had me questioning his plans.

Ben drove us around the back and parked. A short distance away stood a smallish glass-enclosed atrium, lit up inside by strands of fairy lights.

"Down this way, I suppose." He motioned for me to follow him along the small path.

"We're eating in the greenhouse?"

He looked back with a twinkle in his eye. "It's very private."

"Sure is." I looked out into the darkening landscape and listened to a nearby stream sing its song. Glad he didn't try to grab my hand, I tucked it into my jacket pocket and went along, nervous and dreading this whole night. I wanted him to be my friend, I really did, but I still worried he was playing for my dad's side. And *that* I could never forgive him for.

Inside the glass structure it smelled exactly like a florist's shop. I inhaled, enjoying the earthy scent. Around us were various houseplants and flowers, obviously loving the warmth. A large pothos hung from a white brace and its long tendrils curled and looped around the perimeter of the circular room.

Ben and I sat at the central table. Water goblets and long crispy breadsticks were already waiting for us. After my large lunch with Preston I wasn't super hungry. Just thinking about him sent worry through me, making me feel queasy. I had to figure a way around the gag order so I could explain this to him. Or just take the risk and tell him. It wouldn't be long before it was all over the press.

Clearing my throat, I looked around. "I can't help but notice that this feels . . . romantic."

"It does, doesn't it." He looked away and polished a spot on his fork.

"I know we're in a strange situation, but are you hoping for this . . . whatever it is, to actually turn into something?" *Please say no.*

"Are you?" He asked, turning the tables, his green eyes worried.

I looked at him and inhaled sharply. "Ben, I don't know what's going on or why my dad needs us together so bad, but I . . ." I sighed, hating every second of this and not knowing what to say to him.

"I don't know if this has anything to do with it, but one of the studio heads, Kyle Mason, came out to the set a couple weeks ago. He didn't look happy. They locked themselves in a trailer and had it out. Walking by you could hear them yelling at each other." His eyes widened. "When it was over your dad stormed out and Mason followed yelling, 'It's over, McKendrick.' And your dad's been . . . I don't know, it's like he's panicking or something."

I shook my head. "But why us? I don't understand."

He reached over and patted my hand. "I don't either, but it might not be all that bad, you know. I don't bite."

"It's not that, I like you, I do. You've been nothing but kind and fun to be with since I met you, but, I just, I don't feel that electricity. I mean, do you?"

"Being blackmailed into dating each other isn't exactly the most romantic thing, is it?"

A huge smile filled my face and a sense of relief washed over me. "He's blackmailing you too?"

He nodded as he said, "What did you think? That I was working with him or something?"

"I honestly hadn't a clue. I hoped you and I were a team in this, but you could've been his secret lover for all I knew."

"Ew, no." He laughed, then shook his head bitterly. "No, he's got me right where he wants me and I'm his personal puppet."

"So then we're in the same position." I gestured to our surroundings. "Too bad this romantic atmosphere is totally wasted on us."

He tilted his head and ran a hand over his short dark hair. "Well, I don't know about that."

"What?" Nervous energy filled my mind with a crackling buzz.

"Honestly I don't know how I feel, we haven't even kissed yet." He shrugged. "I like hanging out with you and I know your father is gonna make sure we both follow through with this. I figure we might as well make the best of it and enjoy it. We can figure out the after part once we get there."

The waiter silently came and delivered salads to us. Even when thanked, he only nodded and walked out.

I looked away, unsure what to say. He was keeping his options open. I wasn't. I knew who I wanted after this debacle was done with. Stabbing a few lettuce leaves, I said, "Well, whatever our situation, we are both good and stuck with each other."

"Completely." Ben's hand rubbed down his face and he looked at me.

What does Dad have on him? Knowing Dad was holding something over Ben's head made me feel so much better. Which sounded horrible, but at least I knew I could trust him, and right now that felt like a major victory.

"I'm guessing you regret signing on to this movie."

He shrugged. "If it hadn't been me, your dad would've forced some other guy on you. So, in a weird way I'm glad it was me. I actually do care about you. At least this way I know you'll be safe."

"That's sweet." I took a sip from my water goblet. "So, can you tell me what he's holding over you?"

A smirk curled his lips and he shook his head. "Not yet. I need to know you better before I reveal that. You?"

"If I don't do this he's threatened to drag out the divorce and make sure Mom gets nothing. He said he'd fight her tooth and nail for everything and that he'd make sure she was tied to him for a very long time."

"I'm sorry. He's a prick."

"Yes." I laughed. "He really is."

We chatted through dinner and he told me more about his father abandoning them and how his mom supported them. In turn, I told him about Dad and what he was like growing up with. I couldn't look Ben in the eye as I told him how he'd abused all of us. We bonded over the fact that we both had crappy father figures, but also amazing moms who fought to make up for the deficit.

"I guess the good news is we only have to do this through the spring."

I swirled a piece of steak in my mashed potatoes. "Have you told anyone?"

He shook his head. "He threatened me that if I did, he'd release the info he has on me."

"He's got me under a gag order too."

Ben sucked in a deep breath and reached across the table to squeeze my hand. "We'll get through this. Together."

I nodded.

"Let's just get it out of the way now." The determination on his face threw me.

"What?"

"We're gonna have to kiss at some point and I'd rather it be in private than in front of a horde of photographers. Plus, you never know, we might find there's something there."

I raised an eyebrow, now nervous and thinking only of Preston. I knew I'd have to kiss Ben eventually, and I'd rather do it in private too, but still. After the kisses I'd just shared with Preston I didn't know how I'd get through this.

A smile cracked his lips. "I'm going to kiss you now." With a laugh, he added, "You know, for your dad."

"That's wrong on so many levels." I nervously chuckled and set my fork down.

Ben stood and came to my side of the table, offering me his hand. "If we're going to do this, we should do it right."

Unsure, I put my hand in his. He pulled me up to stand. My stomach went queasy and icky. *What if I like it?* With a painful slowness Ben leaned his face to mine. So close together our breaths now mingled. *Oh, God, this feels wrong.*

Preston.

"I'm seeing someone," I blurted and squeezed my eyes shut.

Ben tilted my chin up with a finger until I opened my eyes and saw matching confusion on his face. "So was I."

"Was?" I asked softly.

He nodded and lifted one shoulder. "It was still new and when I mentioned what we have to do . . . well, I understand the choice that was made, but it still sucks."

And that's why I'm terrified to tell Preston.

"Shall we try this again?"

I nodded and steeled myself for his kiss.

An arm came around my waist, pulling me closer. I closed my eyes as he slowly leaned in. His lips pressed onto mine and I jumped at the initial contact. My hands, which I'd rested on his shoulders, curled around his neck as the kiss got more serious and he got more demanding.

• • •

Daisy sat cross-legged in her desk chair, iPad on her lap, sketching. Andrew was sprawled out on my bed, reading a fashion magazine. I was about to cross the threshold, but stopped when they started talking.

"Do you think Preston knows about this thing with Ben Chambers?" Daisy's voice floated through the opening.

"I sure hope so. I wouldn't want to find out the person I was totally falling for was dating someone hot, famous, and rich on the side."

The chair Daisy sat in creaked as she popped one leg out to dangle. "He's got to know, right?"

I stepped into the room, wanting to clarify things. "Preston doesn't know. I don't know how to tell him. He knows my dad is Scott McKendrick and that's about it."

Dropping my bag and shedding my coat, I plopped on the bed next to Andrew.

"Are you planning on tellin' him about this Ben thing? What *is* the Ben thing?" Daisy set her electronic tablet on the desk and crossed her arms.

Andrew snickered and flipped a glossy page. "Whenever you choose the one you want, can I have the other one?"

"It's so not like that. If I had to, I'd choose Preston every time."

"Really? But Ben's so hot." Daisy tucked a clump of hair in her mouth and chewed on it.

"That's totally cool with me. I've got no complaints with Ben Chambers." Andrew winked at me.

"Ben and I aren't exactly together by choice." Sighing, I pulled my pillow up, clutched it to my chest, and launched into an abridged tale of my "relationship" with Ben. They'd find out soon enough anyway. "You guys can't tell anyone. I mean it. My dad would kill me." After they nodded, I told them about Dad being abusive and his forcing me to date his lead actor. "I've said way too much."

I prayed trusting them was the right move.

"Whoa." Andrew's eyes were wide and his jaw dropped, the magazine pushed aside. "That's seriously messed up."

"How could he do that?" Daisy asked. "Why?"

"I can't tell you that. And seriously, you can't say anything. I can't even tell my mom or brother."

They both nodded, looking a little rattled. Normal dads just don't do this kind of crap.

"And there's no way out of it?" Andrew rubbed his nose.

I shook my head. "I don't see how."

Daisy gave my shoulder a rub, then shook out her hair and shot me a cheeky smile. "At least they're both hot."

"'Cause that matters." I rolled my eyes, annoyed, yet grateful she was lightening the mood.

Andrew snorted and slung his arm over my drooped shoulders. "Which one's the better snog?"

"Have you snogged them both?" Daisy squeaked. "Oh my God, what's it like kissing Ben Chambers?"

I tossed the pillow aside and pulled my robe off the corner of the bed and draped it over my legs, needing to stall. "A lady never kisses and tells."

"Well, you may not have told, but you sure gave us quite the show in the parking lot, so we know you've kissed Preston." Andrew smoothed the front of his Ramones T-shirt and smirked at me. "And it was *good*."

Daisy squealed. "You've totally kissed Ben Chambers, I know it. Maybe you don't realize how fine he is, but I sure do. I need details." She glanced at Andrew. "*We* need details."

I sighed, resigned. "It was . . . okay. Not bad by any means, but also nothing like Preston." Kissing Preston felt like one of those big firecrackers that shoot way up high into the sky, then burst into a million sparkles. Ben was more like a sparkler. Fun to try and write your name with, but nothing that really took your breath away.

"I find that hard to believe, but okay, to each her own. Just put in a good word for me. Then when you guys are done with your . . ." she waved her hands around as she searched for a word, "show, I can have him."

"I already called first dibs, get in the queue." Andrew popped a hand on his hip and stared her down.

She shook her head. "Nope, he's mine. He's my Mr. Right. I can feel it."

"Well, your feeling is wrong." Andrew snickered and bopped her on the arm with his rolled-up magazine.

"Yeah, well, you don't know your arse from your elbow." She stuck her tongue out at him.

I had to tell Preston, and soon. I'd be seeing him on Friday for his birthday, but it just didn't feel like the best gift to give him—"Hey, happy birthday, by the way I'm totally dating a major Hollywood hottie, no biggie, I promise."

A queasiness settled low in my stomach. This was going to end badly, I just knew it. I couldn't shake the feeling that when everything was said and done, I was going to come out of this alone.

Chapter Nineteen

Highs and Lows

Andrew stood beside me behind the counter at The Bolt. Since I was the newbie on staff, he was still basically my babysitter. Not that I needed one anymore; the job wasn't super difficult to begin with. Shelves lined with colorful rolls of fabric surrounded us in a rainbow assortment. This place just felt magical; full of untapped potential and possibilities. I snipped off eight yards of tulle a customer wanted, and spun to ring her up.

"I think you're really getting this down. Such a good thing Millie listened to me." Andrew puffed up his chest and squared his shoulders. "I rock."

Millie limped into the cash wrap area, her air cast squeaking, and patted his cheek. "Yes, you do. It also helped that I watched her help an older customer before she even spoke to me and she's verra kind. I'm a good judge of people, wee Andrew, don't forget that." Her Scottish accent was now easy to decipher, thanks to my roaming around Inverness all summer.

"Here you are, ma'am." I handed a cloth tote, stuffed with the neatly folded tulle, over the counter. "See you next time."

"Okay, I'm sending you two into the back. We've just gotten a new shipment in and I want you to sort it, tag it, and get it in the areas it needs. This ankle of mine won't cooperate enough for me to do it." She'd tripped over Calico, the store cat, and had a small stress fracture as a result.

"We got it, Millie, sit and relax your foot." Andrew motioned for me to follow.

As we walked away Millie scooted the cat off her chair, muttering under her breath, "Bloody nuisance you are, Calico."

In the dingy back room unopened boxes were stacked on one side along with a couple long, worn tables. The other side had a mini fridge and hooks for our personal items.

Andrew's kohl-lined eyes roamed the stack as he assessed our work. "Let's open these up and sort by fabric type, then we can work on getting them out to the floor. Go grab the trolley in the hall, yeah?"

With a nod, I popped out of the room and grabbed the metal cart. On my way back my phone vibrated in my pocket. Pulling it out, I saw a text from my dad and my heart sank.

Dad: Leaving tomorrow evening. Need to see you before I fly out. No exceptions.

Tomorrow was Friday. It was Preston's party. There was no way I could miss that.

Me: I have classes and work.

Okay, the work part wasn't entirely true, but this party was important to Preston. He'd *asked* me to be there. How could I possibly blow his birthday off?

Dad: Cancel it.
Me: With no notice?
Dad: We have a situation that needs dealing with. I don't care how you do it, find a way to be at the manor house or the deal is off.

He seriously wants me to go all the way to Scotland? *Unfreakingbelievable.*

Me: Can't I just call you after my shift?
Dad: What do you think?

I think you're a power-hungry jerk who has to try to exert control over everyone. That's the real reason he probably wanted to see me in person. To prove that he could make me do it.

"What's got your face looking like it wants to hurt something?" Andrew had started stacks of fabric on the tables.

"Just my dad being his selfish prick self. He needs me in Inverness tomorrow over some cryptic issue."

"But tomorrow is Mr. DreamyMan's party, right?"

"I know." I grabbed a bolt of pale pink seersucker and slid it on top of the cotton pile. I couldn't disappoint Preston. My stomach coiled with nerves. I hated my father for springing this on me. "Oh crap." My eyes clenched shut as a thought hit me. "It's also when they're announcing that big thing they've been hinting at all term in Design Studio. There's no way I can miss this. He couldn't possibly have picked a worse day for this if he tried."

"What'll your dad do if you skive off?"

I sighed. "He'd kill me and basically make my life miserable." Not to mention what he'd do to Mom. He'd immediately set to making the divorce and her world a nightmare. If he wasn't already.

Andrew's eyebrow rose and he looked nervous. "What if you *have* to cancel on the birthday boy?"

"Then that's what I have to do." I rubbed my forehead, hating the situation all around. "I'll have to find some way to make it up to him I suppose."

I'd really been looking forward to seeing Preston this Friday. I'd found what I thought would be the perfect present for him. I came across it a couple days ago. It was a beautiful architecture art book of Louis Kahn's work. When I saw the minimalist designs, something I knew my structural engineering major Preston was interested in, I snatched it up.

Sighing, I grabbed another bolt, imagining the worst-case scenario. Dad would call Thrippletons, throw his name around, and get me excused from class. He'd probably even have a car outside waiting for me before my morning alarm went off.

Maybe I should just tell Mom and Marc and get it over with. I shook my head, scratching the thought. Last night Mom had called to check in with me and she'd sounded so happy that I just couldn't bring myself to say anything. She was excited because she was working on an adaption of Elizabeth Gaskell's *Wives and Daughters* and it was going well. I couldn't ruin this for her with the truth of what Dad was doing. But mostly, I couldn't let Dad destroy her second chance.

• • •

My phone rang and I smacked the bed, near my pillow, trying to find the damn thing. Once I had it, I folded the white coverlet back, cracked my bleary eyes open, and answered in a groggy voice. "Hello?"

"Miss McKendrick, your car is waiting out front."

"Wha? Car?"

"Yes, miss, the car your father sent." The man on the phone sounded like it was something I should obviously know.

Ugh, I called it. Dad was never one to leave anything to chance. *Dammit.* I cleared my throat. "Um, are you the driver?"

"Yes, miss."

"Okay . . ." My brain scrambled for a solution. "Um, park and wait for me to finish with my studio class. I can't skip it. We can leave right after."

There was a momentary lull in the conversation. "Um, I'm under strict instructions, miss."

"I'm sorry. I'll be as quick as I can." Anger coursed through my veins as I tossed my phone back on the bed. It bounced and fell to the floor, where the back popped off and the battery fell out. Growling, I retrieved it, reassembled it, and turned it back on. I wasn't going to bother texting my dad about the delay; I knew the driver had probably already done that.

Daisy flipped over in her bed and grabbed her digital clock. "Why are you up so early?"

"My dad sent a car for me. Just like I knew he would."

"Ugh, that sucks. So you're going?"

I sighed and tucked my arms back under my blankets, burrowing in. "I don't see that I have a choice. I'm gonna hit the studio, then head out. What am I going to tell Preston?" I *wanted* to tell him everything.

"The truth." She lifted her head and raised one eyebrow as if challenging me. "Why add another lie? Might as well start somewhere, eh?"

I opened my text thread with Preston. It took twelve erase and restarts but I finally got a text sent.

> Me: Bad news, I've been summoned back to Scotland by my very angry and disappointed father. As much as I don't want to say this, I might miss your party. :(

Not waiting for a reply, I buried my head under the covers, soaking up the last of the heat, and fell back asleep until my alarm startled me awake twenty minutes later.

Daisy and I scrambled to get dressed and were running through the halls, praying we wouldn't be late. Mr. Walker, our Design

Studio instructor, was not one for tardiness any more than he enjoyed using nicknames.

I slid to a stop at the doors and pulled one open just as the bell rang. Andrew sat to the side of the large room at a table long enough for the three of us. We quietly walked over as Mr. Walker stood at the front, rolling and unrolling a tape measure.

With a deliberate slowness he turned to look at us. "Glad you could join us, ladies."

My eyes darted to Daisy's. She just rolled hers as Walker began his lecture.

"All right class, now that we're all assembled, we have a special treat for all our studio students this term. It's my pleasure to introduce you to the Duchess of Westminster, Evangeline Gray. She's with us today to share an exciting opportunity."

From the front row of the class a tall, redheaded girl stood. She walked up, looking poised and polished, and turned to us with a smile.

How is she old enough to be a duchess?

"Hello, everyone."

She's an American? And she's a duchess here? How does that even work?

"I'm so excited to be here with you all today. I'm actually skipping a few of my classes so that I can. But that'll be our little secret." She leaned against the front table and I felt a pang of jealousy for how at ease she looked in front of a room of people. I'd be a shaking, stuttering mess.

"I'm here because I have the pleasure of attending a gala in December. It's for a charity I work with, the Westminster Wildlife Foundation. It raises awareness and money for endangered species."

Daisy leaned into me as the duchess ran through a list of animals on the brink of extinction. "I'd kill for her hair."

"Those curls," I whispered back. They were the perfectly soft and wavy kind. My short brown hair had a slight wave to it, which only succeeded in making it look messy and kinky.

She nodded and softly added, "The color. Those highlights."

"So, it's my intention to pick one of you to design my gown for the event. Both first- and second-year students can enter. There are a few things you need to keep in mind. I'd like it to be a full-length gown as it'll be pretty chilly then."

It was November now, which meant we didn't have much time to pull this off. I started scribbling her list on a piece of scrap paper I pulled from my bag.

"The charity's colors are blue and yellow, so if you can incorporate them it'd be wonderful. Sadly, I'm not an animal print person." She chuckled. "And if at all possible, make it comfortable; I'll be in your fabulous creation for hours. I need to sit, dance, eat, you know . . . basically live in it for a night." She smiled warmly at us.

Mr. Walker cleared his throat beside her and puffed up his chest.

A small smile curled the duchess's pert lips. "Mr. Walker has kindly put together the competition's rules and created a brilliant handout outlining them for you."

Walker smoothed his skinny tie. "If you intend to enter, I want your preliminary design sketches in my hand at the beginning of class next Friday. I will then meet with each of the entrants individually and we will discuss your sketch. You'll have a week to revamp and get it back to me."

"That's when he'll give them to me," the duchess said. "I will meet with the applicants and go through and discuss changes I'd like made. I'll then pick the three I'm most interested in and give you each two hundred pounds to bring your design to life. Then, I select a winner and that'll be the gown I'll wear to this *highly* publicized event."

Our teacher stepped forward. “I’m sure I don’t have to elaborate on how good this would be for your career. To have the duchess wear your design would be quite the boon.”

“Yes, this event will hopefully help a worthy designer and endangered species all in one. We’re certain this competition will draw the interest of the press, and word of the event and the charity itself will spread. The winning designer will also be attending the event as my personal guest.” She smiled and leaned forward. “I’m looking forward to seeing what you all come up with.”

This was my chance. My dress had to be the design she chose. When photographers and interviewers asked her who she was wearing, I wanted her to say “Maggie McKendrick.”

As quietly as I could, I grabbed my notebook and bag and snuck out the back door. I’d kept Dad waiting far too long as it was.

• • •

The town car pulled up to the manor house in Inverness. The rainy weather didn’t help my mood. I knew Dad would be ticked I’d made him wait, but I was pissed too, not that it mattered. As the driver hopped out to open my door, my nerves shot into a frenzied action and rooted themselves deep inside. The house loomed before me and I really didn’t want to be by myself with him in there. Last time we were alone I’d walked away bruised.

I’d spent the whole drive up rough sketching designs for the duchess’s dress. It helped me keep my brain on something other than Dad and this moment.

Tucking my sketchbook in my purse, I exited the rain-spattered car. My feet crunched on the gravel and I looked up, noticing Ben’s car in the drive. *Thank God he’s here.*

I opened the door and called out to Dad. There was no reply. I took off my damp jacket and dropped it over the banister before heading for the office. If I knew him at all he'd be perched behind the massive desk, like a demigod just waiting to pass judgement on Ben and me.

Outside the door to the wood-paneled office, I stopped, took a deep breath, and turned the knob. Just as I'd expected, Dad sat behind the mahogany desk and Ben in one of the leather wingback chairs opposite him. Knowing my place, I went and sat in the chair next to Ben.

When I glanced at Dad, his brows lifted and he tightly smiled. "Margaret, nice of you to finally join us."

He wasn't looking for a response, so I folded my hands in my lap and kept my mouth shut.

"Ben tells me the two of you have talked."

I nodded. "We have."

He steepled his fingers under his chin. "This plan of ours needs to begin right away. Ben's going to stay around for a few weeks and I want you photographed together, a lot. Then we can discuss the next phase."

There are phases?

"So, can you tell us *now* why this is important enough to blackmail people for?" I asked, not daring a glance at Ben.

"Mostly publicity purposes. What better way to get headlines than a lead actor dating his director's favorite daughter. You met on set and it was love at first sight. Ben's rather . . . quiet lifestyle wasn't doing the film any favors."

Looking to Ben, his face was screwed up. Clearly he wasn't following Dad's logic either.

Inside I was shaking, but Ben being there gave me added strength. "Well, I'm not your favorite daughter, I'm your only."

"Semantics." He used the tip of a letter opener to scrape under his nails.

I shook my head. "Okay, then are you saying you *want* Ben to be some partying playboy?"

"I'd rather him be banging every hot chick in Hollywood and anything else that gets his face on every magazine than whatever the hell it is he does with his free time. Sex sells, Mags, and he's not having nearly enough."

My mouth popped open at the crassness leaving his lips. "Well then why drag me into it at all? Why not just have him date a bunch of people back in L.A.?"

"It's more believable to say you met when you were on set and a romance developed from there. I mean, Mags, you aren't exactly the obvious choice for an A-list actor like Ben here. Everyone will be interested in why he's with you. And be curious how I feel about it."

Ben's jaw clenched and he gripped the armrest until his knuckles turned white. "Why do you need us to publicize your movie this way? The studio covers that stuff. My only obligation is personal appearances and promoting the movie. This is—"

"Any publicity is good publicity." Dad's eyes slivered as he stared Ben down. "And this'll have an even bigger impact if I publicly disapprove. But of course you two darling love birds insist on being together." He stood, walked around the desk, then leaned against it, like he was pitching his next great movie idea. "There'll be a feud between me and my daughter's boyfriend. That'll make for great headlines."

I shook my head, unbelieving he'd put this much thought into his scheme. It all seemed a bit much to me. Then again, my father was blackmailing me; I probably shouldn't be that surprised.

"Maybe get an apartment together. Oh, Mags, it wouldn't hurt if you gained a little more weight either." He motioned his hands over his belly in a bump. "A pregnancy rumor will do just the trick."

My mouth popped open in disgust. *There is no way in hell I'm pretending to be pregnant.* I turned to Ben, trying to gauge his reaction to see if I actually heard what I did. "I'm only eighteen. Is that really what you want people to think of your daughter?"

This is going to destroy everything with Preston.

"Come on, Mags, catch up. You won't really be pregnant, obviously. Just think of this as an acting gig. Plus, you being eighteen will add even more fuel to the fire. The press will be all over that."

"I'm not an actress, I'm your daughter."

Ben cleared his throat, his brows low over stormy green eyes. "I don't think I can do this."

"If you want this movie to be successful you damn well better do it. I can easily make sure you never work in the entertainment industry in any capacity again."

I hadn't forgotten Ben mentioning his love of special effects. Dad wasn't only threatening to take his acting career away; he was going for all of Ben's passions.

"And as I remember, Ben, you've got your mom to take care of, am I wrong?" Dad glowered between the two of us, not waiting for his reply before adding, "And don't forget the alternative if you choose not to date Maggie."

Ben's hands were now fists and he looked away, clearly tangled in Dad's tightly woven snare.

My overwhelmed brain struggled to process everything. How could my father put me in this position? Why did he want so much depth to this lie? "I'm curious, where exactly are you suggesting we live together? We're not exactly close geographically with me in Bampton and Ben in California."

"L.A. of course. They have the best press possibilities."

Shaking my head, I stood. This wasn't adding up for me; there were still too many missing pieces. "Dad, I can't. I'm in school. There's no way I'm going back to California right now. And I don't want people to think I'm just another teenage pregnancy statistic. Come on, this is insane. I'm not going to do this."

Dad silently looked between the two of us, his jaw tensing and releasing. "But you will."

"This isn't something you make your other actors do. Why are you doing this to Ben?" I continued, anger pooling inside me.

"You don't know what I've made my other actors do, now do you? This is just the first time I've had a daughter the right age to put in a relationship with my male lead." He raised an eyebrow, little emotion on his face. "And if you must know, the funding's been completely cut. If I want to see this film to completion I've got to do it out of my own pocket."

"Really? But why?" I glanced to Ben and even he looked shocked. Dad's movies always had plenty of funding, primarily for the sheer megabucks they always brought in.

Dad went back to his seat. "*That* is not something you need to concern yourself with."

I stood and turned to leave, but stopped. A part of me still hoped he'd come to his senses and see what he was asking of me. "Is this really what you want us to do?"

His eyes met mine and for a moment I thought I caught a flash of uncertainty in them. It was quickly replaced with a chilly stare. "Yes."

Chapter Twenty

An Open Book

The car carried me back to Thrippletons and farther away from my father. *Thank God.* As soon as Ben had given me an awkward hug and drove away I hopped in the town car, not wanting to spend another second near my dad, and took off. Slumped in my seat, I pulled my phone out to take it off Silent. *I missed five texts.* My foul mood only worsened when I saw who most of them were from. Not because of the sender, but for what I was missing.

Preston: So, how'd it go?
Preston: Any chance you'll make it? I'd really love you to meet all my friends.
Preston: I'm guessing it's not going well.

A quick glance at the clock told me it wasn't going to happen. His party was in two hours and I still had a three-hour drive to Thrippletons. Then I'd have to change and catch the bus to Oxford. Aside from the obvious time issue, I wasn't in a celebratory mood. Anyone I met right now wouldn't see normal Maggie; they'd get the I-hate-my-asshole-father Maggie. She wasn't fun to be around.

My frustration and anger had congealed in my stomach, leaving me sick. This wasn't going to end well. With my dad behind the wheel we'd no doubt collide in a fiery inferno. The more I thought about it the more upset I got. If this went south, not only could it destroy everything with Preston, it could also affect Thrippletons and the career I so badly wanted.

Running a hand through my hair I imagined what Ben and I'd be forced to do. It killed me not knowing what Dad had over Ben.

Sighing, I typed a response to Preston.

Me: I'm not going to make it. I'm so sorry. We'll have to get together soon so I can give you your present.
Preston: Seeing you is present enough. Tomorrow work? ;) I'll drive over.

He wants to see me. I smiled, wanting to see him too.

Me: I would love that.

My phone vibrated in my hands as the ringtone went off. Preston's name popped up on the screen. I closed the privacy glass between the driver and myself. I certainly didn't want an audience, definitely not one that reports back to my father.

"Hey."

"Hi." His low voice sent a shudder through me. I don't think he even had the foggiest clue what his voice alone did to me.

"I'm so sorry about tonight. I'm just now leaving Inverness and I . . . it's been a rough day." I blew out a deep breath.

"Want to talk about it?"

I shook my head and inhaled sharply. "There's so much I should tell you, and I want to . . ." A lump formed in my throat, making it difficult to sound normal. The gag order swam in my mind, stopping me. "But it's your birthday, and the very last thing I want to talk about is my dad."

"Don't worry about my birthday. You sound upset. What's going on? If you want to talk, I'll more than happily listen."

Eyes closed, I leaned my head back on the town car's leather headrest. "My dad just doesn't get it. He's . . . selfish and has completely lost touch with reality." I bit my lip, tears threatening. "It doesn't matter. I just have to get through this, then everything will be fine."

"I'm sorry." He blew the air from his lungs and in the background I heard a door close. "I bet I could take your mind off of it."

"I'm sure you could." I sat up and opened my eyes. "If only I were in better shape for company, but right now, I'm liable to snap at anyone. I don't want your friends to see me at my worst."

He sniffed a laugh. "This is your worst? You're pretty tame. When my sister gets upset she swears a blue streak. I think she could *actually* make a sailor blush."

I laughed. Just talking to him had lifted my spirits. "I miss you. I wish I could be there."

"What time do you want me there tomorrow?"

The corners of my lips curled and I sighed. "How early can you get up?"

• • •

Early the next morning, I sat at my desk and refined my design for the duchess's dress. I grabbed my colored pencils, trying to decide how to incorporate the yellow she'd requested. In the end, I decided to leave it out. It looked more elegant without it.

I glanced at my phone. Preston would be here any minute. Giddy happiness swarmed my stomach and unfurled through my body in a warm golden glow. He couldn't get here soon enough.

My phone pinged and my heart tripled its pace.

Preston: I'm out front.
Me: Be right down.

I snatched my brightly colored poncho coat and darted for the door.

Daisy stopped me in the hallway as she was heading back to our room, arms laden with fabrics. "Where are you rushing off to?"

"Preston's here. Oh, crap, I forgot his present." I zipped back, found the silver-wrapped book, and darted out again.

"That explains the giddiness. Don't stay out too late. Andrew decided to let me dye his hair tonight." She raised a brow and smirked. "It'll be a blast. I grabbed a box of purple, just in case."

"Fun." I glanced at my watch and nodded. "I'll try to be back in time."

"Oh, just go, I know the delay is killing you. I'll talk to you later."

As I spun away, I heard her holler, "Tell him the truth while you still can."

I flew through the hallways, only walking when my History of Fashion teacher scowled at me. Pushing the front door open, I practically hopped down the stairs.

Leaning against his Land Rover, Preston smiled when he saw me and started in my direction. In the middle of the parking lot he met me and picked me up, twirling me around in a hug.

"I came so close to driving out here last night. But Edmund convinced me it'd be rude to leave a party being thrown for me." He sat me down, put his arm around my shoulders, and led me to the car.

"I know I've already apologized, but still, I'm so sorry I missed your birthday."

"I'm just glad we're together now." Pulling me close, he kissed my forehead then leaned me against the side of his SUV, pressing his body against mine. His lips parted in a smile that made his much-loved dimple appear.

Slowly his head moved toward mine. Maybe it was because he was so tall, but it felt like ages before our lips finally met. Tingles swiftly spread throughout my insides.

I wrapped one arm around his neck, the other I pressed against his back, still holding on to his gift, and pulled him tight against me. He made a growly noise in the back of his throat that had me wanting things from him I couldn't have right now. This was it; the feeling Ben and I just didn't have. *This* was fireworks, badass explosions, and choirs singing all at once.

This was what I didn't want to lose.

Preston leaned back and took a shaky breath. "Why don't we get in the car before we give your whole school a show."

He opened the door for me and I climbed in. When he joined me his nose was red from the cold. Running a hand through his hair and rubbing the back of his neck, he looked at me and asked, "Where should we go?"

"Anywhere you want. We're celebrating you."

"Brunch? I'm starving." His eyes twinkled at my nod and we were off. Reaching over, he grabbed my hand and twined our fingers together, then rested them on my denim-clad knee.

I looked over at him and a stab of guilt coursed through me. I needed to tell him. If I didn't tell him about Ben the press would. *Screw Dad's gag order.* With Daisy and Andrew knowing it felt especially wrong keeping it from Preston. Especially when it'd affect him way more than either of them. And if I could trust them, I could definitely trust him.

He may not understand, but at least I wouldn't be lying any more. I just didn't want him to come away from this hating me. Deep breath in, I blew it out in a rush. "You know how I told you about my dad the other day?"

"Yeah." He glanced between me and the road.

"Well, I kinda have a little bit more I need to tell you."

"Okay, what's that?"

I kept my eyes focused out the windshield, my palms sweaty and itchy. "You already know my dad isn't the nicest of guys. He's used to doing whatever it takes to get what he wants and . . . well . . . he's kinda blackmailing me."

Preston flinched back, his brows pulling together, but stayed silent, listening.

"The thing is, what he wants me to do is going to get splashed all over the press and just be . . . everywhere. I can't see a way out of it. And I wanted you to find out from me rather than reading it on some sleazy magazine cover."

He quickly met my eyes. "Should I pull over for this?"

"No." I shook my head. "Keep driving, please. It'll be easier." He did as I asked and I tried to find the best way to word it. "You know who Ben Chambers is, right?" I shook my head, feeling silly. "Of course you do, everyone knows who he is. Well . . ." I glanced at him and cleared the lump from my throat. "Um . . . in the press, it's going to look like we're a couple."

He slowly nodded, eyes still on the road. Opening his mouth to speak, he shut his lips and opened them again, looking a little like a guppy. "Is this your way of telling me you're seeing someone else?"

"No . . . but, well, I guess yes, kinda? But not like that." I ran a hand over my face and angled myself in my seat to better see him. "Ben and I are friends. *Only* friends. I actually met him around the same time I met you."

Shooting me a glance, he slowed down. "I'm going to pull over."

"My dad is hoping to use us to drum up publicity for his film. Something happened between him and the studio, at least that's what we think. He won't tell us. He mentioned losing funding and . . . he's . . ." I didn't have the words to describe my father.

"So, you're going to date Ben Chambers?" He shook his head, brows drawn together. "How in the bloody hell can I compete with him?"

I filled my lungs to capacity, sickness turning my insides into tight knots. I wanted to reach out and touch him, but I wasn't sure how he'd react. "It's not a competition. If it were, you'd easily win. I just . . . I don't have a choice."

"Why don't you have a choice?"

The words slipped from my lips of Dad's blackmail. Making the divorce draw out, freezing Mom's accounts, not letting her move on.

Preston sat, digesting for what felt like forever before he looked me in the eye. "I'm guessing your mum has no clue he's doing this to you, does she?"

I mutely shook my head.

"Do you really think she'd want you to do this?"

"No, probably not. But she's been beaten, bullied, and humiliated by my dad, we all have. She deserves to have a fresh start and be happy. I can fake-date Ben Chambers for a few months to make that happen."

Preston sucked in a breath. "What does your brother think of this?"

"He doesn't know either." I bit my lip, hating all the worry and dread surging through me. Ben lost his relationship when he came clean; I so didn't want to lose Preston.

"Maggie, you've got to tell them." Preston's hand slid over mine.

I shook my head, tears welling. "I can't. My dad said if I told anyone it'd void our agreement, and he'd make my mom's life a nightmare."

"But you told me?" His eyes softened.

"I had to. I couldn't hurt you like that and have you thinking I—I didn't care, that I was willingly with someone else. But, *please* don't tell anyone about this."

His hand came up and cupped my cheek and I leaned into it, enjoying his touch, hoping it wasn't the last.

"Your secret is safe with me."

I closed my watery eyes and took a deep breath, hating the words on my lips. But I had to say them. I had to offer him an easy out. I couldn't expect him to go along with this. And I definitely didn't want him sitting there trying to figure out a polite way to end things. "I'll understand if you don't want to see me anymore."

"No." His reply was swift. "That's not what I want. I want you, but only if you want me too."

"I do want you." My words were whispered; it was all I could manage.

A sad smile cracked his lips and his thumb caressed my cheek. "You have to promise me one thing. If you start to fall for Ben, you'll just tell me. Don't drag it out." I started to protest, but he stopped me. "I'd rather know right away than fall for you even more than I already have. As it is, I'm not certain I'd ever fully recover if I lost you."

"I feel like you're already one foot out the door." A tear escaped on a path to hit his thumb, but he wiped it away.

He shook his head. "Both feet are firmly planted. I'm where I want to be."

My heart faltered in my chest and I leaned over to press a kiss to his cheek.

Capturing my face in his hands, he tilted my head back and stared into my eyes. "Maggie, I-I . . . I—" He shook his head and pressed his lips into mine, stopping midsentence and leaving me wondering.

We held each other in a lingering kiss. I wanted so much more of him. Everything about him was so damn wonderful. *I can't lose him.*

Fingers twisted in my hair, he released his seat and I squealed against his lips as we whooshed back. The sudden motion pulled me onto his lap, and I felt his mouth curl into a grin. When I tried to straighten up, he held me tight and pulled me so I was sitting fully on him with my legs draped over the center console.

Leaning back, I looked into his eyes as his hand slid to my neck, rubbing the muscles there and gently tugging me back to him. With a small smile, I bit my lip and resisted momentarily before letting him kiss me again. I wanted to savor the sight of him like this. My effect on him. Wanting me.

Just before his lips took mine, he said, "One thing you should know, I always fight for what I want."

Chapter Twenty-One

Up Close and Personal

Friday was upon us. The day to turn in our submissions for the competition. I sat in my Design Studio spot, staring at the sketch I'd put together, looking for any mistakes, and trying just to breathe. I'd spent the night before with Ben at a restaurant in London and gotten back late. Tired, I carefully pressed my palms against my burning eyes, not wanting to smudge my makeup.

Reaching back I pulled at my bra, which suddenly seemed way too constricting. The nerves running rampant inside me were having a party. Mentally I'd prepped for a battle, confident in my work and talents, but Mr. Walker was a tough judge.

Class was almost half over and I was the last student to hand in my portfolio. Walker took it from me and I nervously waited while he looked it over.

He raised one manscaped brow. "This is your final design?" he asked, touching the fabric swatches and beading attached to the page.

"Yes, sir."

He nodded, mouth in a straight line. "See me after class and we'll discuss."

Sighing, I turned, the unexpected feeling of failure cascaded over me. He hated it. It sucked. I suck. *Dammit.* I went to my chair and slumped low. Pulling my sketchbook toward me, I started doodling. The instructor rattled on about the competition and how he'd have a sign-up sheet on the desk after class for personal critiques with him.

"I'm expecting a little over one hundred of you to enter. And as you know, only three of you will move on. I hope you all did your best work." He turned and eyed me, making me squirm in my chair.

Maybe Dad was right. Maybe I'm not a good designer.

While the rest of the class went into design mode, some sketching while others worked on dress forms to piece together their final class project, I drew one particular set of brown eyes. Preston's. I propped my feet up on the table and balanced my book on my knees, feeling dejected and like an utter loser.

"Incoming." Andrew leaned and whispered near me.

I dropped my feet, quickly closed my book, and leaned to look at Andrew's design. "Oh, I really like that."

Walker passed by. "Can I take a peek at your work?"

Andrew nodded and passed his book over.

"Hmm, yes, nice. I'm looking forward to seeing your finished project. And Miss McKendrick, what are you working on?"

I opened my book to some sketches I'd done for the duchess's dress that I didn't end up using. My bracelets jangled as I passed it over.

"You're thinking of doing another gown for your class project?"

"Not sure. Mostly just trying out ideas." I turned the pages back and showed him some more casual things I'd sketched up. "I really like the chunky knits and I was hoping to find a way to incorporate them into my project."

He did a slow appraisal of what I was wearing: lace-up ankle boots, a short A-line skirt, leggings, layered slim-fitting T-shirts, and a soft bat-wing sweater I'd made. He fingered the gray knotted threads and met my eyes. "Hmm, and is this something you concocted yourself?"

My gaze fell to his hand. "Yes, sir."

"Interesting."

He handed me my book and spun on his heel, returning to the front of the class. "All right, start cleaning up. You're dismissed."

I packed up and waited for the rest of class to finish signing up for the duchess design critiques.

"We'll wait in the hall for you." Daisy smiled, looking back at our teacher with trepidation.

When Mr. Walker and I were the only ones left, I approached the front. While I waited for him to finish packing his bag and gather all our competition entries, I signed up for one of the consultation spots.

He shook his head. "That won't be necessary."

Oh, God, he's kicking me out? Am I that bad? I crossed off my name and looked at him, trying to hold back the tears.

"Come, walk with me."

We swept up the aisle to the door and left the room. Andrew and Daisy looked on with questioning gazes. I shrugged and waved, walking in the opposite direction of where we needed to go.

"Margaret, do you know why I asked you to stay after?" He walked briskly down the corridor and I struggled to keep pace with his long lean legs.

My nose wrinkled at his use of my full name. "Um, no, I'm not sure."

He stopped at an arched doorway, pulled his keys out, and pushed it open to reveal a minimalistic office. Everything was black and white. Along the back, behind his desk, he had a row of dress forms, all classic examples of the little black dress. It looked like there was a dress style for every decade. The 1950s tea length with big circle skirt was my favorite.

After he set down his armful of designs and satchel, he took off his blazer and hung it behind the door. "You have a lot of promise,

Miss McKendrick. The most I've seen in a long time. Your design is brilliant."

"Really?" *Oh, thank the stars.*

"I think the duchess is going to be particularly impressed with your work. I do have a couple notes I wanted to discuss. Would now be okay?"

I picked my jaw up off the floor and bobbed my head silently. My sourpuss mood flipped to elation. I had a class to get to, but I didn't mind being late on account of this.

"Your style is very contemporary and quite on trend." He pulled my design off the top and looked at it. "She's going to love the pockets you added and I like the draping. The silk chiffon and organza will give it wonderful movement."

I grinned and nodded. "I chose them because I wanted it to be very fluid and light."

"Excellent. The deep V neckline might be a bit drastic, but she could love it. I really think it'll be flattering and emphasize her curves. Really beautiful job."

"Thank you." My shoulders rolled forward, unsure how to respond.

"Here, take this." He handed my design back to me. "Start thinking about different necklines that would look okay with the silhouette, just in case. Also, maybe consider keeping the bead work to a minimum. I'm looking forward to seeing your revision." His smile startled me. It was the first one I'd ever seen from him.

"Okay, thanks." I backed out of the room, bumping into the doorframe. In the hall I spun and ran to my History of Fashion class, ecstatic. The hope I'd momentarily lost had amazingly resurfaced, and brought its friends.

• • •

It was the morning of the duchess's return. I paced my room, chewing on my pencil and wracking my brain for anything to make my design stand out and ensure that she'd pick me. I bit hard, leaving teeth marks in the soft wood.

My midnight-blue ball gown still boasted a plunging V-neck. It tapered down to a cinched waist, defined by a matching thin satin ribbon. Just below was a flowing floor-length skirt. The sheer overlay material I'd picked would show her movement as she walked and twirled around the dance floor. She'd be a picture of perfection.

I picked up the delicate Solstiss lace and glass seed and bugle bead embellishments I'd selected to make it look ultra opulent. Smiling, I imagined how the small beads would catch the light and how the lace would give it an extra little feminine touch and texture.

With the duchess's red curls, she would look beyond stunning. The dark sapphire would be perfect on her pale skin. I found myself curious if she was single. If she was, this dress had the potential to turn that around.

I really hope I get to make this dress.

Daisy came to my side and grabbed my shoulders. "I know you're nervous, but you have to stop with the pacing. You're driving me crazy."

"I'm sorry, I'm just super tense. I want this so bad."

"We all do."

"I know." I grabbed my portfolio and sketchbook and clutched them to my chest. As Daisy walked away, I softly added, "But I *need* this."

We made it to class with minutes to spare. When I glanced over, Mr. Walker was crouched down in front of the duchess, chatting. Looking a little besotted, he stood and cleared his throat.

"Ladies and gentlemen, you will each have five minutes with the duchess. This is the only chance you have to get her opinion. Make sure you listen. Remember, only three will advance."

The duchess stood, a single white sheet of paper in her hand, a soft smile on her lips. "Mr. Walker's given me a class list and I'll be calling each of you back. Try not to worry and let's just have some fun."

"The winning students will be posted outside the classroom at seven. Good luck, everyone," our instructor added.

The duchess called the first student, Rosalyn Adams, and they walked into the room that housed the sewing machines. In less than five minutes, Rosalyn was back out.

I watched as the next girl went in. Adjusting my position, I, like the rest of the class, waited nervously. Pulling up a fresh page in my sketchbook, I started doodling Preston's eyes again. I just couldn't get them out of my mind. Softly I said, "I wonder what it's like being a duchess."

"In her case . . ." Daisy leaned toward me, whispering. "Amazing. She's very wealthy and has an absolute dreamboat for a boyfriend."

Andrew's name filled the room. With nervousness shining in his eyes, he looked to us for encouragement so I gave him a thumbs-up and flashed him a smile.

"How do you think he'll do?" Daisy asked as he disappeared through the doorway.

"I liked his dress, although, it might be a little on the short side."

She nodded. "I told him she wanted a ball gown and he said he was taking a risk."

I ran my hand over my sketch, flicking off a few stray eraser bits. "I hope at least one of us three move on to the next round."

"That'd be so cool." She stood and turned to plunk her bum on our tabletop. It groaned, startling her. "I promise to be happy for either of you if it's not me. Hey, maybe all three of us will move on."

Laughing, I shook my head. "Yeah, not likely. She wouldn't pick three first-years. There has to be some seconds in there too."

"You never know." Daisy raised a brow, a hopeful look in her eye.

Students were excused as soon as they'd finished with the duchess. The room steadily emptied until it was only me, Daisy, and a couple girls in the back.

"Margaret McKendrick." A smiling face framed in red poked out the arched door.

I waved my hand and stood.

"Come on back."

Grabbing my stuff, I rushed to the door, not sparing a look for Daisy, I was wholly focused on the task at hand.

Wait, how am I supposed to address a duchess? Highness? Lady? Just Duchess?

"Hi there. Please, sit and get comfortable. I know it's hard, but try not to be nervous. I promise I don't bite."

I performed a shaky curtsy and said, "Yes, Your Highness." Hoping it was the right way to address her, I sat in the chair across from her.

"Oh." She leaned back with a wide grin on her rosebud lips. "You're American too?"

Nodding, I flexed my fingers around the edges of my portfolio. "California."

"Washington." She reached out and patted my hand. "It's always nice to come across another West Coast girl. Do you miss home?"

Making a face I shook my head. "Not really."

She chuckled and my nerves settled slightly. I relaxed my grip and sat my portfolio and sketchbook on my lap.

"I miss it sometimes, especially when I think of my dad, but England is my home now. I'm trying to convince him to move over here." She smiled. "Anyways, I'd love to take a look at your work." As she leaned toward me her necklace dangled and caught the light, sparkling. The large, light blue, cushion-cut stone was encircled by diamond baguettes.

"Oh, that's beautiful." I gestured to her necklace.

Reaching up she touched the pendant, a soft smile filling her face. "My boyfriend gave me this. It was actually his grandmother's."

"Wow. Nice boyfriend." I opened my sketchbook to take notes with and sat it on the smooth, white table between us, then opened my portfolio.

"He is pretty amazing." She slid my sketchbook closer to her. "Well, those are a lovely pair of eyes. Do they belong to anyone special?"

I glanced down and saw Preston's eyes.

"Oh, sorry, I meant to open it to a blank page." I took it and quickly flipped it.

"It was a beautiful drawing. They actually looked familiar." The duchess smiled, then turned her focus on my design in my portfolio. Slowly, she bobbed her head. "Yes, this is very good. I love the fabric you've chosen." Her fingers touched the samples. "Really, really beautiful work." She looked up and her brilliant green eyes met mine. "I only have one request."

"Okay." I leaned forward, pencil in hand to jot down notes.

"While I love the plunging neckline, it's just so not me. I'd be scared the girls were going to make an unscheduled appearance."

I laughed. "That's understandable. And there are several options. I can bring it up all the way and widen it like a boatneck, which is also a bateau. Or maybe relax it a bit into a scoop neck."

I did a couple quick sketches just to show her my thoughts. "Or do you have another idea?"

She leaned over the page, her red hair pooling on the table. "I think a boatneck might be the way to go. It's always been a flattering cut on me. What do you think?"

"I think it'd be perfect."

"All right then, boatneck it is."

I circled the word "bateau," left my portfolio, and prepared to leave. "Thank you, Your Highness."

She smiled softly and appeared to be debating something. "Normally I wouldn't say anything, but since you're an American, I want to help any way I can. So, please, don't take this the wrong way."

"Okay." My heartbeat sped up as nerves started popping all over my body in an itchy heat.

"This took me a while to learn as well, but I think I've got it now. It's all so confusing." She chuckled. "The address of 'Your Highness' is reserved for the monarchy, like king, queen, prince, princess. Dukes and duchesses are 'Your Grace.' Then everyone else is pretty much 'Lady' and 'Lord.' Of course there's other ways to address them as well, but that's pretty much the basics."

"Ah, I was wondering about that. Thanks for giving me a heads up." I tucked my sketchbook to my chest and stood.

"It's been lovely chatting with you. Good luck." She stood and escorted me to the door. She stopped as I continued through. "Daisy Michaels."

As I passed Dais, I gave her a thumbs-up and walked up the aisle and out of the room. The duchess had been so kind and friendly, that had to be a good sign.

She has to select me.

Chapter Twenty-Two

Stronger

The handle of the Design Studio door rattled and the mob of waiting students froze, barely daring to breathe. It was almost seven and soon we'd know who was moving on to the next round. I'd been saying prayers and crossing my fingers and toes. I wanted this so badly.

Leaning against the wall across from the door, I tapped my fingers against the gray stones holding me up. Daisy sat on the floor and Andrew didn't come at all. He said he didn't think he had a chance in hell after he'd told the duchess he wouldn't alter his design. He *really* didn't want to make it long. I guess you could say he had an uncompromising artistic vision.

The door pulled open and Mr. Walker stood there, a piece of stark white paper in his hands. "Ladies and gentlemen, please clear the way and make room."

From my vantage point I could see our ginger muse still in the classroom. I was surprised to see she'd stayed so late. Slight smile on her face, she quickly typed something into her cell, stuffed it in her pocket, and stepped into the hallway.

"Before I go, I just wanted to say thank you to everyone for sharing your wonderful designs with me. There were so many good ones, it was nearly impossible to select just three. So, best of luck to the finalists and I look forward to working with you." With a swift wave, she disappeared down the corridor, her boots clacking against the wooden floor.

Mr. Walker pinned the list to the corkboard near the classroom entrance, then scrambled through the door, knowing he was on the verge of getting crushed. Voices filled the hall and chairs scraped the ground. I stayed back, waiting until I could make my way safely up there.

"Stop pushing!"

"Who the bloody hell is that?"

One girl broke down crying. "This sucks."

Several students slumped away, looking disheartened.

"That's me! She picked me!" A tall slender boy jumped and fist-pumped the air. Daisy smiled at him and gave him a thumbs-up. He returned the gesture.

"He's cute." Daisy mumbled in my ear.

"She actually chose a first-year. They shouldn't have even been able to compete." A girl with long black hair stormed past me surrounded by a couple friends. "It's not fair."

Just hearing that the duchess picked a first-year gave me hope. I raised a hand to sweep my hair back and noticed a slight shake to it. I stuffed it in my pocket instead.

Daisy stood and straightened her sweater. "Wish me luck, I'm going in."

"Wait for me." I grabbed on to her sleeve and followed her into the mob. I couldn't see around Daisy's head, but I heard her mumble something.

She turned, huge smile on her face and her blue eyes wide as saucers. "It's you. You did it. You're one of the three."

"What?" I didn't believe her. Craning my neck, I tried to see around her. "Scoot over, I need to see."

Daisy switched places, now hovering behind me. Grabbing my hand, she gave it a squeeze. There it was, on the bottom of the list in a feminine cursive script, Margaret McKendrick.

I rubbed my eyes, not believing it. *Holy shitballs.*

A giggle burst from my lips and I turned to Daisy, throwing my arms around her neck with a squeal.

"Congratulations!" she squeaked as a classmate nudged in front of us, eager to see the list. "Come on, let's get out of here and celebrate."

On the way to our room she knocked on Andrew's door.

He poked his head out a crack. "If I didn't win don't bother me. I'm sulking."

"You didn't get picked, God love ya, but Maggie did. Come on, come celebrate with us."

The door opened a little more and his eyes widened as he looked at me. "Really? You made it to the next round?"

I nodded, still not believing it myself. *How the hell did this happen?* Maybe it was simply because I was American and she felt a camaraderie with me. I was scared to want this as much as I did. It had the potential to turn bad in a heartbeat and send me spiraling into the funk to end all funks. If I made the dress and she didn't choose it . . .

No. She has to pick me. *Has to.*

• • •

Marc's scruffy face filled the video screen of my iPad and I smiled as he waved at me. For the first time in a long time I felt a little homesick. During our last video chat he'd met Daisy. She'd been disappointed to learn he was in California. She'd told him he was super hot and then informed him of her determination to find Mr. Right this year. She quickly added that if he ever found himself in the UK to give her a call. Subtlety was not her forte. I was glad to have the room to myself this time.

"What is that, Mags?" He pointed to his screen, at my head.

"What do you mean?" I leaned forward in my desk chair so I could get closer to my laptop.

He laughed. “Is that a purple streak in your hair?”

I sighed and fingered the dyed strands. “Yes, Daisy talked Andrew and me into being more adventurous. Andrew’s got blue.”

Preston had yet to see my new color, but this weekend I’d been invited on another investigation with Haley’s team and I couldn’t wait to show it to him.

Marc scratched his neck. “Your friends, they sound . . . interesting.”

“They’re crazy, but I love them.”

“I like the hair, it’s fun.” He smiled, his eyes crinkling at the corners. “So, aside from the funky new ’do, how’s things in jolly ol’ England?”

I shrugged. Just seeing him and hearing his voice made me want to jump through the screen and hug him. “Um, things are pretty good.”

Quickly, I filled him in on my finalist position and on things with Preston.

“I take it things are going well with you two? Hey, whatever happened to Ben? Dad seemed pretty obsessed with pushing you guys together before we left?”

“Ugh, that’s a long story.” I looked to my inspiration wall. Photos I loved, fabrics I thought were pretty, cool doodles and designs I’d done, art that sparked my imagination, and some of my sketches. Essentially all my favorite and most-loved things. My gaze scanned the images and stopped on a pair of brown eyes with flecks of gold, ripped from the pages of my sketch book. Preston.

Marc zipped his gray hoodie, the sound pulling my attention back. “I’m here and I’ve got some time.”

Grabbing a pen, I made swirls on a scrap piece of paper. I needed to tell him about Ben and me fake-dating. With it coming out in the press any day now, he’d be calling me and grilling me anyway. I never could lie to him. "You have to promise you won't be mad at me that I waited this long to tell you?"

"What's going on, Mags?" He leaned closer to the camera.

"You also have to promise you won't say anything to Mom. Or anyone."

"Mags!"

I didn't look up. "Dad's blackmailing Ben and me so we'll pretend to date."

Marc fell silent, probably processing. My eyes darted to the screen.

"How is he blackmailing you?" He stared back, his face scrunched and confused.

"He threatened to drag out the divorce and fight Mom for . . . well, everything. He'll make things as difficult as possible for her." I told him all the details I knew and the further I got, the lower his jaw dropped.

Running a hand through his dark hair he blew out a long breath. "Son-of-a-bitch. You should've told me this. God, that explains why I saw you and Ben on a magazine yesterday."

Crap, it's started. Truthfully, I was surprised it'd taken this long.

"You're right. I should've told you, but Dad told me if I did it'd void our agreement. And I felt like such a coward for giving in and not being brave enough to stand up to him." Tears burned the backs of my eyelids. I *still* felt that way. Inside, the six-year-old me was still terrified he'd hurt me, even if there was an ocean and an entire continent between us.

Marc turned his face from the camera. "Mom's been saying there's some strange guys following her, not paparazzi. We don't know what they're doing, but I think Dad's having her watched. Like digging for dirt to use against her kind of stuff." He cleared his throat. "And God, Mags, Dad's lawyer is like a . . . a pit bull.

Even if he tells you he'll make it easy if you do his bidding, well, let's just say it doesn't look like easy is what he wants."

"Wait, how long has this been going on?" I'd agreed to Dad's scheme, so why was he doing this?

"Mom noticed the guys trailing her right after she filed and Dad hired his lawyer."

My heart raced. "Did you call the cops?"

"We did. They're chalking it up to the increased attention from all the divorce talk in the papers."

I rubbed a hand over my face. "What should I do?"

"You should probably tell Mom what's going on, Mags."

I shook my head, hair slipping into my eyes. "I can't. If Dad finds out I told her . . . he'd unleash his pit bull lawyer in an instant. I'm taking a huge risk telling you."

"We've told her lawyer about the guys following her. He thinks we should hire someone to follow Dad too, see what he's up to."

"What a mess." I tucked my bangs behind my ears; they were finally getting long enough that they stayed where I put them. "Listen, you absolutely *have* to tell me what's going on. I can't not know. If he's being a prick and torturing Mom, then I'll stop playing his game."

"Same goes for you." His voice sounded strained. "I'll try to figure a way for you to get out of this."

I swallowed over the lump in my throat. "Even if I could, it's not just me. Dad's got something on Ben. I can't just throw him to the wolves."

"We'll think of something."

If Dad was having Mom followed and already preparing for a war, then he and I needed to have a serious conversation. If he wasn't going to hold up his end of the deal, I wouldn't hold up mine. At least over the phone, I didn't have to worry about him decking me.

• • •

As the afternoon sunlight streamed through our window I plopped down on the bed, exhausted. Stretching, I grabbed my water from my desk and saw a magazine on Daisy's nightstand. I got up, grabbed it, and carried both back to bed.

Shivering from the early winter chill, I pulled the throw off the bottom of my bed and wrapped it around my shoulders.

I took a sip and set the cup on the floor. The first few pages of the mag had nothing that interested me. Flipping through, I stopped at a picture of my parents and read the blip about their divorce:

> "Diana McKendrick, highly sought after director of photography, filed for divorce from director Scott McKendrick, citing irreconcilable differences. Sources close to the pair say the couple have been having marital problems for years. Mr. McKendrick is well-known in the industry for his volatile temper on set. Rumors have swirled for years that it often extended into his home life. Top studio execs aren't happy with the situation and are growing tired of the unstable director's antics. Mr. McKendrick has yet to respond to the filing."

Deep breath in, then out, then back in. I'd known it was out in the media. I'd just been in a bubble between school, Preston, and this Ben situation that I hadn't actually seen it. Also, I was kind of avoiding the tabloids; I didn't really want to see it. Turning the pages, I continued reading.

A gasp caught in my throat. Ben and I kissing in the atrium filled a double-page spread. Smaller photos showed us sitting, smiling, and eating. Others, the largest ones, were me in his arms, his lips pressed to mine. Some jerk with a telephoto lens must've been camped not far from where we'd parked. They referred to me as Margaret, which meant Dad's fingers were definitely all over this.

"So much for privacy." Ben had had his assistant choose a secluded spot. Or so he'd said. I didn't know what to think anymore. Disgusted, I tossed the magazine to the floor and pulled the blanket over my head, not wanting to deal with this today, and wishing I'd stuck with ignoring celebrity magazines.

Grabbing my phone, I pulled up my text messages and tapped Ben's name.

Me: Pics of us in *Celebrity Today*. I guess it's started. :(

I tossed my phone on the bed and took a deep breath. Dad wanted me to help him create a buzz. It scared me just how far he was willing to take this. He'd have no qualms intentionally sabotaging the life I was creating for myself. This had the potential to damage everything I was building at Thrippletons. *My career.*

Yes, Ben and I were in this together, but he was still hiding something, and I wasn't completely sure I could trust him. Why wouldn't he tell me what Dad had over him? But most of all, Preston would see this; this would be the first test to see if he could handle it. My stomach churned as an overwhelming exhaustion enveloped me and made me want to sleep until the drama was gone.

The rest of the day passed in a blur of classes. Thanks to my new media attention, I was now more than a blip on my fellow students' radars. Between trying to act normal and staying focused on my classes, I managed to squeeze in time to talk to Dad just after lunch. Late that evening I found myself in the design lab, pinning my muslin pattern pieces for Duchess Evangeline's gown to the dress form. *Even her name sounds fancy.*

Nearly ready to cut into my dark blue silk chiffon, my brain refused to cooperate. I couldn't focus on anything but the phone call I'd had with Dad earlier.

I glanced over to Ethan, the only male finalist. He was starting to piece together his light blue bustier. His design looked more structured than my soft willowy one. With a huff of breath he blew his long straight bangs out of his face and pushed his dark-framed glasses up his nose. Daisy thought he was cute. I suppose I could see it, but he couldn't hold a candle to my tall British hottie.

Preston and I hadn't talked or texted today. I was too afraid to. He'd probably seen the pictures and had now changed his mind, wanting nothing to do with me. How could I blame him? I was kissing another guy.

Dad's rough voice floated through my mind as I remembered our conversation. "I haven't done anything to your mom . . . yet. I'm just setting things in motion should you disappoint me. But, you know better than to cross me, don't you, Maggie?"

I physically shook at the threat in his voice. Memories of him hitting me, all the bruises and scars rushed to mind. The last time it'd been his belt. I'd carried the welts across my back for weeks. The scars where the edges had cut were still visible. That'd been Marc's last straw. He vowed then that if Dad ever hurt me again, it'd be the last thing he ever did.

"If you make Mom fight you or try to make this anything but smooth sailing, I'm done. I'll tell the world what you're doing." My voice trembled and the overwhelming urge to hide pulsed in my mind.

"You're awfully brave when there's thousands of miles between us, aren't you?"

My sweaty hands struggled to keep a firm grip on my cell. "Not at all. Just reminding you that you have a part to play in this deal as well."

Chapter Twenty-Three

Pulled Under

The train rocked back and forth, lulling me into a vegetative state. It was just after four in the morning and I was on my way back to Bampton, my eyes burning with exhaustion. I'd gone on an investigation in London, hoping Preston would be there. He wasn't.

I leaned my head against the window and closed my eyes, wishing I were cuddled up in the guest room at Preston's flat. He'd canceled at the last minute. Something came up with his family. My brain couldn't stop thinking it had way more to do with the pics of Ben and me kissing than anything else.

When I'd tried to talk to his sister she was aloof and chilly. Part of me wanted to go home, but the other was determined to stick the evening out. I may be a coward when it comes to my father, but I could damn well survive an evening with Preston's sister and a few ghosts.

"Our mum needed Preston, so he dropped everything." Haley's words were clipped and tight.

"Is your mom okay?"

She sucked in a breath through her nose. "She battles with depression. Preston's her ray of sunshine."

"Aw, he's such a sweetheart."

She turned away from me and gave a noncommittal grunt.

Either she's pissed at Preston or she's seen the photos? If the latter, he couldn't tell her the truth about Ben because I'd asked him not to. I squeezed my eyes shut. This was such a mess. Surely his friends would see them too and hate me. *I don't even know how to begin navigating this.*

The darkness around us masked my utter disappointment at his absence. I'd been so excited for a chance to be near him. Not gonna lie, I'd also fantasized about kissing him. "I was so looking forward to seeing him. We've both been so busy we haven't had any time to get together."

"Mm." Haley nodded and shined the beam of her flashlight to a far corner. "Well, ghost hunts aren't really his thing."

Yet, he'd promised that if I went, he'd do everything he could to be there.

Uneasiness flooded my senses. She made me nervous and I couldn't shake the feeling she was judging me. Or worse, hating me. She'd been so friendly when we first met. This was a complete turnaround. I said the first thing that popped into my mind: "I'm so glad I met him. He's really amazing."

"He is." Tension rolled from her in tight, small waves. "That's why I can't stand to see him get played. So many girls seem to think they can use him and make him their doormat. I hate it. And them for it. He has such horrid luck with women."

"Any girl would be stupid to treat him like that."

A scoff sounded next to me. *Okay, she's definitely seen the pictures and she's pissed. Shit, shit, shit.* She didn't directly call me out, so I didn't know how to tell her that Preston knew and we were cool. Instead, I decided to keep my mouth shut and avoid any personal conversation. I just wanted to get through the night and go home. I did manage to shoot off a text to Preston telling him I missed him. I kept checking my phone, but no response.

Ben hadn't replied to my text either, about photos of us being in a magazine. But I knew he was still in London. Dad had made sure he stayed and was footing the hotel bill. I'd received a text from Dad saying he expected me with him every weekend at the very least.

I may not have to lie to Preston about Ben any more, but I still felt icky. Nerves tangled my stomach into a nasty knot as I worried over Preston and how he'd really react to this. Knowing it was happening and seeing it were two totally different things. And I wasn't so sure I believed Haley's story about where he was. Then again, maybe I'm just not trusting him enough. He said he'd be cool with this. *God, please let him be cool with this.*

All night long I'd fought off tears. Haley had jumped at every small mistake I'd made. She sent the message loud and clear that I was unwanted and in the way. To think I'd even had to switch shifts at The Bolt so I could make tonight happen. *I'd have much rather been at work.*

When we wrapped for the night I let out a sigh of relief. Grateful to go home, where I could cry in private. My emotions swirled and keeping them in check was wearing thin. I really didn't want his friends and family to hate me, but what choice did I have?

Dropping me at the train station, Haley bid me farewell. I didn't expect to get invited on another investigation, and that was fine.

"Will you say hi to Preston for me?" My foot nervously scuffed against the sidewalk.

With a curt nod she hopped back in the van and drove away. I waved at the retreating vehicle, then turned to find my train and get back to Thrippletons.

Safely seated and completely drained, I stared out the window, questioning all my choices.

What am I even doing anymore?

The darkened landscape blurred as my eyes watered, weariness seeping through my pores. My life was dragging me down, trying to drown me. It was just getting to be too much. I had my monster father who I'd been struggling to keep at bay so I could keep my mom in a bubble of ignorance. My new fake relationship had my real one, if I could even call it that, feeling as fragile as eggshells. Add in that Friday the duchess would be back and ready to try on her gown and I was completely and utterly frazzled.

If this Ben thing went south, it'd bring me a lot of unwanted attention. Knowing my luck these days, Thrippletons, and even the Duchess of Westminster would get pulled into the mess with me. I couldn't have that. My education and career felt like it hung on a series of what-ifs. I didn't like it.

Yet, I was most stressed that Preston wasn't responding to me. Neither was Ben . . .

I yanked my phone from my jacket pocket to fire off a text to actor boy. Tired, frustrated, I couldn't take much more. Tendrils of anger seeped through my veins.

Me: You know, I thought we were in this fake-relationship together. You could at least reply to my texts.

As of right now, it looked like Ben was abandoning me, and Preston . . . well, I just hoped he hadn't changed his mind.

Closing my eyes, I leaned my head back, letting sleep envelope my weary senses.

Thunk. My phone slid off my lap, waking me up. The conductor's voice filled the cabin. The next stop was mine.

I picked my cell up off the ground and saw a reply from Ben, sent about two minutes after I'd sent my message, waiting for me.

Ben: Sorry, things were really busy here and I've been meaning to reply, but keep getting pulled away. What's going on?
Me: *Celebrity Today* ran an article about us.

Ben: Yeah, I saw it. My mom says our fake relationship's all over the States too.
Me: How did they get pictures from our dinner? Kissing pictures.
Ben: Probably your dad. I'm assuming you're coming into London soon?
Me: Next Saturday. I've got to finish the dress.
Ben: Your dad warned me, he's not happy. We need to make it easier for the photogs.

Shit. An unhappy Dad was a scary thing.

• • •

The sparkly blue gown hung from the dress form, and I smiled. Done. My competition, Ethan, had finished earlier in the day. And the third contestant, Ana? Well, neither of us had a clue about how she was doing or what her dress even looked like. She must've been keeping it hidden away in her room. In fact, I'd barely seen her around at all lately. And she wasn't one of those girls you didn't notice. She was tall, tan, and eye-catching.

Behind me the door opened. I turned and smiled at Mr. Walker. He came over and wordlessly did a lap around my creation. He lifted a hand to his chin and pondered what he was seeing.

"How do you feel about this?" he asked.

"My work?"

His look said: duh, what else would I be talking about? My mind had been scattered far and wide lately, concerned with my mom, Dad, Marc, Preston, and Ben. There wasn't enough room in there to worry about everything.

I shrugged and cocked my head, really looking at the gown for the first time in days. It'd been a while since I'd stepped back and taken it in. *Maybe that's what I need to do with my life—take a step back.*

"Um, I'm pleased with how it's turned out. I think with the duchess in it, that's when it'll really shine."

A slow smile curled Mr. Walker's lips. "Margaret, it's fabulous." He scanned the room and leaned into me and whispered, "Out of the three of you . . ." He then leaned back, pointed to my dress and gave me two thumbs up.

I grinned, unsure if he was saying he thought mine was going to win or if it was just his favorite. Either way, it was a good thumbs-up.

"You should get to bed. Tomorrow's bound to be a long day." With that he turned and headed out of the room.

I took out my phone and snapped a few shots, sent them to Mom, then slumped onto my stool and put my head down, using my arms as a pillow.

My phone chimed.

Mom: BEAUTIFUL! She's going to love it!
Me: Thanks. :)
Mom: So, what's the deal with Ben?

Um . . . crap.

Me: ???
Mom: Don't even try, I've seen the photos all over the magazines. What happened to Preston, I thought you liked him.
Me: Nothing happened to Preston.

Well, at least I don't think so. We'd only texted a few times since the ghost hunt he'd missed, trying to sort out a time to get together, but he was still in London. Apparently his mom really had needed him.

Mom: You aren't the kind of girl to date more than one guy at a time. Why do I feel your father's behind this?
Me: I gotta run and meet Daisy. I'll talk to you later.

I set my phone on the table and drew in a deep breath. *I can't tell her. I can't tell her. Don't even think about it.*

Shaking my head, I looked to my finished piece that stood in front of my table and I soaked it in, trying to push aside all other concerns and feelings. Just a moment of peace, that's all I needed. A sense of accomplishment shot through my veins. I was proud of what I'd created. It was really good. And no matter the outcome, I'd done my very best.

With my phone still in front of me, I pulled up Marc in my FaceTime and hit the Call button. I needed to see his face and find my sense of grounding that'd been lost in the wake of the past few weeks.

A messy haired Marc popped on the screen. Shirtless, he had earbuds stuck in his ears and a tired look in his eyes. The room behind him didn't look familiar to me, so he couldn't be at home. "Hey, Magpie, how's it going?"

My brows scrunched together. "Something tells me I don't want to know what I just interrupted." An ultra feminine giggle reverberated through the earbuds I'd popped in and my eyes widened. "Is this girl someone special that I should know about?"

Marc shook his head and shot a glance at his unseen companion. "Oh, um . . . we're friends."

"With benefits," I scoffed. Behind Marc, a lithe blonde clad only in a T-shirt crossed the room and went into the bathroom.

He looked over his shoulder and shrugged. "It's easy and that's what I need. I just can't handle a relationship right now. Not with everything going on."

"Is everything okay?"

"Don't freak out, it's just tough to have a normal relationship when there's a thin wall separating me from Mom. It's cool though. We're fine."

"I'm sorry. I wish I were there to help."

"You're right where you should be. Hell, if you were here I'd just have more worries. At least I know you're safe."

"Did you see the pictures of Ben and me? Mom apparently did."

He nodded and scratched at his bare chest. "Yeah, it's everywhere here. Mom was asking me what was going on. I told her I hadn't a clue and she'd have to ask you. What did Preston think?"

"He knows about Ben and the whole situation. He's not thrilled by any means, but right now, he's willing to go along with it."

"At least you told him. But honestly, I don't know that I could handle seeing the girl I was into dating and kissing another guy. I'd be thinking of his lips on her every time I saw her."

I shook my head. "How is that helpful, Marc? I didn't even realize Dad had someone spying on us that night."

Marc scowled. "I know, I'm sorry. I just don't want you to be blindsided if he decides he just can't do it. How would you feel if you had to see him all over another girl?"

A pang of pain reverberated in my chest. I remembered how I felt when I'd thought he had a cute blonde girlfriend. I hated it. "It's not like that. I'm not with Ben out of choice."

"Just . . . just be prepared."

"I am, Marc." The skimpy T-shirt girl reappeared and smiled for the camera before slipping out of the frame.

Marc's attention was pulled off screen and the smile he shot the girl I could no longer see was absolutely feral.

"Hey, Marc, I know I interrupted something, um . . . personal. Why don't you call me back when you're alone? Tomorrow's totally fine."

A sly smile crossed his face. "Thanks, Mags."

Tucking my phone away, I went and took my dress off the form, prayed I got the duchess's measurements correct, and hung it inside a garment bag. Tomorrow was the big day.

Chapter Twenty-Four

Perks

It was after classes when Ana, Ethan, and I stood at our usual work stations in the empty Design Studio classroom, garment bags in hand. The duchess was due any minute. This would be the first time she set eyes on our finished pieces and actually tried them on. I'd double and triple checked that I'd dialed her measurements correctly on my dress form, but it didn't stop the fear that the gown wouldn't zip.

I stiffened and straightened my shoulders as I heard Mr. Walker approaching, talking to a female. "Here we go."

Ethan smiled at me. Ana's face had no expression. I couldn't tell if she was worried or knew she had this in the bag. There was just no reading her, which drove me crazy. With all Ethan's fidgeting, I knew he was just as nervous as I was. That simple tidbit of knowledge made me feel infinitely better.

He reached over his table and grabbed my hand. "No matter how this unfolds, we're both awesome designers."

I didn't know Ethan well at all, but I kinda loved him for saying that. "Totally."

Studying him, a thought formed in my head, Daisy still hadn't found her Mr. Right. I knew she thought Ethan was cute. *Hmm, maybe I can get them together.*

Pushing all thoughts of Daisy's love life aside, I leaned around Ethan and eyed the third finalist in the room. "Good luck, Ana."

"I don't need luck." She kept her gaze focused forward as she spoke. "I have talent."

The door swung inward and our instructor, accompanied by the duchess, two burly guys dressed in dark clothing, and a tall blond guy, stepped through the doorway. I did a double take. Holy crow, isn't that the *prince*?

Ana didn't appear fazed. Ethan took a step back in surprise.

Mr. Walker, the duchess, and the prince came down the aisle. The guys who looked like they should be named Butch and Brutus hung back, taking their positions on either side of the doorway. I couldn't stop smiling. Okay, the prince was cute. Like super cute with his wavy locks and bright blue eyes. He was wearing a three-button hoodie, exactly like Preston wore for our picnic, even down to the gray color.

God, I miss Preston. I'd called him this morning and he'd sounded so exhausted and stressed. He'd been hopping between London and Oxford all week.

"Ladies and gentlemen, may I introduce to you His Royal Highness, Prince Edmund." Walker guided him toward each of us in turn. "This is Ana Pendergast."

The prince stepped forward and shook Ana's hand. "Lovely to meet you."

A very slight smile turned the corners of her mouth. "Nice to meet you."

Edmund moved away and Ethan took a step closer as Walker intro'd him. Immediately Ethan offered his hand. "It's a pleasure to meet you, Your Highness."

A warm smile filled the prince's handsome face. "The pleasure is all mine."

When he stepped in front of me my knees wobbled under his intense gaze. "And that means you must be Margaret." He clasped my hand, the corners of his eyes crinkling in a smile. Turning to include Ethan and Ana, he said, "I'm so looking forward to seeing all your designs."

He stepped back to the duchess's side and she smiled up at him with a look of such love on her face, it made me a little jealous. Beautiful, kind, and completely in love with someone, and a prince at that. Not that I wanted a prince by any stretch of the imagination. I just wanted a certain tall, blond guy who made my heart pitter-patter and whose kiss had nearly been my undoing.

"I decided I couldn't possibly choose a winner on my own, so I brought along an impartial judge to help me out." She slipped her arm through the prince's and beamed. "I cannot wait to try on your gowns."

Mr. Walker stepped forward. "Ana, you're first."

With a curt nod she led the way in to the sewing room, which had been temporarily turned into a dressing room.

The prince waited outside while his duchess changed into Ana's design. Minutes later she appeared and motioned for the prince and Mr. Walker to join her. That left Ethan and me in the workroom.

I hopped up and took a seat on the front table while Ethan paced. My heart raced as I ran down my mental checklist, making sure I hadn't forgotten anything.

"You ready for this?" I asked, needing something to do.

He shook his head. "I'm not sure, you?"

"I am, and I'm not. I'm worried I missed something or it's too small."

"Can you imagine winning this? We're so close! My mum would just die if I won." His wide lips curled in a smile and he pushed his glasses back up his nose.

Ana left the room carrying her garment bag, not bothering to spare Ethan or me a look. Following close behind was the prince and Mr. Walker. I jumped down from the table and clasped my hands in front of me.

"Ethan, you may go in now," our teacher informed him before sitting down to wait.

My eyes darted to his as he nervously smiled. I grabbed his hand and gave it a squeeze as he passed by. "You're going to do awesome."

"Thanks." He straightened his shoulders and walked through the door.

"That was very kind of you." The prince approached to stand beside me. "You must not be very competitive."

I chuckled, a little nervous at his attention. "With an older brother I'm actually quite competitive. Well, at least with him I am."

He smiled. "Are you and Ethan close?"

"Not really." I shook my head. "We've just been working together a lot. He's a nice guy. I guess I feel a camaraderie with him more than anything."

The duchess's head popped out again. "'Kay, guys, I'm ready."

Both men jumped at her call and disappeared, leaving me alone. I unzipped my garment bag to peek at my dress and reassure myself it was still in there and doing okay.

As if it's going to grow legs and run away. I shook my head. The stress was clearly getting to me.

My phone alerted me to a new text. Zipping the bag back up, I laid it across the front table and proceeded to grab my phone.

Mom: Marc spilled the beans. You better call me when you get a chance.

Mom: Oh, and good luck today! :D

Crap. I didn't want to think of what she'd have to say. She'd probably be ticked off, definitely at Dad for being a jerk, and me for not telling her. *Dangit, Marc.* Trying to clear my mind, I jumped up the steps leading to the door, skipping one riser every other hop. I nearly face-planted when the guys exited the room. Ethan smiled and mouthed, "Good luck."

Mr. Walker nodded to me and gestured to the door. "Miss McKendrick."

Deep breath in, I retrieved my dress, squared my shoulders, and marched in, the door automatically closing behind me.

"Margaret." The duchess came to me, wrapped in a silky lavender robe, and grabbed my free hand. "I can't tell you how excited I am to see your dress."

I hung the bag on the rolling rack and smiled at her, my heart ricocheting off my ribs like a bullet. "I really hope you like it."

The zipper made its zippy sound as I pulled it down. When I took the gown out she gasped. That had to be good, right?

She came over and fingered the fabric. "Oh, Margaret, it's even lovelier than your sketches."

Chill, she probably said that to Ethan and Ana too.

"You ready to try it on?"

She nodded with a grin, grabbed the dress, and darted behind a changing screen.

The fabric rustled and her silhouette was just visible through the paper partition. I crossed my fingers. *Please fit. Please fit. God, please let it fit.*

I heard the side zip pull up, a soft sigh, then she stepped out into the open. My frazzled nerves popped and zapped inside me like electricity. *Was that a good sigh or a bad sigh?* The blue bodice clung to her curves with precision, and the organza and silk chiffon of the skirt floated to the ground in a shimmery cascade. She looked incredible.

With an unsure heartbeat, I stepped toward her as she turned toward the mirror, anxiously awaiting her reaction.

Her green eyes widened as they traveled from her feet up to her face. Fluffing the skirt, she turned to the door.

She never smiled. My pulse stuttered as my hope cracked and crumbled into tiny pieces.

I looked at my lace-up brown boots as she told her prince and my teacher she was ready.

When the prince walked in his jaw dropped and his eyes widened. He went to her, grabbed her hand, and twirled her. The fabric moved in a graceful dance around her legs. My eyes watered. *If she won't wear the damn dress I will. It's perfect.*

His eyes took her in and he smiled when his gaze fell on her face. "You always look incredible, but . . . wow. That's . . . that's just bloody brilliant. You look amazing."

She turned to me. "I expected this to be much more of a challenge, but . . . this is it. This is my dress."

She went to the mirror and twirled as my brain struggled to process what she'd said. *Does that mean . . .*

"I won?"

The prince closed the space between them and pulled her into his arms. Holding her close, he led her in a music-less slow dance.

"It appears so." Mr. Walker came to me with a smile on his face, watching the happy couple.

My mouth fell open and tears built up in my eyes. I couldn't hold them back. Once one trickled out, the others couldn't be stopped. This dress, *my* creation, would see the light of day. My name would be heard. This could lead to so, so much more.

Holy shit!

The duchess stopped in front of the mirror and smoothed out the skirt, a grin on her lips. "I can't believe how comfortable this is." Her face frowned. "Hang on, what's this? You gave me pockets?" Her face brightened. "It's so perfect. I can't wait for the gala now."

"I'm glad you like it."

She rushed to me and grabbed my hands. "I can't wait to show you off at the gala. You're brilliant with a needle and thread."

"Oh, right, I forgot, the gala." My brow wrinkled and I shook my head, not sure I wanted to go. I wasn't good at parties.

"I'm not going to take no for an answer. It's your prize for winning. That way people can meet the new upcoming designer who dressed me for the night. You can bring a date if you like. It'll be a blast."

Preston.

"That sounds perfect." I loved that people would see me and associate me with dressing this incredible girl.

"I'm just curious, and of course you don't have to answer, but are you seeing anyone? If not I think I might have the perfect guy for you." She gave me a look from head to toe, her eyes narrowing as she looked at the prince. "Don't you think so?"

His brow furrowed and he shook his head. "Yeah, no. He's still seeing someone. Remember?"

"Yeah, but . . . I just get the impression things aren't going well, don't you?"

I looked between them and their unspoken communication. "Um, I appreciate the thought, but I'm kinda seeing someone."

"Hmm." Her lips scrunched on one side. "I still think you'd be perfect for our friend, but I promise I won't play matchmaker. Although, if something happens between now and then and you need a date, let me know."

Edmund shook his head and put his hand on her shoulder.

I snickered. "I will. Um, when is the gala?" What I really wanted to know was how long I had to sort out my dress.

"Two weeks. Just before Christmas."

Mr. Walker cleared his throat and came to stand behind me. "She'll be there."

• • •

Phone up to my ear, I laid on my bed, iPad propped up in front of me, waiting for Mom to answer. When I'd returned to my dorm Daisy had been nowhere to be found, so I figured it was time to face the music.

I scrolled through more pictures of Ben and me. Some were recent and some were from over the summer. No wonder Dad had been so giddy whenever we'd spent time together. I clicked on an article and it popped up with pics of us from the pizza place, that first night we got dinner together. Still calling me Margaret, and no mention of my interest in fashion. Just Ben Chamber's girlfriend or Scott McKendrick's daughter.

"Hello, baby girl." Mom actually sounded pretty chipper. As much as I didn't want to hear a lecture, her voice cuddled me like a warm blanket. I'd missed hearing it.

"Hey, Mom."

"So, how'd it go?"

A grin spread across my face. "I won."

"I knew it! I knew you'd do it. I'm so proud of you, sweetie."

I recapped the moment and she couldn't believe I'd actually met Prince Edmund. It was so nice to just talk to her again. We gossiped for a few minutes as I told her what he was like and that yes, he was super cute. She then shared with me that Marc had been dating up a storm lately.

"Any of them redheads?"

She paused. "I don't think so, why?"

"Just a little inside joke between the two of us."

"So . . ." She cleared her throat. "What's your plan for your father?"

"Plan?"

"Mags, I can't have you doing this for me. It's not fair to you. I can't have you sacrificing so much. Your father . . ." She let out a heavy sigh. "He and I can sort out our divorce. Even if he tries to drag it out and keep me in limbo, freeze my assets, fight me over everything, whatever it is he's telling you he'll do, that's between him and me."

The snap of Ben and me on my iPad screen darkened and I rolled to my back. "But, Mom, if I can make it easier, if I can do some small thing to help you through it, it's worth it."

"You want to help me through it? Be happy; live your life your way. Prove to me that all the years I stayed with him and all the abuse didn't permanently scar you."

"But, Mom."

"No. No buts. I don't want you to do this. I'm so incredibly touched that you care, but Mags, this is final. You're not doing this."

"Are you happy?"

She paused. "What?"

"Are you happy? I want you to have a second chance at happiness and I don't want Dad to get in there and destroy that."

"I'm en route to happy. I'm free, which is a fantastic start. For the first time in years I'm not walking around trying to hide my bruises with scarves, glasses, or makeup. I don't have to tiptoe around anyone. I know you and Marc are safe. I'm working on a project I actually feel passionate about. I haven't been able to say that in . . . God, over a decade. Mags, I'm getting there."

Her words lifted my spirits and they just as swiftly plummeted when I realized it was too late for me to do anything. "I don't know how to get out of it. The photos have starting surfacing, our dating is getting press coverage, and if I bail, Dad would use whatever he's holding over Ben's head. I can't get out if it'll hurt Ben."

"I don't want you doing this for me. But I get you wanting to help Ben." She paused and thought. "Tell me about Preston. How's he handling this?"

"I don't know." I shrugged, not that she could see it.

"Does he know *everything*?"

I sucked in a sharp breath. "Yup. Every dirty detail. When I told him about Ben and the blackmail he seemed to understand. But since then, I don't know. He's pulling away. We're talking less and less, he's always super busy. The more photos that release the further away he seems."

"Aw, sweetie, I'm sorry. We've got to get you out of this." She paused, then softly snickered. "You know, your Dad only said you had to date Ben. He didn't say you had to do it happily."

Chapter Twenty-Five

Crushing Blows

Sitting on the window seat of our dorm, I read through Marc's text. The sun had just barely breached the horizon, and I should still be in bed, but I couldn't sleep. I was still riding the high from winning the competition. That is until Marc and I started texting. His date was in the bathroom and he was killing time.

Marc: Mom had offered to buy Dad out of his half of the house, but he refused.
Marc: He doesn't want her to have it. He's basically forcing her to sell it.
Me: But why?
Marc: Because she loved that house and really wanted it.
Me: That jerk. He promised me he wouldn't fight her.
Marc: What did you think of the article in *People*?
Me: I haven't seen it. Avoiding the tabs. What's going on?
Marc: Dad's got a girlfriend.

I scrunched my face in displeasure. Dad . . . dating? A girlfriend? What the hell? There's no way that can be correct.

"What's wrong?" Daisy groggily raised her head.

I shook my head and held up a finger before tapping out a reply. "Sorry, I'm just texting with Marc. I'll be quieter."

Me: Seriously?

Marc: She's in her mid 20s. She's only a few years older than you and me. :(
Me: I think I'm going to be sick.
Marc: I'm sorry. Although, I guess it's better coming from me than seeing it spattered all over the news.
Me: I suppose. Wait, how's Mom handling this?
Marc: She's not surprised.
Me: I hate him.

Yes, he was my father, but he'd never really and truly been a dad. I'd only heard stories of the kind man my mom married. Marc and I certainly never met him. Well, Marc may have, but he was too young to remember. There was nothing for us to miss, except the idea of a loving father.

Marc: We all do. I think he's losing it.
Me: Clearly.
Marc: I've been thinking about your Ben situation.
Me: I'm listening.
Marc: You'd have to get Ben on board, but I might have a plan.

My alarm blared and I slammed a hand down to silence it. I had to get ready for school, but I wanted to hear Marc's plan.

Me: What is it?
Marc: Nothing groundbreaking. I'll call you a little later. Gina just got back. Bye!

Seriously? Way to leave me hanging. I set my phone on my desk and grabbed my bathroom caddy from the bottom of my armoire. "I'm gonna hop in the shower. Start waking up, princess."

Daisy grumbled as I closed the bathroom door behind me. Stripping, I hopped into the now steaming shower. As the warm water hit me, my thoughts turned to the gala and to Preston.

I needed to call him and see if he was able to go with me. Plus, things had been weird lately and I wanted to talk to him.

Outside the shower, I dried off and pulled on my gray sweatshirt with the big black heart. I wiped away an oval of steam from the mirror over the sink. I looked to the digital clock on the wall. I had enough time, I could call him now. Spinning around, I finished dressing, wrapped my towel on my head, and grabbed my cell off the shelf below the mirror.

Phone to my ear, it rang and rang until his tired voice answered. "Maggie, hey."

"Preston, how's it going?" I stepped from the bathroom and paced the length of our dorm room, nervous. Daisy opened one eye, grumbled, and tucked the blankets over her head.

He blew out a long breath. "It's going. Trying to catch up from the days I've missed."

"How's your mom?"

It took him a moment to reply. "She's okay. Did Haley tell you much?"

"Not really, only that she struggles with depression." I didn't want to pry and ask questions, but I hoped he'd offer up more of the story on his own.

"Yeah, she's always dealt with it, but a few years ago it got really bad. Whenever she needs me, I do what I can to be there for her. I always have. My dad tries, but with work, well, it's just not quite the same, I suppose."

Yanking my sweatshirt away from my body, I turned and paced back to the window. "Haley said you were her ray of sunshine."

A soft snicker filled the phone. "Ever since I was a baby Mum called me 'sunshine' 'cause I was such a happy child."

"That's sweet." And she was right, there was something about him that felt like warm sunbeams curling around you.

"So, how are things with Ben?" A creaking noise sounded in the background, like he'd leaned back in his chair.

Ben was the last thing I wanted to talk about. My thoughts were so jumbled on what to do about him. I sighed, needing to steer the conversation to the gala, somehow. "Fine, I guess. I'm heading to London on Saturday to see him."

"Mm." He didn't sound thrilled. His whole demeanor seemed off.

"Are you doing okay with this? Really?"

Preston sucked in a deep breath and slowly blew it out. "I get why you're doing it, I do, but . . . I don't know. I never considered myself a jealous guy before, but maybe I am." He paused and I feared his next words. "It's just, seeing him holding you and you kissing him and knowing that the world thinks you're his. It's tougher than I thought it'd be."

"I'm sorry." I squeezed my eyes shut, hating that I'd dragged him into my mess. "I swear there's nothing real between us."

"Perhaps."

He doesn't believe me?

"Haley's seen the photos and I can't even explain it to her. I tried to tell her there was nothing to worry about, but I know she didn't believe me. Mags, I just . . . I don't . . . I can't . . ."

I sat hard on Daisy's bed, just missing her feet, and grabbed a pink satin throw pillow, holding tight to brace myself. Heart thundering, I asked, "What are you trying to say, Preston?"

The pause on the line nearly killed me. His voice sounded rough when he answered, "I don't think I can do this."

My breath caught in my throat. What happened to him fighting for what he wanted? My lungs wouldn't fill. I was slowly and painfully suffocating.

He doesn't want me.

"You can't?" I struggled to speak past the lump in my throat but couldn't. Instead my head bobbed in a nervous nod, as if he could see me.

"Maybe once you're finished with *Ben* we can talk, but . . ." He trailed off, thought unfinished.

Maybe? A frizzle of anger popped in my chest and mingled into my sadness.

Tears threatened to fall and I shook my head, trying to stem the tide. As much as I hated it, my voice came out strangled. "Mm, yeah . . . maybe."

"Mags, are you okay?"

No, he didn't get to act all concerned after ending things. He couldn't do us; I couldn't do this conversation.

"Take care, Preston." I hit the End Call button and buried my face in my hands. The door to our room flew open and my head snapped up.

Andrew rushed in, carrying a magazine. "Ohmigod, you slept with Ben Chambers?"

"What?" Daisy sat up and eyed me, rubbing the sleep away.

A picture of Ben and me smiling and entering his hotel, lit only by the glow of its neon sign, graced the cover. The caption read: *Hot Lovers' Tryst.*

Lovers' tryst my ass. It'd been taken the night we'd rented videos and hung out in his suite over the summer.

Oh, God, Preston thinks I'm sleeping with Ben.

Anger at my father flooded my system. How could he have had us followed and photographed like this before we'd agreed to his scheme? It now looked like I'd been sleeping with Ben since we first met. In reality, I'd been too busy falling for Preston to really notice the A-list celebrity in front of me.

I lobbed the magazine toward the trashcan, but it smacked the wall and landed on the floor with a *thwack*. Thanks to Dad, Preston was done with me. That left my schooling and my career. And I had my suspicions that Dad wouldn't stop until he'd completely decimated everything that made me happy.

• • •

With Preston bowing out of my life, I invited Ethan to the gala. I figured since he went through the experience with me, he deserved to go. Andrew and Daisy weren't pleased with my decision. They sat on her bed, giving me the cold shoulder as they read gossip magazines that had Ben and I splashed on the covers.

I'd gotten a warning text from Ben earlier in the day. He'd done several interviews for Dad's movie and talked about us and admitted to our *relationship*. Up until now it hadn't been confirmed. Tomorrow the press would be all over us when I went into London.

"You know, the two of you are going to have to talk to me eventually."

They ignored me.

"How many times do you want me to say I'm sorry? It wouldn't have been fair to only invite one of you. Since I couldn't ask Preston or pick one of you, Ethan was my next logical choice."

I sighed, throat constricting as I watched them. "Come on. My world is crumbling, I can't lose you guys too."

"You're not losing us," Daisy finally spoke and lowered her magazine. "I'm annoyed. I was sure you'd take me since Preston's out. I wanted to meet Prince Edmund."

Daisy had been pissed when she'd heard about Preston. Called him an "eejit" who wasn't worth my time. I loved her for being so protective, but I also tried to stay neutral. It was a difficult situation to be in. In truth, I was sad, and okay . . . a little angry. I thought he liked me and would fight for me. Apparently I wasn't worth it for him.

Andrew scoffed. "Whatever, she was supposed to take me."

"Roommate." One of Daisy's sculpted eyebrows rose as she pointed to herself.

"If I could take both of you I would."

"I know you would've." Sighing, Daisy came and sat by me. "Hey, why didn't you ask Ben?"

My eyebrows rose and my eyes widened. *Seriously?* "Fake relationship, remember?"

"But he's still a friend, right?" Andrew tossed his rag mag on the bed.

"He is, I suppose. I just don't want what's real and good in my life to get tangled up with the dirty fake part. Plus, he's not exactly a date that would go unnoticed."

Daisy shook her head with a smile. "He'd get you noticed all right."

"I suppose I get it." Andrew put his arms behind his head and leaned against the wall. "Although, what I don't get is why you're letting your dad blackmail you. I'd try to find a way out. Well, then again, if it was Ben Chambers maybe I'd tough it out." He snickered and gave me a wink.

"How's the divorce going?" Daisy looped an arm around me and gave me a squeeze.

Shrugging, I caught them up on the drama. "Marc told me that they met with their lawyers to try to settle out of court and it ended up being a huge shouting match."

"Been there." Daisy chuckled. "One time my parents were at a funeral for a friend. He died in a car accident and they ended up arguing in the middle of his wake, with my dad accusing her of sleeping with the guy. It was so humiliating."

Andrew's nose scrunched up in distaste. "Oh that's bad."

"Yikes." My phone pinged and I hopped up to grab it off my desk, hoping it might be Preston, changing his mind. It wasn't. I blew out a deep cleansing breath. "I've got to get my mind off this. So . . . should I make my own dress for the gala? It's two weeks away."

"You made the duchess's dress in less time than that. You could totally come up with something beautiful. Come on, let's go to the workroom and see what we can do." Andrew jerked me up off the bed.

"You know," Daisy clutched onto my arm, "I say we make you an amazing dress, catch the eye of some hot guy, then when that Preston fellow comes crawling back, 'cause he totally will, you can tell him to go screw himself."

A new guy? I wasn't ready for that.

The duchess clearly had someone in mind; maybe I *should* let her hook me up. A rebound. A chuckle burbled at the thought. *Me, getting set up by a duchess.* Yeah, right.

• • •

Ethan stood in the entryway decked out in a tux, his blond hair slicked back and looking rather dapper. I stopped at the top of the tall staircase and turned to Daisy, who was fiddling with the part of my hair I'd pulled up. Probably making sure my purple streak peeked out properly.

"Take a look at that, Dais." I pointed down the stairs. "He looks pretty hot."

Glancing up, she smiled wistfully. "If only he were straight."

I looked at him again and shook my head. "I never got that vibe. In fact he told me about one of his exes, Beth, while we were working."

"Hmm, really?"

"Come down and say hi with me."

"No way, I look like shite and he looks *amazing*."

My hand clutched her wrist. "I doubt he'll care."

We went down the stairs and Ethan looked up at us, smiling. "Maggie, you look lovely."

I did a quick spin. "My own creation. And Daisy helped."

My roomie did an uncharacteristic meek wave and smile. "I just suggested the color, really. It matches the streak in her hair. She looks grand in that deep purple."

"She does." He took in Daisy and grinned. "From the first moment I saw you I thought you must have an eye for color."

"Oh, why is that?" She looked up at him, eyes flirty and chin tilted down.

He gestured to her hair. "'Cause your hair is so awesome."

And that did it. Her cheeks flamed bright pink and she looked away. "Thanks."

"Um, we should probably get going." He reluctantly turned his gaze from Daisy. "We've still got an hour and a half drive to get into London."

"You're right." I took his offered arm. "'Night, Daisy."

She waved and twisted the toe of her right foot on the floor. "Have fun, you guys."

Outside the snow swirled in the December air and I pulled my thick cape around my shoulders. Cold air seeped through my dress, making my teeth chatter.

"Sorry it doesn't match our attire a bit better." He pointed to an old beater car.

"Hey, as long as it runs and has a heater, it's great. I just hate to think of all the wrinkles we'll have by the time we arrive."

"At least we'll be wrinkled together."

We climbed in, snowflakes clinging to our hair, laughing, and took off. As we tore down the motorway, the car protested his lead foot. I gripped the door handle, praying we wouldn't get in a wreck.

I glanced down at my dress and smiled. The bottom was a dark violet mermaid skirt, which gradated lighter as it went up into a silvery lavender waist, where it began to darken again up to the off-the-shoulder neckline. All of the gown, including the long sleeves, had been embroidered with small stones, pearls, and sequins. It was a massive amount of work, but if it caught the lights like I thought it would, it would be totally worth it. Thank God Andrew and Daisy had helped with all the embellishments or it would've never gotten finished.

The car gave a clunky groan and I pitched forward, clutching onto the dash. "Is everything okay?"

"Um, no." He looked up to me, panic in his eyes. "It seems I've lost power." He pulled us over to the side of the road with a fight, and tried to restart her. A few stuttering attempts led to only a clicking sound as the key turned in the ignition.

When his gaze lifted to mine I said, "Cab?"

He nodded. "Thank goodness I have my mobile."

We were on the outskirts of Oxford, which brought a certain guy to mind. I slipped my hand in the pocket of my dress and palmed my cell, tempted to call Preston and beg him to help us. It'd be more of an excuse just to see him again. It'd been two weeks since we'd ended things. In that time more and more pictures of Ben and me kissing and parading around together had filled the press, the stories made worse by suggestive headlines.

Marc's idea had been to start getting in the press with all different people, but Ben and I couldn't see how that would help the situation. It would just garner more press for Dad. Mom told me we should look like we didn't like each other; we didn't have to be happy to fulfill Dad's plan. But, honestly, Ben was a friend and I did enjoy being with him, so it was actually a challenge to not smile around him.

I didn't even want to know what Preston's opinion of me was now.

• • •

Ethan and I stood outside a tall mirrored glass building taking in the glittery scene inside. The snow had stopped, but there was an icy wind still blowing. I pulled his arm, and we stepped toward the large doorway.

Leaning in, Ethan whispered, "We're only a little late."

"Considering we just had to get a cab to the underground, take a train, and then get another cab to get here, I think we're doing great." I smiled up at him. "Come on, let's go." We walked inside and promptly checked our coats.

After being greeted I spied the duchess twirling around the floor with Prince Edmund. I watched her move, loving the way the dress moved with her. I couldn't believe I'd made that. A satisfied grin curled my lips. I felt a little like a fashion rock star. *She looks incredible.* Her red hair fell in long waves and her makeup was perfection. She didn't look like a duchess; she looked like a freaking princess.

"Do you want to dance?" Ethan made a move to pull me to the floor.

I shook my head. "In just a little bit. I need to find something to drink first."

"There's a punch station just over there." His extra height was quite a bonus right now. "Let's go." Clutching my hand, he pulled me along behind him, navigating the crowds nicely.

A cup of punch pinched between my fingers, I prepped to toss it back when the duchess popped up beside me.

"Margaret, I thought that was you. You look fabulous!" She motioned for me to twirl, so I obliged after sipping down my drink. "Oh, I love your dress."

"Oh, thanks." I glanced down and smoothed the front of my skirt, more out of habit than necessity.

She looked over to Ethan and gave me a side-eye look. "Is Ethan the guy you're seeing?"

I met Ethan's eyes and we both shook our heads. "No, we're just friends. I figured since he worked just as hard as I did, he deserved to be here."

"That's wonderful, and so kind." She grabbed my hand and gave it a squeeze. "Ethan, do you mind if I steal her away?"

Ethan shook his head. "Not at all, go show her off."

"Come with me." She pulled me away from Ethan. In a much softer voice, she added, "I know you're taken and I promised that I wouldn't set you up, but I can still introduce you to someone. I think the two of you would get along splendidly. He's been in such a funk lately. You'd be perfect."

"Umm . . ." I followed along, panicking and looking for places to run. *I'm not ready for this.*

She stopped and grinned. "It's okay, I promise. At the very least, you'll walk away with a new friend. Preston is such a sweetie."

Preston?

I glanced up across the room and there he was. *My* Preston. The duchess pulled me along behind her and I couldn't think what to do. My brain shut down. As if he were suddenly in slow motion, he turned. His eyes clapped on to mine.

Oh shit.

Chapter Twenty-Six

Eye Catching

The ballroom tilted in my vision and the shimmering chandeliers left streaks before my eyes. I gently pulled on the duchess's hand, not taking my eyes off Preston, who now was open-mouthed, looking between the duchess and me. *But how?* Dancers swirled past us on the floor, turning into colorful blurs as we made our way toward him.

My mind flashed to Preston calling his best mate Edmund, who had a girlfriend named Evie. Surely he hadn't been talking about the prince and the duchess. Was he? *Oh God.* I pulled back, forcing her to stop in the middle of the dance floor. I just . . . I couldn't do it. I couldn't face him, not when he'd made it clear he didn't want to be with me anymore.

"Um." I tore my eyes from Preston. He looked positively amazing in his tuxedo. I momentarily squeezed my eyes shut. *Focus.* "I'm curious, do you go by 'Evie' a lot?"

She nodded with a puzzled expression. "It's what all my friends call me. Why?"

"Oh boy." I sucked in a breath, all the pieces snapping into place. Preston and Edmund even had the same three-button hoodie. Maybe it was the same damn one. *I'm so blind.* Why the hell hadn't he told me? No wonder he understood my not wanting to tell him who my father was.

"Margaret, are you okay?"

My eyes opened and they darted to Preston, who was now walking toward us only to be stopped by Edmund. I couldn't face him, not yet, not feeling so unwanted. And most definitely not here.

Shaking my head, I looked into the duchess's green eyes and whispered. "I think we have someone in common. And I really can't be here . . ."

"What?" The duchess glanced to Preston, then back to me.

"Most people call me Maggie."

"Maggie?" Her eyes narrowed and I could almost see the moment when understanding hit her. She flinched back. "Wait, Preston's Maggie? Oh my stars, I thought you looked familiar. You're dating Ben Chambers."

A tremble started in my core and spread though my limbs. "I'm not Preston's any more." I couldn't lie to her, even if it changed her opinion of me. Above all, I needed to stay professional. "I should probably go . . . and find Ethan." Then we could hightail it out of here and avoid a nasty, career-crushing altercation. "Excuse me."

I spun, my dress swishing around me, and moved toward the entrance, searching for Ethan.

When he saw me, he came to my side. "Hey, are you all right? You look . . . off."

I glanced behind me, the duchess in pursuit and Preston watching. He turned to Edmund and gestured in my direction. *Is he mad that I'm even here?* "Um, something's come up and I can't stay. I'll understand if you're not ready to go. Feel free to stay and enjoy your night."

"What?" Ethan grabbed my arm and stopped me. "You can't leave. We just got here."

"Maggie?" The duchess caught up to me and rested her hand on my arm. "Forget Preston for a moment. And I know there's two sides to every story. I'd really like to introduce you around. My dress has people curious about my new designer. Plus, I wanted to talk to you about more pieces I'd like made."

"You . . . you still want me to make something else for you?" A small smile cracked my nervous façade. "Even after . . ."

"Are you kidding? With how fabulous this dress is, of course I want you to do more for me."

I couldn't stop the grin. She wants more. *Ohmigod.* Ethan nudged me with his arm in quiet congratulations.

My eyes scanned around the room. Looking for Preston, wanting to run and tell him my news, but he wasn't where he'd been earlier, or anywhere else that I could see. *Wait, he doesn't even want me.* That small reminder cut the urge to run and find him.

Knowing we possibly were in the same room had me on edge. I didn't like the feeling churning in my stomach. Instead of friendly butterflies, it felt more like a stampeding herd of rhinos. I still wanted to leave, rather than have to face him.

"I'm flattered, and I definitely want to design more pieces for you, but . . . I'm sorry, Your Grace, I really should go."

She cocked her head to the side. "Please, call me Evie. I'd like to be your friend, especially since we're going to be working together."

"Thank you, I'd like that . . . Evie." I met her eyes and felt the kindness there, which was unbelievable considering the circumstances. "How about I give you my number and you can call me next week." I pulled a scrap of paper from my glittery clutch, scribbled my number on it, and handed it to her.

She stuffed it in the pocket of her skirt and looked at me as if she were trying to figure something out. "You really don't have to leave. You can tell me what happened between you two. I'll listen, see if I can help."

Ethan cleared his throat. "Um, I think I'm going to . . . yeah, just . . . over here." He gestured uncomfortably, then fled.

Shrugging, I blinked back tears. "I can't, not really. It's a weird situation and everything's so messed up. It's too late for us now."

She frowned. "It's never too late. We could go talk to him. I'm sure we could sort it out in a minute."

I shook my head. "I can't. I don't even know what I'd say to him." Across the dance floor a slightly wavy blond head came into view and my pulse jumped. When it turned, it wasn't Preston. "It's pretty straightforward; I wasn't enough. I'm sorry, but I have to go."

With that, I turned and hurried to the coatroom to retrieve my cape. Tossing it around my shoulders, I ran out the door. Outside, I inhaled deeply. The cold air hit my lungs, making me cough. Determination in my steps, I walked to the nearest underground station, boarded a train, and went home.

• • •

A couple days after the gala, I sat in my History of Fashion class and held my phone under my desktop, scrolling through the line of old texts between Preston and me. It may be stupid, but I missed him. We'd had no contact since that horrid phone call. I wanted to text him or call and talk to him, but I couldn't. *He ended us.* Were we ever even an actual "us"?

My phone buzzed in my hand, alerting me to a new text. I no longer held any hope it'd be from Preston.

Evie: Hey, I'm coming to Bampton this afternoon. Can we meet for coffee?
Me: Of course, when and where?
Evie: 3:00 at Starbucks okay?
Me: Perfect.

From that point on the day dragged endlessly. I hoped she wouldn't want to talk about Preston, but undoubtedly she'd bring him up. I liked the duchess. She seemed straightforward, which I normally didn't have a problem with, but when it involved my love life, that's when I had issues.

I tied the belt of my thick maroon fleece jacket around my waist. The cafe wasn't too long a walk from Thrippletons, so I pulled the large hood over my head and set off. The clear sky meant it'd be getting super cold.

My feet crunched along the side of the road, my family on my mind. My birthday had just passed and Christmas was just around the corner. I'd never celebrated either without them. But with finances super tight it seemed irresponsible to spend money on an expensive flight home. And I refused to touch Dad's money. I didn't even want to think about what he'd be doing. Undoubtedly it would involve his new girlfriend.

Outside Starbucks, I took a deep breath and shifted gears, putting thoughts of my family on hold. Yes, I'd be away from them for Christmas, but I'd make do. Daisy and I'd be together at least. Andrew offered to take us home with him, but we'd both told him we'd be okay. I was glad I wouldn't be alone, and it helped that Dais was pretty awesome.

Opening the door, a wave of warmth engulfed me as I stepped inside. Christmas decorations filled the cozy spot. A sprig of mistletoe hung above the cash register. A quick glance around told me I'd gotten here before the duchess. Behind me sleigh bells jangled and I spun to see a friendly smiling face.

"Maggie! So sorry you had to wait." She came toward me, unbuttoning her gray jacket.

"I actually just got here."

She stuffed her gloves in her pocket and unwrapped her blue scarf. "Have you ordered?"

I shook my head and we both got in line. She ordered a tea and I got a peppermint mocha. We found an empty table in a back corner and sat, drinks in hand.

"Okay . . ." Evie jumped right in. "I have another event I need a dress for. It doesn't have to be a gown. It's for a museum opening. So I'm thinking black, pretty, and classic."

I nodded and pulled out my sketchbook from my brown satchel. "I can do that, no problem."

"What about casual wear?"

"Definitely. Anything specific?"

"Jackets, simple dresses, fun tops, anything really."

I jotted down notes, excitement bubbling in my veins. *I have a client!* "Okay, I'll start sketching up some stuff."

"Fabulous. Now, do you think you could scan your designs and email them to me?"

I nodded. I had an electronic tablet to design on; I just never used it much. I preferred the scratch of pencils on paper. But I'd pull it out for this. "Yeah, no problem. Jot your email down for me."

She scrawled her address down in my sketchbook and passed my pencil back to me. "Brilliant, now that we have business out of the way we can have a little girl chat." She took a sip of her tea.

Swallowing hard, I nodded and took a gulp of my still-scalding coffee. My tongue and throat felt raw and fuzzy afterward.

"I think you know what I want to talk about."

My head bobbed involuntarily, hating the direction this was going. *Preston.*

"Please, don't panic." She held up her hands. "I just want to help. The way you looked the other night at the mere mention of him . . . you seem to be suffering just as much as he is. Which is hard to imagine, because he's pretty miserable."

The idea that he was just as unhappy as I was made me feel a little better. At least he hadn't simply written me off and gone on his merry way.

Looking down, I ran my finger in the wet circle left behind by my cup. "I'm in a weird situation that I can't really . . . divulge." I hated being so secretive. "Preston knew about it and it just got to be too much. So, I'm not really sure there's even a point in trying."

"If you like him, if you still have feelings for him, if you still think about him, then there's a point to it."

I couldn't stop the smile. "Okay, so maybe there's a point from my angle, but him?" I shook my head, my grin fading. "He told me he always fought for what he wanted, but in the end, he decided I wasn't worth the fight. He doesn't want me."

"The way he looked at you the other night didn't say that at all. Quite the opposite actually." Evie inhaled deeply and paused, thinking before she spoke. "I don't know much of the details, because Preston won't say anything about it. But I do know he hasn't had much luck with girls. Don't get me wrong, he's a huge flirt and he's always willing to take a chance if he likes someone, but from what I understand, any time he's gotten serious, he's been really hurt."

"Hurting him is the last thing I wanted to do."

She took a swig of her tea and dabbed at her lips with a napkin. "About a year ago I overheard him asking Edmund what it was he lacked that made girls feel he wasn't enough. Why they always cheated."

My cheeks puffed out as I blew a heavy breath. He'd never told me about his past. I really knew very little about him. I'd been so self-absorbed all summer that I hadn't really gotten to know much about him. "I thought he was more than enough. But I wasn't enough for him."

"Do you want me to tell him anything?"

"Yeah, tell him to call me."

Green eyes met my blue ones. “I’ll do that, if you answer one thing for me.” At my nod, she continued. “What’s the deal with Ben Chambers?”

Chapter Twenty-Seven

Determined Decisions

The air in the cafe comforted my nerves with the scent of coffee and cinnamon. My conversation with Evie, however, was anything but comfortable. The duchess looked at me, waiting for my answer to her question: what's the deal with Ben and me?

"Ben and I are just friends." I held my hand up, stopping her before she said anything more. "It doesn't look that way, I know. And it's probably only gonna get worse. But the way things are . . . there's nothing I can do."

I'd met up with Ben in London a couple days ago and we'd acted like a perfectly in love couple. The whole time I'd felt awful and guilty and ashamed of what we were doing. According to Marc, Dad was losing it. He'd moved his girlfriend into our house and given her everything that'd been Mom's.

Evie's lips puckered, and she looked like she was stopping herself from saying something. "I don't understand."

"It's hard to explain, and I've only told close friends." My brow furrowed and I blew out a deep breath. Averting my gaze, I allowed the sordid story to spill out. Who my father was, the abuse, the divorce, the blackmailing, the fake dates, everything. I wanted her to understand. Maybe because I knew she was my only link to Preston, and he needed someone to understand what he was going through, or maybe it was simply that she was easy to talk to.

Her mouth fell open. "Your own father?"

"Yeah, pretty awesome, right?" A tear ran down my cheek and I quickly wiped it away. "He actually just moved his girlfriend, who's close to my brother's age, into our house."

Evie's eyes widened. "I'm so sorry."

"It's been a little stressful." A bitter laugh slipped through my tight throat and I realized just how much anger I had pent up inside. What surprised me, though, was the amount now aimed at Preston. Yes, I'd asked a lot of him, but he'd abandoned me when I needed someone in my corner the most. No wonder I felt so lonely. And that's when I knew *I* was done. "You know what. Don't bother talking to Preston for me. I know he's your friend and you think he's great, but he's actually a bit of a shit. I don't want anything to do with him anymore. *That's* what you can tell him."

Wide green eyes took me in. "And Preston knew all this?"

I nodded. "He knew everything and he made the decision to leave."

"Maggie, I don't know what to say."

I shook my head and stood up. "You don't have to say anything, it's okay." I slipped into my jacket and zipped it up, then grabbed my bag and notebook. "I'll get the designs to you by the end of the week."

She stood. "I'll look forward to it. See you soon."

The bell on the door jangled and bumped the glass with a clack as it closed behind me. I needed to get out of there and walk. The antsy feeling coursing through me made me want to move.

With everything going on in my life, I didn't have time to chase after the might have beens.

• • •

My body plopped onto the bed with a soft whoosh and I kicked off my shoes. My feet were killing me. The whole way home I'd either run or stomped off my anger as I kicked stones off the roadside.

Daisy eyed me warily; she must've sensed I was in a mood. "How did it go?"

Sitting up, I smiled. "I'm designing another dress for the duchess, and some casual clothes."

Her eyes widened. "That's fabulous. Congrats!"

"She asked if she could take a message to Preston for me."

One of her pale, slender brows rose. "Oh?"

"I told her I was done. That I wanted nothing more to do with him."

"Good for you! Does this mean we can finally go out guy hunting together?"

"What about Ethan? I thought you liked him."

"I've been hinting to him, but he's just not getting it." She threw her arms in the air. "What is it with guys these days?"

I flipped onto my back and blew out a deep, pent-up breath. I may have a less than stellar love life, but perhaps I could get the ball rolling for her. "You know, I actually need to talk to him, so I could mention something, try to give him a little less of a hint and more a suggestion."

She smiled at me and picked up her tablet and sat to sketch. "He's in the workroom. At least that's where I left him."

With a stretch, I stood and headed down the hall, running my fingertips along the gray stonework. I poked my head through the door, and sure enough, he was standing next to a dress form, working on a pattern. "Hey, you got a minute?"

His head snapped up and his fair hair fell into his face. With a puff of air and a smile, he looked at me. "Of course, I've got loads of time for you."

"Aw, thanks." I hopped and sat on the table near his dress form. "I mainly wanted to apologize for ditching you at the gala."

He waved me off. "Aw, it wasn't a big deal. I could tell you needed to get out of there."

"It wasn't my finest moment, that's for sure." My legs dangled below my perch like a little kid on a tall swing.

He snorted a breath as he chuckled.

"So, what are you working on?"

He took a step back and eyed his design. "A piece for my Advanced Portfolio class."

"Hmm, I like it." I jumped down and did a quick circle, fingering the white Peter Pan collar. "So, what do you think of my roommate?"

"Daisy?" He easily followed my subject change. When I nodded, he continued. "She seems very sweet."

"Do you think she's . . . pretty?" I deliberately dragged out the last word.

He smiled and I noticed how straight his teeth were. "Of course she is. She's got those great big blue eyes and her hair . . . I love the pink. And it's awesome that she got you and Andrew to do some too." He reached up and gave a little tug to my purple chunk.

It certainly sounded like he was interested. "I think you should ask her out."

His eyes widened. "Oh you do now, do you? And why is that?"

"You like her, she likes you, I'm just putting the pieces together."

He paused in the middle of pinning a sleeve. "Daisy fancies me?"

I nodded, pulling out my ringing cell phone. The smile on my lips vanished and my heart accelerated when I saw who it was. *Not talking to you.* Silencing it, I slid my phone back into my pocket and pasted a happy face on. "You know, she's up in our room right now. Alone."

Ethan grinned and nodded. "You want me to do it now?"

"Is there any time like the present?" I gave him a small grin.

"I'll be back." He set down his pin cushion and strode for the door.

When I returned to my room, neither Ethan nor Daisy was there. I emptied my pockets and changed into my pajamas, so done with the day. My emotions were all over the place, happy for Daisy, excited for more work, angry with my dad and Preston, and just freaking exhausted.

My cell sat on my desk, the little red circle telling me I had a voicemail torturing me. I folded my arms over my chest, refusing to pick it up. When Preston's face had filled my screen I'd been so thrilled and so angry at the same time. I knew, without a doubt, the message was from him.

Like hell I'm going to listen to it.

Two text pings came in shortly after the call. I could guess who they were from. *Not going to read them either.* Evie must've talked to him.

Daisy floated back into our room with a smile on her face. "I love you."

I snickered. "I know *who* you were with, but where were you?"

"We went for a little walk and he asked me out." She bounced with excitement, her voice squeaking at that end.

I smiled at her happiness. Better to focus on her than on that damn little red notification. I went to sit by her on her bed. "So?"

"So, we're going to get dinner Friday night and maybe see a movie. I'm so excited, he's so nice, Mags."

I put my arm around her and gave her a hug. "He is a really sweet guy. I'm happy for you."

"Even with all the boy drama in your life?"

"Of course. Why wouldn't I want great things to happen for you? It's not like I want everyone to be as miserable as I am."

I placed my head on her shoulder and tried to ignore the little niggling jealousy. I *was* happy for her. I just wanted to be happy for me too.

She leaned her head on mine. "I really don't like that Preston fella."

"You're my friend, you have to say that. Granted, I'm not his biggest fan right now, either. But, he did finally call me tonight."

She shot upright and turned me to face her. "Shut your gob! What did he say?"

Shaking my head, I told her I hadn't answered. Nor had I listened to or read his messages. "I'm not touching my phone. I don't care. He can call and text all he wants, I'm not replying. I'm done."

"Want me to block him?"

"You can do that?"

She nodded. "Oh yeah, I've blocked loads of people on my mobile." The look I gave her must've encouraged her to elaborate, as she added on, "What? I have a lot of annoying family members."

I gave her a pat on the knee before standing. "I'm so happy you're my roomie. I don't want him blocked, at least not yet."

"Want me to listen to it then?"

Shaking my head, I leaned away from her. "No, I'm just gonna let it sit for a while, I think. I'll let you know if I change my mind."

"Okay. And seriously, thanks again."

"Happy to help. At least one of us needs an awesome love life, right?"

That night as I lay in bed, my brain lingered on the messages on my phone. Hadn't he said enough? Yanking the covers over my head I slipped my earbuds in, hoping music would take my mind off him.

Didn't work.

I reached out and grabbed my phone. *I shouldn't do this.* The darkened screen lit up at the push of a button, hurting my eyes. In a white box on the screen was Preston's face and a little red dot with a two inside. I could see only the first few words: *Maggie, I need* . . . I could think of a lot of things he needed, but none of them were flattering.

Daisy's bed creaked as she rolled around, but her breathing remained steady. Up in the top corner of the screen was the icon for voicemail. I didn't know which to do first.

I opened the texting app, my fingers hovering over Preston's name. At the last minute I chickened out and tapped on Marc.

Me. How're things back home?

It was eight in the evening there, I didn't expect the swift reply I got.

Marc: Hi, Magpie. Things are good here. What about you?
Me: Good. The duchess wants me to design some more stuff for her.
Marc: Nice! I always knew you were a total fashion badass. Good for you!
Me: How's Mom?
Marc: Really good. She's planning a big Christmas dinner. Grandma's coming into town for it, so is Aunt Tilly.
Me: Nice, that'll be fun. Dad'll probably be holed up in our house with his girlfriend.

I'd seen pictures of them together on online sites. She was the complete opposite of my classy and amazing Mom. I had to wonder when Dad would start hitting her, too. At least she provided a distraction for him. But I knew it wouldn't last. His focus would turn back to Ben and me in no time.

Marc: How long do we think that'll last?
Me: lol, I see him marrying her quickly and divorcing her just as quickly. She's probably pregnant.

Marc: Ow, thanks for that mental picture. >_<
Me: Aw, I'm just sharing the love.
Marc: Keep it, dear God, please keep it.
Me: lol, love you.
Marc: Love you, too.

Forcing my phone to sleep, I leaned out of bed and put it on the desk again. The farther away the better.

Maybe I'd break down and read it in the morning, but as of right now, I was still done. Something told me tomorrow wouldn't be any different.

Chapter Twenty-Eight

Revelations

I stepped from the shower and towel-dried my hair. Today was the last day of classes before Christmas break. I wished I could fly home and be with Mom, Marc, and our family, but I'd have to make the best of it here. At least Daisy and I would be together. Her mom and stepfather decided to go on a romantic couples cruise.

As I sat down on my bed, groggy eyes peered out of the blanket nest across the room. "Don't wanna get up."

I stretched. "Well, if you do, you'll get to see Ethan."

"I'm up, I'm up."

Smiling, I tossed my pillow at her. "Don't you just love that one boy who makes getting up for school so worth it?"

A blissed-out smile crossed her lips. "Absolutely. You know, he just might be the one. I get a good feeling about him."

"You and your feelings." Chuckling, my gaze went back to my phone. There was another message from Preston. The little red circle now held a three. *I wonder how high I can let that number get before I break down?*

It felt like a challenge. I liked to be challenged. Hell, my whole life was a challenge lately.

Daisy reappeared from the bathroom with a toothbrush in her mouth, muddling her words. "You 'bout ready? I don't want to be late."

My phone pinged and I glanced at it again.

Ben: We need to get together again.

I sighed and reached up to rub my stiff shoulders.

Me: No, we really should find a way to put an end to this. No offense, but I really don't want a fake boyfriend anymore.
Ben: Fabulous, got any ideas?
Me: What if we didn't give them photo opportunities?
Ben: Your dad would find something to release and up the threats.

Tossing my phone on the bed, I slid into some old jeans and a cowl-necked sweatshirt. Hair still wet, I hurried out the door behind Daisy.

All through class my fingers itched to read Preston's texts. *I could always read them and not reply.* That'd be a new challenge. I glanced up at our History of Fashion teacher. I really needed to pay better attention in here. Finals were scheduled for just after winter break and were sure to be a nightmare.

Class wrapped and I pulled out my electronic tablet to carry to my Design Studio class. I wanted to work up my designs for Evie. It would help me keep my brain focused and off the waiting messages.

We had to finish our final projects today, but I'd finished my bateau-necked navy cocktail dress over the weekend, so I had plenty of time to work on my preliminary sketches.

Behind Andrew and me, Daisy trailed, flirting with Ethan. The way they nervously looked at each other made me long for the days when Preston and I shared those looks. My hand moved for my pocket, but I yanked it back as Andrew gave me a side glance.

"I don't like him for what he did to you, but put yourself out of your misery and see what he has to say for himself."

"I shouldn't have even told you he contacted me."

"Probably not, and what he has to say will most likely be complete and utter bollocks." As we sat at our tables Andrew turned to face me and grabbed on to my shoulders. "But at least you'll know. I don't want to see you pining for this arsehole any more, you got it? He's not worth your time. He let you go. Read it, listen to it, whatever, just do it and get over him. Then you can make this thing with Ben Chambers real." He waggled his eyebrows.

That got a laugh from me. "You dork." Mr. Walker went to the front of the class and I leaned over to whisper. "You working tonight?"

Andrew nodded and I flashed him a thumbs-up. It meant we'd have the closing shift together and that made me happy. I loved working with one of my best friends. He silently pretended to clap his hands.

Daisy plunked down into her seat beside me just before Walker started addressing us. I looked over at Ethan, who was still watching her with a smile on his face. Realizing he was caught, he looked away, his cheeks pinking. They'd have fun on their date tonight. It was their third. Daisy was counting.

• • •

Andrew and I sat on the counter that lined the wall behind the cash registers at The Bolt. We'd only had a few customers so he'd started telling me stories of his family Christmases as we shot baskets with crumpled pieces of paper into the garbage bin we'd moved to the other side of the counter.

I laughed as his shot missed and rolled toward the front door. "Dude, you better stick to fashion."

"You're one to talk." He smacked my shoulder with a loud snort. "Most of yours have ended up down that aisle."

I hopped off the counter, grabbed all our outliers and tossed them at him. "I'm running to the restroom. Be right back."

"Loo, it's called the loo," he hollered as I headed to the back. I smiled and shook my head. That was one I didn't think I'd ever adjust to.

After washing my hands, I headed to the break room, glancing back to make sure Andrew wasn't coming. I tucked the wrapped gift in his coat pocket. He always complained about his crap scissors, so I'd gotten him a nice pair of Gingher shears. On my way back to the front, I was about to push the swivel doors open, but Andrew's raised voice stopped me.

"What could you possibly want?"

"I was hoping I'd find Maggie here. Is she working tonight?"

I froze. The low voice hit me straight in the chest and I couldn't breathe. *Preston.* Lifting up on tiptoe, I tried to peer through the small square window. If I wasn't careful I'd fall through the gray swinging doors. I nibbled my lip and braced myself on the doorframe, savoring the sight of his tall form.

God, he looks good.

"She's not here." Andrew's words were tight and he scowled at Preston. "Door's right there, mate."

Preston's jaw clenched, but he still pleaded with my pissed-off friend. "I get it, you don't like me, and rightly so. I know I'm a complete tosser and I've probably made too big of a mess of things. That's why I'm here. To apologize. I have to see her. I've . . . I've made such a mistake."

The look on his face was pained, but Andrew didn't care. I loved that he was so willing to defend me, but I was tempted to go out and put Preston out of his misery. I leaned into the door and stopped as Andrew's words stung me, sucking the air from my lungs.

"You let her go, didn't you? You knew exactly what she was going through and you just completely ditched her."

I wasn't enough to fight for.

Preston pressed his palms flat against the counter. "What are you? Her gatekeeper? I just need to see her."

"I already told you, she's not here."

Rubbing his forehead, Preston asked, "Do you know where I might find her?"

"Nope." Andrew's lips popped on the "p." "Even if I knew, I wouldn't tell you. You don't deserve her."

"Yeah, so I've been told." Preston nodded and looked around the store and lightly smacked the counter. "All right, thanks."

The bell on the front door rang as Preston stalked out, but I couldn't move. Emotions that I had no clue how to control swirled inside me. I struggled to steady my heartbeat and even my breathing. Andrew made a beeline for me. The doors almost hit me as he blew through them.

"Do not come out front. Work on stock or something. I'll take care of the floor, it's slow enough."

I nodded. Too discombobulated to speak.

"Hey, I got your back, always."

Up on my tiptoes, I planted a kiss on his smooth cheek.

"The way I see it, you can deal with him on your terms, when you're ready, not when he just shows up."

"Thank you."

The two remaining hours of our shift flew by. When it was time to close, the back room was spotless and super organized. I hoped Millie liked it when she got there in the morning.

"Come on, let's go out this way." Andrew grabbed my arm and pulled me out the back door, locking it behind us.

"Why did you want to go out the back?"

His shoulders lifted. "Just in case he was watching the store."

I put my arm through his, resting my hand on his shoulder. "I don't get the stalker vibe from Preston, so I think it'd be okay."

"He seemed awfully desperate to talk to you."

We walked in silence as his words penetrated my tired brain. "Should I have come out and talked to him?"

"No. Why do you think I told you to stay in the back?"

I squeezed my eyes shut for a moment. "It was so hard not to run from the back at the sound of his voice."

"You know I'll support you any way you choose, but I still don't think he deserves you."

Andrew had driven his small Fiat, refusing to walk home at night in the cold, even though I'd tried to convince him otherwise. Sitting in the heated vehicle, I was glad he hadn't listened.

"So, who's the craziest relative you have to deal with when you go home?" I held my hands up to the heater vent. The warm air blowing out stung my icicle-like fingers.

"My auntie Bev. The woman is out of control with a camera. I have so many pictures of me with my mouth wide open, taking a bite, it's insane." He laughed. "She's sweet, though. I really wish you and Dais were coming home with me."

"You just want everyone to think you're bringing home two girls."

"Ha, ha. No. They wouldn't believe it for a second, they all know I don't swing that way."

I chuckled. "Well, that just foils all my long-term plans."

He pulled to a stop under a lamppost at Thrippletons and heaved a tired sigh. "Let's get inside."

My boots crunched on the snowy gravel as the wind whipped past me, catching my scarf and flapping it into my face. Pulling it down, I ran to the steps with Andrew, laughing as the cold air seemed to push at our backs and grapple for the very air in our lungs.

"Hurry, hurry, brrr." He shut the door behind us with a smile. "When are you heading out tomorrow?"

"Maggie?"

My fingers froze on the buttons of my jacket.

Preston.

He was behind me and sounding so close I suddenly couldn't move. His footsteps approached and I squeezed my eyes shut before looking up at Andrew, hoping he'd show me what to do.

"She doesn't want to talk to you." Andrew stepped around me, putting himself between us. I still didn't turn.

"Why don't you let her decide and speak for herself? She's perfectly able. Maggie, please listen to me."

I turned and faced him, ignoring the weakness in my knees that being so near him brought on. His eyes met mine and he offered me a shaky smile, which I didn't return.

"Why are you here?" Just looking at him made a lump form in my throat. "You made it pretty damn clear that you didn't want anything more to do with me." I took a step back as he took a step forward. I knew that the moment he touched me, my calm façade would crumble.

Dropping his hands to his sides, he pleaded with his eyes. "I made a mistake, a huge, massive, gigantic one. I shouldn't have let you go. I should have trusted you, but I was scared and I . . ." He looked down to his toes and added, "I've never been enough for anyone before. And the way I felt about you, it's—it's something I haven't felt before."

Andrew looked at me, waiting for me to signal that I needed help. He was like my super-fashionable bouncer.

Keeping my distance, I looked into Preston's face. It'd been a couple days since I'd met with the duchess, and now here he was.

"And yet, you're not really here because of me. You're here because of Evie. If she hadn't intervened, you wouldn't be here right now." I looked away and shook my head. "I meant what I said to Evie. I'm done . . . with all men, not just you. I took a chance on you. I let you in and trusted you. You were supposed to be different. But I was right, you're all the same. Clearly, *I* was the one who wasn't enough."

Preston sucked in a sharp breath and took a step back. "Maggie, please."

I shook my head, my vision blurring from unshed tears. "No, I'm sorry."

Turning, I bolted toward the stairs, not waiting for Andrew.

"I took a chance on you too." Preston's voice was filled with hurt.

My step faltered, but I didn't turn back. *He didn't want me enough to fight for me.* I'd done it. I'd stood up for myself and *really* ended it. I refused to examine the feelings of regret surging through me like an overwhelming tidal wave.

At the door to my dorm I went to turn the knob and stopped. A sheer yellow scarf hung limply from the knob. *Is this a signal?* I'd seen it in movies, but Daisy and I'd never worked out what we'd do if we brought someone back to the room.

This sucks. Daisy was in there happily making out with Ethan and I'd just sent Preston away. I missed him already. Hell, I never stopped missing him even though he'd shattered my heart.

Did I just make a huge mistake?

Turning, I was tempted to run after him. Instead I slid down the wooden door and sat on the floor, tears now spilling onto my cheeks. My breath shaky and hitching in my throat, I felt so lost. I didn't know how or when it happened exactly, but somewhere along the way I'd fallen in love with Preston. *No wonder this hurts so damn much.*

My life was in chaos and there was just too much going on. With nothing to ground me I was like a kite blowing in the wind, lost, lonely, and hoping someone would find me before I tangled in a tree.

My phone pinged and I squeezed my eyes shut, knowing it was Preston without even looking.

Footsteps echoed at the far end of the hallway and I glanced up to see Andrew coming toward me, a wrapped present in his hand.

"Um, he asked me to give this to you."

I took the shiny red-wrapped gift and held it tightly. The glittery green bow sat neatly in the center. With a gentle tug the ribbon came apart.

"He said to tell you he did it from memory."

My hands stilled. "Did what?"

Andrew shrugged. "He didn't say, just said to tell you that."

I swallowed and slid my fingers under the flap in the back, popping the tape free. As the paper fell to the floor it revealed a black wire-bound notebook, just like the one I'd bought in Scotland when I'd run into him. Smiling, I opened the front and gasped when I saw a stunning pencil drawing of my face staring back at me. How did I not know he could draw like this? *This is something I should know.*

"Let me see." Andrew leaned over and saw it. "Damn, that's good. It looks exactly like you. He's even got the little mole near your hairline."

I lifted a hand to touch the small brown spot at the far right, letting Andrew take the book from my hands. Should I run outside to see if he was still here?

"Good Lord, he must've studied the hell out of your face. It's actually pretty romantic to think he knows you that well. I don't think he forgot anything about you. Did you read what he wrote here?" He pointed to the page he was looking at.

My eyes darted to his and I shook my head.

"It says: I tried to push you from my mind so many times, but you just kept popping up like you were right where you were supposed to be, with me. Merry Christmas, Maggie. Love, Preston."

Tears filled my eyes as I took the book back and ran my fingers gently over the nearly photographic picture. "I didn't even know he could draw."

"He's into architectur-ey things, right? He has to have some skills to do that."

Turning, I made a beeline down the hall and flew over the stairs, clutching the notebook in my hand. When I stepped out the front door Preston was no where to be seen, and neither was his Land Rover.

Chapter Twenty-Nine

Friends

The sunlight streamed through the windows right into my face. *What the hell?* I pulled the blankets over my head, trying to block out the light. One sniff of the masculine cologne on the sheets and I knew I wasn't in my bed. I shot up and looked around. All my groggy memories came cascading back.

Andrew's room.

Which explains why someone was spooned up behind me. Feeling defeated, drained, and not wanting to wait for Daisy and Ethan, I'd let Andrew drag me back to his dorm.

Across the room his roommate let out a loud choking snort. I winced and slowly lifted Andrew's arm off, which he'd draped over my stomach.

Slowly, I slid out of bed and grabbed my phone and Preston's notebook. While waiting last night, I'd finally listened to Preston's messages and read his texts. I'd yet to respond, but I intended to. My phone told me I had two new texts, both from Preston.

I left Andrew's room and padded down the hallway, carrying my shoes. Thankfully, the scarf was off the doorknob. Sneaking inside, I stripped and climbed into my soft flannel sheets. I took my phone into the little igloo I'd created for myself and pulled up Preston's text thread.

Preston: Maggie, I need to talk to you. Please call me back.

Preston: Please, we need to talk.

Preston: I made a huge mistake. The pictures of you going into a hotel with him freaked me out. It made me think you two were much more serious.
Preston: I was wrong. I know that.
Preston: If I could do things differently I would. I hope you'll give me the chance to make things right.

My eyes teared up and I sniffled. The last two had come in this morning.

Preston: I see your face in my dreams and when I close my eyes. It's like you're seared into my mind.
Preston: I told you once that I'd fight for you. But I let my fear get in the way. You are worth fighting for.

I smiled as a tear trickled down my cheek. Reaching for a tissue, I wiped my runny nose.

He does want me.

And I wanted him. But as much as I wanted him, I couldn't just drop him back into the same position as before. Nothing had changed in my life. It hadn't been fair then and it wasn't now. Until Ben and I sorted our situation out, I couldn't be with Preston.

What felt like seconds later, the alarm I'd set on my phone blared and I quickly swiped the screen to turn it off.

"Unh, make it stop." Daisy folded the covers down and covered her eyes with her hands.

"That's what you get for kicking me out last night."

She smiled, practically purring. "In that case it was so worth it."

"Did you two sleep together?"

"What? No, it was only our fourth date. But there was serious snogging going on. He's an amazing kisser." She closed her eyes and kicked her feet against her mattress with a surge of excited energy.

Laughter left my lips. "I'm happy for you."

"This probably never would've happened if it weren't for you. I can't ever repay you."

I waved her off. "I'm glad you're happy, but the two of you would have gotten together without me. It was just a matter of time." Lying on my side, I put my arm under my head, needing to talk. "So, um, I saw Preston last night."

"What?" She sat up.

"Look at this." I leaned over the side of my bed and slid the journal across the soft carpeted floor. It spun out of sight, under her queen-sized bed.

She dangled out of her sheets and retrieved it. Opening the front cover she gasped. "Jayzus."

She looked to my wall covered with pictures, some cut from magazines, some I'd drawn. Preston's face was up there several times. Especially his wonderful brown eyes. After he'd ended things I never took them down. Or maybe it was more that I couldn't. Somehow I needed him there.

"I know."

"Okay, this has to be a sign."

I nodded and breathed in deeply, filling my lungs to near bursting.

"You're calling him, right?"

Meeting her eyes, I struggled to find the words. "I want to, but I'm wondering if I shouldn't wait until my life gets less crazy."

"Will that ever happen? Think about who your family is."

I sat up. "I don't know, but I need to get some stability in my life."

"Maybe *he* could be your stability."

I shrugged, not knowing just how stable he'd be. "At the very least, I have to get through this Ben thing."

"Then you better figure a way out of it right quick."

• • •

The day before Christmas—two days after Preston gave me the journal—I found myself in the deserted workroom, FaceTiming with Evie. She'd received my final designs and we'd made arrangements to discuss fabrics and any changes she wanted to make.

Smiling, her face filled the screen as she looked through the designs and nodded. I loved that she'd printed them out and studied them.

"These are wonderful. I love the dress, it'll be perfect for the opening. It's sexy, but still elegant and refined. I love how feminine your work is."

"Thanks. I had a lot of fun designing for you."

"This draped hoodie is gonna be my new favorite, I can already tell. Can you find a really soft material to use?"

I nodded and jotted down a note. "Of course. I could do a brushed fleece or even a cashmere."

"Oh, cashmere would be fabulous."

My pen scratched on the page. "Perfect, it'll be cozy and cuddly, you'll never want to take it off."

Smiling, she set the designs down and looked into the camera. "Okay, I promised Preston I wouldn't say anything, but I just can't keep quiet. Are you going to get in touch with him? He's been so miserable and mopey."

"I've started so many texts and emails." I sighed. "I can't seem to find the right words."

"Are you going to give him another chance?"

Looking down at the keys of my laptop, I couldn't meet her stare. "I want to. I do. But, with Ben still very much a part of my life, I can't put Preston in that situation again. I don't want to hurt him." I paused. It wasn't just that. "And I'm also a little terrified to take another chance on him. What if I let him back in and he decides he can't deal with the craziness of my world again?"

"He wouldn't do that. You're too important to him. I really hope you talk to him soon. He needs to hear from you. You could always be friends for a while." A wistful smile crossed her lips. "Just don't leave him hanging."

"I won't."

She sat up straight and nodded. "So, when can I expect the pieces?"

Behind her was a wall of pictures, much like my own. It made me smile and feel a tiny connection to her.

"I'm thinking I'll work on them over break and we can do a fitting in the new year, then go from there."

"Sounds perfect."

When we disconnected I leaned against the workroom table and opened my text thread with Preston. It didn't have to be perfect, but I did have to say something.

Me: Your Christmas present was beautiful. I didn't know you could draw like that. Thank you.

After a summer spent in high drama and being so self-absorbed by my life, I promised myself, if given the chance, I'd get to know him better. I packed up my stuff and was about to slip my cell in my pocket when it chimed.

Preston: I'm glad you liked it. I originally drew it to try to get you out of my mind. But it didn't work, in fact it did the exact opposite.

My stomach fluttered and tensed up. I sat back on my stool and started my reply only to delete it, then repeat the process over and over.

Me: When did you start drawing?
Preston: Ever since I was a kid. My dad never thought I'd make money at it. My mum always wanted me to try.
Me: Why didn't you?
Preston: I thought structural engineering would help more people, and I really do love it.

I sucked in a deep breath and ran a hand through my hair. I wanted to lay it all out for him, so he understood where I stood, but I knew I'd fumble my way through it. *I can do this.*

Me: I'm not sure how to say this . . .
Me: Right now, with my life the way it is, I can't be with anyone. Not while Ben and I are forced to fake a relationship.
Preston: Hmm, think I could be a friend?
Me: You are my friend.
Preston: Thank God.
Me: :)
Preston: And just to make sure, do you think we could hang out sometime as friends?
Me: I think that's a definite possibility.
Preston: That's perfect.
Preston: I'm glad we're talking again.
Preston: I've missed you.
Me: I've missed you too.

I put my phone away, picked up my stuff, and left the workroom. The smile on my face had everything to do with Preston.

Daisy sat on her bed, watching a Christmas movie on her tablet. We'd gotten a tiny tree and decorated it with mini paper chains and a single strand of twinkle lights. A couple presents to each other lay underneath. It wasn't much, but it added a bit of holiday festivity.

"Surprised you're not making out with Ethan right now."

She stuck her tongue out at me. "He's home with his family for Christmas."

"You must wish you were in Dublin."

She shook her head. "Even when my mum and my stepdad, Frank, aren't ditching my sister and me for a cruise, it's not that exciting. Mum always ends up in a row with her mum and two sisters. I'm not missing anything."

I plopped down beside her and grabbed a handful of popcorn from her bowl. "Well, I'm super glad you're here. It would've been lonely and creepy without you."

"Aw, I'm glad I'm here too."

"What's your sister doing?"

"She's spending it with her husband's family." She looked at me strangely. "You talked to Preston, didn't you?"

Nodding, I grabbed another handful. "After that gift, how could I not?"

"True. At least you're smiling. That's a good sign."

"We're gonna do the friend thing." I popped it piece by piece into my mouth.

She laughed. "Yeah, right. I'll believe that when I see it. The way you two look at each other is anything but just friendly."

I shook my head and looked away, trying to hide my smile. Preston and I definitely had some obstacles left to overcome, mainly if we could trust each other again. But at least we'd gotten back on the path. Hopefully it was the right one. And hopefully we could stay on it.

Chapter Thirty

Second Chances

History of Fashion exam now over, I stepped outside the lecture hall and took a deep breath. My brain was still on Christmas break. Whoever chose to do finals after the holidays was an idiot. Ethan told me at breakfast that it was something they were trying this year to see what the students thought. My thoughts? It sucked. Three weeks off and I felt like I'd forgotten a lot.

My phone buzzed and rattled against the wood top of my dorm room desk. I smiled at Marc's face staring at me and snatched it up. "Hey, how's it going?"

"You won."

My face scrunched in confusion. "What did I win?"

"The bet you didn't know we made." He chuckled. "Remember when we were talking about Dad and his girlfriend?"

"Yeah?"

"You called it."

I squeezed my eyes shut, a sudden headache throbbing. "Please tell me Dad isn't engaged."

"He apparently proposed at Christmas. The divorce isn't even near finalized yet."

My jaw dropped. Marc blew out a long breath.

"You okay?" His low voice made me ache for home.

"Um, I'm . . ." I shook my head. "You're serious? What . . . how . . . what did Mom say?"

He cleared his throat, sounding tired. "Just that she thinks he's an idiot. You might want to call her."

"I will. How's the divorce going?"

"They got into a big fight at the lawyer's office over him moving his . . . well, his new fiancée into the house. Dad lost it and ripped the front of Mom's dress. They had to call the cops. Mom's getting a restraining order, finally."

Standing, I paced the room. "I wish there was something I could do. God, I miss you and Mom so much." My voice faded in emotion.

"Well, what happens now is, we start a pregnancy pool. It's only a matter of time before we have a baby brother or sister."

I suppressed a shiver at the thought. "Just another life for Dad to screw up."

"Well, he's just so damn good at it."

A wry smile curled my lips as a thought popped into my head. "How did Grandma like the apartment?" Just the idea of Mom entertaining at Marc's place seemed crazy.

"You should've seen Aunt Tilly and Grandma, they were pissed. A couple glasses of wine and they were telling all these horrible stories about Dad. Neither of them ever really liked him. They thought he was too cocky the first time they met him. Complained that they didn't know why Mom couldn't see it."

"Well, Dad can turn on the charm when he wants to."

"True."

"And Gram's always hated how he treated us. She tried to get Mom to move in with her in Portland when we were younger."

"Really?" Marc sounded confused.

"Yup." Sighing, I rubbed the back of my neck, hoping to ease the stiffness. "What about you? How's school and the love life?"

"School's good, I'm working on a big project and keeping busy. Nothing really to report in the romance sector."

"Aw, really? No redheads?"

"Yeah, unfortunately not. What about you?"

I filled him in that Preston and I were talking again and starting over as friends. Marc and I hadn't been able to talk much when we'd FaceTimed at Christmas thanks to Grandma and Aunt Tilly.

"Hopefully he doesn't freak out again. I mean I kinda get it, but . . . I don't know. I just don't want to see you get hurt again."

"I'm being careful." Outside my window the wind kicked up, making the naked tree branches dance and shiver.

"Good. You know, I've been thinking about your situation. Dad's getting some seriously bad press here, what with his crazy behavior and all." Papers rustled in the background. "And Mom's turning into quite a hot commodity, everyone wants to work with her. From what I've heard, Dad's not in that position any more. People are refusing to work with him. I don't think he has any future projects lined up."

"Okay." My brows pulled together in confusion. "What are you getting at?"

"Think about it; he's not sticking to his end of the bargain. He's fighting Mom, moving his new girlfriend into our house, and just making things more difficult than they need to be. He actually had her car towed back to the house yesterday, saying it was his, even though it'd been a Christmas gift two years ago. He's hired people to follow her, and is just being an asshole. So, why are you going along with his game?"

I paused, trying to think of why. "'Cause I don't know how to end it. Or what he's got on Ben."

"Really?" He sounded like he couldn't believe what I was saying. "You haven't even the slightest idea why Ben's going along with this?"

"Okay, Mr. Sarcasm, clearly you know something I don't, spill it."

Marc, sighed. I could just picture him running his hand through his floppy dark locks. "Ben's . . . well, at least *I think*, he's probably not interested in the same kind of people I'm interested in, if you catch what I'm saying."

"Wait, are you saying he's gay?"

"Duh, Mags."

How had I never considered this as a possibility? "But, he's kissed me. A lot."

"Right . . . he's still an actor, Mags. He knows how to turn it on for the cameras."

I was silent a few moments, processing his words. "What should I do?"

"Stop putting your world and your life at risk for Dad's. Don't play his game any more."

We hung up and I leaned against the creaky chair back, my brain a mess of thoughts. *Could Ben be gay?* That time he'd met Andrew, I thought I'd detected a little something between them; maybe it was a spark. Maybe if he *was* gay I could set them up? I shook my head, needing to focus. *How do I stop playing the game?*

The night before classes started up again, Ben had texted me. He was attending Dad's movie premiere and wanted to make arrangements to go together. I was dreading it. Dad would probably be there.

My gaze traveled across the room, thinking of all the work still to be done. In my wardrobe was a garment bag filled with goodies for Evie. I needed to do a fitting on her. Maybe a trip into Oxford was in order. If I did that this weekend I could easily get it finished up. Somehow I had to squeeze that in *and* Ben's premiere.

I pulled out my phone to call Ben. *Wham!* I jumped as the door to our room flew open and slammed against the wall. In came Ethan and Daisy, pressed together, kissing fervently. He pushed her against the wall, his hands wound in her pale pink hair.

I cleared my throat and they broke apart, guilty smiles on their faces. "Hi, guys. I'm here."

"Hey . . . sorry, Mags." Daisy blushed prettily and covered her lips with a hand. She looked up at Ethan and giggled. They started whispering to each other, then slowly backed out the door with a wave.

It was sweet, how into each other they were. It made me think of Preston and me. The time in his car when he dropped me off after our punting trip. It'd been so perfect. The way his lips felt pressed to mine and how his hands curled in my hair. I let out a shaky breath, the memories too real.

God, I miss kissing him.

With a shake to clear my thoughts, I shot a quick text to Evie.

Me: Can we do a fitting soon? Saturday? I can come to you or would you prefer to come here?
Evie: Do you mind running into Oxford? Saturday morning works for me.
Me: I might have a Ben thing in the evening, but if we're early enough it should work.
Evie: 10:00?
Me: Sounds good. Where should I meet you?
Evie: My dorm isn't a very good place. Edmund's flat would be perfect. I'll text you the address.

It was strange to think of a duchess living in a dorm room. I would've pictured her in a fancy house. Then again, I wouldn't expect a prince to have a flat share either.

Me: I've got it, I'll see you then.

Of course I had the address. He's Preston's flatmate.

• • •

I stepped off the train and made my way to the busy streets of Oxford. Wanting to take my time to get there, I decided to skip the cab. *I wonder what she'll pay me for these?* Glancing to the garment bags draped over my arm, I smiled. This would be my first paying gig. Hopefully, more would come.

Mental checklist in my head, I ran through it to make sure I had everything. Pins, thread, needles, more embellishments, measuring tape, small pair of scissors, notebook . . . all checked off. I should be set.

But I wasn't.

As I neared their flat my gait slowed. *There's a chance he might not even be there.* But what if he was? I nibbled my bottom lip, stressing over something that might not even happen. *We're friends, it's cool.* At least that's what I kept telling myself.

No matter how much I tried to convince myself that I was ready, in reality I knew I was nowhere near it. One look from his brown eyes and I'd turn into a mushy mess, thinking only about his lips and kissing them.

Just around the corner from my destination I paused, my nerves in tangles. As I peeked around the side of the building, the front door opened and two of his friends came out. One I remember had poured my coffee the morning after I'd crashed there, Marissa. The other, her girlfriend . . . I drew a blank on her name.

I straightened myself up and adjusted my wool duffle jacket in case they came my way. Sure enough, they rounded the corner and saw me. Marissa waved and leaned in to say something to the girl with the black bob. Now if only I could ask them if Preston was home. Would that be too obvious?

"Maggie, why are you still out here?"

My brain tried to scrabble up a response, but nothing popped to mind. A panicky sensation worked its way up my throat until the truth burbled out. "Just prepping myself to go in." Then a thought hit me and I smiled, probably too big. "Making sure I have everything."

The girl with the dark bob grinned and looked up at Marissa, then turned her gaze back to me. "He's home."

A wall of nerves hit me and I stuffed my free hand in my pocket, grasping the small heart-shaped rock I'd picked up a few moments ago. "Oh." I looked between them, exhaling as my shoulders slumped. "I'm not even going to pretend I don't know what you're talking about. Thanks for the heads up."

Marissa reached over and squeezed my shoulder. "He's nervous too. You'll be just fine."

"I've known Preston for years, and I've never seen him this into anyone." The girl with the bob smiled at me and threaded her arm through Marissa's. "It's actually kind of nice to see him unnerved and not his super-confident self."

"You've definitely got him all sorts of topsy-turvy." Marissa grinned.

"Maybe we'll see you when we get back." Marissa's girlfriend pulled her down the path and I watched them leave.

Deep inhale, I turned and made my way to the front door. It was a couple minutes before ten, but I needed to get this over with. With a shaky hand, I squeezed my eyes shut and pushed the doorbell. The chimes sounded through the door, along with what sounded suspiciously like several sets of running footsteps.

The door pulled open and Evie's smiling face greeted me. "Maggie, come in, let me take your coat."

I stepped in, surprised to see no sign of Preston. Behind her on the stairs sat Prince Edmund, a knowing grin on his face.

Standing, he said, "Lovely to see you again, Maggie. Do you ladies need any help?"

Evie turned her head to him and shook it, mouthing something I couldn't see.

A guard with an earpiece stepped forward. "May I check your bags, miss?"

Nodding, I handed them over, wondering if I'd get a pat-down too.

While he began looking through the bags, I took off my jacket and scarf, Evie grabbed them from me and hung them up.

Edmund tucked his hands in his pockets and ambled his way toward his girlfriend and me. "Sorry about Sebastian, here. My brother's visiting and . . . well, he likes his entourage."

Evie lightly smacked his arm. "Be nice and go. Your brother is waiting for you." She turned to me. "Let's go upstairs. There's an extra bedroom we can use for the fitting."

"I'll leave you girls to it." Edmund disappeared around the corner toward the kitchen.

The guard quickly finished his search of my garment bags and satchel. With a curt nod, he handed them back to me. "Have a nice day, miss."

Nodding, I gathered my things and looked around, wondering where Preston was. *Is he avoiding me?* My stomach coiled in anxious knots. The idea of him hiding away in his room until I left made me feel sick. The front door held my escape just behind me. As soon as Evie started climbing the steps, I knew my window of opportunity had closed.

Hangers tight in my grip, I pulled my slipping messenger bag full of supplies back up on my shoulder and followed her. *Apparently I don't have to worry about seeing Preston after all.*

Knowing he was avoiding me was so much worse than not knowing if he was home.

Right now, I had to stay professional. I couldn't succumb to the tears burning the backs of my eyes. Evie opened the door to the spare room. Waiting inside was a tall, slender woman with long smooth blonde hair.

I looked to Evie, waiting for an introduction.

"Maggie, this is Edmund's sister-in-law, Princess Lauren. When she found out I was meeting with you today she begged me to let her come." She grinned at the graceful blonde. "You see, she of course saw my dress at the charity event and was hoping you could make something for her."

My lips formed a silent "o" and I nodded. This was the woman who would one day be the queen of England. I went over and shook her hand. "Of course, I'd be thrilled to design something for you . . . Y-your Highness."

"Please, call me Lauren." Her smile was warm and as soft as her voice.

"Okay, you guys can chat about ideas in just a bit. I'm dying to try on your new stuff." Evie rubbed her hands together, her green eyes twinkling.

I hung the bags inside the empty closet, then unzipped and slid off the protective covers. Evie and Lauren came forward and looked everything over. I held my breath waiting to hear what they thought. Never have I felt more vulnerable.

"Nothing's completely finished yet. I still have some cleaning up to do after I make sure everything fits perfectly."

Evie slipped into the black sheath dress. It fell to her knees. The piece was comprised of black lace over a flesh-colored under layer. Bead and sequin embellishments gave the appearance of modesty, even though they technically weren't needed. The jewel neckline went up to the base of her creamy throat and the long sleeves stopped at her wrists. Her pale skin peeked through the lace on her arms and chest. She looked incredibly beautiful.

"Let me pin up the bottom so I can hem it." I stuck a few pins between my lips, knelt down, and did a swift loop around her, pinning the fabric where I wanted it.

"Wow, the dress is really quite sexy, yet very elegant." Lauren looked down at me with a grin. "Philip would love this. Could you make me something similar? Maybe in a dark blue? Less lace?"

I nodded and jumped up to make a quick note. "Of course."

Lauren continued, "I know several women who'd love your style."

My heart flipped in my chest. *Several women? Is this seriously happening?*

Evie made her way through the pieces. Only minor adjustments were needed. She pulled the draped hoodie around her and smiled, rubbing it against her cheek. "Oh, I love this. The cashmere is so soft and cozy. I wish I could have it right now."

"I should be able to get them to you by the end of the week."

"That's awesome." She clapped her hands. "I can't wait. And we haven't really discussed payment. Should we do that now?"

I swallowed and nodded. I hadn't a clue what a just-starting-out designer should charge, especially since I was still in school. With a smile, and in a much higher voice than normal, I said, "Sure."

Footsteps stopped just outside the door. I froze mid-motion as I hung up the black dress.

Is that Preston?

Chapter Thirty-One

Plans Not Quite Set in Stone

Evie sat on the bed in the spare bedroom as I zipped the garment bags back up, a very satisfied smile on her face. My brain reeled from what they'd convinced me was a fair price for the pieces. It'd give me everything I needed for my final term of the year at Thrippletons.

Now I don't need Dad's money. I couldn't wait to give it all to Mom.

It was Lauren, Prince Philip's wife, who ultimately persuaded me when she said, "I've worked with numerous designers and your pieces are exquisite. You need to charge not only for your time and materials, but also for your talent. Soon, people will want to pay just so they can say they're wearing a Maggie original."

"You're too kind, and I sure hope you're right." I smacked my hand against my thigh. "Okay, if you guys think this is a fair price, then so be it."

Tape measure in hand, I took Princess Lauren's measurements, then jotted the numbers down just under where she'd scribbled her contact information. Evie excused herself while Lauren and I discussed what she was looking for. Sitting in a room with royalty felt beyond surreal. Celebrities were one thing; this was . . . incredible. Even though really, they weren't all that different.

Once I was all packed up, I grabbed Evie's pieces and started to leave. Under my excitement bubbled fissures of disappointment.

I swung the door open and nearly barreled into a very surprised-looking Preston.

Stomach somewhere in the vicinity of my knees, I took a couple steps back.

Lauren scooted around us. "I'll give you two a moment."

I broke eye contact to watch her leave, then glanced up. "Hi."

"Hey." His lips curled into a smile. "How'd it go?"

"Um, really good." I bobbed my head and tightened my grip on my bags, my legs a little wobbly.

"I never got a chance to congratulate you on winning the competition." He tucked his hands in his pockets and rolled his shoulders forward.

"Oh, yeah, thanks."

"I didn't realize it was you. Well, not until the night of the ball. Evie kept calling you Margaret so I didn't make the connection until I saw you . . . there."

I swallowed hard, nervous to talk to him. My mind flashed to the night of the gala and how he'd looked in his tux.

He gave me a grin. "You looked incredible."

"Thanks." I looked away as my cheeks flared with heat.

"I, um, I like the purple." He gestured to my streak. "Daisy got you to do it, huh?"

I chuckled and tossed my hair out of my face, my hands still full. "Yup. The three of us all have a little something."

Preston cleared his throat and shot a glance to the stairwell. "Look, I don't know if you'd be interested, but do you want to grab dinner? Just as friends."

Scrunching my face, I shook my head. "I can't. Dad's London premiere is tonight and Ben and I have to put in an appearance." My heart constricted as his smile faltered. "But . . . I think I might actually have a plan to put an end to this. I'll need Ben's help to pull it off, of course."

"Oh?" His brow furrowed as his gold-flecked eyes studied me.

Did I look different than he remembered?

"Walk me out and I'll tell you about it?"

"Here let me take those." He held out his hands for the garment bags and I gladly handed them over. Backing out of the room, he gestured to the staircase, letting me descend first. "So what are you thinking?"

"Well, both Ben and I hate how he's using us. Obviously. The big problem is, Dad's not keeping up his end of the bargain." I filled him in on all the drama he'd missed of Dad purposely doing things to make Mom's life hell.

Preston's eyes widened and with his free hand he pulled my coat from the closet and handed it to me before grabbing his own. "So, what's your plan?"

"Well, Marc tells me that Tinseltown isn't as enamored with our father as they used to be. In fact, Mom's gaining popularity and people are siding with her in this whole mess. Essentially, my dad's being blackballed. Marc says he's totally oblivious to it, though."

Preston paused at the door, his hand on the knob while I slipped into my jacket. "What are you going to do?"

"I've decided since he can back out on our deal, so can I. Tonight at his premiere Ben and I just might let the world know the truth about what he's forcing us to do."

Opening the door, he stepped out and walked down the stairs with me as I adjusted my chunky knit cowl, hoping he'd walk me to the train station so we could keep talking. I'd really missed his company.

"Has Ben agreed to this?" Tiny bits of snow started to fall as wind whipped around the corner we'd just turned.

"I haven't told him my idea yet, so I don't know. I figure even if Ben doesn't want to do it *that* way, we can come up with a way to use the press for our gain." I chuckled and side-glanced at Preston, who was watching me. "We could always stage a massive fight and break up, make sure the press get loads of photos and hear us arguing. Dad couldn't keep claiming we were a couple any more. I mean, he never stipulated we had to be a happy couple."

Preston smiled. "That might work. How's your mum and Marc doing with all this? Do they know?"

I shrugged and focused on the scuffed toe of my brown boots as we walked down the sidewalk. "Yeah, I told them. None of us are really speaking with Dad, and honestly, we're all doing really well. Better in fact than we ever did with him around."

"Was your father always like this?"

I shook my head. "Mom says he's not the same guy she fell in love with. He used to be really kind and funny. Then it was like a switch flipped."

"What do you think caused the change?"

"His fame." I shrugged, trying to brush it off, knowing I'd never fully be able to.

His lips curled. "I'll admit, I was surprised when you told me he was your dad. And shocked that you'd be friends with someone like Ben Chambers."

I eyed him warily. "What's that supposed to mean?"

"Well, they're both huge celebrities, and yet you're so down-to-earth. I'd never have guessed you got to hang out with movie stars."

The corners of my lips twitched. "Imagine my surprise when I found out your best friend is a prince and you hang out with a duchess."

"Touche, but it's not quite the same."

Wasn't it? Celebrities were basically America's version of royalty. Both Evie and I were fated by our genetics to be in the public eye. I certainly never had an option, and I imagined Evie didn't either.

Preston ran a hand through his hair, making his blond waves stick up in odd, but charming, spiky peaks. I had to stop myself from reaching out to straighten them.

Just ahead of us the train station loomed. "You're right, Ben could fade from the limelight, but your friends will be in their roles presumably until they die."

"What are you doing tomorrow?" He stopped walking, as if buying us more time.

"Um." I shook my head. "Probably just working and hanging out with Andrew and Daisy. Why?"

"What if I were to drive into Bampton and pick you up for lunch? Dinner?"

Nibbling my bottom lip, I nodded. "Be there at seven and I might be able to get dinner with you. Andrew may want to tag along as my bodyguard though."

"Yeah, he doesn't like me much, does he?"

I opened the heavy glass door and took a step inside. "He's definitely not your biggest fan."

"Then it'll be my goal to win him over." Reaching out, he held the door for me and passed the garment bags back, our hands grazing on the exchange.

Shyly I looked down, feeling butterflies at his touch.

"See you tomorrow." He waved and waited for me to leave.

"Tomorrow. But you have to promise me something."

He shrugged. "Anything."

"I want to know more about you and your family. I realized that all summer I was so caught up with the chaos in my life that I never really got to know much about you, and I feel bad."

His lips turned up into a smile. "You can ask me anything you want. I'm pretty much an open book."

• • •

The premiere was over and Ben sat across from me in the modern sushi restaurant, looking tired. I took a sip of my hot tea and leaned back against the black vinyl booth. The spots from the camera flashes had finally disappeared from my vision. Dad had been there and totally in his element. He schmoozed the press and made sure he got pictures with his arms around Ben and me. Luckily his fiancée hadn't come with him.

The only silver lining was I got to wear one of my own creations and got asked about it several times throughout the evening. Dad hadn't been pleased, which was a definite added bonus.

"I'm sorry I couldn't call him out at the premiere." Ben twirled his napkin around a pointer finger and sighed.

I shook my head. "No, don't apologize. I don't know what he's holding over you, and your name and career are wrapped up in his movie. I get it, I do."

He nodded with a weak smile. "So, your other plan, stage a fight and break up. Do you think it'll really work?"

"It's worth a try, isn't it? We can use the press, just like he has. You can't be his daughter and not learn a thing or two."

Ben shrugged. "He'll retaliate. He'll tell the world my secret and he'll make your mom miserable."

Scoffing, I said, "He's already doing that to my mom. He *never* held up his part of the bargain with me."

He took a drink from his water glass and cleared his throat before looking away. "He has with me."

"Would it really be so terrible if people knew you were . . . gay?" I probably shouldn't have said it, but we needed to end this. And frankly, I was getting sick of his runaround.

Ben's eyes widened. He leaned over the table and frantically whispered, "How did you know that?"

"It was a guess."

He closed his eyes and rubbed his forehead. "I'm actually bi. My last serious relationship was with a woman. But just before this all started," he gestured between the two of us, "I was seeing a man who I thought might be the one. But, as you know, he couldn't deal with this little situation of ours and called things off."

"Why don't you just come out?" I picked up an avocado roll with my chopsticks and popped it into my mouth.

He scoffed. "It's not as easy as you think. Yes, the world is way more tolerant, but it's still . . . it can ruin a career. I've seen it happen. My agent doesn't think it's a good time, and all the studios I've worked with have agreed. Especially since I tend to get cast as the romantic lead. And really, it isn't anyone's business who I love and choose to be with."

"Why didn't you just tell me?"

"I guess I was scared of your reaction. I've lost some friends and family members as I've gradually come out."

I shook my head and reached across the table to grab his hand. "You are who you are; who you love doesn't change that. I'll always be your friend."

"Thanks, Maggie." His blue eyes looked suspiciously watery.

"I'll understand if you don't want to go through with my plan. Maybe we can find another way to get out of this."

He pushed around a piece of rice with his chopstick. "Can I think about it? Coming out on such a massive scale is a pretty big decision to make."

My eyes widened. "Oh my goodness, of course you can. But can I say one thing?" I continued at his nod. "If you do it of your own volition, you'd never have anyone trying to use it as leverage to make you do something you don't want to do."

"I know." His voice was soft and sad. Clearing his throat, he gave me a weak smile. "Enough about me. What happened with that guy you were seeing?"

"Preston? We tried to stick it out, but it just got to be too much. His family and friends saw the pictures and he couldn't explain it. It was too hard."

Closing his eyes, he shook his head. "I'm guessing he didn't like that I've gotten to kiss you so much either."

I wrinkled my nose. "Yeah, not really."

"This is such a mess. When it's over, do you think you'll try to get back together?"

"We'll see. I mean, I'd like to, but what if he ditches me again when something gets tough?"

"Good luck with that." He chuckled and ate a tuna roll.

"Meaning?" I sipped my small cup of hot tea, enjoying the warmth as it slid down my throat.

"Consider your family. I'm sure your dad's going to be an issue for you for the rest of your life. At the very least, the rest of his."

I blew out a heavy breath. "That's exactly what I'm worried about."

"Look at it this way. You're a very sweet, attractive, intelligent woman. If Preston can't cut it, you'll have no trouble finding a guy who can stay with you through whatever your dad throws at him."

I shook my head and chuckled. "That's sweet of you to say, but I think you're full of it. Never in my life has that happened."

"No?" He cocked his head to the side. "Just this summer you had your Preston and me interested in you."

Scoffing, I looked him straight in the eye. "You were only interested in me because my father told you to be."

"That's not true." He shook his head, his lips curling in a crooked smile. "I was very interested in you. I got the impression that you didn't feel the same. Especially after our first kiss, in the greenhouse. I felt something; you didn't."

• • •

Seven on the dot, Preston knocked on the door to my dorm. Andrew jumped up from my bed, straightened his button-down and opened the door. I closed my laptop and struggled to fill my lungs. I spun in my desk chair just in time to watch their greeting.

"Hey, Andrew, how's it going?" Preston offered a hand, which Andrew ignored.

Andrew gave a grunt. "Preston, oh yay. I hear we're all getting dinner tonight." He leaned close and whispered with menace, "Just know this, I don't think this is a good idea. I still hold that you don't deserve her."

Preston nodded. "She's too amazing for me to just give up on. If she'll give me another chance, I bloody well intend to take it. I never meant to hurt her or make an enemy out of you. But I'm glad she has someone like you on her side, especially when idiots like myself leave the spot vacant."

Andrew stood stock still and eyed Preston. Clasping him on the shoulder he pulled him into my room. "Hurt her again, there's no coming back. Understood?"

Preston grinned. "Understood."

"So where are we going?" Andrew yanked me up off my chair.

"Anywhere but sushi."

"Don't like sushi?" Preston asked. He grabbed my heavy peacoat off the bottom of my bed and held it for me to slip my arms into.

"Ben and I went last night. I'm sushi'd out."

Preston took a step back and glanced at his hands. "How was that? Is your plan a go?"

I shrugged. "He's not sure. Dad's threatening him with some pretty heavy stuff. I'll know in the next couple days."

"I wonder what your dad will think of this kink in his plans." Andrew checked his reflection in the mirror, smoothing out the sides of his dark hair before grabbing a can of hairspray off Daisy's vanity to help solidify the height he had going on.

Heading toward the door, I wrapped my octopus scarf around my neck. "I couldn't care less what he thinks. I hope it royally screws things up for him."

Preston opened the door and out we went. Daisy and Ethan came scrambling down the hallway. Her lipstick smeared on Ethan's face.

"You weren't thinking of going without us, were you?" she hollered.

"Never." Andrew motioned to Ethan to wipe off his face, which he quickly did.

Daisy reached up and ran a finger around her lips. "Where are we going?"

Preston came up behind me. The warmth of his body seeped through the back of my jacket and I closed my eyes, loving the sensation. In that moment I didn't want to be just friends. *Only a little longer.*

Chapter Thirty-Two

Set Free

Preston sat next to me at the pub that Daisy and Andrew finally settled on after much arguing. The wooden table was laden with yummy foods and drinks. I opted for a mushroom burger and chips. Well, they were fries, really. I took a sip from my glass and turned to Preston, who gave me a grin. Wiping my lips, I decided it was time to get to know him better.

"So, tell me about your family."

"Okay, um . . ." He chuckled. "Well, you already know what they all do, what do you want to know?"

"What was your childhood like?"

He shrugged. "I grew up in Derbyshire; Matlock, actually. Pretty normal childhood, really. We had a small cottage and a garden that my mum loved. It wasn't until my father came into an unexpected inheritance that things really changed."

"Unexpected inheritance?" I dipped a fry in ketchup and took a bite, intrigued.

He wiped at the corner of his lips and swallowed his mouthful. "Yeah, a great-uncle my father never knew about died. I guess there was a long-standing family feud between my grandfather and his older brother. So, long story short, this great-uncle had no children and all his estate and wealth reverted to our side of the family. My father was an only child, so he got it all."

"Wow." I chuckled. "That must've been a pleasant surprise."

Andrew chimed in. "Now if only I had a rich uncle who'd leave me everything, I could quit school and start doing what I really want to do."

"Oh? And what's that?" Preston asked.

"Start my own label. This school hasn't taught me anything I don't already know."

I shook my head at Andrew's cockiness and turned my attention back to Preston. "Did your life change much after the inheritance?"

He raised a shoulder. "I was about sixteen at the time, so I got sent to a prestigious boarding school, that's actually where I met Edmund. Soon after that my family sold the cottage and moved to London. It was closer to Dad's job. Mum made some pretty high-society friends. Then, after a time, one particular woman pretty much forced her out. All her friends followed the example. That was kind of the start, at least that I can remember, when she really started struggling with her depression."

"That's awful."

"Our family rallied around her and have always looked out for each other. She's got new friends now through her various charities she volunteers for, so that's good. But honestly, her depression comes and goes." He grabbed his pint and took a gulp.

I glanced over to Daisy and Ethan. They were feeding each other, completely ignoring the rest of us.

Andrew crossed his eyes and stuck out his tongue, pretending to choke himself.

Leaning away from Daisy, Andrew steadied his attention on us. "Well, I think you'd be hard-pressed to find a family as screwed up as Maggie's, here."

"Probably true." I sighed and shook my head. "I got a text from my dad the other day, telling me to start wearing loose clothing, especially when I'm around Ben. He actually wants the world to think I'm pregnant."

Preston's brows drew together and he opened his mouth to reply, but Andrew beat him to the punch. "That's just sick."

"I know, right?" I took a bite of my burger.

Daisy giggled and leaned into Ethan. They were so lost in each other. A pang of jealousy washed through me and I shot a glance at Preston. My teeth tugged at my lip. I wanted that with him. What wouldn't I give to have the Ben situation resolved so that I could finally move on.

"So, Preston . . ." Andrew cleared his throat and sawed off another bite of his steak. "How'd you and the prince become friends?"

A smile crossed Preston's face. "We were in the same dorm, neighbors actually. One night he was coming back from a disastrous date and was trying to get in, but couldn't find his key. There were a few paparazzi around snapping pics and I happened to be leaving the commons area when he saw me and knocked. I let him in and we've been friends ever since."

"So, you've got to tell us, do you think he's going to marry the duchess?" Andrew's eyebrows lifted, ready for juicy gossip.

"Um, well . . ." Preston paused, one corner of his mouth tweaking into a crooked grin. "Let's just say I wouldn't be surprised."

Andrew set his fork down and smirked. "That means you don't know."

I bit my lip and held back a chuckle. Andrew could be tactless when he wanted information.

"I wouldn't say that." Preston sat back and took a drink.

"Ugh, you're killing me." Andrew propped his chin on his hand. I could tell that he was warming up to Preston again, which I was glad for.

Preston chuckled. "Sorry, mate."

A phone chimed at the table; it wasn't mine. Daisy roused from her oblivion and pulled hers from her purse. "Not mine."

Preston reached and pulled his phone from his pocket. He illuminated the screen and frowned. "Can you guys excuse me a second? I need to um . . . get this."

Before anyone could reply, he was up and heading to the door, phone to his ear. It sounded like he'd said "dad" before he was out of earshot. My gaze lingered on him, hoping everything was okay.

"That was weird." Ethan sat, arm slung around Daisy.

"You look worried," Daisy said to me, snuggling into her boyfriend.

I shrugged, watching for him to come back. "His voice sounded, I don't know, kind of odd."

Andrew smirked and shook his head. "Hmm, looks to me like you're still in love with that boy."

My eyes narrowed and I shot him a look. "Who said I was ever in love with him?"

"Oh, lovey, anyone who saw you together or heard you talk about him would know. I think the only person in the dark about it was you."

Daisy leaned toward Andrew and bobbed her head in agreement. "He's so right. You were totally gone over him from the first moment I met you."

My gaping mouth closed with a soft pop. I hadn't realized I'd been so transparent. Before all this drama had gone down I thought there might've been a possibility for the L-word, but now . . . okay, yes even now. Even when he'd called things off, through all that hurt, my heart had been his. I just needed to be sure he'd be there for me. That I could trust him before I fully acted on these feelings.

From the front of the restaurant Preston hurried toward our table, glancing at his watch, his hair a mess of pieces poking out haphazardly. When he reached the table, he pulled out his wallet and tossed down a chunk of cash, enough to cover the whole meal.

"I've got to run. It's a family emergency . . . it's my mum." His gaze latched on to mine, his eyes worried. "I'm so sorry."

"Ohmigod, no. Go." I shook my head. "Take care of your family. We can walk back; it's not that far."

Andrew, Daisy, and Ethan all nodded in agreement.

"Thank you." He looked to everyone, then turned to me. "I'll call you."

"Um, can I walk you out?" When he nodded, I turned to the group. "I'll be right back."

Preston led the way outside and to his vehicle. He ran his hand through his hair again, then rubbed the back of his neck. "I'll call when I can, I promise."

I reached out and put my hand on his arm. "I hope she'll be okay. You drive careful."

He looked at me like he wanted to say something, but stopped. Instead, he placed his hand over mine and squeezed. "Thank you."

Leaning in, he gave me a quick peck on my cheek. My fingers knotted together as he hopped into the car and gave me a wave before he drove off. A shiver coursed through me. I'd left my coat inside and only had a light sweater on over my robot T-shirt.

Back at the table, Daisy and Ethan were whispering and chuckling. From the looks of it I was probably getting kicked out of my room tonight. Andrew, on the other hand, was looking everywhere but at the two of them.

"Is everything okay?" he asked.

Shrugging, I shook my head. "I don't know. He said he'd call later."

My phone pinged and I grabbed it from my bag.

Ben: My phone's been hacked. Our secret's out.

• • •

My phone trilled out an incoming call. The last two days it'd rung incessantly. I grabbed it off the bed and checked the caller ID to make sure it wasn't Preston, then sent the call to voicemail, intending to go back to my sketches for Lauren.

"I don't want to talk to you. Stop calling me," I growled at my cell.

"More press?" Daisy turned her head away from her armoire to look at me. She had a hot date with Ethan she was getting ready for. She'd also recolored her hair. It was still pink, just much brighter.

"Who else?" The press were camped outside Thrippletons, waiting for me to make an appearance, which I hadn't. Never in my life had I experienced anything of this magnitude. I was at the center of a Hollywood scandal. And everyone wanted to talk to me. It was overwhelming.

To make matters worse, I still hadn't heard from Preston and I was worried. I hadn't texted him aside from a quick "I hope you're okay," because I didn't know what he was dealing with and I didn't want to interfere, but my good intentions were slowly crumbling.

"Arsehole press." Daisy grumbled and went back to rummaging. "Ugh, I have nothing to wear."

Thumbing through my contacts, I dialed Mom. It only rang once before she picked up.

"Maggie, sweetie, what's wrong? Are you okay?" The worried note in her voice brought a soft smile to my lips.

"I'm fine. I just wanted to call and see how you're doing."

"Probably better than you are." Just talking to her calmed my nerves.

Shrugging, I sighed. "I'm doing okay."

"Has Ben figured out how they hacked into his phone?"

"He didn't understand it enough to explain it to me, but basically they got to it somehow through the cloud. A lot of celebrities were targeted. Even Dad, I think."

She sighed. Marc's voice echoed a greeting in the background. "I'll tell you one thing, this has killed your father's career. People can't believe he'd use his own daughter like this. This coming on the heels of the world discovering he was abusive was just too much."

A huge part of me was pleased to hear it. Another, the small part that wished he'd been a normal father, hated he'd made such a mess for himself.

"Are you going to give an interview to anyone?" Mom asked.

"Right now I haven't a clue. I really don't want to do it. It feels like such an invasion of my life. I don't want to be known as the girl whose dad prostituted her out."

"It's such a mess. Maybe you and Ben should do an interview together."

One eyebrow rose. "We actually talked about that. But I think he's kinda scared to. He's not sure if Dad's going to out his secret. So he wants to be careful."

"I wish I knew what to do."

"It's okay." I sat up and adjusted my pillow behind me. "How's the divorce coming?"

She scoffed. "Slowly. Although, with all this it might play in my favor. Perhaps I could at least get my accounts unfrozen."

"Are you strapped for cash?"

She sighed and I could almost picture her running a hand through her dark hair and shaking it to flow behind her. "I have been since I filed for divorce. Your father cut me off, of course, and froze all our joint accounts. Apparently, the money I made working on his films he feels is his. Lovely, huh?"

Typical jerky behavior I'd expect from him.

I could make things easier for her. Thanks to Evie and Lauren, I didn't need Dad's money, not even for tuition. That meant I had quite a lot of cash stashed away. I'd always intended to give it to Mom, but I wanted to wait for her to get separate accounts set up that Dad couldn't touch or freeze. "You've got your own accounts set up now, right?"

"I do, but they're still under scrutiny until the divorce finalizes."

"Hmm." I bit my bottom lip and tucked my hair behind my ears. "You know Dad gave me money for school, well . . . to bribe me to date Ben, right?"

"Yeah?"

"I have a bunch saved up and I want you to have it. I always intended to give it to you. I just wanted to find a way that Dad either wouldn't find out or make sure he wasn't able to touch it."

"How much are you talking about, Mags?"

Sucking in a breath, I blew it out. "About three hundred and fifty thousand dollars."

Mom was silent, undoubtedly processing my words.

"Mom?"

A whoosh of air crackled in my earpiece before she said, "I really appreciate the thought, Mags, but I can't let you do that. The money is yours. You dated Ben. You put your world and the people you love at stake. This is your money. Use it to start your label. I've got work and I'm getting paid. I just can't access it easily. But I'm making do. And best of all, I'm happy. This will be over before we know it."

"I don't know if I'll even *have* a career after all this. Who's going to want to buy a dress from the girl with the psycho pimp for a father?"

With a laugh she said, "You'd be surprised. Especially if you give interviews, you might be able to swing this to your advantage."

"Huh, I never thought of that. It's kinda brilliant."

• • •

Curled in bed, lights off, my mind whirled uncontrollably. Daisy was off with Ethan; presumably they'd decided to cut me a break and use his room for once. So, I was alone with my thoughts. My jumbled, confused thoughts.

Preston had texted me earlier to let me know his mom was okay, but I still didn't know what happened. What I really wanted was to talk to him. I picked up my phone and pulled up his number, my finger hovering over the Call button. Chickening out, I tossed it next to me. I didn't know what he was dealing with and I didn't want to disturb him.

As if he read my thoughts, a text pinged in from him.

Preston: I just saw the news. You okay?
Me: Um, lol, that's kind of a tricky question right now. You?
Preston: I'm breathing. That's about all I can hope for.
Me: Can you tell me what's going on?

His response didn't come as swift as the others and I'd wondered if I'd crossed a line in my curiosity. I set my phone aside, nervous he wouldn't reply. An exhale of relief left my lips when my phone chimed.

Preston: Can I call you?
Me: Of course!

The phone rang and Preston's deep voice was on the other end. "Hey."

"Hey." I pushed the covers off as a wave of heat hit me.

"So, um, that night I was with you, the call I got was from my dad. He'd been at work and when he came home . . ." His voice sounded tight and strained. "Um, my mum had overdosed with sleeping pills. He called me from the hospital in a panic. Hal and I rushed into London to be with her. That's where I'm still at, actually."

"Oh, Preston, I'm so sorry."

"The doctors are trying a new med combination to manage her depression. Her sister, my aunt who lives in Scotland, is coming to stay for a while so Haley and I can get back to work and school."

"Is she going to be okay?"

He cleared his throat. "She is, and that's all that matters. So tell me about you. I could really use something to get my mind off everything."

Inhaling a sharp breath, I caught him up. "My mom thinks I should do some interviews."

"I think you should do whatever you're comfortable with." A creak sounded on his side of the line and a soft groan left his lips. I wondered if he was lying down.

I laid back on my pillow. "I'm leaning toward doing them."

"So, this means the Ben thing is over, right?"

Maybe it was his voice or maybe it was simply the question, but a small tingle coursed over my skin. "Yeah. We're officially just friends."

"And are you . . . happy about it?"

Snickering, I nodded. "I am. It's a relief. I feel like I finally have my life back."

I knew the situation he was in was horrible, and this wasn't the time to talk about us, but it didn't stop me from wanting to. Nibbling my lip, I waited for him to speak.

"Well, I'm glad things are looking up for you." He paused and a sudden worry hit me.

What if he's changed his mind again?

"Thanks." My voice came out soft.

He cleared his throat. "I don't know when I'll be in Bampton next. I've got to play catch-up with school."

"No, it's okay, I get it. Next time I'm in Oxford I'll get in touch." My heart fluttered. "I hope your mom starts feeling better soon. And I hope you don't have to put up with Tanner while your aunt's there."

Chuckling, he said, "No, he's away at school, thank goodness."

We hung up and I can't explain why, but a gray mental haze descended on me. I couldn't shake the feeling that we were drifting apart. *Maybe I should've told him I wanted to be with him?*

Chapter Thirty-Three

Into the Unknown

I clasped my shaking hands together in my lap as I sat in a short-backed, cushioned chair. Ben sat in an identical one at my side, looking relaxed. We couldn't be more opposite. I really didn't want to do this interview, especially since it was live. But at least Dad wouldn't be here. It's why we'd gone with Bianca Wilder. She was the journalist celebrities flocked to when they needed to get the story straight. But our main reason was she hadn't mentioned Dad being a part of the deal.

Two large cameras pointed at us from different angles. The pristine set was a hotel room made to look light and airy. The overcast London weather gave a soft glow through the white sheers hanging from the window.

"All right you two, we go live in just a few moments," Bianca announced. "This'll be simple. We'll just go through what happened, the allegations, and what your plans are now. It'll be painless, I promise."

I nodded and Ben looked to me, his eyes asking if I was okay. With an infinitesimal bob of my head, I blew out a pent-up breath.

Bianca sat across from us on the matching couch and sat a small stack of notecards on a mirrored table before a makeup artist touched up her lip gloss.

"Okay, let's do this." She smiled.

Ben and I exchanged a quick glance. I sat up straighter and smoothed the front of the navy blue sheath dress I'd made for the occasion.

Bianca intro'd the live show and posed the first question to Ben and the next several after, mostly about what it was like working for my father. I sat there, nerves ratcheting up, not wanting to have my private life so exposed.

"Now, Maggie, your father's abuse is becoming widely known as more and more celebrities and crew members come forward with allegations of his mistreatment of them. What was he like to grow up with?"

I inhaled a sharp breath. "Well, my brother and I learned from a very young age not to cross him. If even one of us got in trouble, it'd trickle through to the rest of us." I paused, pulling my thoughts together, then continued to give a little more insight into what our home life was like.

Our interviewer nodded, a pensive look on her face. "What were your first thoughts when he approached you with his plan for you both to fake a relationship?"

Ben answered first. "I was surprised. I mean, we've all heard rumors and rumblings of co-stars dating each other solely for the publicity of the movie they're in, but I've never experienced that. And I certainly didn't expect him to have me date his daughter."

"Had you two met before this?"

I shook my head. "Well, I met him at the beginning of the shoot and we hung out as friends."

"Do you think there could've been something more there had your father not pushed you together?" Bianca's eyes took me in, a small quirk to her lips.

"I don't know." I shrugged and glanced at Ben. *Do I mention Preston?* "I guess I just never really looked at him that way." My gaze darted to the doorway, wishing this was over.

She laughed. "You might be the only girl alive who wouldn't look at Ben Chambers like that."

Ben smiled and crossed a leg over the other. I just shrugged with a grin, as if to say, you're probably right.

"Were you both single when this started?"

"No," Ben answered for us.

"Really? Interesting. That must've caused problems."

Did it ever.

Ben smiled. "It did, but that's the past."

"So, Maggie, how did you feel about your dad asking you to date Ben?" Bianca adjusted her position, watching me.

"He didn't ask me. He told me. Or . . . really . . . he threatened me. I just couldn't believe my own father would want me to do something like that. I felt trapped . . . and ashamed and embarrassed."

We spent the next hour recapping the experience and reliving the whole ordeal in every little painful detail.

"What was his reasoning for blackmailing you two?"

"He'd lost funding and the studio refused to do any publicity for our movie, *The Moons of Angalside*. So he was using us to entice the press to get coverage."

"That doesn't seem like a very good reason to go to such extremes." Bianca looked between us. "Now, we know that Maggie went along with everything to protect her mother, but Ben, can you explain why you agreed to this?"

Ben inhaled deeply; his eyes darted to me and back. "I'd rather not. But, what I would like to do today is announce my plans to retire from acting."

Way to go Ben! That was one hell of a redirection.

"Retire?" Bianca's head tilted to the side, her short blonde bob swaying with the motion. "Why would you retire when you're at the pinnacle of your career?"

"There's several reasons. I have other passions that I'd like to pursue. And quite frankly, this whole experience has shown me how very un-Hollywood I am."

She inquired about his new direction and he evaded, saying he needed time to get everything sorted first.

Picking up her cards, she flipped to the next one and smiled.

"Now, I have a bit of a . . ." She looked up as if searching for the right word. "Curve ball, you might say."

A burst of nerves coursed through me and my palms began to itch. I glanced behind the camera crew and sucked in a sharp breath.

No. Why is he here?

I couldn't look away from my father.

"Okay." Ben sounded wary; he obviously hadn't spotted him.

"We have Scott McKendrick here." Bianca's gaze settled on me as I tore my eyes from the devil on the sidelines.

I sat back, trying to act calm, but inside everything was exploding. Dad stepped forward and joined Bianca on the couch, a smile on his freshly shaven face.

"Mr. McKendrick, we're delighted you could join us."

One camera followed Dad's movements while the other stayed glued on Ben and me, trying to capture our reaction. I kept my face straight, with no outward signs of distress.

My eyes settled on my father in his flashy dark suit. His blue eyes met mine and a small sneer curled his lips.

Bianca led Dad through the retelling from his perspective as Ben and I sat there watching the spectacle.

"I was desperate, what else can I say. If I'd thought it through more, I wouldn't have used my own daughter or played Ben's sexuality against him."

Ben flinched in his seat and a fury of anger unleashed inside me.

"Wait, what did you just say?" Bianca leaned forward.

"That I'd do it differently if I could." He looked solemn.

"No, about Ben?" she persisted.

"Oh . . . how awkward." A faint smile played at the edges of his lips. "Oh, Ben, I must sincerely apologize. I'd thought you'd come out recently."

Ben sucked in a breath and opened his mouth to speak, only to close it again.

Leaning forward, I shook my head. "You are unbelievable and *so* fake. What, you didn't get your way and your life is crumbling so now you have to take others with you? How dare you!"

"Calm down, Margaret."

"No. I won't calm down," I shouted. "You no longer have any control over me. You lost that a long time ago. I'm not afraid of you anymore. Why don't you crawl back to your fiancée and leave the rest of us alone? Mom, Marc, and I, we're all so much better without you. No one wants you."

"Stupid girl, that's what you think. I'm untouchable. My name alone sells tickets and fills seats. Studios won't give that up. No matter what I do." He leaned his arms on his knees, closing the gap between us.

"Right, which is why your last film did so stellar."

"It's early days," he barked at me. "Plus, I've plans to open my own studio."

A scoff left my throat. "Oh, good luck with that. Tell me, are you planning on starring, writing, producing, and directing everything from now on?"

Bianca's wide-mouthed stare followed the volley between us. I glanced to Ben and saw that he'd regained his composure, his mouth now a tight line.

Reaching out, Dad clutched my arm in a painful grip and growled. "You're just like your mother. Don't know when to shut up."

"Oh, this interview is gonna do wonders for your image." Reaching up, I grabbed his hand, taking it off me. "Don't ever touch me again." My eyes never left his. "Better yet, don't ever talk to me again." I wanted to hit him, but I didn't dare. "I'm done here."

Standing, I walked behind the camera and yanked off my mic. My hands shook as I handed it over to the sound guy, who gave me a reassuring smile.

"So, um, Ben . . ." Our interviewer struggled to regain control of this live situation gone awry. "Would you care to address what Scott has just revealed?"

Ben smiled and stood, unclipping his mic pack from the back of his pants. "Why the hell not." He laughed. "I'm bi. Big fucking deal. See ya later." Strolling my way, he tossed his mic where I'd just dropped mine off. "Let's get out of here."

I laced my hand with Ben's and we left the fancy suite at the swanky hotel.

"It's over." He grinned down at me.

I returned the smile. "That actually felt pretty damn good."

• • •

My heavy feet clomped up the staircase, dragging my drained body to my room. Ben and I'd grabbed dinner and parted ways as good friends. Hopefully, this whole debacle was finally and completely finished.

I couldn't stop wondering if Preston saw the interview. Would it change anything if he had? I knew he was still dealing with family stuff and busy, but I was worried about where we stood.

Lost in my thoughts and not paying attention, I nearly ran into Mr. Walker.

"Miss McKendrick, you're coming in awfully late, aren't you?"

"Just getting back from London, sir."

"That's right, the interview. How did it go?"

"Okay."

"Well, I couldn't sleep, so I decided to go for a walk. Try to clear my mind." He straightened his gray suit coat. "Since you're here, I do have something I've been meaning to speak with you about."

"Oh?" I gave a longing glance down the hallway toward my room, so not wanting to talk to him right now.

"I've been receiving calls about you."

My face scrunched in confusion. "Calls? About me?" Was it the press?

"Yes, it would seem the Duchess of Westminster has been talking you up quite a lot. As well as being seen in your designs everywhere. And your recent press, well, let's just say it hasn't hurt you one teensy bit. Quite the opposite, actually."

I'd handed over Evie's garments and collected my check about a week ago and just this morning received final confirmation from Lauren that she was pleased with my designs and wanted me to put them into production.

"What are you saying?"

He clasped his hands together, steepling his pointer fingers and touching them to his chin. "It's not often that this happens, but I think you might be a candidate for early graduation. Every once in a while someone like you comes along and you're just ready and opportunity presents itself so beautifully that we'd be mental to ignore it."

"What does graduating early entail?"

His eyebrows rose. "Well, a heavier course load next term and a collection in the second-years' fashion show."

"I could do that."

"If I were you, I'd graduate and get your label launched. Lord knows you've got the skills and some *incredibly* powerful backers in your court. Don't waste it." He tucked his hands behind his back and eyed me.

"How do I sign up to do this?"

"Come to my office next week and we'll get you sorted."

I was left in shock as I watched him continue down his path. It took me a moment to remember how to walk. With a little more pep in my step, I made my way to my room, where a purple scarf was tied on the doorknob. I threw my head back and growled. These two needed to get an apartment.

Jealousy surged through me. I wanted what she had. I wanted a reason to put a scarf on the doorknob. At least my career seemed to be on an upswing. I had to stay focused on the positives.

Turning, I trudged down the hall and knocked on Andrew's door.

Bleary eyed and messy haired he answered, his roommate snoring in the background. One look at me and he opened his door all the way. "Come on in."

He crawled into bed and I curled up next him, letting him pull the covers over us. "I'm graduating early."

"What?" He recoiled back, then leaned up on his shoulder so he could better see me. "What happened? Is your dad making you come home? Did the interview flop?"

I shook my head. "Walker thinks with all the interest I'm getting right now I should strike while the iron is hot."

His eyes widened. "Whoa, really?"

Head on his pillow, facing him, I nodded.

After a long pause, he said, "I want you to hear me out on something."

Nodding, I met his eyes. "Of course."

"Take me with you."

"What?" Now it was my turn to be shocked.

He sighed. "I hate school. I love designing, but this . . . it's just not for me."

"Why didn't you ever say anything?" I whispered as his roommate stirred.

His eyes dropped to the sheets. "I didn't want you or Daisy or anyone to think I was stupid and couldn't cut it."

"Andrew, no one would have thought that."

"I won't let you down, I swear. You know I can sew like a badass demon. I've got the skills. I'll stick with you while you build a name for yourself, then maybe I can do some designing under you, then branch out on my own. What do you think?"

"It's definitely not a fast track."

He laughed. "No, but think about it, 'cause as you get more popular, with the duchess and Princess Lauren rallying behind you, it's only a matter of time. You're going to need help completing orders. I'm your man."

My man. The thought made me laugh. *Just what I need, another gay man.* "I can't pay you right away, at least not anything resembling a salary."

"We'll both keep working at The Bolt. We can get a manky flat together and you can share a portion of your sales, the ones I help you on of course. Please say yes." Everything about him pleaded with me.

"If it's really what you want, then yes of course, let's do it. But don't be afraid to change your mind at any time. 'Cause I just can't believe this is really what you want."

"It is."

Ever since the phone hack, things had been insane. My life had transformed, in very good ways. I could do this. I was on the road to fulfilling my dream, and I was doing it *my* way.

"You sure you okay?" Andrew laid down and looked at me, his brow furrowed with worry.

Silently, I contemplated his question, then nodded. "You know what? I'm better than okay."

I pulled the covers over my shoulder as his roommate grumbled something and rolled to face the wall. "You know, Andrew, I think I've got just the perfect guy for you."

For the first time in a long time I could see things clearly. Maybe it was the freedom of having my life back, or knowing my career was progressing in the right direction. Whatever it was, I knew one thing with absolute certainty. *My* way included Preston. And I wanted to make sure he knew it too.

Chapter Thirty-Four

A Magical Love

The cold air chapped my cheeks as I stood outside Preston's flat. Unable to sleep the night before, I'd gotten up and taken the bus into Oxford, still in the navy dress I'd worn for the interview. I needed to see him. I looked up at the tall white townhouse and shook my head. *What am I doing here? This is crazy.* It was still early in the morning and I doubted anyone in the house would be awake yet. I didn't even know if Preston was in there. He could still be in London for all I knew.

But I had to take the chance. Finally I was sure about him and I had to make it clear that I didn't want to wait another single second. I'd been so worried about him leaving again that I hadn't stopped to realize that he'd come back to me, Ben and all. Yes, he'd made mistakes, but so had I. And we'd probably make many more mistakes in our relationship. What mattered was right now.

My heart had long been his. Even when I wished it wasn't, and I'd wanted to yank it away from him, I couldn't. If I continued to protect it and lock it away, it still wouldn't stop me from getting hurt. I'd just be lonely.

Plus, Preston was worth the risk. And with great risks come some pretty freakin' awesome rewards.

I took a step back and remembered a cafe nearby. Deciding I needed to wait for a reasonable hour, I went and got myself a peppermint mocha.

In a booth near the window, my heels bounced with nervous energy. Caffeine might not have been the best idea. I hadn't quite sorted out what to say to Preston; my brain was too frantic to pin down a plan. I wasn't all that positive he'd even want to talk about us being an *us*, with everything his mom was going through.

I grabbed my phone, scrolled Facebook, and hit Like for several pictures of Marc surfing. He looked happy, and I was thrilled for him. He'd tagged me in one of the pictures of him at the beach, knowing how much I loved going there. I added a comment: Miss you like crazy!

The longer I sat, the more people arrived and filled the cafe. Now I was just stalling. My nerves were taking over. My only plan was to run if Preston looked at me like I was insane. It wasn't a good plan.

"Maggie?"

I turned to see Evie and Edmund, coats draped over their arms and red cups in hand, making their way toward me. Bodyguards trailed behind them. She wore the drapey gray hoodie I'd made for her. She looked fabulous and stylish.

I tucked my messy hair behind my ear, suddenly wishing I'd bothered to check a mirror in my haste to get here. What the hell was I thinking, coming to Preston looking like I'd just crawled out of bed . . . 'cause I totally just did. "Oh, hey."

"What are you doing here so early? Is everything all right?" She sat down across from me and Edmund slid in next to her.

"Do you want me to call Preston? He got back late last night and is probably still at the flat. He'd love to see you," Edmund offered, pulling out his phone.

"Oh, no, that's okay. I'm just . . ." I looked between the two of them, wondering what they thought of me and wondering what I could say to explain why I was here. I shook my head and turned my focus to the lid of my mocha. "I'm just realizing the idea I had in my head this morning wasn't as good as I thought it was. I should probably catch the next bus back to Bampton."

Evie looked up to Edmund, smiled, and gave him a conspiratorial look. "You have class now, right?"

He nodded slowly and said, "Yes, and so do you. We have it together, remember?"

"Then you can take notes for me." She put her hand on his shoulder and leaned in to kiss his cheek, but he turned just in time so they were lip to lip. After a second little peck she said, "Why don't you head to class and I'll sit with Maggie for a bit."

"All right, I'll see you later. It was nice to see you again, Maggie."

"You too."

Evie took a sip of her tea. "I'm guessing you're in Oxford for a reason. And I'd feel pretty comfortable placing a substantial bet on that reason being Preston."

At the look in her green eyes I had to avert my gaze. "I guess you could say I had a bit of an epiphany this morning and I ran off completely unprepared."

"Hmm, this epiphany of yours, is it going to make Preston happy?"

I raised a shoulder. "I hope so."

"Good." Her eyes scanned the visible part of my torso. "Do you want to freshen up before you see him?"

"Um, you know, I think I'm gonna head home and just call him later."

"Absolutely not. Come back to my dorm and between Suze, Caroline, and me, we should be able to get you looking a little more presentable."

"No, I couldn't." I shook my head and took a pull from my now lukewarm coffee.

Reaching across the table, she rested her hand on my arm, a soft smile on her face. "You could. If you wanted to see him badly enough that you left the house so early, looking as rumpled as you do, then trust me, you definitely could."

"Why would you do this for me?"

"I saw how happy Preston was after summer break. It was because of you. And then how miserable he was through this whole Ben Chambers mess. I watched your interview. I think you guys deserve another chance. You make him happy." She patted my arm. "Plus, with all the amazing clothes you've made for me, I'd like to think we're at the start of our friendship."

"I'd like to think so too." Her kindness touched me, easing the weight of my insecurity just a bit. *I make him happy?*

"Come on then, let's go get you ready to surprise Preston."

Evie stood, grabbed my hand, and pulled me from the booth. A girlish giggle left my lips. I had to come up with a plan.

We left the coffeehouse and with her phone to her ear, it sounded like Evie was asking someone to meet her at her dorm. "Are you both together? Okay, meet me in ten minutes. I'm by Edmund's so we've got to get back to St. John's. Yeah, see you then."

Looking both ways, she darted across traffic. My heart beat an erratic rhythm in my chest. I was really going to do this. By the end of the day Preston would know that I . . . that I . . . oh God, that I was in love with him.

"We've got to book it. Preston usually comes this way and we probably want to wait to surprise him."

I jogged beside her, the cold air making my lungs ache. I pulled my scarf up to cut the pain. We passed lots of old stone buildings and swerved onto cobblestone streets. Oxford was actually quite beautiful. This was by far the most I'd seen of it.

"Just this way." She pulled me through an archway and glanced back to give me a giant smile.

Through the door of a modern-looking building and up a flight of stairs, we burst out into a hallway with gray carpet. Leaning against a door was Marissa's girlfriend, with the black bob. Beside her stood the girl who'd been so upset that morning at Preston's flat.

"Maggie, have you met Caroline and Suzy?"

Caroline! That was Marissa's girlfriend's name.

"We've met." Suzy smiled warmly at me. "She was there that morning I was so upset because of Leo, remember?"

I met Suzy's blue eyes. "I've been wondering about you ever since. Did you guys work things out?"

Averting her gaze, she shook her head. "No. It wasn't meant to be, I suppose."

"I'm sorry."

"Oh, don't be, I'll be fine." She perked up and her eyes sparkled. "Besides, we're here for you and Preston. Come on."

Evie opened the door to her room, and I was struck by how normal it was. It wasn't fancy or posh, in fact it looked a lot like mine, but significantly smaller. With the one twin bed I figured out they must not share rooms. Under a long shelf was a wall of pictures. Several were of her and Edmund. The rest of the gang was interspersed in there as well. I smiled when one of Preston making a goofy face popped out at me.

"Okay, you definitely need a little . . . perk up. Go to the bathroom and wash your face. We'll fix your makeup when you come out," Caroline ordered me.

I spun and followed Evie to a small room with a shower, toilet, and sink, nothing fancy. She handed me a brush and smiled.

She pointed to the counter. "Here, try this stuff, it'll give your hair a great shine."

"Okay, thanks."

When I looked in the mirror my reflection horrified me. Bits of my hair were sticking up and out where they definitely should be down and in. I ran a finger under my eyes, trying to erase the mascara-smudged bags. I looked exhausted. Then again, with the amount of sleep I didn't get, I was seriously fatigued.

Quickly, I washed my face, then brush in hand, I got to work. In a few minutes everything was smoothed and I used some of the shine stuff Evie suggested. I now had soft chunky waves framing my face.

"Okay, come over here and we'll freshen that makeup." Caroline was clearly the girl with the plan.

Hmm, maybe she can help me with my plan.

"Oh, give your dress to Suze, she can run to my room and steam it."

Evie offered me a robe so I wouldn't have to sit in my bra and undies, which I appreciated.

By the time Caroline was finished I looked incredible. Gone were the dark circles, and my complexion looked flawless. She'd even managed to make the blue of my eyes pop.

"Wow." I leaned closer to the mirror and examined her work. "You're amazing."

She nodded. "Well, I had a good base to work with. Slip back into your dress and you're ready to go get him." Caroline handed the navy dress to me, holding it out to get a better look at it. "Did you make this? I love it."

"I did." I slid into the sheath dress and turned so someone could zip me up.

"Hmm, I may have to buy one from you, it's fabulous."

I swallowed, feeling so not ready. "I don't know what to say to him."

Evie leaned against her desk and crossed her arms over her chest. "Well, what did you want to say to him this morning?"

"Um, just that I realized I want him in my life." I closed my eyes and took a deep breath. "He needs to know that I'm in love with him, and that being with him makes me feel . . . like I can fly." I giggled, feeling completely silly.

Caroline had a soft smile on her dark burgundy lips. "Well now, that sounds pretty wonderful."

"I can already tell we're going to get to know you much better." Suzy leaned in and gave my shoulders a squeeze. "And I for one am looking forward to it."

"You ready?" Evie asked and looked at her watch. "Preston should be on his way to the dining hall for lunch."

"Take a breath. Your eyes are so big you look like you've just seen a ghost." Caroline stood me up and grabbed my shoulders.

"What if he's changed his mind about me?"

"He hasn't." They all three answered in unison, then laughed.

I shook my head. "I don't think I can do this."

"Yes, you can." Evie grabbed my hand and squeezed it. "If you leave now, you'll surprise him on his walk over. Come on, let's go."

"Okay," I nodded, my breathing shallow. They slipped me into my coat and led me downstairs, back out the double doors we'd come in. "Which way?"

Suzy showed me the path and I set off, praying this didn't turn into a disaster. Around the corner, I pulled my scarf up to cover my neck from the freezing wind. When I looked up I saw him, coming in my direction, hands stuffed in his pockets, watching something across the street.

I froze and stared at him.

When he looked my way, he stopped walking and squinted his eyes, like he was making sure he was really seeing me.

"Maggie?" He came toward me, big smile on his wonderful face.

"Hi." My voice came out breathy.

He shook his head and pulled me away from the edge of the sidewalk and out of the way of foot traffic. "What are you doing here? Shouldn't you be in class?"

I nodded and bit my lip, forcing myself to go on. "I needed to see you."

"Me?" His brows rose. "What do you want with me?"

"I, uh . . . well, there's something I need to tell you." My palms began to sweat in my gloves.

Preston looked around us, then up at the tall stone building we stood next to. "Let's go in here."

I followed him, wondering if we were allowed to be in here. From inside the foyer I could see a large lecture hall just steps away. It must be part of the university.

"What did you want to tell me?" He smiled down at me, and I could see the tiredness etched in his face.

I wanted to hug him, but I wasn't sure I should. "First, I wanted to apologize again for dragging you through this whole Ben thing."

"Okay." He looked confused.

"And, well, I suddenly had a realization and . . . um, I didn't want to wait a second longer to tell you."

His eyes silently met mine and he cocked his head, waiting for me to finish.

"I just, I feel like we've wasted too much time and . . . oh, God, I'm botching this up horribly." I ran a hand over my face, feeling like a complete idiot.

A smile cracked his lips as he reached out and brushed my hair from my face. Tucking it behind my ear, his fingers grazed against my cheek and my breath caught in my throat.

"You're doing just fine."

My voice now a whisper. "Preston, I *really* like you." *No that's not right.*

His hands came up to cup my face. "Are you saying what I think you're saying?"

I nodded, my eyes welling with tears. "I'm so completely in love with you."

He didn't need words. Instead, his lips crushed against mine and he dropped his hands from my face, pulling me tight.

When he leaned back he chuckled and kissed my forehead. "I love you, too." He slid his hand behind my neck and pulled me forward so he could kiss me again. "God, I've missed kissing you."

I kissed him back, my heart soaring. Behind me I heard clapping and cheering. We both turned to see his friends just outside the door, making a scene and celebrating us.

Hiding my now flaming cheeks against his chest, he held me in his arms and I heard his low laughter rumble through his jacket.

When I looked up, he kissed my forehead again and grabbed my hand. "Come on, let's get out of here. These people are crazy."

With laughter on our lips, he pulled me toward another set of doors and we took off. I didn't know where we were going, but wherever it was, it was sure to be better since he was at my side.

From here on out, I intended to make sure my life was a life well lived. And well loved. And all my own.

Epilogue

One Year Later

Ducking behind a rack of clothes, I took a deep breath. A moment, I just needed a second to recenter myself. Closing my eyes, I started a cleansing inhale then broke into a happy dance. *I'm at London Fashion Week!*

Andrew's face popped around the rack and he snapped, "Oi, princess, get a move on. I can't do this by myself."

"Hey, who's the boss here?" I laughed and he winked at me.

I'd been invited to exhibit in Fashion Week after my show with the second-years at Thrippletons. Which had come as quite the shock.

"Do you have any idea how busy we're going to be after this?" Andrew pulled a yellow empire waist, linen sundress and headed for the steamer.

We'd already been busy, what with Evie and Princess Lauren—the latter who I'd just done several maternity looks for—as regular clients. Even the girls in the gang bought several pieces. My style was a little too prissy for Marissa, but she did get a funky wrap hoodie. On top of that, several of their posh friends had contacted me. Business was steadily coming my way. At this rate it wouldn't be long before I'd saved enough to pay Dad back for his dirty bribe money.

The unfailing support of my new group of friends was amazing. And Preston? He was like my own personal cheerleader. The way he believed in me was astounding.

When the lead in Mom's newest film, super celebrity Julianna Blackmoor, wore a sexy red dress I'd made to a premiere, we'd received more attention than I'd expected. Our phone had rung nonstop after that. If we did well here, there'd be no question about it, I'd have to hire more help. Andrew had been bugging me to hire someone since we'd moved from Bampton into London, but I'd wanted to play it safe.

"Hey, steam this too, please." I pulled out a long tunic and handed it off to him.

I walked past the row of makeup stations filled with scantily clad models and went to check with the show's producer that we were still on time. I also wanted to get a peek at the audience. Mom and Marc were flying in this morning and I was dying to know if they were here. I'd only taken a quick trip home last June and it'd been nearly nine months since I'd last seen them.

At least Mom had been settled into her new place when I'd visited. The divorce had been final ages ago and Dad had managed to get the house. Mom got the pets and was now busy refurbishing a little cottage with an ocean view and was always busy with work.

"Hey, Leena, are we still on schedule?"

She pulled her headset mic away from her mouth and smiled at me. "Yup, you've got . . ." She glanced at her clipboard, then her watch. "Thirty-seven minutes."

Oh, holy hell.

I didn't have time to take a peek. Turning, I ran back and immediately started prepping the models, helping them get in their many different types of dresses, from gowns to maxis and the casual-wear pieces. I checked and double-checked, making sure everything fit perfectly and laid correctly.

Before I knew it, the girls were lining up, ready to walk. I took a deep breath and shakily blew it out.

"This is it." Andrew grabbed my shoulders and gave me an excited shake.

I looked onto the catwalk. The white backdrop now had my black logo for Maggie Mack Designs, and I grinned. The audience looked packed from my limited view. Music filled the venue and we were on.

One by one, the girls made their way down the runway. Our last look was about to go out, a beautiful and sexy deep-V princess gown, and I struggled to breathe. Up to now had been the easy part. Once the final model returned they'd all take one last lap, and I'd have to bring up the rear. Under my breath I whispered, "I will not trip. I will not trip. I will not trip."

Andrew leaned against me. "Hey, when you see my boyfriend give him a wave for me."

I put my foot on the bottom step. The last model was nearly back and we were ready to do our loop.

"Don't trip." Andrew snickered.

Shooting him a glare, I set off with the final model.

The spotlights made it nearly impossible to see the audience, as did the photographers' flashes. Smiling, I waved my way along, trying to see where my family and friends were sitting. At the end of the catwalk, I paused with the model and stood there as the thunderous applause reached its pinnacle. With a gracious nod and a hand to my heart, I waved one last time and turned to head backstage.

On my return walk I spied them. Marc waved as Mom wiped a tear from her cheek, smiling. Just past them was Preston, Evie, Edmund, and the rest of the gang. Preston stood and clapped. My cheeks flushed and I had to look away.

This past year he'd helped me ride the aftershocks of the Dad debacle. He'd also been there helping Andrew and me launch my label. The late nights and take-outs . . . he'd been there. Sitting on the couch, just being with me while I worked on designs, he was there. I couldn't have gotten through it all without him. He was my rock.

Daisy let out a whoop as a smiling Ethan clapped. His eyes glanced to her and you could see the utter love there. They had plans to get married after her graduation in two months. I was already busy making her wedding dress.

At the end of the group sat Andrew's boyfriend. With another wave and a smile, I continued my walk, feeling incredibly blessed. Once safely backstage I was able to fully fill my lungs.

"That was awesome." Andrew wrapped me in a hug. "You did it."

My nerves were simultaneously frazzled and numb, but I still managed to shake my head. "No, *we* did it. I couldn't have accomplished all this without you."

"Did you see my boyfriend?" He leaned back with a grin.

"Yes." I nodded. "I saw Ben."

Mom and Marc were the first to reach me. Something told me Preston held the others back to give us just a moment together. I loved him for it.

"I'm so proud of you." Mom hugged me.

"Way to go, Magpie." Marc put his arms around both of us. "Life's a little different from a year ago, isn't it?"

He was right. None of us had spoken to Dad in ages and we were all the better for it. And unfortunately I'd called it. Dad married his fiancée, they had a baby, then about a minute later they were working their way through a messy divorce with a newborn. I knew none of this firsthand, but the tabloids still occasionally mentioned him, especially as more actors and crew members came forward, shedding light on his abusive and controlling antics. He was thoroughly finished. And he'd brought every single bit of it on himself.

After his second wife filed for divorce, he'd tried to come back to Mom. Calling her and trying to remind her of their good times. She hadn't been amused.

With a slightly heavy heart, I pushed Dad from my mind. He didn't belong there, not today. "I'm so glad you guys made it. It wouldn't have been the same without you."

"We wouldn't dream of missing it." Mom leaned back and smiled. Marc gave my shoulders one last squeeze before the gang descended on us

Congratulations and hugs surrounded me, but the one person I really wanted to see hung back. Preston stood behind the group, smiling and patiently waiting his turn.

He must've come to the show straight from the architecture firm he'd been hired at before graduating last spring. I loved how on casual Fridays the only difference in his attire was that he paired his button-down and tie with a pair of dark jeans instead of chinos.

Once everyone had backed off, Preston stepped forward and wrapped his arms around me in a bear hug. He whispered in my ear, "You were brilliant. But, I must say, I can't wait to get you home."

Leaning back, I put my hands on his chest and smiled. "Neither can I."

Preston had moved out of Edmund's townhouse after graduation and now had a flat in a London high-rise. It had incredible views of the city and the Thames. Compared to Andrew's and my place it was pretty freaking posh.

The flat Andrew and I had shared served not only as our living quarters but also as our studio and headquarters for Maggie Mack Designs. We'd outgrown the space in no time. In the months of prepping the collection for Fashion Week we'd come to a conclusion . . . one of us had to leave. Either that, or we'd kill each other. Luckily, Preston had the perfect solution.

Two months before the show we'd moved in together at his flat.

"You and Andrew finish up here, then let's all go to celebrate and grab some dinner." Evie draped her arms around Preston and me. "I knew you'd be a huge success."

With a quick hug, Evie and the gang headed back to the front to wait, chatting and smiling. Preston stayed backstage with me, and I was glad he had.

Marc leaned in to me before he followed the others. "The redhead, Evie, is she single?"

"No." I laughed. "She's dating a prince. You don't have a chance."

"Damn." He tucked his hands in his pockets and headed after the group.

"Hey, Maggie?"

I turned to see one of the makeup artists coming toward me, carrying a floral scarf in her hand. "Yeah, Hannah?" A thought popped in my head and I held up a finger to hold her off. "Hey, Marc, come back a second."

Hannah was a redhead, and a sweet one at that. She'd be perfect for Marc.

Shortly after Ben decided to leave Hollywood, he'd opened his own special effects studio in London, The Chamber. Hannah had been one of his first hires. When I'd told him over dinner with Preston and Andrew that I was looking for a makeup artist for my show, he'd immediately suggested her.

"Hannah, have you met my older brother, Marc?" I shot a glance to Preston, who just grinned and shook his head.

Hannah gave Marc a shy smile. "I don't think I've had the pleasure."

I made the introductions and stood back while they chatted. "I'm gonna go help Andrew. I'll see you two later."

"Oh, wait." Hannah stopped me. "Do you need me to help with anything?"

"No, go, have fun." I turned from her and patted Marc on the shoulder, then went to Preston.

"Just couldn't help yourself, could you?" He kissed my forehead and I laughed. "That's just one of the many things I love about you."

"Come on, help me pack up." I grabbed his tie and gently tugged him toward me, nipping at his lips. "It'll get us that much closer to heading home."

"Promise?" He leaned so his face hovered just above mine.

My breath caught in my throat and I nodded. With a small quirk to his lips, he lowered them to mine. It started off slowly, but quickly escalated to my fingers twined in his hair and his hands grabbing my waist, yanking me closer.

Taking a step back, his voice rough, he said, "I think Andrew can handle this."

"No, Andrew can't," Andrew hollered from nearby, bagging the clothes.

Laughing, we pulled apart. I grabbed his hand. "Come on."

• • •

Preston pulled his key from the lock and opened the door to our flat. *Ours.* I loved the sound of that. It still felt surreal and a little like we were playing house, but it was all real and all wonderful. Dinner had been lively and full of laughter, but I was glad it was over and it was just the two of us again. Mom and Marc were back at the hotel and we'd made plans to get together tomorrow, but right now, all I could think about was Preston.

Reaching over, he helped me out of my jacket and hung it up. "So how do you feel about the show?"

"Good. I hope it's as successful as Evie seems to think it was."

"I don't think you have anything to worry about. You're insanely gifted. The only thing you need to be prepared for is the onslaught that's sure to happen tomorrow."

"If I'm lucky." This past year felt like a dream; it pulled together too easily. Like magic. I was terrified it could all blow apart with a sneeze. And at just nearly twenty, I felt so beyond blessed to have this life.

"You don't need luck. You've got what it takes—talent." He lifted my hand to press a kiss to the back of it.

Glancing at him I smiled, my eyes burning at the buildup of emotions.

With a sideways look he said, "Now I don't know this for certain, of course, but you might be getting a *huge* job soon."

"What do you mean?" I kicked off my shoes and settled on the couch. Preston sat beside me and leaned forward, kissing my neck and collarbones.

"Well . . . let's just say . . ." His lips trailed along my shoulder. "Something big's about to go down."

Confusion furrowed my brow and I tried to stay focused on our conversation. "Way to be vague and cryptic."

"I can't say much." He lifted his head and looked in my eyes. "But I may or may not have just helped someone pick out a pretty important piece of jewelry."

"Seriously?" My eyes widened and my lips cracked into a happy grin. I knew exactly who he was talking about.

He gave me a worried look. "You can't say anything to anyone. Not Andrew, Daisy, Marc, your mum . . . no one."

I pretended to pull a zipper across my lips. "I wouldn't dream of it."

My brain flooded with ideas for dresses that would make her look like a fairytale princess and I smiled, giddy with all the fun I could have with this. She'd be breathtaking.

"You're already designing the dress in your head, aren't you?" He put an arm around me and pulled me against him.

Blushing, I met his gaze. "Guilty."

His hand threaded through my hair, coming to rest at the nape of my neck. With a satisfied grin crossing his lips, he tilted my head so my mouth met his.

A soft sigh escaped my lips and my arms twined around his neck as I pulled him tight. A low growl reverberated from him, sending tingles shooting down my spine to settle low in my tummy. Pressing me back into the couch, Preston's lips curled against mine in a smile before thoroughly kissing me again. This was exactly where I wanted to be.

Leaning up, he studied my face. "Do you remember when we went stargazing at Chillingham?"

I nodded, my fingers twirling in the soft curls of hair just above his neck.

"I was right."

"About what?"

He brushed my hair off my face. "When I said that true love was the closest humans ever got to magic." His thumb grazed my cheek. "This. Us. We're magic."

"I love you." I leaned into his hand.

"I love you too."

Kissing me again, I lost myself in his touch and the feel of him.

It'd been a rocky road to get where I was now. I'd managed to escape the crazed celebrity world of my parents for a much calmer life, and one that I'd carved out all my own. Now I had my wonderful family, an amazing group of friends, and the best boyfriend I ever could've hoped for.

Preston believed true love was the closest humans ever got to magic. But he's only partially right. Magic doesn't solely come from true love; it's around us every day, in the love of our friends and family as well. And I've been beyond blessed to create a life all my own, overflowing with magic.

THE END